"Filled with colorful characters and voices, Uncle Sam's blends history, espionage and race relations into a lively and imaginative tale that brings St. Augustine alive during the early days of America's entry into the Second World War."
                                    Brian Thompson, columnist
                                    The St. Augustine Record

Praise for Humphreys' "Seasons of the Sea":

"The written equivalent of a glass-bottom boat... Seasons is a keeper."
                                    The Florida Times-Union

"... delightful...deftly covers the strange migration of the tarpon, the season of the dead fish."
                                    The Tampa Tribune

Printed in the United States of America

First Edition

MATANZAS PRESS
P.O. Box 940
St. Augustine, FL 32085-0940
www.MatanzasPress.com

ISBN: 0-9745920-0-5

Cover design: John Potter
Escape Key Graphics
www.EscapeKeyGraphics.com

JAY HUMPHREYS

UNCLE SAM'S

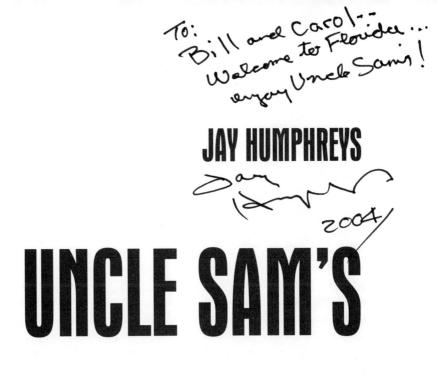

MATANZAS PRESS  **ST. AUGUSTINE**

ACKNOWLEDGEMENTS

In many ways, St. Augustine is a time capsule of Spanish and American history. Within the historic district of this ancient (by American standards) city, a visitor can get a true feeling of what it was like to live in this part of Florida many centuries ago. But to re-create a specific time and place takes much more than feelings--facts are needed to build the skeleton on which the story can be hung. Fortunately, the extensive holdings and kindly people of the St. Augustine Historical Society helped provide a wealth of materials essential for creating fiction that contains a heady dose of fact. For their help, I am particularly grateful. In addition, the U-boat operations described in this novel would be sadly lacking in authenticity if not for the enthusiastic support of the many fine scholars and dedicated enthusiasts who provided their expertise via U-boat.net -- undoubtedly, the richest repository of U-boat lore and facts in the world today. For all who helped, I offer a hearty "Good Hunting!" Also, for more than a century *The St. Augustine Record* has been documenting events, both mundane and extraordinary, in the Oldest City. The back issues of this exemplary newspaper provided the essential details, as well as the intriguing possibilities, that made this story possible.

Of course, no novel of the Second World War would be complete without the distinctive music of that era. My thanks go to the publishers of the following songs for their kind permission to include them in *Uncle Sam's:*

All of Me, original words and music by Seymour Simons and Gerald Marks, copyright 1931, Marlong Music Corporation (ASCAP). International copyright secured, all rights reserved.

Bei Mir Bist Du Schoen (Means That You're Grand), original words by Jacob Jacobs, music by Sholom Secunda, English version by Sammy Cahn and Saul Chaplin, copyright 1937. Renewed 1965 Cahn Music Company (ASCAP) and Warner Bros. Inc. (ASCAP). Rights for Cahn Music Company administered by Cherry Lane Music Publishing Company, Inc. and Dream Works Songs. International copyright secured, all rights reserved.

Jay Humphreys
November 2003

Uncle Sam's

For my wife,
DARLENE,
who showed me that reality
can surpass the most fanciful dreams.

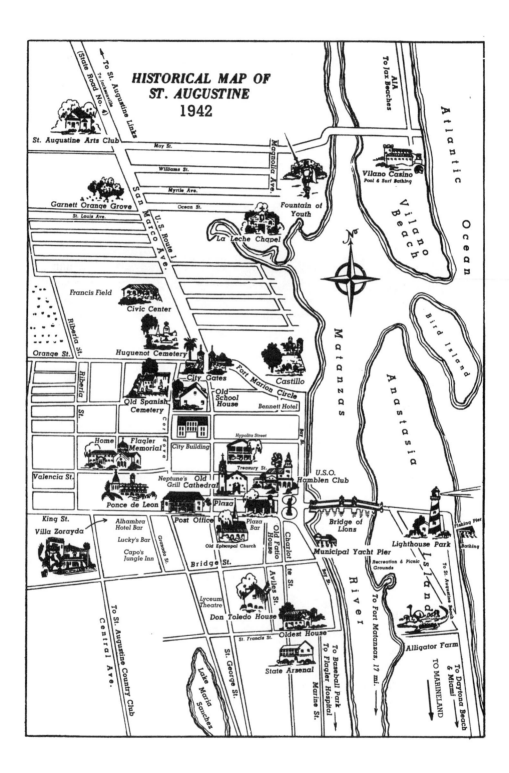

HISTORICAL MAP OF
ST. AUGUSTINE
1942

To St. Augustine Links
(State Road No. 4)
To St. Augustine
To Jacksonville

A1A
To Jax Beaches

Atlantic Ocean

St. Augustine Arts Club

May St.

Williams St.

Myrtle Ave.

Ocean St.

Magnolia Ave.

Vilano Casino
Pool & Surf Bathing

Vilano Beach

Garnett Orange Grove

St. Louis Ave.

San Marco Ave.

U.S. Route 1

Fountain of Youth

La Leche Chapel

No

Bird Island

Francis Field

Civic Center

Riberia St.

Orange St.

Huguenot Cemetery

City Gates

Fort Marion Circle

Castillo

Matanzas

Anastasia

Old Spanish Cemetery

Riberia St.

Old School House

Bennett Hotel

Home
Flagler Memorial

City Building

Hypolita Street

Treasury St.

U.S.O.
Hamblen Club

Valencia St.

Neptune's Grill

Old Cathedral

Ponce de Leon

Plaza

Post Office

Bridge of Lions

Municipal Yacht Pier

Lighthouse Park

Fishing Pier

Bathing

King St.
Villa Zorayda

Alhambra Hotel Bar

Lucky's Bar

Capo's Jungle Inn

Granada St.

Plaza Bar

Old Patio House

Charlot

St.

Old Episcopal Church

Bridge St.

Recreation & Picnic Grounds

Island

To St. Augustine Beach

Lyceum Theatre

Don Toledo House

Aviles St.

te St.

River

To Fort Matanzas, 17 mi.

Alligator Farm

St. George St.

St. Francis St.

Oldest House

State Arsenal

Marine St.

To Baseball Park
To Flagler Hospital

To Daytona Beach & Miami

TO MARINELAND

To St. Augustine Country Club

Central Ave.

Lake Maria Sanchez

PROLOGUE

Las Vegas
March 6, 2002

As far as Rachel Rubinstein was concerned, Marty Edelman was a genius. How else could she explain his decision to give her this assignment? Marty simply knew talent when he saw it. Sure, she reasoned, he could have picked any of the six more experienced writers on the staff of *Diva Life* magazine to do this exclusive interview, but he had chosen her.

Of course, the other writers were jealous and the rumors about her providing some sort of sexual favors in return for the assignment had already begun. Although she had noticed Marty looking at her strangely one morning as she bent over to load paper into the copier, Rachel was convinced that it was her enthusiasm for the written word that he admired, not the shape of her thighs. As the elevator doors slid open on the 34th floor of the Malay Princess Hotel, Rachel took a deep breath and stepped out into the hallway. She was determined to show everyone that Martyís faith in her talents was more than justified.

One of the first things Rachel had noticed about Las Vegas was that day and night were synonymous. The subdued lighting along the long corridor signaled her internal clock that it was late at night, but a quick glance at her watch confirmed that it was just a couple of minutes before four in the afternoon.

"No need to hurry," she told herself. 'You're right on time."

Rachel's footsteps were muffled into silence by the thick beige carpet as she walked confidently past the gleaming black doors of a dozen suites before stopping in front of the one with the polished brass 3416 beside the doorbell. She paused to straighten her dress, gave a confident toss to her head and brushed an errant strand of auburn hair away from her face before pushing the button. From somewhere far behind the heavy door she could hear the faint melodic chime of the doorbell followed by the click of a lock being opened and the rattle of a deadbolt. The door opened a mere six inches.

"Yes, may I help you?"

"Oh, hello Miss....," Rachel said and then realized that even though she was speaking to a black woman, there was an excellent chance the face peering at her from behind the door did not belong to the subject of her interview. In fact, she was now certain that she had almost mistaken a maid for one of the most beloved and successful American singers of the Twentieth Century.

"Uh, yes, my name is Rachel Rubinstein from *Diva Life* magazine. I have a four o'clock appointment with Miss Greer." Rachel wondered why her voice suddenly sounded as if she were asking her kindergarten teacher for permission to go to the bathroom. The maid slowly looked her over from head to foot while Rachel fought back a feeling of panic as she wondered what she would do if this woman simply told her to go away.

"Of course, we've been expecting you," the woman said and swung the door open. "Please come in."

Relieved, Rachel stepped inside and the maid, a short bulky woman in a gray suit, closed the door behind her.

"Miss Greer is out on the balcony....she likes fresh air this time of day," the maid said and started down the short foyer. Rachel stepped forward to follow her, but the woman turned and gave her a look that left no doubt that she took her job as maid, doorkeeper and bodyguard very seriously. "You wait and I'll tell her you're here."

Rachel obediently waited and watched as the maid moved across the elegantly appointed suite and disappeared around a corner. She could hear a patio door slide open and closed. Rachel again felt helpless—getting this interview was not a sure thing, at least not yet. She heard the door slide once more and was relieved when it obviously remained open. The maid stepped from behind the corner and there was a hint of a smile on her ebony face.

"Miss Greer will see you now," she said and like a traffic cop, waved her forward.

As Rachel rounded the corner in the maid's wake, she felt

herself passing from the cool air-conditioned room into the dry heat coming through the open balcony door. The maid bowed slightly and beckoned her guest to step outside.

"While you're out here, you keep an eye on Miss Greer and if she needs anything—anything at all, you come get me at once. My name is Mae."

Rachel mumbled a "thank you" and the door slid quickly shut as the maid retreated into the cool confines of the hotel suite.

For a moment, Rachel thought there had been some mistake and that she was actually alone on the balcony. But then her eyes adjusted to the harsh glare of the Nevada sun and she saw the subject of her interview sitting at a wrought iron table tucked into the balcony's shaded corner.

"Hello Miss Greer," Rachel said nervously. "I'm Rachel Rubinstein from *Diva Life* It's really a pleasure to meet you."

Winifred Greer smiled. She had not expected someone so young...so obviously inexperienced...to conduct this interview. But perhaps, she told herself, this young woman is some sort of literary genius—or at least very good at getting her way. Either way, Winifred was anxious to finally tell her story.

"Well, it's nice to meet you too. I hope you don't mind talking out here on the balcony. Sometimes I just have to have some fresh air. Please, have a seat."

Rachel put her notebook, handbag and tape recorder carefully on the table. She winced when the recorder fell over as she pulled out the chair and quickly settled in.

"This is really nice of you to give us this interview," Rachel said as she hit the "record" button and watched the level indicator jump to life. "I know how busy you must be and I'd be the last person to bother you. I saw you on TV last night getting your award and I must say it was really something. I'll bet you're so proud of everything—especially that award. I mean it was so nice to see you win something like that. It just seems like..."

"Child. How old are you?"

Rachel stopped fiddling with the recorder and looked up. For the first time, she made eye contact with the world's most famous jazz singer and she saw that Winifred Greer without her makeup was quite different from the mature black woman seen on television and in front the adoring audiences at her always-sold-out-concerts.

Not that 76 years of life, most of it spent performing around the world, had treated her harshly— far from it. Her dark eyes still sparkled and her blue silk dressing gown hung loosely around a firm figure that had none of the bulkiness so often associated with women her age. There was, however, a slight sag beneath her chin and along the line of her jaw. And there was that unmistakable tightness at the corners of her eyes that showed the aftermath of at least one serious facelift. But her skin still had the milky glow that reminded Rachel of the French vanilla-flavored cream her mother always added to her coffee. And while looking at least 25 years younger than her age was quite an accomplishment, it was obvious that it took several makeup artists and probably some very flattering lighting to give her that mature, but still attractive look that millions of fans assumed was her natural, unaltered appearance.

"Well, I'm waiting," Winifred Greer said with just a hint of annoyance. "I'm guessing you're not a day over eighteen."

"Yes I am, Miss Greer." Rachel stopped the tape, sat up straight in her chair and tried to project a sense of professionalism. "I'm much older than eighteen. In fact, we just celebrated my twenty-second birthday two weeks ago."

The recipient of last night's "All Time Favorite Singer - Female," smiled at the girl who somehow thought twenty-two years of living qualified her for some sort of merit badge for maturity.

"Twenty-two? I have shoes that are older than that."

Rachel said nothing and her obvious discomfort made Winifred Greer feel just a bit guilty.

"Well, child, here I am asking the questions—that's supposed to be your job. Your editor told me this story was going to be Winifred Greer—The Early Years' or something like that. So let's get to it before I forget everything—not that I haven't already."

Rachel nodded and slid the tape recorder to the center of the table and pushed "record".

"Testing...testing...this is Rachel Rubinstein. It's March sixth and the subject of this interview is Miss Winifred Greer. We are..."

"Stop that thing!" Winifred Greer glared as Rachel turned off the recorder. "Before we go any further with this, I want you to call me Winnie—all my friends back in the old days called me Winnie. I think it would help my memory if you did too."

"Of course....Winnie. I'll make a point of it." Rachel smiled as she realized that she had already come up with new information. Winnie. She had never seen a reference to that nickname—Marty was going to like this story. She turned on the recorder once more. "All right then Winnie. Why don't you tell me about your childhood? When did you first realize you had a gift for singing?"

For the first time in decades, Winifred "Winnie" Greer felt as though she were going to be struck by stage fright. She was excited about the prospect of telling this story—she had often wondered why no journalist had ever asked her about her childhood. But now that she had the opportunity, the story seemed confused and disjointed. In her mind, silent images swirled and danced.

"I really don't know the answer to that one...it was all so long ago. So very long ago."

She looked down through the metal railing to where cars were moving slowly along The Strip far below. The desert heat was beginning to dissipate and the shadow across the balcony was lengthening. She sighed as she searched her memory for a starting point and then a silvery flash of light caught her eye. The desert sun had begun its long slide toward the coolness of the mountains and its golden rays slanted down to shimmer across the surface of an Olympic-sized swimming pool nearly forty floors below. Winnie's vision was drawn to the spectacle of light on the water and as she watched the sparkling sideshow, her mind was drawn to another day and time when she had seen a similar flash and twinkle... a light display that seemed so far away in space and time that she wondered if it had really happened.

Uncle Sam's

SUNDAY
April 12, 1942

BUTLER BEACH: 0745 hrs.

Winnie squinted her eyes against the harsh glare of the Florida sun. As she tried to move to the edge of the crowd gathered on the beach, she struggled to answer three questions: Why did the service have to be held at this time of morning? Where was the cool shade? What happened to the sea breeze?

"Like John the Baptist at the River Jordan, we are here to wash away sin!" Reverend Amos Fulmer's voice was filled with the Spirit this morning and his words were answered with a chorus of "Amen!" from the congregation of the Moses Creek African Methodist Episcopal Church.

"We are here to bring new life...new life in the Lord Jesus Christ! Salvation sweet as honey and a soul as pure as the Lamb of God!"

As usual, the way the reverend said the word "God" caused goose bumps on Winnie's arms. When the crowd roared "Amen!" she could feel a tingle at the base of her spine—and she knew it wasn't caused by the trickle of sweat that suddenly ran down her back. Last Sunday's Easter call to the altar had been particularly fruitful and more than a dozen new converts waited patiently to receive salvation. Winnie felt a tinge of guilt when she realized she had wished that the service would soon end so they could go home where it was cool.

Jerome Manly was first in line to be baptized and as he reached out for the reverend's hand, Winnie could see that he was scared. His eyes were wide and shining white from his black face—somehow it didn't seem right that he should be so frightened. He hadn't looked that terrified when Sheriff Hartson had accused him

7

of stealing a pack of cigarettes from the City Gates Market up in St. Augustine.

"Praise the Lord! Praise His precious name!"

The shout of exultation came from so close behind her that Winnie flinched and spun around to see Jerome's momma looking up into the hot sky, her large brown arms were spread wide and her eyes were closed. The harsh sunlight that filtered through her white straw hat made a strange pattern of light and dark on her broad face. She seemed about to swoon and Winnie stepped back. She had seen that happen before and she had no intention of letting Mrs. Manley's three hundred-pound bulk come crashing down on top of her. Fortunately, two men stepped forward and as the big woman's knees began to buckle, they struggled to support her by her armpits.

"Praise Him! Praise Him! Praise Him!" The crowd took up the chant as the reverend led Jerome into the surf. At first, they tried to step over the gentle rollers that hissed up the beach. But soon the two of them, hand-in-hand were bucking through each wave until they reached a point beyond the break and the crests rose nearly to Jerome's chin before falling to below his waist as they passed. Both of them were soon soaked by the warm sea, their black trousers glimmered with wetness and their drenched white shirts were tight against their torsos. Winnie hoped God wouldn't punish her for noticing how firm the reverend's chest looked beneath the wet shirt that clung to his skin.

Reverend Fulmer raised one arm skyward and encircled Jerome's shoulders with the other. If he hadn't, Winnie was sure the next wave would have sent the boy stumbling toward the beach. The crowd stopped their chanting—they knew from long experience that the moment of baptism was close at hand.

"Our Heavenly Father," the reverend began, his voice booming above the unruly rush of the waves. "I bring to you your humble servant Jerome Manley who, through the act of baptism, publicly professes his love for you in return for your precious gift of eternal life!"

It was at this point that Winnie first heard the growl of a speedboat's engine and despite the approaching climax of the baptism she couldn't help but look to the left where she saw the sleek hull skimming the surface of the sea and heading directly for Reverend Fulmer and Jerome.

"....in the name of the Father, the Son and the Holy Ghost...." The reverend was speaking, but his words were overpowered by the snarl of the boat's engine. Winnie saw the reverend dunk Jerome under. He came up with a broad smile on his face and in the rapture of the moment seemed unaware of the boat hurtling toward him. The sound of the engine was beating against her eardrums and the crowd began to move up the beach toward the safety of the dune as though they expected the boat to come ashore and hunt them down. Winnie had never seen a boat move that fast...she could see it was made of polished wood and shiny metal. Two white men were seated up front and a small American flag snapped over the stern.

The reverend held up his right hand as though he could somehow convince the two men to simply stop and with his other arm he pushed Jerome roughly toward the shore. At that moment, the boat swerved away from the beach and both the reverend and Jerome disappeared beneath the rooster tail of spray it created. The boat was so close Winnie could smell its hot exhaust fumes and as it turned seaward, she could see the two white men looking back at them over their shoulders. They were laughing.

Several young men rushed past her and dashed into the water where they helped Jerome and the reverend regain their feet and stumble to the beach. There were angry voices all around and Jerome's mother was sobbing:

"How could they do that? It was my baby's special moment with the Lord and they done messed it up!"

"It was that bastard Joe Miller and that little white pig that works for him!" Benny Sharples snarled and he rushed toward the water as though he could somehow catch the speeding boat that was already a quickly receding dot on the horizon.

"I ain't takin' no more of this sh....stuff!" Charles Lewis said. But Winnie knew that anyone with enough sense to censure his language at a time like this was not likely to do anything rash.

"We could go burn that pier right now! That would show him. Burn him right out!" Old Man Pell was hopping mad and he punched wildly at the air. "Even a white man can't get away with that—messin' with the Lord. They done be messin' with the Lord!"

"Mr. Pell, please calm yourself," Reverend Fulmer said as he stood with hands on hips and watched the speedboat disappear from sight. "As you know, the Lord says 'vengeance is mine' and

9

we have no right to interfere with the Lord's will."

Old Man Pell didn't argue. The lines of anger on his ancient face slowly faded and he seemed almost embarrassed by what he had suggested. The reverend's words, however, seemed to have little effect on Dwight and Lively Fishburn. Winnie could see their blood was boiling and she knew from past experience that they were the congregation's leading exponents of violence. Reverend Fulmer walked over to the brothers and gave them a hard stare until they were forced to look at him.

"That's right boys, vengeance is mine sayeth the Lord," the reverend said. "You do believe the Lord's teachings don't you?"

Dwight and Lively nodded slowly.

"Then give up those thoughts of anger and rejoice in the beauty of the Lord's Day. Besides, we still have some more baptizing to do this morning."

Lively dropped the driftwood club he was carrying and he and his brother slowly turned and walked away.

"Winnie! Winnie Greer!" The reverend shouted her name and Winnie's heart skipped a beat. "How about a song? Everyone! Winnie's gonna sing for us!"

Winnie was surprised. She had not planned to sing. There was no piano here on the beach. It was hot. She could think of a dozen excuses, but as she went over her mental list of reasons not to sing, she noticed something strange. The members of the congregation suddenly seemed to forget the ugly incident that had just occurred. They began moving toward her. The children stopped whimpering. Even Mrs. Manley seemed to regain her composure and Winnie heard Old Man Pell say: "Damn! That girl can sing."

It was at that moment that Winifred Greer realized for the first time that her voice could do more than just produce pleasing sounds—it could affect people... make them happy...or sad if she wanted them to be. The realization that she held such power brought her the same rush of adrenaline Jerome had felt at the moment of his baptism. She was ready to sing for these people... she wanted to sing for them!

"Go ahead Winnie," Reverend Fulmer said encouragingly. "The Lord has blessed you with that voice. Share His gift with us."

A cleansing gust of wind seemed to sweep away the anger and frustrations of the congregation... even the teenaged boys in the back of the crowd stood quietly and waited for Winnie to sing.

She cleared her throat once…then twice. What to sing? What message to give? She moved away from the crowd, kicked off her shoes and climbed several steps up the crumbling slope of the dune. As she turned to face them, the wind pulled at her white dress and sent sand dancing across her bare feet. Over the heads of her audience she could see the blue Atlantic's gentle waves rolling toward the shore. Above her, two seagulls swirled in the hot sky and one laughed loudly before sweeping down the beach.

The song came to her from a memory far back in her childhood—a memory of a bright day just like this when she had stood on this same beach sheltering from the sun's glare in her mother's cool shadow as they had listened to the choir. Since that day, the words of that song had always brought her a sense of comfort and security. As she began to sing, she hoped the song would work its old magic on the angry crowd.

Shall we gather at the river,
Where bright angels he has brought,
With its crystal tides forever,
Flowing by the throne of God.

The words and the melody were the same as the author had intended nearly eighty years earlier, but Winnie gave them a new, up tempo, bouncing quality that had faces in the crowd smiling and nodding in agreement.

Yes, we'll gather at the river,
The beautiful, the beautiful river.
Gather with the saints at the river,
That flows by the throne of God.

Hands began to clap in rhythm and bodies started to sway together beneath the Sabbath sun. By the time Winnie reached the chorus, the "Hallelujahs!" began and Old Man Pell let out a loud "Praise the Lord!"

Ere we reach the shining river,
Lay we every burden down,

11

Uncle Sam's

Praise our spirits will deliver,
And provide our robe and crown.

Reverend Fulmer felt Winnie's energy sweep through the crowd and for a brief moment he wanted to join in the dancing on the beach or play tag with the children who were now splashing in the surf. Instead, he looked at Winnie and told himself to remember this moment for it would be something he would someday tell his grandchildren long after Winifred Greer had gone on to the fame he knew was waiting for her. Although the members of Moses Creek A.M.E. assumed Winnie would always be there, he knew better. She was just sixteen, but her talent could never be confined to St. Johns County or even to the State of Florida. She would soon be on her way to stardom and none of them could follow her.

"Make her go in the path of Thy commandments," he whispered.

Joe Miller felt no more guilt about disrupting the baptism than he would if he had sent frightened rabbits scurrying to avoid the wheels of his Lincoln sedan. For him, the local colored folk were just part of the Florida landscape—much like the wading birds and pelicans that inhabited this stretch of shoreline. But as he looked back over the stern of the speeding Chris Craft, he couldn't help but wonder if the Greer girl was among the crowd. He had first heard her sing nearly a year ago at the 7th Annual Music Festival held at the colored Florida Normal and Industrial Institute in St. Augustine. She had, of course, won the soloist competition and ever since then he had slowly formulated a plan for taking advantage of her talents.

"Did you see the looks on their faces?" Luigi Carbone yelled above the roar the Hercules flathead six. "Them niggers are hoppin' mad now!"

"I don't care about them," Miller shouted in reply, "but ease back on the throttle! You have to be gentle with her!"

Carbone's smile revealed a line of nicotine-stained teeth framed between lips that even in the bright morning sunlight seemed to have a purplish hue. He pulled the throttle back slightly and as the engine's roar fell an octave, so did the bow of the twenty-two-foot *Lady Liberty*. He throttled up slightly to keep the boat on plane, checked the wet compass mounted above the dash and turned slightly to starboard. Their destination would be coming up shortly.

Miller's training and experience had shown him the value of letting subordinates run out on their leases occasionally—just as long as the exercise was finished with a firm yank that let them know you were still in command. Miller intended to deliver that yank within the next few minutes by immersing his underling in a smelly task. For now he was content to let Carbone amuse himself. Besides, Miller had to admit the man's simple approach to life was something he could learn from—the stress of his work was beginning to make Miller feel far older than he should at age fifty-one.

"So boss," Carbone said suddenly, "are them niggers the lowest form of humans? I mean are they what's lower than them under-mens or whatever it is you call them?"

"*Untermensch...* I think that's the word you're seeking." Miller was surprised at Carbone's interest in things that might possibly be categorized as... intellectual.

"Yeah, that's what I said – under mens. I saw it in that book in your office--the German one with all them pictures of people over in Europe. You know the book I'm talking about? Its got pictures of them Jews, Slavs...goofy-looking gypsies. So would you say that niggers is in the same class with those poor bastards or are they a whole step lower down the ladder?"

Miller was surprised by the question. For a moment, it was as if he were looking at a completely new and different Carbone. The man still had the same pockmarked olive complexion ...the same bushy black eyebrows... and the same oily black hair sticking out from beneath the ever-present yacht captain's hat he had found years ago and which had long since exchanged its original whiteness for a greased-streaked shade of ochre. But despite the familiar exterior appearance, Miller had to admit that the question posed by Carbone revealed a depth of character he had not previously seen in his employee during the four years they had worked together. For a moment he was concerned about this newly discovered aspect of his employee. But then he smiled as he realized that even this "depth" of character was so incredibly shallow that it was little cause for concern.

"I would say we have a job to do this morning," Miller said

firmly. "We can discuss racial purity later."

As always, Carbone yielded to his employer's opinion, but as his powerful arms turned the wheel slightly to bring the boat back on its proper heading, he couldn't help but mumble: "At least I'm Italian. My papa always said, 'son, you might hear people talking bad about your heritage, but at least God made you better than a nigger'."

Miller was in an exceptionally fine mood this morning. The wind on his face... the sun sparkling on his boat's freshly waxed Philippine mahogany... an obedient servant at the helm...and an actual mission to perform! It was almost like the old days. But as he looked back to see that the coast had become visible only when they topped one of the gentle waves, he had to admit that none of the old days had ever been this warm and he had never before had a boat that moved as fast as this 1939 custom runabout.

"Phew! What the hell is that stink?" Carbone exclaimed and screwed his Mediterranean face into a snarl of disgust. "That wasn't me Boss. I can cut some good ones—but nothing that will hang in the air like that smell."

Miller knew at once that the heavy odor of rotting eggs meant they had reached their destination.

"Engines all stop!" Miller barked, but when Carbone hesitated, he translated his order into language his helmsman could better understand. "Cut the engines. Now!"

"Do we have to stop here?" Carbone protested. "Can't we get out of this stink before...."

Miller was in no mood for debate. He leaned across Carbone and yanked the throttle back to the idle position. The engine roar fell to a happy gurgle and the boat wallowed into the swell.

"I'm gonna be sick," the helmsman groaned.

"Nonsense. You have work to do—it will make you forget the smell." Miller pointed toward the rear cockpit where two sterilized metal containers had been lashed together beneath the gunwale. "Fill those jugs and make sure they are sealed tightly." He saw Carbone hesitate. "Get busy! The sooner you fill them, the sooner we can get out of here."

Carbone mumbled something in Italian as he swung himself over the decking behind the front cockpit and worked his way astern. He fumbled with the rope holding the containers in place and as the boat dipped and swayed in the rolling sea, he nearly fell overboard. Recovering, he quickly unscrewed the top from the first container.

Miller had regained his sea legs—just like riding a bicycle, he thought, you never forget. He stood in the cockpit and jotted down his observations in a small spiral-bound notebook. He recorded that the water had a strange color here—it had changed abruptly from the deep blue-green of the springtime Atlantic to a garish greenish-yellow that bubbled up from somewhere deep below the surface. The odor had become even more pungent and his eyes began to water. "Hydrogen sulfide—very intense," he wrote.

"One filled," Carbone grumbled as he pulled the first container, now filled with seawater, back on board. "This stuff is terrible."

"Taste it," Miller ordered.

Carbone looked as if he had been asked to sip from a toilet. "I'm not drinking this... it's probably poison."

"Nonsense, four hundred years ago Spanish galleons stopped here to refill their water casks," Miller said. He realized that he could easily lean over and taste the water himself, but remembered that an officer would never assume such an undignified posture in front of a subordinate. Besides, he was suddenly feeling very... authoritarian ...and this little exercise was just what was needed to remind Carbone who was giving the orders.

Carbone realized that drinking the water was just one more thing he would have to do for Miller in order to maintain his job. He took the cap from the second container and used it to scoop water from the crest of the next little wave that bobbed past on its way to the shore. He sipped the seawater and was surprised that its taste was nothing like its smell. The taste was more metallic than salty—like drinking water from a ladle made of lead.

"So?" Miller asked. "Report on the taste."

The little Italian shrugged. "I'm no water expert— it's drinkable, but it tastes like metal. I'm sure a cold Bud will wash the nasty taste away in no time."

Miller wrote: water is potable—but has metallic aftertaste. "Very good. Fill the remaining canister and we can return to port."

Carbone shook his head and he lowered the second container over the side. Sometimes Miller seemed like a completely different person—like the naval officer he once was, giving orders and marching back and forth on the deck of some battleship. Sometimes his boss' behavior was so odd that he thought the man must have been shell shocked back in the Great War.

"All right. I've got both jugs filled," Carbone said as he tied down the second container. "Anything else you need?"

"Very good Mr. Carbone," Miller said and snapped to attention. "Return to your post. All ahead one-third and come to course two-eight-zero."

Carbone scrambled forward and settled in once more behind the wheel. He eased the throttle forward and the engine responded with a deep guttural roar.

"What are your orders? Captain Miller," Carbone said jokingly, but he could see that for the moment, Miller seemed to take him seriously. And then the moment faded, and the tall, blond man with the thin face that reminded Carbone of some sort of hawk dropped his rigid sea captain routine and a faint smile crossed his face.

"Just get us the hell out of here," Miller said. "But run us directly toward shore before turning north. I want to make sure of our coordinates."

"Aye-aye Cap'n," Carbone said and made a sloppy salute before gunning the engine. The Lady Liberty leaped ahead and left a cloud of blue exhaust smoke drifting above the smelly patch of ocean. In less than thirty seconds, the rooftops of the scattered houses that made up the hamlet of Crescent Beach came into view dead ahead. Miller continued to stand in the cockpit and took notes for a few moments longer. Finished at last, he tucked his notebook into his shirt pocket and dropped heavily into the leather seat. He tapped his helmsman on the shoulder and pointed north. Carbone swung the boat to the right until another tap told him he had reached the desired course so he centered the rudder. They were now racing along just outside the breakers that were crashing on to the sand of Anastasia Island.

"See that house up there?" Miller was practically shouting above the roar of the engine and the wind. Carbone followed Miller's pointing finger and saw a low house perched on top of the second row of dunes. He nodded.

"Marjorie Kinnan Rawlings lives there," Miller said matter-of-factly.

Carbone gave him a quick glance and then turned his gaze directly ahead.

"She's a famous American writer," Miller added. "Her books are in all the best bookstores. Haven't you read *The Yearling*? It won the Pulitzer Prize for the best novel a couple of years ago."

"Oh yeah," Carbone said and his face brightened. "I remember that one—it's about that thirteen year-old blonde who goes to work in a New Orleans whorehouse! That's one of my favorites!"

Miller laughed—not long and not loudly. He slapped Carbone on the back to show his appreciation for a man who wasn't ashamed of his ignorance. But even though they were at opposite ends of the intellectual spectrum, both men were now thinking of one thing—getting out of the hot sun and back to the pier and nightclub both of them thought of as "home".

WASHINGTON, D.C.: 1145 hrs.

Special Agent Bill Spencer had been with the Bureau for three years, but this was only his second visit to the fifth floor of the massive Justice Department Building on the corner of 9th Street and Pennsylvania Avenue. That would not have been so unusual if he had been assigned to a regional office in Atlanta or San Francisco—but the fact remained that he had spent his entire FBI career within the confines of this building. For him, the infrequency of his visits to the floor where the Director and the Attorney General had their offices had always served as an accurate reminder of where he ranked in the G-man pecking order. In fact, his only other visit to the fifth floor had been for a Christmas party the first winter he had worked for the Bureau. It wasn't until two days later that he realized the chilly reception he had received was due to the fact that he wasn't supposed to be there at all. The gala had been intended for senior staff only—he still blushed at the thought of how J. Edgar Hoover had looked at him with disdain and then delivered a whispered, but obvious reprimand to Clyde Tolson regarding the presence of a "junior G-man" at a function of such importance.

As Spencer made his way down the long corridor, he couldn't help but think this Sunday summons must mean he was moving up the Bureau's food chain. But to his surprise, he found himself only mildly excited by the prospect. Over the past few months, it had slowly dawned on him that being a Special Agent wasn't all that "special". So far, his experience at the Bureau had not been much different from that of any reference librarian. His "office" was a cubicle in the basement where he spent most of his time compiling background information on members of Congress. Even the occasional research into mistresses and gambling addictions had failed to maintain his interest for long—Congressional indiscretions had become so common that behavior once deemed outrageous was now simply categorized as routine.

Spencer stopped outside the door to office 564 and checked to make sure the name on the frosted glass was indeed "Frank Masterson— Deputy Director, Southeast Region." Convinced that he was indeed exactly where the telephoned instructions had told him to be, he straightened his tie, turned the doorknob and stepped inside.

"May I help you?"

The question came before he had closed the door behind him— so quickly, it reminded him of his neighbor's yappy Boston terrier. The dog would start barking even if someone thought about coming to the front door.

"Special Agent Bill Spencer," he said to the young redheaded woman seated behind the receptionist's desk. "I was told to be here to meet Mr. Masterson at noon."

The girl blinked back at him from behind spectacles that made her blue eyes look much larger than normal—like a goldfish staring out from inside a fishbowl.

"Oh very good!" she said. "I know Mr. Masterson is anxious to talk with you. Just have a seat. He has someone in his office right now."

As Spencer sat on the leather sofa that seemed much too luxurious for a government office, he was tempted to make small talk with the girl. There was undoubtedly something sensually appealing about the way her white blouse gapped open at the top just enough to reveal the pale line of her throat descending into the faint shadow of cleavage. But at the same time, there was a certain oddness about her that, despite her fashionable appearance, made him think of the poor little Jones girl back home who could sit motionless for hours staring at nothing. At least the Jones girl always seemed to be concentrating on something, he thought as he tried to avoid the receptionist's stare, this girl's mind seems to be just like the top of her desk—completely empty.

He picked up the front section of the morning's *Washington Post* and began reading the lead article about the final collapse of American defenses in the Philippines. The Japs were overrunning Bataan, Spencer thought, and he was sitting in an office in Washington, D.C. doing essentially nothing. Not that he hadn't wanted to join the military--at age 28, he was fine physical specimen of American manhood. But the Bureau had frowned on the concept of sending highly-trained agents into combat. According to the Bureau's press releases, they were much too valuable to the War Front at home to risk them on the battlefield. In fact, the Director had arranged draft deferments for all of his agents—even the ones working in the basement.

Spencer was trying to compare the value of gathering information on the drinking habits of a Massachusetts senator with fighting hand-to-hand with Japs in the South Pacific when the door to the inner office opened and an elderly black man and Frank Masterson stepped out into the reception area.   The black man was wearing a shabby, but clean, dress suit and clutched his battered fedora in both hands. Masterson, on the other hand, was wearing one of his many "Sunday best" suits. This one was double-breasted slate gray with a bright blue handkerchief peeking out of the breast pocket. His tie was a matching blue with a diagonal burgundy stripe and a gold tack in the center. His lightly-oiled blond hair was combed back above his finely chiseled face and if Spencer had not known better, he would have guessed the FBI man was actually the president of Boeing or General Motors.

"Yes, Leroy, that will be fine," Masterson said as he patted the man on the shoulder much like he were petting an old, but loyal, coonhound. "You just get her all shined up by this evening and everything will be fine."

"Yassuh, Mister Masterson, suh, I be gettin' right to it," the black man said as he shuffled his way to the door. "Don't you worry none, suh, you gonna have the finest lookin' automobile in all of DC when I get done with it."

Masterson opened the door and guided his guest into the hallway.

"You tell the missus I said hello and I hope you have a fine Sunday—what's left of it," the FBI man said. "Oh and don't forget to scrub that spare tire."

"Yes boss... I'll get to it and don't...."

The black man's reply was cut off in mid-sentence when Masterson closed the door in his face.

"There goes the only colored fellow in a town full of niggers," Masterson said as though Spencer and the receptionist could both benefit from his evaluation of the man who had just left the office. "Now, Agent Spencer, come on in and let's have a talk. I appreciate your interrupting your Sunday to come here."

"Well sir, it's my job to be here," Spencer said as he stood and followed Masterson into his office. "Besides, it's not that far to come."

"I know," Masterson said as he walked behind his desk and glanced down at the file lying on top of the dark green blotter. "You live over in Arlington—one-seven-oh-four Lee Terrace I believe." He motioned for Spencer to sit in one of the two leather chairs facing his desk. Despite the brightness of the day, the curtains were drawn and the only light in the office came from a brass desk lamp and another lamp sitting atop a wooden filing cabinet in a corner of the office.

"Yes sir," Spencer said as he took his seat. This was not going as well as he had hoped. It was beginning to sound more like an investigation into his background instead of an assignment. And apparently there was nothing special about being called into the office on a Sunday. After all, the man who washes Masterson's car must have received a similar summons. But as he watched the region's deputy director leaf through what was obviously the personnel file of William A. Spencer, he knew his being here must be something more than doing yard work over at the Masterson home in Foggy Bottom. Not that he had ever been there, but he had driven past it, as well as the homes of the Bureau's other big dogs. Although the homes were not mansions by D.C. standards, from the perspective of a young man from the Southern Appalachians, they were palatial.

"So, do you mind if I call you Willy?" Masterson asked without looking up from the file.

"Sir?"

"It says here that your friends call you 'Willy'." Masterson was now staring at him as though he were being accused of impersonating an FBI employee.

"Well, I'm sorry sir, but I've never been called by that name... never. I don't recall anyone in my family ever being called that either."

Masterson continued to stare at him as though waiting for him to change his story. When he didn't, the deputy director returned his attention to the file, flipped back through several pages and carefully drew a line through an entry.

"So what do your friends call you?" he asked.

"Bill. Just plain old Bill."

Masterson's shoulders sank and he looked at Spencer as though he couldn't believe anyone would give such a stupid answer. "No, I mean what do your friends down there in West Virginia call you? You know, when you come home from up here in the big city, what do all those hillbillies say? Here comes....? Here comes ....?"

"Billy."

"Very good!" Masterson said in a condescending tone and neatly penciled in the answer above the information he had just crossed out.

Spencer was annoyed. He wondered why he had come here to have his native state and family ridiculed by this jackass? Not just to this office and the FBI, but to Washington in general. Why hadn't he just stayed down there in Logan County? He had asked himself that question hundreds of times during the past three years and he knew the answer—no jobs for young lawyers there or even over in Charleston. Plus he had always wanted to travel... have big adventures. He was in DC working for the FBI because that was what he wanted and, as always, the truth left him with an ugly feeling of self-loathing.

"Hmm...the other information looks good," Masterson said as he continued to review the personnel file..."height five-eight...weight one-seventy...eyes..." Masterson looked up to study Spencer's face, "yes, eyes blue. But your hair color is listed as red. Looks more like blonde to me."

"Well, I reckon some the Bureau's boys didn't do their homework on me," Spencer said and let a little of his natural Southern drawl creep into his voice in hopes of annoying the stuffed shirt from…from.. he glanced up at the Harvard diploma on the wall above Masterson's head – Boston, of all places!

"It's irrelevant," Masterson said with a cold smile. "Really inconsequential information."

Spencer knew what the man's tone of voice was meant to convey—"irrelevant – just like you."

Masterson withdrew a thin folder from the drawer to his right and tossed it into the puddle of harsh light in the center of his desktop.

"I thought I would give you this file and let you take it down to your office in the basement to review it," Masterson began. "But there's really no need for that. So rather than worry about you losing it, I'll tell you everything you need to know about it."

Now Spencer was intrigued. An honest to God secret folder— surely this was something more challenging than snooping through Congressional mail. It was probably even more interesting than sitting at the "Nut Desk" and talking to all the crackpots who called the Bureau to report Nazis hiding in their attic or little green men frolicking in the woods. In exchange for the information he was about to receive, Spencer was even willing to temporarily overlook Masterson's rude Yankee upbringing.

"Basically, this is the story," Masterson began. "J. Edgar… The Boss… the Director to you, is no friend of the Limeys. We work with their military intelligence folks, or at least we did until Wild Bill Donovan and his OSS clowns got into the act. Now we just take what they give us…not much reciprocation on our part if you know what I mean."

Spencer clung to every word—even if this assignment involved sorting the garbage at the British Embassy it would be better than anything he had done before.

Masterson continued. "Last week, we received this file from the Brits. It's top secret as is everything else I'm about to tell you. You share it with no one. Is that understood?"

"Yes sir! You can count on me sir," Spencer said and immediately hated himself for his ill-concealed enthusiasm.

"We're working on a project with them that's too technical to go into here. But essentially it involves a method of intercepting radio signals from Nazi U-boats and then tracing them back to their point of origin. Apparently, if we can master this technology, it may be possible to do this so accurately and quickly that our bombers or ships can be sent immediately to attack the U-boat that just transmitted the message. Got it?"

"I'm with you so far sir," Spencer said and refrained from asking the man to drop the intellectually superior routine.

"Among the interceptions the Brits have made has been a recurring... anomaly, I guess you would call it," Masterson continued. "The source of these Nazi transmissions can, under ideal conditions, be narrowed down to an area of about twenty-five square miles—they think they will soon be able to do even better than that. So they've been making these radio intercepts for a few weeks now, the report doesn't say if they've actually destroyed a U-boat as a result, but when they plotted the locations of all these transmissions they found one that has remained unchanged. It seems to be coming from somewhere near the Florida coast. As far as a specific location is concerned, their best guess is somewhere near St. Augustine."

"A U-boat in Florida waters. Surely we'd find it." Spencer was beginning to doubt the effectiveness of this new technology. "How could it just be sitting there and not be detected?"

"Who says it's a U-boat?" Masterson said smugly. "The transmissions come from the same area nearly every night around midnight—but the messages are very short. That's apparently why it is so difficult to get a fix on the transmitter. This has been going on for at least the past three weeks—that's when the first intercepts were made. But this transmitter could have been operating for months—or even years. So in all probability, if this transmitter does indeed exist, it operates from a shore station or maybe a boat just offshore from America's oldest city. That's why you, Special Agent Billy Spencer, are going to St. Augustine."

"Yes sir," Spencer said and this time he was able to restrain his enthusiasm, but it was a struggle.

"There's a Navy transport plane flying out of National at four. Be on it," Masterson said sternly. "They're taking some high ranking officers down to Mayport—that's the Navy base at Jacksonville in case you're wondering. The local FBI office will leave a car for you there. Pick it up and drive on down to St. Augustine—shouldn't take you much more than an hour. You're booked into the Alhambra Hotel—sounds exotic. I want you to take the next few days and nose around. See what you can find about this… phantom transmitter… and report to me say, Tuesday. Any questions?"

Spencer knew he should have dozens of questions, but he could only think of one. "Why me?"

Masterson smiled stiffly and stood to signal the discussion was at an end. "Why you? Well, believe it or not, all the other agents have more important things to do."

"More important than catching German spies?" Spencer asked as he stood to go.

"Look, I don't for one minute think there's a German transmitter operating in Florida. No one in the Bureau believes it. But J. Edgar loves this scientific stuff… so he wants to check it out and what he wants he gets. Besides, you speak the language don't you?"

"German?" Spencer was confused – surely his personnel file didn't say he spoke a foreign language.

"Of course not," Masterson and his voice betrayed his annoyance. "If you were smart enough to speak German we wouldn't be wasting you on an assignment like this. I mean you're from West Virginia….you can talk in that quaint Southern accent all of those folks down there use. What do they call those backwoods hicks down in Florida? Snappers? No…crackers! A hillbilly among crackers – you should fit right in."

"Technically, there are nine distinct Southern accents," Spencer said coldly. "The intonation in my voice generally fits the tonal pattern known as Appalachian Highland. I believe the people of St. Augustine would have a Coastal Lowland accent." There, he thought, that should give this pompous stuffed shirt something to think about.

"Oh Billy, don't bother me with that sort of detail," Masterson scolded. "There may be nine different accents down there, but to me they all sound equally ignorant."

Spencer was seething inside, but realized there was nothing he could do about his superior's attitude—at least not at the moment. The trip to Florida suddenly seemed even more appealing.

"And Billy, don't forget. Don't go glory hunting down there. If by some miracle you do come up with something, call me immediately. I'll pass the information on to the Chief and he can decide what to do. Who knows? He might come down there and make an arrest personally. The point is—don't get your name in the papers. We don't need another Little Mel Purvis. Got it?"

"Yes, I've got it. And I've got a plane to catch." Spencer felt as though the walls were closing in on him and escape was just a few feet away through the door. First, Masterson had insulted his heritage. Now he was reminding him about Mel Purvis – the G-man who had become Public Hero Number One after leading the investigation that resulted in the death of the notorious John Dillinger. J. Edgar Hoover had become so enraged by the fact that the media had ignored him and given Purvis all the credit for Dillinger's demise that he had forced Little Mel to resign.

"Oh and one more thing," Masterson said. "Don't talk to those guys at Army or Navy intelligence—there's no need to get them involved. And don't forget to call me Tuesday with a report."

Spencer was already reaching for the doorknob. "Yes sir, no problem sir," he said as he stepped out of the office and firmly pulled the door closed behind him.

UNCLE SAM'S: 1830 hrs.

Joe Miller was glad he had decided to close the bar on Sundays. Not only did it give him and Luigi time to catch up on important management details, it also reinforced his reputation as a decent, law-abiding member of the God-fearing community of St. Augustine. Not that anyone doubted his sincerity, his compassion, or even his patriotism. He was a member of the Chamber of Commerce, the Security Council, and the Lions Club. Although he didn't attend church, he never failed to send a monthly $100 donation to each of the four major congregations in town. And the "Free Beer Night" he sponsored always insured at least one sold out Saints baseball game each season over at Francis Field.

He was also a good employer during hard times. His current payroll included two bartenders, four barmaids/waitresses, a short-order cook, two dishwashers and a janitor. On Saturday nights and on evenings when Army troops were brought over from Camp Blanding to let off steam, he sometimes added as many as twenty part-timers to his staff. In addition, the eight members of the *Patriot Swing Band*, led by Luigi Carbone, were the best paid and most popular group of musicians in all of Northeast Florida.

Miller closed his ledger and he could hear a faint popping as he twisted his head from side to side to relieve the kinks in his neck. He sighed and shoved the heavy book aside to signal another day's work was at an end—at least the work related to running a bar and fishing pier. It was time to savor the results and Miller couldn't help but feel proud of all he had accomplished. Two years ago, Uncle Sam's had been a boarded up derelict, but he had applied himself to its renovation with a zeal that quickly became the talk of the town. For people who liked to say: "in St. Augustine, a day late is two weeks early," the newcomer's devotion to restoring the old seaside property was not only borderline bizarre, it was also inspiring. Not since the heyday of Henry Flagler's resort building fifty years earlier had such ambition been seen in the nation's oldest city. Miller's work was a gentle reminder of the town's past glories.

First, the bar had been completely rebuilt and an entirely new kitchen was added. Pine-paneled booths were built along one wall and an open-air dance floor and covered stage large enough for a 20-piece band formed a new section on the south end of the building. Portholes substituted for windows and gave the bar a ship-like feel. The new boardwalk running the length of the property along the beach had turned out to be one of the most popular additions—nearly every night it was crowded with couples clutching in the darkness or leaning against the railing and looking down at the gentle surf surging up the beach and disappearing beneath their feet before hissing from under the boardwalk as it raced back to the sea.

And for those local residents who frowned on the liquor, the jazz and the groping in the darkness, Miller had rebuilt the dilapidated fishing pier—he had even extended it so that it now jutted nearly one thousand feet out into the Atlantic. The fact that he didn't charge admission to enjoy the fishing opportunities provided by the pier insured its popularity. His only stipulation on it use was that it was off limits after ten each night—but would re-open at eight each morning. Miller explained this "no compromise" closure policy was needed because of his possible liability should someone decide to commit suicide by jumping from the pier in the middle of the night. His story about a California pier operator who had gone bankrupt after being sued by the widow of

26

a jumper was widely accepted by everyone. In fact, not one person had ever asked why someone who was suicidal couldn't simply jump at 9:59 p.m. In fact, Joe Miller was often astonished that no one ever questioned his motives. He assumed that his copious use of red, white and blue paint on *Uncle Sam's Bar and Pier* along with the large American flag snapping in the sea breeze and bathed at night in the glow of a spotlight were enough to discourage any sort of probing questions from the locals.

But it was his office that most pleased Miller. He had drawn the plans himself—the dimensions had come from the memory of countless hours pacing the bridge of the Nassau more than twenty years ago. Mounted like a blockhouse on the roof high atop the bar, the office had a distinctive warship look about it. Included in its design were custom built metal window covers that looked much like blast shields, a ship's wheel and matching bronze binnacle mounted in front of the high windows running down the seaward side of the building—Miller had even included an engine telegraph that instead of signaling "full speed ahead" could be used to summon Carbone from behind the bar if he were needed in the office. As a final nautical touch, access to the office was available only by way of an iron spiral staircase that led to a hatch in the center of the "deck."

For Miller, the office served a far more valuable purpose than simply a place to work amid an atmosphere of seagoing whimsy. For him, this room was a link to his past –a link he was determined would remain unbroken by time or events. In fact, sometimes late at night he could sit at his desk in the dark and almost feel the presence of old comrades. He could hear the Kapitan's orders and on those special, stormy nights of summer, he could easily convince himself that the lightning and thunder in the skies above St. Augustine were actually the flashes and roar of Nassau's main guns firing at targets out of sight beyond the horizon. On those nights, he remained on watch in his office just as he did years ago aboard the old battleship. Then, when the storm faded, he would retire to his quarters—a ship's cabin that occupied the landward side of the office.

"Mind if I turn on a light?" Carbone asked from his desk in a corner of the office. "My eyes just ain't what they used to be and if I could make these last few calls, I'd be finished for the day."

27

Uncle Sam's

"Certainly, go right ahead," Miller said and noticed that Carbone had flicked on the lamp without waiting for his permission. When it came to getting a job done, he didn't waste time on the niceties. As far as Miller was concerned, his assistant was living proof of the fallacy of the common American belief that Italians were, by their nature, incurably lazy. It didn't matter if the work was manual labor or playing the drums, Carbone could always be counted on to give his best performance. In fact, there had been many times when Miller had envied his employee's ability to lose himself entirely in his work. Carbone was not a deep thinker—he was a worker and one of the best drummers Miller had ever seen.

Pounding the tubs, as Carbone called it, was the perfect activity for him. The drums required no vast knowledge of composition or even the ability to read music. What it did require was a sense of rhythm and an enthusiasm for the work that led to an aggressive and often inspired style of playing the drums that left the audience both enthralled and exhausted. Even now, as he held the telephone receiver with one hand, his other hand was busy tapping out a rhythm with a shiny new pencil.

"Mrs. Eubanks? How you doin'?" Carbone's telephone voice seemed especially friendly this evening. "This is Luigi Carbone over at *Uncle Sam's Bar*. Is Pete around?" A brief pause followed before he continued his familiar spiel. "That's too bad. We just drew his name out of Uncle Sam's hat here and he just won ten dollars! Do you know how I can get in touch with him?" Carbone looked up at Miller and winked good-naturedly. "That's too bad. Sailed today on the *Southern Cross*. That's too bad. I wouldn't worry about Pete sailing on that tanker—he's a careful guy." From across the room, Miller could faintly hear Mrs. Eubanks' voice on the receiver. Although he couldn't make out the exact words, it was obvious she was in a talkative mood. Carbone listened patiently before continuing his conversation. "Oh, you say the *Southern Cross* is a freighter, not an oiler....carrying sugar and rubber up to New York." The drumming stopped as Carbone scribbled down notes from his conversation. "Won't be back for two weeks....coming back to Jacksonville with a load of Army trucks. All right then, how about if I just put this money in an envelope and drop it in the mail to you? I'm sure you can find a good way to

28

spend it. OK? Consider it done. What's your address?" Carbone carefully wrote down the Eubanks' address. "I'll send it out tomorrow. Have a good evening!"

Carbone picked up the next index card and quickly dialed another local number.

"Mrs. Pellicer? How you doin'? This is Luigi Carbone over at *Uncle Sam's Bar and Pier*. Is Walt around? That's too bad. We just drew his name out….."

Miller shook his head at how easy it was to get vital information about ship sailings and cargoes by simply asking. Sometimes Luigi would make a dozen such calls and by the end of the telephone session, he would have a fairly accurate accounting of departures and arrivals from Jacksonville and St. Augustine. Most of the local seaman would visit the bar before setting out on their next voyage. They would invariably say something about their impending departure and Carbone was always there to inconspicuously jot down the information in a small black notebook he kept under the cash register. Although few were irresponsible enough to discuss their ship or its cargo with a bunch of drunks, they always shared the details with their wives or girlfriends. Carbone had developed this simple telephone routine for extracting the desired information from the women. Of course, he always mailed the ten dollars just as promised—no need to annoy anyone.

Miller rose from his desk, stretched his thin frame, and walked over to the open ports on the west side of the office. Beyond the Matanzas River, another glorious Florida sunset streaked the high blue vault of the sky with glowing amber. As he watched, the sky slowly faded from a deep blue to a royal purple and then to the final indigo of night. Behind him, Carbone continued his telephone conversations with women who, if he did he job correctly, would soon be widows. Miller savored these moments when everything seemed to be under control and he could allow himself the luxury of simply breathing in the smells of the salt marsh and the sea while listening to the gentle break of waves on the sand. Tonight there was a strange dryness to the air and he tried to remember the last time he had seen rain. Although he missed the heavenly light shows orchestrated by Mother Nature nearly every summer night, he was thankful for the quiet atmosphere of spring—the seemingly perpetual calmness of the nighttime atmosphere greatly increased the chances of success for the work he had scheduled for later in the evening.

Miller's quiet contemplation of the natural world was interrupted by the sound of a vehicle coming up the coast road. He watched the headlights approach and then the battered pickup entered the glare of the bright lights now emanating from Uncle Sam's. The truck was speeding as it passed, but two passengers riding in the bed had time to raise their beer bottles in salute to him while the driver honked a happy greeting.

"Hey Joe! What do you know?" One of then yelled and Miller waved in reply as the truck was swallowed by the night. He couldn't help but smile at the thought of what the truck's passengers would think if they only knew that Uncle Sam's Bar and Pier had been purchased and renovated with cash he had received in a brown paper bag handed to him by the German ambassador to the United States.

MOSE'S CREEK: 2010 hrs.

Winnie Greer loved the feel of cold sand on her bare feet. It reminded her of snow. Not that she had ever touched or even seen real snow. But whenever the path home was lit by the Florida moon, she liked to pretend the soft sand beneath her feet was actually the snow she had heard was often found in the streets of Philadelphia. In fact, whenever she imagined the City of Brotherly Love, it was covered in snow and her father was always happy and singing as he walked along to his office. But like snow, she had neither seen nor touched her father. All she knew of him was that he lived or had lived in Philadelphia. That's all her mother had ever told her about him.

But by combining that fact with the equally irrefutable evidence provided by a newspaper photo showing a blizzard in Philadelphia, she was able to mentally construct an imaginary world in which her father worked as a lawyer or executive in a fancy office. In her imagination, her father often wanted to come south to visit her. Unfortunately, some business emergency would always come up at the last minute to prevent him from coming down. In fact, she could vividly recall how he couldn't come to

Florida one Christmas because President Roosevelt had a special assignment for him. She felt a tinge of embarrassment each time she remembered how several folks at church had laughed at her when she told that story—but even eight years later, it remained one of her favorite Christmas memories.

"Sonofabitch," Winnie muttered and immediately added: "Forgive me Lord." For a moment, she was ashamed of what she had said—especially because her true feelings about her father had made her curse on Sunday. "What would Mama say?" she asked herself even though she knew the answer. Mama wouldn't say anything. Mama was dead and gone—her bones buried in the cemetery behind the church. And her father hadn't even come down for the funeral. As much as she hated to admit it, Winnie had to concede that her father was even less of a man than the numerous other locals who got women pregnant and then never bothered to make a home for their new families. At least some of them would show up on special occasions and some even showed some financial responsibility toward the children they had produced—but not her father.

There had been a time when these confrontations with reality would make her cry—especially at night when no one could see her tears. But now she found great comfort in the fact that admitting the truth about the man who had planted his seed in her mother's womb helped her summon up an inner strength that could sustain her through anything—even the death of her mother. "Sonofabitch," she repeated and this time she didn't bother to ask for forgiveness.

The path darkened as a silvery cloud slid across the face of the moon. The fading of the pale light forced Winnie to abandon her reverie of snow in Philadelphia so she could concentrate on the reality of picking her way through the piney woods of St. Johns County. The final hundred yards of the trip home were always the most frightening for Winnie. The clean sand gave way to a tidal muck that smelled of decay and oozed between her toes in the form of a putrid slime that always seemed reluctant to loosen its grip on her skin no matter how hard she scrubbed. At high tide, the black mud of the trail was hidden from Winnie by six inches of water. But now, the receding tide had exposed the mud flat and the creatures who lived there were busy taking advantage of the darkness to go about their business without the dangers that a daylight excursion from their burrows would bring. Tonight, they were especially rambunctious—faint shadows scurried in the darkness and off to the left there was a loud splash that made Winnie increase the pace of her walking.

She wished she had never gone to the alligator farm over on the island. But it was the only trip her school offered to its seniors and that was available only because the farm's proprietors provided an annual "Colored Seniors Day" with free admission to her school's graduating class. After seeing the huge gators devouring chickens and thrashing about in the mud, Winnie was convinced "Colored Seniors Day" was held just to scare them into thinking that giant reptiles were roaming the mud flats in search of their favorite food—colored teenagers. Still, she couldn't help but agree with her classmates that at least the white folks who ran the alligator farm were thoughtful enough to give them something in recognition of their academic achievements – even if the reward resulted in nightmares for some of the graduates.

Not that anyone had ever seen an alligator running loose this close to the ocean. "Them gators don't like salt water," Old Man Pell had said and his word on questions of nature were taken as gospel. But Winnie couldn't help but wonder what would happen if some of those giant reptiles over at the farm decided to break out and head inland toward the lakes and creeks where their ancestors had hatched. Surely they would stop here for a snack on their way to Gainesville. Winnie forced herself to ignore the shadows that suddenly looked remarkably like the low profiles of hungry reptiles by concentrating on the injustice of white seniors going to a banquet sponsored by the Chamber of Commerce while the reward for colored seniors was a trip to see a bunch of smelly old alligators. At last, she could see the glow of the lamp on the front porch. She pulled her feet out of the muck and hurried toward the house where she was born.

"Winnie?" Verna Washington's eyesight wasn't so good at night. She got up from the rocking chair and leaned over the porch railing. "Is that you Winnie?"

"Yes, ma'm. It's me." Even in the dim light, Winnie could tell the woman was relieved to see her. "It's been a long day."

Verna was a large woman, but she moved quickly as she

gathered up her knitting bag and headed toward the steps leading down to the bare yard. Winnie felt sorry that their closest neighbor had spent most of her Sunday watching over Granny.

"I'm sorry I didn't get here sooner, but the Reverend wanted me to sing at tonight's service too. You know how hard it is to tell him no once he sets his mind on something."

"Oh I know that all right," Verna said as she squeezed past Winnie and carefully went down the rickety steps. "But I'm sure everyone enjoyed your singin'. Next time, I'll try to be there."

"How's Granny? Was she all right this evening?"

"Oh she's just fine," Vera said and without looking back waved a quick goodbye. "I reckon she's still awake waitin' for you."

Winnie had a hundred questions to ask. Did she have one of her spells? What did she eat? Was she awake all day? But Vera's broad expanse wrapped in a tight purple dress had already moved beyond the lantern's glow.

"Thanks for watching her!" Winnie shouted to the darkness and heard Vera mumble something that sounded like "you're welcome."

The screen door screeched on its hinges as Winnie entered the house and she was careful not to let it slam behind her. It was only a few steps down the narrow hallway to her grandmother's room where she found the most remarkable woman she had even known sitting in her wheelchair with her Bible in her lap. The feeble light of a single candle gave the room a spiritual quality and its flickering caused shadows to dance across the woman's white cotton gown.

"Hello Granny. I'm finally home." Winnie wrapped her arms around her grandmother's frail shoulders and gave her a kiss on her forehead. She noticed her hair smelled of strawberries—Vera had obviously given her a shampoo. Winnie felt a tinge of remorse as she realized that simple act had probably been the high point of her grandmother's day.

Granny Greer reached up and patted Winnie's hand. "I'm glad child. I was beginning to worry."

"Oh now Granny, you don't have to worry 'bout me," Winnie said. "I'm a big girl now."

"That's why I worry—big girls can get into all kinds of trouble."

Winnie knew she was referring to her mother—and she wanted to avoid that subject.

"I'm sorry about this Sunday. I really am," Winnie said. "I would have stayed here with you, but the church was expecting me to sing tonight and I couldn't let them down. Bernard said how sorry he was he couldn't get the truck over to pick you up."

Bernard White owned an old flat bed truck that served as Granny's only source of transportation. Every other Sunday, if the tides were right, he would bring it through the mud flats and they would roll Granny in her wheelchair up on the bed and take her to church. But today, Bernard had spent the morning transporting worshippers back and forth between the church and the baptismal services on the beach.

"You tell Bernard not to worry no more 'bout it," Granny said quietly. "I had a fine Sunday right here. Vera brought over some fried chicken and I had lots of time with the Lord. Just Him and me."

"And what did you and the Lord talk about?" Winnie sat on the edge of her grandmother's bed and reached out to hold the woman's bony hands in her own. Granny's cataract-covered eyes seemed to shift toward her.

"Well, I talked to Him about you and Curtis."

Winnie smiled. "Granny, I swear, the Lord is gonna get tired of talkin' to you—it's always the same subject…me and Curtis."

"No He won't. He loves to hear about you and your brother. He watches over the both of you—and I thanked Him because now that Curtis done gone off to the white man's Navy, he needs watchin' out for with the war and everything."

"But you know how Curtis is—he's probably getting' along just fine. Probably workin' for some admiral by now." Winnie seldom worried about her brother. In fact, instead of being concerned about him, she was often envious. After all, he was far away from Moses Creek—'sailing the seven seas' he had written in his last letter.

"I know he's fine, but it never hurts to remind the Lord to keep an eye on him… and you too. We had a long talk about you today."

It had not been that long ago that Winnie had actually believed her grandmother and God had private conversations. Although she still had no doubts that God would hear her prayers, she found it difficult to believe the Lord had nothing better to do than discuss her life for hours on end.

"He says you need to do more with the gift He gave you," Granny said firmly.

"More? I don't know what more I can do," Winnie said in her own defense. "I sing nearly every day at the church. And I won that contest. Reverend Fulmer says I bless the entire congregation every time I sing."

Granny pulled her hands free from Winnie's grip. "I don't know exactly what He wants from you. But He made it clear that the voice he gave you should be heard by the multitudes, not just by the members of the Moses Creek church."

"But how? How am I supposed to…."

"God will provide. But it's up to you to know His will."

Winnie's fondest dream had been to become a famous singer—when she was alone, she often pretended she was Bessie Smith. But she always believed she would spend the best years of her life here taking care of Granny—and she had accepted her fate willingly. Now, the woman who had raised her seemed to be saying that if an opportunity to move on with a career in music came along, she should take it. In fact, she had just said God wills it. Winnie felt that this conversation would be long remembered by both of them.

"You know I want to please God," Winnie said. She stood and leaned down to hug her grandmother again. "Where He leads me, I will follow—I've sung that a thousand times."

"I know you will child…and where He leads me is to bed. I'm so tired."

Winnie squeezed her grandmother as tightly as she dared and for some reason she felt tears welling up in her eyes and running down her cheeks. As she helped Granny out of her wheelchair and into bed, Winnie felt ashamed that she was happy about the prospect of someday leaving this woman who had given her everything.

Uncle Sam's

Monday
April 13, 1942

U-112 OFF MIAMI: 0640 hrs.

As U-112 continued its leisurely circle, the rosy glow of dawn washed across the faces of the six men atop the submarine's sleek conning tower. Despite the fact that the enemy's homeland was less than ten miles away, they were in a relaxed mood. Not that they had lessened their vigilance—that was something that would remain at a high level until the boat tied up once more at their Lorient bunker. But there was something about the warmth of the Florida morning and the hint of tropical islands on the sea breeze that brought a sense of pride and contentment to each of them. Although U-boat duty was often uncomfortable and sometimes terrifying, it was moments like these that made all of the hardships seem worthwhile. They knew that among all the sailors of the world, they were a special breed. As the First Watch Officer Jens Thiele had noted just a few minutes earlier: "Who else gets to go sightseeing in the enemy's backyard?"

Each of the four lookouts continued to scan his assigned ninety-degree arc of sea and sky while *Kapitanleutnant* Theodore "Teddy" Rahn lined up the target. The boat's 32 year-old commander glanced over his left shoulder and watched as the pink hues of sunrise quickly faded into the brilliant blue sky of the new day. When he returned his gaze to the target, he saw it was bathed in the sparkling morning light.

"Glorious!" Rahn said aloud and then quickly shouted his orders down the open hatch at his feet to the helmsman sitting patiently in the tower. "Come to two-two-zero! All ahead two-thirds!"

He could hear his words repeated in the control room and at

once the gentle simmering of the twin diesels changed to a workmanlike throb. Rahn could feel the boat heel slightly in the turn as the screws bit firmly into the warm sea. He polished the lens of his Leica with a handkerchief and then spread his feet on the wooden deck to steady his posture against the roll of the boat. Satisfied with his position, he flipped the camera's switch to "on" and framed the Fowey Rocks Lighthouse in his viewfinder.

Click....ti-ti-ti-tick....click....ti-ti-ti-tick.

Rahn advanced the film with his thumb as he squeezed off a dozen exposures without taking his eye off his subject. Through the viewfinder, he watched the light peak in sharp intensity before fading to a commonplace brilliance that would have been judged to be extraordinary in most other parts of the world. He lowered his camera and as he watched the lighthouse pass abeam, he wiped prickly drops of sweat from the back of his neck with his handkerchief. *"Mein Gott,"* he thought, "there's still deep snow on the ground and great skiing at Oberstdorf."

"Hello girls!" Kovic, the starboard lookout, shouted and waved as the boat's course brought the lighthouse into the sector of horizon he was scanning. "We love you too!"

Rahn brought his Zeiss binoculars up to his eyes and quickly focused on the lighthouse perched all alone atop spindly legs that jutted from the seafloor to a height of more than 100 feet above the deep green sea. Sure enough, he could see two American sailors leaning over the railing that encircled the light platform—the blue denim work uniforms and white sailor caps were clearly visible. As he watched, one of them waved in return!

"All right men, let's say hello to our American cousins!" Rahn ordered and everyone on the bridge waved a friendly greeting to the two sailors high up in the lighthouse.

Thiele swung himself up on the periscope housing and enthusiastically waved his cap. *"Herr Kaleu,* don't you think we should give them a little gift? A couple of rounds through those metal supports and the whole thing will collapse."

"Don't be so rude, Number One, some of us with more sophisticated tastes than your own consider that contraption to be a work of art," Rahn said as he lowered his binoculars and looked up to where his smiling First Watch Officer was precariously balanced with one arm wrapped around the periscope housing. "Besides, after the war, I think I'll come back here with a little boat and take dancing girls from the Miami Beach clubs on daytrips. If you blow up the light, what will we do when it gets dark and we can't find our way back to Miami?"

Even without his binoculars, Rahn could now see that a third American sailor had joined his two comrades. All three of the Americans enemies gave a friendly wave as the U-boat's course now took it away from the lighthouse.

"Idiots," Rahn muttered. He was amazed that the Americans were unable to identify their boat as one of the Third Reich's genuine terrors of the deep.

"*Ja*, that's what I would do…warm nights, dancing girls, lots of rum…" Matrose Peter Weingarten continued to scan his sector while verbalizing one of his favorite daydreams. The bright sun and the warm tradewinds made it difficult for the lookouts to concentrate—their minds sometimes wandered, but based on their off duty conversations it seemed obvious that Weingarten was the only one whose fantasies were exclusively inhabited by dark-haired beauties with names like Carmen and Esperanza.

"Hey, Little Pete!" shouted Klausen the lookout on the opposite side of the tower. "Don't you know there is a height requirement for entering Miami—they wouldn't let you off the dock!"

"And don't forget the minimum length requirement," Thiele added. "Sorry Weingarten, you lose on both counts!"

Everyone laughed, including Weingarten who had long since accepted his diminutive stature and now found most of the jokes about his shortness to be more boring than annoying.

Kapitanleutnant Rahn stepped back to the open *wintergarten* platform and with one hand resting on the breach of the anti-aircraft gun, he watched the lighthouse slowly slide from view beyond the U-boat's broad, fleecy white wake. A raucous flock of seagulls spun and dove, fluttered and climbed just beyond the stern as though they expected him to provide them with a hearty breakfast of raw fish. He couldn't help but think of how different his world was from that cold and nearly colorless world now occupied by Kat. Here there was warmth and sunlit hues that seemed far too splendid to be categorized as mere greens and blues. Rahn found it simple to visualize the day at Kat's home—a solid overcast so thick that even the noonday sun failed to create a shadow from the leafless trees along the canal where pieces of old ice seemed permanently attached to the surface of the motionless black water. The snow would be melting now, but it would still be piled deep against the north side of the two-story stone house where Katrina...dearest Kat...would be looking out the kitchen window and wondering if spring would ever arrive. At this time of day, she would be preparing lunch for her ailing mother—probably some cabbage soup. As he visualized her carrying the tray of food up the stairs, he couldn't help but think of the way the muscles in the calves of her shapely legs had flexed that summer day eight years ago when he had first followed her upstairs to her bedroom.

"All right! Enough fun for one morning!" Rahn shouted to wake himself from his reverie before he slipped hopelessly into its enchanting grip. He pushed himself away from the wintergarten and stepped purposefully back on to the narrow bridge. "Just in case those Amis aren't complete morons, let's take her down—an emergency dive please Number One."

"*Jawohl, Herr Kaleu*," Thiele said as Rahn squeezed past and descended through the open hatch. The First Watch Officer waited until the white tropical cover on Rahn's officers cap bobbed once, twice and then disappeared below before beginning the exercise. He stepped over to the hatch and gazed down to see that the boat's commander had made it to the bottom of the ladder and had disappeared into the brightly lit control room. Seidel, the helmsman looked up at him and smiled from his station in the tower just below his boots.

"*Alaaarrrmmmm!*" Thiele shouted, sucked in another breath and repeated his warning. "*Alaaarrrrmmmm!*" He stepped aside as the four members of the watch scrambled past him and slid down the ladder to the accompaniment of the frantically ringing dive bell. Thiele heard their boots smack the control room deck and in one much-practiced motion, he slid down the ladder while pulling the hatch closed behind him. He quickly spun the hatch wheel to seal fifty-two men away from the world of sunlight and tropical breezes.

"Hatch secure!" he shouted.

Thiele's shoes framed the open hatch in the tower deck through which he could see the tops of heads and caps rushing forward through the control room as the crew scrambled forward into the torpedo room where their combined weight would help speed the boat on her downward plunge. To his right, Seidel busied himself with preparing the helmsman's station for underwater operations. He paused just long enough to give Thiele a questioning and concerned look. The First Watch Officer's answering wink made him smile – "just a drill—we're not about to die."

To Thiele's way of thinking, the process of taking a U-boat beneath the waves consisted of piling orders and reports on top of each other so quickly and in such quantities that the boat had no choice but slide into the depths. The loudspeaker began to crackle as each compartment was reported to be ready for descent. He gave Seidel's shoulder an encouraging squeeze and then slid down the final length of ladder and into *Zentrale*— U-boat *Eins-Eins-Zwei's* control room.

Oberleutnant August "Augie" Wieland, the boat's chief engineer, watched the dive preparations like a concerned parent seeing his children perform in public for the first time. A heavy-set man with one of the best beards in the fleet, Wieland was known for his no-nonsense approach to his job. Although most chiefs would have given the crew excellent marks for their response to the alarm, he had made several mental notes about "corrective actions" that needed to be taken. He had been particularly annoyed by the behavior of one young seaman who had slowed his headlong rush to his duty station just long enough to reach up and squeeze the small rubber doll that hung from a valve in the overhead. As always, the brown-skinned beauty with an assortment of tropical fruit atop her head had responded to his touch by exposing her ample breasts until he released his grip and they popped back into her dress. Despite his concern for the need for additional "professionalism," Augie made his report to Thiele.

"Ready to dive!"

"Very good Chief," Thiele responded. "Let's flood!"

"Flood!" Wieland ordered and his eyes flashed with excitement as a new stream of reports came in.

"Air vents open....flood valves open....diesel air valve closed...."

Along one bulkhead, there was a flurry of activity as two crewmen rapidly closed valves and yanked levers into place. There was a slight shudder as the diesels shut down.

"Diesels off line....e-motors engaged..."

The electric lighting blinked once as the boat switched to batteries and the hiss of released air sounded throughout U-112. Reports continued to squawk from the loudspeaker.

The Chief leaned down and placed his hands on the shoulders of Kovic and Weingarten who had taken their seats at the hydroplane controls as soon as they dropped from their lookout positions topside.

"Bow planes down ten....stern down five," the Chief said firmly and the two men in his grip responded by pressing the palms of their hands on the hydroplane control buttons. The U-boat seemed to teeter on top of the ocean and then it slid downward. Their eyes were fixed on the mercury that began to rise in the periscope depth gauge used for judging precise depths near the surface.

"Ten meters," Kovic said quietly.

"Ten meters!" The Chief repeated loudly for the benefit of those gathered in the control room who could only see the large scale Tiefenmesser depth gauge whose needle had just begun to move across the face of its dial.

"Take us to fifty and hold us there Chief," Thiele said and leaned against the chart locker.

Wieland nodded and watched the depth gauge slide past twenty meters. He stroked his luxurious red beard as he studied the array of gauges in front of him. Normally, he would already be calculating the changes that would need to be made in the boat's trim to bring them level, but this time he was confident that this would be one of those rare occasions when everything was just where it needed to be.

"Forty meters," Kovic said.

As the *Tiefenmesser* slid past 42 meters, the Chief made his call: "Bow planes up ten...stern up five...rudder amidship....e-motors one-third." The hydroplane operators pressed their controls, the helm responded and the electric motors slowed. "Bow planes zero. Stern planes zero."

For the crew, the sudden feeling that they were no longer leaning forward told them the dive maneuver had been completed.

"Fifty meters, Number One, the boat is trimmed," Wieland said as though taking fourteen hundred tons of steel and its human occupants beneath the surface of the sea and stopping at exactly the depth specified was mere child's play.

"Very good Chief! Excellent job Number One!" Rahn said from the position he had silently occupied in a corner of the control room throughout the dive operation. "Let's maintain this depth and bring us around to course oh-seven-oh."

"*Jawohl, Herr Kaleu,*" Thiele said and the smile on his face showed Rahn's compliment had been appreciated.

"Good work gentlemen!" Rahn said so that everyone in the control room could hear him. "We were down to ten meters in less than two minutes—not bad for a broad-assed boat like this one."

He noticed that not one member of the crew had asked whether the dive had been an actual emergency or was it just another practice session-- it was obvious to every man on board that it was all another game of pretend. Rahn knew that sort of complacency could prove deadly in a life and death situation. He couldn't help but hope the Americans would at least send a patrol plane somewhere near by so they could get some live action—it had now been more than two weeks since they had felt that rush of adrenaline that comes from playing cat and mouse with an enemy who could easily kill them all. Although there were few visual signs that his crew might be losing its competitive edge, he could sense that the razor sharp reflexes that had safely brought them here were slowly fading.

ST. AUGUSTINE: 0920 hrs.

FBI Agent Bill Spencer found St. Augustine to be even better than he had imagined. In fact, he had to keep reminding himself that he was on an assignment for the Bureau—not on a vacation. Instead of the lazy, Southern county seat he had expected, the city seemed more like a Spanish colonial port tucked away on some remote Mediterranean island. Although he remembered from Mrs. Brainard's eighth grade history class that St. Augustine was the oldest city in the United States, founded in 1500-something or other, she had not taught them anything about the beauty of the town--the Moorish-Revival architecture, red-tiled roofs, ancient coquina walls, the Basilica, and all the splendor that Henry Flagler's millions of dollars had added at the turn of the century created a setting that was a welcomed change from the cold rain and oppressively bureaucratic architecture of Washington, D.C.

The drive down from Jacksonville had taken longer than he expected, although he had to admit the brand new Chevy coupe the Bureau had provided made the trip far more bearable than it should have been. His first hint that he was arriving at a unique destination came shortly after midnight when he entered St. Augustine by driving through a massive city gate just as travelers had undoubtedly done for hundreds of years. At the end of a narrow street, he came to a central plaza where a moonlit cathedral had nearly convinced him he had arrived in Mexico.

By the time he reached his hotel, he was exhausted and sleep had come quickly. In fact, it wasn't until he had put away a hearty breakfast and finished his second cup of coffee at the Alhambra Hotel's small restaurant that he felt prepared to begin his assignment. After paying his bill, he walked through the hotel's lobby and stepped out into the bright sunlight.

Directly across the street, the sprawling Ponce de Leon Hotel with its stone arches, towering spires, and stained glass windows cut deep within heavy concrete walls was a site that made the G-man pause. Closed for more than ten years because of the Depression, the hotel still possessed a magical charm like some sultan's castle in *The Arabian Nights.*

Spencer pulled the brim of his hat much lower than he would have in Washington. The sun's glare would take some getting used to, he said to himself, as he headed down King Street. Already the shade of the *Plaza de la Constitucion* beckoned to him and he crossed over to this small park that had served as the city's central gathering point for nearly 400 years. This morning, the Plaza was occupied by the usual collection of retirees lounging on park benches or playing checkers at the two tables that had been set up for that purpose in a spacious gazebo. He walked past the iron cannons, reminders of the city's many battles against English invaders and rampaging pirates, and paused at the Confederate Memorial Column just long enough to note that a large percentage of the St. Augustinians who had died defending the South against Northern aggression had Spanish surnames.

Like a tourist in town for the first time, Spencer took in the sites—the magnificent Bridge of Lions glistening white in the morning sun and beyond it the St. Augustine lighthouse with its distinctive black-white paint scheme jutting into a bright blue sky. Traffic hustled past on the broad *Avenida Menendez* while up by the massive old coquina fortress, the *Castillo de San Marcos*, sailboats rode at anchor in the aquamarine waters of Matanzas Bay.

"Special Agent Spencer?"

Spencer was startled to hear his name spoken, but he continued to gaze out toward the inlet where the broad Atlantic had beckoned the town's residents for centuries.

"Yes," Spencer said finally and tried to fix his expression into some sort of intimidating glare before turning to face the person who somehow knew his name.

"Hello, my name is Michael Pomar. Mind if I ask you some questions?"

Spencer could see that his best G-man face had failed to make any sort of impression on the young man who was now extending his hand and smiling in a most disarming manner. He shook the boy's hand much more firmly than necessary in hopes of clearly establishing his physical dominance. When he released his grip, he felt mildly ashamed that he would try such a thing with a kid. He felt better when he realized his childish display had failed to impress young Pomar.

"Generally, I ask the questions," Spencer said in his official FBI tone of voice.

"That's OK, I'll answer your first two questions without you even havin' to ask 'em," the boy said happily. "How do I know you're an FBI man? Some of my contacts at the Alhambra Hotel told me. Why do I want to ask you some questions? Because that's what I do—I find out things and report them."

"You're a reporter?"

"Sort of," Pomar said as he pushed his blue and gray Brooklyn Dodgers baseball cap back from his forehead and fished a notebook from his hip pocket. "I'm an independent... I sell my stories to anyone who will buy them—*The Record*, radio stations, anyone who wants them." The boy quickly flipped to a blank page, pulled the stub of a pencil from his shirt pocket, wet its tip with his tongue and prepared to take notes. "In fact, WFOY radio is letting me work there some in the evenings. Who knows? I might get my own show some day."

Spencer sized up the energetic young man and concluded he was probably not only harmless, but undoubtedly a good source of information—something that he very much needed at the moment. However, he also realized that whatever plans he had for remaining inconspicuous during his visit were being seriously compromised as he stood there in the town plaza while dozens of people watched him being interviewed by a reporter—even an amateur one.

"So, Mike, you don't mind if I call you Mike? How about if we take a walk and find a shady spot to talk?" Without waiting for an answer, Spencer noted a short break in the long line of Army trucks, farm pickups and sedans moving past and hurried across *Avenida Menendez*. He realized that anyone watching would think the boy was chasing him, so he paused next to one of the huge carved lions guarding the entrance to the bridge.

"Actually, I do prefer to be called Michael, " Pomar said as he skipped through the traffic to join Spencer. "You don't hear anyone calling Walter Winchell, 'Walt' do you? It just wouldn't sound right, 'this is Walt Winchell reporting.' Sounds like some sort of Disney character."

"All right then—Michael—or better yet, how about Scoop? That's the perfect name for a reporter—Scoop Pomar," Spencer said as he began walking north along the seawall toward the *Castillo de San Marcos*. He could tell by the fleeting smile on the young man's face that he agreed that the nickname had a certain flair about it.

"So, Agent Spencer, what do you think of our town?" Pomar asked as he hurried to catch up.

"Great town…great scenery…great people. In a word: Great."

Spencer was growing increasingly annoyed by this intrusion. The last thing he needed was a story about his presence in the local newspaper. Jesus, he thought, this was supposed to be an investigation not a vacation. And to make matters worse, he couldn't help but remember Masterson's reminder that the headlines were reserved for the Director and nobody else.

"Look, let's get this over with," the G-man said sharply and motioned Pomar toward a stone bench and the two of them sat for a moment staring out to where an Army dredge was busily reshaping St. Augustine's inlet. They could see a fountain of wet sand shooting upward from the dredge and landing in a battered barge. "I'm sorry, kid, but you're not putting anything about me in the paper. If you do, I'll have you arrested for interfering with a Federal investigation."

"Oh I wasn't going to write anything about this," Pomar said and quickly tucked his notepad into his shirt pocket. "At least I didn't think I would—I'm just trying to get some background information. So...what kind of investigation are you doing?"

Spencer was surprised—most people would back off when threatened with arrest. But this boy was different. Despite his age, which Spencer estimated at sixteen, Pomar was not intimidated. In fact, he seemed to approach his 'job' with bulldog determination, as though he were on some sort of holy mission. As he studied the boy's features, he failed to notice anything that would explain his gung ho approach to his work. His wire-rimmed glasses gave him a studious, bookworm kind of look while his muscular neck and broad shoulders seemed to speak of hidden athletic abilities.

"Dodgers fan?" Spencer tried to change the subject by noting Pomar's baseball cap.

"All my life," Pomar said proudly. "Pee Wee Reese is my hero. In fact, if this reporting job doesn't pan out, I think I'll try to be their next shortstop. Now, as I was saying, why are you here?"

"Pomar? Pomar? Sounds Spanish or something, but you sure don't look Spanish." Spencer tried one last time to derail the boy's train of thought.

For the first time, the young reporter looked surprised. Then his features melted into a warm smile.

"I'm surprised that a Special Agent for the FBI would make presumptions about a person's heritage based solely on appearances," Pomar said. "That must be how you arrest all of those gangsters—he looks Italian so he must be in the mob—put the cuffs on him!"

Spencer refrained from agreeing. In fact, he had often thought that sort of ethnic stereotyping was exactly the approach the Bureau was taking toward the mob. How else could you explain why each time the FBI made a mob arrest, the collar always looked exactly like the Sicilian waiter at *Bernelli's Restaurant* in Georgetown?

"Actually," Pomar continued. "My ancestors were Minorcans, from an island off the coast of Spain. The entire village came over to Florida as indentured servants to work on an Englishman's indigo plantation about a hundred miles south of here. When he tried to treat them like slaves, they walked all the way to St. Augustine for their freedom. That was way back in 1777 and their descendants are probably the most influential group in town—just another fascinating history lesson for you. And by the way, Spaniards are Europeans— we're not Mexicans. If you don't believe me, you should go see the Gonzalez sisters—one blonde, one redhead and both absolutely gorgeous. So now I've told you my story...what's your heritage?"

"I don't know—Welsh I think. Welsh Quakers. At least that's what somebody in the family once said." Spencer suddenly felt guilty that he knew so little about his roots--maybe there was nothing worth telling. "My guess is that they were so busy surviving today and worrying about tomorrow that they never had time to think about yesterday."

"Well you seem to have done all right—just look at you, a Federal agent and all. Your mother must be awfully proud."

Spencer had never heard anyone take such a cavalier attitude toward the Bureau. Most people tended to talk about it in hushed tones like it was some sort of secret order. He had to admit, he liked Pomar's attitude.

"Yes, she's positively bustin' at the seams with pride...and I'll bet yours is too. You know, mother of the town's news hound and all."

"Maybe some day," Pomar said and gazed out across the bay. "Now she thinks I just collect gossip."

"And what's the gossip today?"

Pomar grinned and turned to face Spencer.

"Well, besides the arrival of the FBI agent, it's pretty much the same old thing... sugar's going to be rationed... the mayor's wife is pregnant... there's a U-boat patrolling the inlet..."

"Whoa! Now there's something that might interest the Bureau." Spencer tried to sound amused, but he couldn't help but hope he may have found a starting point for his investigation.

"I'm sure they would. No one has seen her for several days and she's so big it would be impossible to miss her."

"People have seen a U-boat!" Spencer could no longer contain himself. "I can't believe it! Why wasn't it reported?"

"U-boat?" Pomar chuckled. "I'm talking about the mayor's wife. No one has seen her lately and yes, she is big."

Now it was Spencer's turn to laugh. Despite feeling slightly ridiculous, he decided Michael Pomar was going to play a valuable role in his investigation—if he ever got it started.

"I'm sure the condition of the mayor's wife is the talk of the town, but I'm more interested in things that might involve national security—like a U-boat, for instance?" Spencer tried to sound as casual as possible. "You say someone might have seen one around here?"

"It would be hard to find someone who hasn't... everybody thinks he's seen a U-boat or two. I thought I was looking at a Nazi periscope yesterday until it flew away." Pomar looked at Spencer as though examining an unusual specimen. "I'll bet you haven't spent a lot of time around the water."

"Well no, not unless you count the Potomac River."

The young man dismissed the river with a wave of his hand. "No. I mean real water like out there." He nodded toward the inlet and the sea beyond. "The light in the morning... or evening ... or even at midday for that matter. Combine it with a playful dolphin or two, throw in some sand churned up by a riptide, add a couple of diving pelicans and the next thing you know, you're looking at Hitler in a rowboat."

"So, with all of your contacts you don't know anyone who has actually seen a U-boat?" Spencer had hoped for more from this conversation—at least a lead on where to ask more questions.

Pomar shrugged. "I'm afraid not. I don't think anyone really believes the Germans are out there. A few weeks ago, they might have worried about it...but now all you read in the papers is about how many U-boats the Navy sank this week. It all seems pretty far away now that the military has eliminated the so-called U-boat menace."

"And you? What do you think, Mr. Ace Reporter?"

"That's a switch. I'm usually the one asking the questions," Pomar lifted his Dodgers cap and pulled it back down firmly while he contemplated his answer. "Well, I'd say their record speaks for itself—there's apparently not much the Germans can't do militarily if they set their minds to it. And despite all the hoopla, I don't think we pose much of a challenge for them—at least not yet anyway."

"Hey, aren't you afraid I'll report you for that kind of defeatist talk?"

"Me?" Pomar said in mock innocence. "What do I know? I'm just a kid. If you want to find out what's going on to defend our little piece of paradise, you need to visit with the members of the St. Augustine Security Council. Now there's some fellas who can tell you about military tactics, strategic planning, how to make the Hun say Uncle—you know the type."

Yes, Spencer thought, he did know the type—civilians with dreams of saving the world from some ghastly evil—pretty much the same as most of the people he worked with in Washington. He could already see it in his report— "established liaison with St. Augustine Security Council." The bean counters back at headquarters loved that sort of thing.

"Security Council? You're right, those are the guys I need to meet. Where can I find them?"

"Well, FBI Special Agent William Spencer, you're in luck— they meet every Monday morning over at the City Building," Pomar said as he stood. "They won't let anyone else attend—all those secrets and things. They have to be careful, but I'm sure they'd be delighted to have a genuine, J. Edgar Hoover-certified G-man sit in on their meeting. C'mon, I'll take you over there and I think we've got enough time for you to buy me a Coke on the way. I don't provide all this information for free—I'm a professional you know. Hey, you can even tell me how I can become a bona fide FBI Special Agent just like you."

"Trust me Scoop," Spencer said as he hurried to catch up with Pomar who was already wading into the traffic on *Avenida Menendez.* "This job is not what it's cracked up to be."

SIX MILES EAST OF MIAMI: 0952 hrs.

Oberfahnrich zur See Oskar Beinlich had carefully noted the exact spot on the Atlantic seafloor where U-112 had come to rest for the day. Like all good navigators, he was obsessed with accuracy. But on this voyage, he was equally interested in making every notation as neatly as possible. Someday, after the war, he intended to obtain the chart, frame it and hang it above the mantel of his parent's home in Lubeck.

His father had once captained a cruise ship on the Hamburg-New York route and a large chart from one of his voyages hung proudly in the library of their home. Throughout his childhood, Beinlich had gazed at the chart and his father in awe. But now, he happily concluded, a mere voyage across the North Atlantic in a giant steamship with all the comforts of home was hardly worth mentioning in comparison to the adventure he was documenting.

The neatly drawn lines on his chart told the story—departure from the U-boat base in Lorient, out across the Bay of Biscay, through the British defenses, down the North American coastline and into the heart of the Caribbean. St. Kitts... Martinique... Aruba –the names on his chart were the same as the ones that would show up on the chart of any respectable pirate. And while cruising these waters within the steel confines of a U-boat was not quite the same as sailing on a brigantine armed with cannons and cutlasses, they had indeed wreaked havoc on the enemy beneath a tropical sky. In his mind, he could see generations of yet unborn Beinlichs looking up to see the chart of his adventure hanging on the wall and thinking of just how brave and...

"Cosinus, are we lost?"

The Kapitanleutnant's questions snapped Beinlich out of his reverie and back into the world where he was responsible for knowing their precise location, where they had been and perhaps, more importantly, what course to steer whenever he was told where they were heading. Of course, it was also a world where Rahn and the other officers felt completely at home calling him "Cosinus" – a moniker reflecting his math abilities and one that he thoroughly detested.

"*Nein, Herr Kaleu,* I know precisely where we are," Beinlich said as he inked in the information he had previously entered in pencil. "Stopping at each lighthouse makes it easy to keep track."

"That was a great shot this morning of Fowey Rocks," Rahn said proudly and leaned against the bulkhead so he could get a good look at the chart. "The lighting was superb."

"Congratulations sir." Beinlich completed his notation and put his pen aside. "How many does that make now?"

"Let's see..." Rahn's finger began tapping its way along the Florida Keys. "I got the Dry Tortugas... I couldn't get a really good shot of the Garden Key light at Fort Jefferson because it's so small, but I think we'll be able to see it on the shot of the fort itself...then there was Sand Key... American Shoal... Sombrero Key... Alligator Reef... Carysfort and now Fowey Rocks. Damn, I wish we could have run in there and gotten a good shot of the Key West light."

"I wouldn't worry Sir, that's a very good collection you've gotten so far." Beinlich was quick to compliment Rahn's accomplishments in photographing Florida lighthouses. He didn't want the U-112's commander to dwell on the fact that the Key West light wasn't included—most of the crew was concerned that he would decide to turn around and sail right up to the American naval base to complete his collection. They had nearly run aground at Sombrero Key—even the Americans would have eventually discovered them stuck there on the reef and both the voyage and many of their lives would have come to an end. Normally, Rahn was not one to take unnecessary risks, but since their arrival in Florida's waters, he seemed obsessed with photographing lighthouses--the crew's latest explanation for their unusual sightseeing trips was that their commander had spent too much time in the tropical sun.

"Not a bad collection of scalps either," Rahn noted their victories — each of which was clearly marked on the chart – a Dutch freighter off Curacao, a big American tanker blown sky high as she nosed out of the harbor at Caracas, a brand new Canadian reefer carrying tons of Argentinian beef sunk off Barbados, and an English tramp steamer sent to the bottom between Trinidad and Tobago.

The last had been a bittersweet victory. Displacing less than one thousand tons, the little old steamer had undoubtedly been a common sight shuttling between the islands. They had come across her just before sundown and the chase had been short and the outcome thoroughly predictable. The first round for their one-oh-five had sent a towering plume of water cascading on to the steamer's deck. The second round had struck her stern just below the waterline and efficiently gutted the old girl. A cloud of brown smoke burst from her funnel, she rattled to a halt and began to go down. The *eins-eins-zwei* had closed in quickly and Rahn had allowed off duty crewmen to come topside to witness their victim's final moments—he continued to regret that decision. As soon as the U-boat's diesels went to idle, they could hear the screams coming across the water and as they approached the dying steamer they could clearly see their source—a young man, probably not more than twelve years old, had been seared alive by a steam line. He was writhing in agony aboard the doomed ship's only lifeboat and as the survivors pulled their oars to clear the sinking wreckage, the boy clutched at the captain and screamed: "Father! Father, help me!"

As the U-boat eased closer, Rahn ordered the engines reversed. But it had been too late. His men's cheering and good-natured banter turned to silence as they looked down on the lifeboat passing along the port side. The English captain looked up at them and they could easily see tears streaming down his soot-streaked face as he held his dying son close. There was no bitterness on his forlorn countenance—just an expression of utter sadness as though asking each of them why this had to happen.

The sunset that evening had been one of the most spectacular of the entire voyage. For a long moment, the hot red orb of the sinking sun sent a glowing pathway across the dark waters and at its center the tiny black silhouette of the lifeboat bobbed forlornly. It was an image that Rahn knew would remain in his memory forever.

"Herr Kaleu?"

Rahn looked up to see *Funkmatt* Andreas Timm, one of the boat's two radio operators, standing quietly at attention. Rahn welcomed the interruption of his thoughts.

"Sir, I was just wondering if perhaps some music might be appreciated by the crew," Timm said. "I could keep the volume low….not that the Americans are listening."

"An excellent suggestion," Rahn said. "Just make sure you don't annoy Cosinus here. I'm sure he has lots of complicated computations to perform."

"Of course, *Herr Kaleu*," Timm said quickly and snapped off an enthusiastic salute. "You can count on me to select just the right tunes." He ducked through the control room's forward hatch and hurried down the passageway to his station in the radio shack where he took his seat and began to search through his extensive collection of records. It had become common knowledge throughout the flotilla that U-112 possessed the very best selection of American jazz in the fleet and for Timm, each song he played was a tribute to his brother Uli – one of Hamburg's swing kids.

At first, it had all seemed like harmless fun. Uli and his friends mimicked the American swingers, dressing in baggy zoot suits, trenchcoats, floppy hats and silk scarves. They even had a large following of girls in short skirts and silk hose who could recite all the female dialogue from the most popular movies from the States. By 1935, the Nazi Party had had enough of Germans dancing and laughing to the sounds of Negroes like Louis Armstrong and Jews like Benny Goodman. Overnight, jazz was banned from German radio stations—a development that motivated Timm to learn everything he could about radio receivers. Within weeks, he had established a listening room in their parent's spacious home where his older brother could bring his friends, including some of the most beautiful girls Timm had ever seen, to listen to the BBC jazz broadcasts.

The Hamburg clubs stayed open and live jazz could still be heard. In fact, Timm had even seen the Kapitanleutant in the *Trocadero* and Lamprecht, the second watch officer, was a regular at the *Alsterpavilion.* But when the war broke out, the Gestapo got busy. Timm could clearly remember a cold Saturday afternoon when Uli made his big mistake. A company of infantry on a recruiting drive had gone down the street and the crowd had responded with three "*Sieg Heils*" followed by a single voice shouting "Swing *Heil!*" Timm knew he could never forget the look on his brother's face as the Gestapo thugs dragged him away—he was smiling, but his face was as pale as death. The family had heard from Uli only once in two years--he was in a labor battalion in Poland.

But now Uli's record collection was safely stored aboard U-112 and each time Timm played a selection he pretended his brother could hear it. This morning, it was the dreamy melody of Duke Ellington's *Mood Indigo* that Timm sent swinging from the U-112's loudspeakers. With the exception of *Oberfahnrich* Beinlich, the entire crew appreciated their radio operator's musical selections. Beinlich, however, shook his head in disgust before entering the date, time and name of the artist in a small notebook that he quickly stuffed into his shirt pocket.

ST. AUGUSTINE: 1135 hrs.

Even after eighteen years of living in the States, Joe Miller never ceased to be amazed by the predictability of Americans. No matter what the situation, he found he could always count on them to put their personal interests first. Although he found their spoiled and childish approach to life despicable, he had to admit it made his work so much easier. He smiled as he thought how a meeting such as this would be run in Germany. There would be little or no debate and the agreement would be unanimous—do whatever is necessary to protect the Fatherland. Here it was very different. The prevailing, but unspoken, attitude at these weekly Security Council meetings seemed to be: "let's see what I can get out of this... and if I can't make a buck off it, maybe I can arrange a profit for a friend who will then be indebted to me... and, oh yes, let's throw in some talk about the war so the Old Woman can brag about me down at the church."

The only thing that made this week's meeting any different was the presence of an FBI agent. When introduced as a "special guest" by Chairman Homer Cooper, the man merely nodded pleasantly and took a seat in a far corner of the room. At first, Miller had been concerned about the Fed's intrusion into the council meeting. But after a few minutes had gone by, he concluded he had nothing to fear from the G-man—the young agent from Washington seemed to have the same "golly gee" expression frozen on his face that Miller had so often seen on the faces of tourists visiting the Ancient City. He couldn't imagine what the young agent could find so fascinating about this group. Except for himself, of course, Miller considered his fellow members of the St. Augustine Security Council to be...what was that colorful American saying? Oh yes. "Useless as tits on a boar."

"....so in conclusion, my fellow council members, I urge your support for passage of this proclamation that will affirm our commitment to the defense of the nation's oldest city and our own hometown—St. Augustine."

There was silence in the small conference room on the third floor of City Hall. If St. Johns County Commissioner Jerry Strickland had hoped his speech would inspire the other four members of the council to action, he was sadly disappointed.

Instead of applause, he was met with bored indifference.

"OK, Jerry, I think we got the gist of what you were saying there," said Chairman Cooper who, despite the fact that his four years in the U.S. Army had been spent inventorying supplies at various warehouses around the world, considered himself to be a bona fide military genius. "What you want us to do is go on record as supporting your contention that we should stop the Nazis from blowing up our town and making sex slaves out of our wives and daughters."

The laughter and snickering that went around the table stopped when it reached Commissioner Strickland whose jaw clenched and face reddened.

"All right...all right Jerry. Don't blow a gasket," Cooper continued. "I think we can support the sentiment of your words. All those in favor say 'Aye'." The vote was unanimous and accompanied by wide smiles from everyone but Strickland. "All right then, did you get that recorded Mr. Coleman?"

Jeremy Coleman, the St. Augustine Chamber of Commerce's representative on the Council and its official secretary, nodded as he scribbled the results of the vote in his shorthand tablet. "I've got it, Mr. Chairman, and if I may say so it's a pleasure to record such harmony—a rare occurrence."

Coleman had meant for his remark to add to the light-hearted atmosphere, but as usual, the effeminate tone of his voice made his fellow council members... uncomfortable. Not that anyone could confirm Cole's sexual orientation. He was married, but had no children. He was a walking encyclopedia of baseball statistics, but as Miller noted, Eleanor Roosevelt's hands were more masculine than Cole's. And then there was his pale skin... as though he never went out into the bright Florida sun. And why wasn't he in military service? Cole said he had a medical deferment because of "upper respiratory allergies" but most people simply assumed that he wasn't military "material".

"Thanks for your support," Strickland said coolly. He realized the public would never know the Council considered his proposal to be frivolous grandstanding. All they would know is what they would read in tomorrow's edition of the St. Augustine *Record*. He intended to make sure his patriotic sentiments were adequately reported by the paper. In fact, he had a press release in his pocket that he had written in a way that left no doubts about his genuine concern for the city. From past experience, he knew the city editor would make sure the release ran verbatim.

"All right then," the Chairman said as he adjusted the reading glasses balanced precariously on his perpetually sunburned nose. "Let's move on to the main item on our agenda. This could take awhile."

"Excuse me Mr. Chairman," Joe Miller interrupted. "Before we start, I was wondering if you were able to get that dredging information we requested last week?"

Cooper glanced over his spectacles at the nightclub operator. He started to note that Miller was the only member of the Council who had asked for the dredging details, but decided he just wanted to get on with the meeting.

"Sure Joe, I've got it right here." He dug into his briefcase beneath the table and came up with a thick brown folder. "I don't know what you're gonna do with this... have a Guess-the-Channel-Depth contest over at your bar?"

Miller smiled as he leaned across the table to take the file that contained all the latest information on the U.S. Army project that had created a new inlet by dredging through Vilano Point and into Matanzas Bay.

"I think we would be embarrassed if someone from the military asked about the new inlet and we didn't have the facts," Miller said. "And I know you fellas aren't about to take the time to go through this file. I'll look it over and give you a report next week."

"That's fine with me, we've got more important things to deal with than dredging," Cooper said and motioned as though waving away a fly. "I want to talk about this lighting issue. Who wants to go first?"

"Oh I do...I do!" There was no hesitation on the part of Chamber of Commerce representative Coleman. "Mr. Chairman, the Chamber has discussed this issue at length and we have adopted a position which is my pleasure to present to the Council. We want you all to know we gave this a lot of thought and it seemed clear to us that based on..."

"What's the Chamber's position on this?" Cooper made no effort to conceal his dislike for Coleman. "We don't have all day to listen to a bunch of background information."

Coleman was like a happy puppy—Cooper's rebuff was no more than a playful swat with a rolled up newspaper. "We're against any sort of dimming of lights here in the city or at the beach. People come here for fun… for a vacation. And while they're here they spend money—lots of it! If we turn out the lights and they start bumping into each other in the dark, they'll just pack up and go to Jacksonville Beach or down to Daytona—places that aren't afraid of some phantom U-boat. Besides, all of us at the Chamber are more worried about gas rationing. Now there's a threat to our economy."

"Coleman, you and your souvenir stand buddies will be singing a different tune when one of those Nazi boats comes into the bay and puts a torpedo up your ass," said Hank Duke, the rotund representative of his self-appointed Defense League. He was tempted to say that Coleman might find such an event to be extremely pleasurable, but decided to at least keep the meeting civil. Besides, he was a man who was accustomed to getting his way and assumed this debate would soon be resolved in his favor.

"So Hank, I reckon this means you… I mean the Defense League, is in favor of cutting back on the lights," Cooper said. "I'm glad someone here realizes we've got a war on our hands."

"You're damned right I know there's a war on!" Duke leaned forward, his corpulent bare forearms rested on the tabletop and his beady eyes flashed. "That's why the Defense League is ready to begin patrolling just outside the inlet and down the beach from Vilano to Matanzas Inlet. We're just waiting for the Navy to deliver a couple of machine guns and we'll be all set for action."

Miller couldn't help but smile at Duke's naïve enthusiasm. A U-boat gun crew would easily blow his matchstick cabin cruiser out of the water before he and his glory-seeking friends could get close enough to open fire with their useless popguns. Not that there was any chance of such an encounter.

Despite his contempt for Hank Duke, Miller had always found it to be to his advantage to placate the man. After all, despite his pomposity, Duke was a person with considerable influence in the town. A former district attorney, Duke now had his own law practice and had made a small fortune keeping his friends out of jail. Plus, he was smart enough to marry into the Montcrief family—his wife was loaded and the knowledge that her money would always be there gave him the sense of financial security he needed to indulge himself in distractions like the Defense League. Not only had he organized the League's St. Augustine chapter, he had convinced the district's Congressional delegation to write letters of support for his efforts to the Secretary of the Navy. As a result, he now "commanded" a fleet of three privately-owned vessels that had been volunteered by their owners to provide security for the City of St. Augustine. Thoughtfully, he had included the Security Council's members in the League. But today, Miller couldn't wait for his opportunity to make the fat man squirm.

"All right then, who's next?" Cooper looked directly at Jerry Strickland. "How about we hear from the County Commissioner—what's your take on this Jerry?"

Strickland was on the spot. He had been so busy with his proclamation that he really hadn't given the lighting issue the attention it deserved. Not that he hadn't had time to formulate an opinion—it was just that the issue had so many sides to it that thinking about it for more than a few minutes gave him a headache. As a result, he had adopted his usual approach to controversial issues. He merely delayed his decision for as long as possible in hopes that the "best" decision for him to make would miraculously appear. Obviously, that was not going to happen this time. His dilemma therefore was whether to annoy local merchants and call for a partial blackout or should he make a speech about the need for everyone to work together to dim the lights in the name of national security. Even if that approach proved unpopular with the business community, it would help solidify his position as a man who takes America's defense seriously.

"I think I'm going to side with Hank on this one," Strickland said thoughtfully and shifted the knot of his red, white and blue tie with one hand. "We can't shirk our duties to the nation just to make a little more money. Besides, I can't imagine that dimming the lights will cause that much economic chaos."

"All right then!" Cooper smiled –he could see himself patrolling the streets and ordering "Lights out!" Strickland and Duke in favor of a blackout and his vote would make three—a simple majority. "Let's hear from Joe—he's the one with the well-lit business right on the beach. What do you say Joe? Should we turn out the lights?"

Miller flashed his best American smile—he always found that if he started his comments with a smile, people were more likely to see things his way—not that he was too concerned about being able to get exactly what he wanted.

"Turn them out? Every time I've gotten into trouble in this life, I was in the dark when it happened." He waited for the chuckles to subside. "Yes. You're right—my place is really well lit and I've always felt it was good for business. You know the story," he made a sweeping gesture with one arm and repeated the well-known advertising slogan for Uncle Sam's Bar and Pier, "…a little island paradise in a sea of darkness. Without the lights, I'd have to change my advertising. Hell, just reprinting the matchbook covers would cost a fortune. You know you can't find a more true blue patriot in this town than I am, but what good would it do to turn off or even dim the lights? If the Germans are gonna sink our ships, they'll do it anyway. Besides, according to the papers, Admiral King and his boys have got the U-boat problem solved. How many did they sink last week? Five? Or was it six? Sounds to me like we need the lights to make it easier to machine gun any kraut survivors who might come floating past after the Navy puts a depth charge down their hatch."

"So I take it your vote is a No," Cooper said. "But mine is a yes and that makes it three to two, so we can move on to developing a plan for enforcing a blackout."

"Just hold on there a minute, Mr. Chairman." Miller was smiling as he spoke, but the tone of his voice indicated he definitely wanted to make his point. "I didn't say how I was voting. I don't want to go on record as being the only man on the council who wants to keep the lights on—if there's evidence the lights help the enemy." His obvious exclusion of Coleman from the "men" category was not lost on the other council members. Coleman shifted uncomfortably in his chair and the others thought about how much they liked Joe Miller. "It's almost lunch time," Miller continued. "How about if we put the vote off until we come back? I'm expecting some information from the Navy in just a few minutes. Let's see what it says after lunch and then we can vote. How about it?"

"That sounds good to me…I'm ready to eat now," Duke said as he pushed his bulk back from the table. "What do you say Chief?

60

Can we go to lunch now?"

Cooper liked to keep a tight rein on the Council, but after moving into his retirement years, he had found there were other priorities in life...things like eating, long naps, fishing and, well, eating.

"All right then. We'll reconvene at one-thirty sharp to take a final vote on the blackout. Then we'll spend the rest of the afternoon working on the details. I want to make sure we come up with regulations that can be clearly understood and I want it made clear that I'm in charge of enforcing them. So, gentlemen, it could be a long afternoon. I suggest you eat a big lunch—I know I will." He brought his gavel down with a loud crack. "Dismissed!"

From his seat in a corner of the room, Special Agent Spencer had closely watched the morning's proceedings. As he stood to make room for the council members to squeeze past him and out the door, he mentally summarized his impressions of each of them. Chairman Cooper: a self-important windbag who was determined to make locals give him some respect. Councilman Strickland: would do anything to win favor with the voters. Coleman: Some sort of sexually ambiguous fellow who has never fit in anywhere. Duke: a pompous clown for whom serving on the council had become boring because it didn't offer the immediate gratification he had become accustomed to receiving. Miller: Defies easy analysis, something odd about him, but seems to have mastered the art of getting people to like him.

"Agent Spencer. It's so good to meet you," Strickland said and thrust his hand toward the FBI agent. "What brings you to St. Augustine? You know they repealed prohibition... you won't find any moonshiners down here."

As Spencer shook hands with Strickland, he noticed that Duke did not even acknowledge his presence. Instead, he struggled into red, plaid jacket and left the room. Chairman Cooper nodded, but hurried out the door with Coleman in close pursuit.

"Oh, I'm sure the fine folks of St. Augustine would never get involved in any sort of illegal activity," Spencer said.

"Then why are you here?" Strickland asked bluntly.

"I'm just passing through actually...on my way to Miami," Spencer lied. "The Bureau just wants to find out if there's anything we can do to help local defense organizations—a sort of FBI wave the flag kind of trip. I'm sure you know how important those things can be."

"Indeed I do and I know just how pleased the St. Johns County Commissioners would be to have you say a few words at our next meeting—it's a week from tomorrow and you could tell us what you like about us and maybe we could come up with some things J. Edgar Hoover could help us with."

Spencer could see his photo in the local newspaper with the caption: "Jerry Strickland introduces G-man to County Commissioners". He wasn't about to play that game.

"I'm really sorry, but I'm afraid I'll be long gone by then. But maybe you could give me a written list of law enforcement help you need down here—I'd be happy to pass it on to the Director."

Strickland's disappointment was readily apparent until he realized what a coup it would be for him to announce he had made arrangements for the FBI to provide the county with direct assistance. That should certainly get some favorable publicity –and votes! But before he could come up with a response, Joe Miller squeezed past to stand directly in front of the Council's visitor.

"Agent Spencer. It's a real pleasure to meet you. I'm Joe Miller."

As they shook hands, Spencer couldn't help but feel that despite the man's winning smile, there was something odd, something staged perhaps, about the bar owner. It was as though the man were operating on a different wave length than everyone else.

"It's good to meet you Mr. Miller," the G-man said.

"Just call me Joe—everyone else does. Even the dogs in this town think of me as just plain Joe."

Despite his friendly words and smile, Spencer couldn't help but notice that Miller maintained an unusually rigid posture. His tall frame bent slightly forward when he had introduced himself, but it quickly snapped back to its ramrod straight position. Spencer searched for a word to describe it. Continental? Yes, that was it.

"So, Mr. Mil—I mean, Joe. My young friend, Michael Pomar, tells me you have quite a bar somewhere nearby."

"Unfortunately, not close enough for lunch," Miller said and sighed in feigned disappointment. "It's only about seven miles away—directly across the Bridge of Lions to Anastasia Island, down A1A past the lighthouse and out to the beach— *Uncle Sam's Bar and Pier*. You can't miss it."

"Well, I think I'd be derelict in my duty if I didn't get over there before I leave."

"That's the spirit! In fact, come over tonight. It's our monthly 'Sock It to the Nazis Night'—there's no cover charge if you donate a pair of white cotton socks. We send them to Bundles for Britain—just our way of helping out. Hell, I'll even give you a meal on the house."

"Sorry, but the Bureau has a strict policy about accepting gifts—even food," Spencer said. "But I think I can come up with a pair of socks. It sounds like that's the place to be."

"It sure is," Miller said proudly. "Just ask anybody and they'll tell you there's no better place to get fed and entertained than at Uncle Sam's. So, I'll see you tonight?"

"I certainly hope so. Unless Washington sends me on some new assignment like arresting Public Enemy Number One."

"I'm sure they would understand if you put that off until tomorrow. Come by this evening—you'll enjoy it." Miller turned and started toward the door.

"Oh Joe," Spencer said suddenly. "I do have one question. Where did you get that accent?"

Miller froze for an instant and then he turned slowly. His face melted into a broad smile that Spencer thought was purely mechanical.

"Accent?" Miller seemed to be suddenly amused. "Whatever do you mean?"

"Oh I don't mean to pry," Spencer said apologetically. "It's just a hobby of mine—trying to guess where people are from based on their accents. Yours kind of threw me because it doesn't really sound like anything I've heard before—it's almost as though it lacks any sort of regional quality. Then I noticed something with your W's—kind of like Pennsylvania Dutch. I'll bet you're from up there around Lancaster. Am I right?"

"That's close—but I think my accent was created by the beer bottle I took in the face about ten years ago." Miller rubbed his jaw. "My mouth and teeth have never been the same since then. I'm surprised I can speak at all." He suddenly glanced at his wristwatch. "Jeez Louise! I'm late. Will you be back for the rest of the meeting?"

"I wouldn't miss it for anything," Spencer replied.

"I'll see you later then—I've got to go!"

Miller hurried through the doorway and as Spencer listened to the man's footsteps receding down the hallway, he realized the owner of *Uncle Sam's Bar and Pier* had deftly avoided answering the question about his place of origin.

As instructed, Luigi Carbone was waiting for his boss at the bottom of the stairs in the City Building's lobby. As Miller came down the stairs, Carbone was surprised to see he was a bit flustered— a condition he had seldom seen in the years they had been working together.

"Something wrong?" Carbone asked.

Miller looked down at his chunky assistant and saw an expression of genuine concern on the man's broad Italian face. For one brief moment, he thought he would blurt out the fact that he had just had a talk with a very inquisitive FBI agent. But he quickly decided there was no need to alarm Carbone—quite possibly, there was no need for either of them to be concerned.

"No, nothing to worry about—nothing at all," Miller said as he dabbed sweat from his forehead with a handkerchief. "Damn it's hot for April—you have the package?"

"Right here," Carbone said and patted the breast pocket of his rumpled sports jacket. "Some of my best work, if I may say so."

Miller stepped quickly across the lobby with Carbone close at his heels.

"I just saw our good friend head out the side door. You should be able to catch him easily," Miller said as he opened the big double doors and the two of them stepped out into the bright midday sunlight. It only took a moment for his eyes to adjust to the glare and then he caught sight of Hank Duke's bulky figure squeezed into a red jacket and topped with a white Panama hat waddling down the street toward the waterfront. "There he goes now. Make the delivery, but don't scare him—he looks like he's on important business."

"I'm on my way," Carbone said as he descended the front steps and took up a diagonal course that would allow him to intersect Duke at the corner of St. George and Hypolita Streets.

As Miller watched Carbone overtake Hank Duke, he couldn't help but compare his assistant to some of the enlisted seaman he had known aboard the Nassau. Carbone had all the tools necessary to make it as an obermatrose or even an obermaat. Unfortunately, the ships where he could make the most of his talents were now rusting on the bottom of the sea.

The chunky, little New Yorker waved his arm and hailed Duke as he approached down his wake and closed on the attorney's broad stern. Even from this distance, Miller could see that it took Duke several more steps to check his forward progress as he turned his head to see who was approaching from behind. "There are no brakes on a manure barge"—the phrase came from somewhere deep within Miller's memory and he smiled at how appropriate it was for Duke.

He could see Carbone making a fine presentation—hands and arms gesturing wildly as he told his tale. Finally, he reached into his pocket and pulled out a small manila envelope and handed it to Duke. The big man looked at the package for a long second before accepting it. Carbone quickly doffed his cap and with an abrupt about face, headed back toward the City Building. As he crossed St. George Street, he gave Miller a happy thumbs-up signal. The delivery completed, Miller watched as Hank Duke's bulk disappeared around the corner on its way to the city marina.

NAUGHTY BOY: 1220 hrs.

It was warm inside the big cabin cruiser moored at Slip 12. Although the *Naughty Boy* was registered to a prominent Jacksonville attorney, the payments on the boat were shared equally by Duke and two other men. Each had his own nautical needs— one wanted the boat for deep-sea fishing, another used it for entertaining clients on quiet cruises. And although Duke had visions of impressing local women by arming the boat with machine guns and patrolling for U-boats, he was quite content to let the spacious interior serve as his little home away from home during hectic workday lunch breaks. The polished brass and varnished woodwork made the boat's interior seem both elegant and comforting. Combined with WFOY's "Mellow Midday Moods" program coming from the radio, the boat's features created a pleasant diversion from stuffy meetings.

"Hey Babe, the lemonade is almost ready! You just relax and cool off."

Judy Parker's voice coming from behind the galley's swinging doors caused a stirring in his groin and the inviting aroma of freshly grilled tuna steaks made his mouth water. Sex and food, he thought—what more could a man want?

"How can I cool off when I'm around you?" Duke asked playfully.

"Oh Hank, you just say the sweetest things," Judy's voice bubbled with an enthusiasm that most people would have considered out of place for a woman nearly forty-five years old. "You just get comfortable. I'll be out just as soon as I finish the salads."

Duke knew from past experience that when it came to satisfying the needs of the flesh, Judy was always right. If she said "get comfortable," then that was what he should do. Squeezing into the bench seat behind the small table had been difficult and it was obvious to him that he would never be comfortable wearing his jacket. He tried to squirm out of it, but the envelope in his inside breast pocket seemed to bind the cloth to his broad chest. After a short struggle, he was able to free the envelope and he tossed it on the table in front of him. Although it wasn't easy, he eventually removed his jacket and threw it across the aisle to where it landed on the leather sofa that ran the length of the cabin. Looking at the sofa reminded him of what would be happening there in a few minutes and he allowed himself the luxury of anticipating what was to come.

As always, Judy would choreograph the entire routine. The first time they had met on the boat, they had gone to the bed in the small stateroom. Having to squeeze through the narrow passageway and door had made Duke feel a bit self-conscious about his weight. And then the coupling on the bed had sent the boat pitching at its mooring so violently that it not only attracted a crowd of curious onlookers, it had given him a touch of nausea. Judy now avoided a repeat of that fiasco by simply having him sit on the sofa while she took care of everything. She was even thoughtful enough to ask him how much time he had before returning to the office so she would know how much of his clothing to remove. Of course, she always had time to take off everything she was wearing.

Duke suddenly realized his reverie had become so graphic that it could cause the actual event to end too quickly. As a result, he looked for a diversion and the envelope on the table seemed like just what he needed. Besides, he thought, Miller's flunky had indicated the man who had given it to him to deliver had said there was some urgent need to open it. Duke roughly tore open one end of the envelope and shook it—a neatly folded note addressed to "Mr. Duke" and a small packet that was taped to hold its contents in place fell on to the table. He unfolded the note and read the message written in a childish scrawl: "Keep the lights on—or else!" It was signed simply "Armando."

"Who the hell is this guy?" Duke mumbled as he ripped the packet apart and six photographs tumbled on to the table—it only took a quick glance for him to realize the photos had been taken through the porthole above his head last Saturday night.

"Sonofabitch!"

"What is it baby? What's the matter?" Judy asked as she stepped quickly into the cabin. Duke's face was devoid of color and he eyes bulged as he stared at the photos on the tabletop--she had wondered when those photos would arrive.

"Those goddam Minorcans! They've really got me by the short hairs this time!"

"Relax sweetheart," Judy said as she stepped over to him and pressed her bare thigh against his trouser leg. "It can't be that bad."

When Duke failed to notice her red teddy, she leaned over to take a closer look at the photos. When he paid no attention to her breasts suspended just inches from his face, she knew the photographs had done their job. Judy tried to hide her smile as she looked at the black and white prints. She had to admit they were really well done—Luigi was quite a photographer. The first two showed only the back of her head and her bare backsides as the knelt between Duke's knees. If not for her tan, her features would have been lost in the immense white blob of the man's flesh. For the next two photos, she had purposely positioned herself so the camera would capture her left side—she had always felt that was her best profile. In the final two photos, her face was out of the frame, but she was pleased with how her body looked as she rode atop Hank Duke—he was obviously pleased too, his corpulent facial features were clenched in an unusually tight expression of pure ecstasy.

"Oh Honey, what are we going to do?" Judy moaned. "This is so embarrassing."

"If my wife sees these, I'm ruined!" Duke angrily shoved the photos aside. 'Her family will cut me off without a dime—and that's just for starters."

"Hank! How can you even think of that...that...woman?" Judy stamped a high-heeled foot and even in his current despair, Duke couldn't help but notice the delightful jiggle it produced.

"Damn it! Don't worry...I'll take care of you." He tried to stand, but his belly jammed under the edge of the table and he plopped heavily back into his seat. "Goddam it!" He grabbed the table with both hands and shoved. There was a groaning of metal as the flange holding the table in place slowly bent. Judy thoughtfully grabbed the photos as they went sliding toward the deck.

Free from the table's constraints, Duke rose and angrily stepped over to the sofa and grabbed his jacket. He tried to pull it on, but scraped his hand on the overhead. Frustrated, he clenched the colorful jacket and headed for the door.

"Hank! Please Hank, I'm serious," Judy pleaded. "I can't stay here...it will be just too humiliating if those photos get passed around town. But I don't have any money. Please help me get away from here." She summoned up a tear and sent it trickling down her cheek.

Duke shook his head and reached for his wallet.

"You're right. It probably would be best if you left town." He pried open the wallet and pulled out all the money it contained. Duke counted it quickly and handed the bills to her. "Here's two hundred and ten dollars. That's all I have with me, but that should be enough to get you some place far away from St. Augustine."

"Oh Hank, you're wonderful!" Judy threw her arms around his neck and snuggled her breasts against his chest. "I know this will all be over soon so we can get back together."

"Yeah, sure." He was already backing toward the door. "I'll call you soon."

Bright sunlight flooded briefly into the cabin as Duke opened and closed the door leading out to the main deck. Judy waited until she felt the boat tilt to starboard as Duke pulled himself up the steps and on to the dock. Free from his weight, the boat rocked gently once....twice...and then settled on an even keel.

Judy also felt as though she had been relieved of a heavy burden. Not only did she feel relieved, she felt giddily happy. Three hundred dollars from Luigi for the photo shoot and now two hundred more from Duke! That was the easiest money she had ever made and it was more than enough to get her settled in with her sister in Miami—Linda was making a fortune down there working the Cuban millionaires and she couldn't wait to get a piece of that action.

And to make things even sweeter, Hank had left the photos behind. She would keep those just in case she needed some quick cash some day. Plus she really liked one of the photos—her hair, her face, her left breast—everything was perfect in it. She wondered if she could get additional prints made? They would make great advertising for her down in Miami. As she hurried to get dressed and pack her few belongings, it never occurred to her that Hank Duke thought so little of their relationship that he had not even bothered to ask where she was going.

ST. AUGUSTINE: 1325 hrs.

The Security Council re-convened promptly at 1:30 and Special Agent Bill Spencer immediately realized that a long meeting would find him struggling to keep awake. He had hoped to have lunch alone with Michael Pomar so the young man could give him more background information on the council members, but unfortunately County Commissioner Jerry Strickland had invited himself to their table at the noisy little *St. George Tavern*. Most of the next hour was spent listening to Strickland's plans for new highways and schools and his dreams of making the area a wintertime vacation destination for wealthy Yankees—much like it had been at the turn of the century.

Spencer noticed that the lunch was even more uncomfortable for the rookie reporter. While the FBI agent could find some relief by savoring his fried oyster sandwich, Strickland frequently paused in his oration to urge Michael to take notes on what he had just said or was about to say. Despite the boy's repeated contention that "this isn't an interview, it's supposed to be lunch", Strickland continued to ramble on about growth projections and tax bases. A full stomach, the unaccustomed heat and the droning politician had all combined to make Spencer long for a siesta. He was wondering just what these folks would think if he feel asleep during their meeting when the crack of Cooper's gavel snapped him out of his stupor.

"The St. Augustine Security Council is back in session," the Chairman announced. "I think our discussion of the blackout regulations could take all afternoon, so I'd like to get started as soon as possible. Mr. Miller! Do you have anything to share with us?"

Miller cleared his throat and glanced down at his notes. When he looked up, the owner of Uncle Sam's wasn't smiling.

"Unfortunately, the numbers I was hoping to get from the Navy haven't arrived. But I did bring this." He waved a clipping from the local newspaper. "This was in last week's paper and I'm sure you all saw it—'Navy Claims 28 U-boat Sinkings in Our Coastal Waters' and I'd like to point out there hasn't been a German attack along Florida's coast since February."

"And your point would be?" Cooper asked.

"My point would be, Mr. Chairman, that the Navy has already defeated Hitler's U-boats. Plus, if you will notice, the lighthouse is in full operation every night. Don't you think that if the Navy or Coast Guard thought there were U-boats out there they would at least dim the light? Don't you think we could just follow their lead and avoid putting a big dent in our local economy just so we can say we're helping protect America?"

Coleman nodded in agreement, but the Chairman was unmoved.

"Nothing else then?" Cooper asked. "Although I think we can assume your arguments haven't changed anyone's mind, we'll go ahead and take a formal vote anyhow."

"Just one more thing," Miller added. "I was talking to a couple of Minorcans and their entire community is dead set against any kind of blackout. The sea turtles will start coming ashore any day now to start nesting and the Minorcans need their lights to slaughter them. They said it's really hard to cut one of those monster's throats by moonlight. Plus they use their truck headlights to find freshly laid nests—they said the fresher the eggs the better the turtle bread."

"C'mon now, that's about enough," Commissioner Strickland said. "I like a fried loggerhead steak as much as the next man, but the Minorcans can't believe we'd compromise the nation's security just to make their butchering a little easier. Hell, they can load live turtles on their trucks and take them home to butcher."

"Frankly, I can't see how you fellas can eat those...those reptiles," Coleman said and a shudder went through his bony frame.

"You don't know anything about them Coleman," Hank Duke said with a surliness that surprised everyone. "You should eat some turtle—it'll put hair on your chest and some lead in your pencil."

Cooper's gavel put an end to the laughter. "That's enough. I vote we impose at least a brownout of some sort and look into imposing a complete blackout. What about you Jerry?"

Strickland unfolded a sheet of paper and began to read aloud: "In this, one of our nation's darkest hours, it is of the utmost importance that we work together to preserve the security of America's coastal waters. During recent months, Nazi submarines have moved unchecked along our shores. They no doubt benefit in their navigation from the many lights blazing from our coastal community. Should this aid and abetting of the enemy continue? Here are some key points to consider. One..."

"I take it you're in favor of a blackout then?" Cooper asked and when Strickland nodded, he went on to the next member. "What about you Coleman?"

"On behalf of the Chamber of Commerce, I vote no to the imposition of any sort of lighting restrictions," Coleman said and entered his vote in his notebook.

"Joe Miller?"

"No. Restrictions aren't warranted."

Cooper smiled. "OK. It's all tied up at two and our best hitter is stepping up to the plate. What do you say Hank? When do we get started on that blackout?"

"We don't. I vote no," Duke said and looked down to intently study the meeting agenda.

A murmur of disbelief went around the table.

"Hank, are you confused?" Cooper asked. "A 'no' vote means we won't be having a blackout."

"I understand the voting process Homer," Duke snarled. "And I vote 'No'—no blackout...no brownout...keep the lights on. I agree with Miller and Coleman. They make perfectly good sense to me."

Chairman Cooper glared at Hank Duke in disbelief and shook his head in disgust. "All right then, meeting adjourned!" He smacked the table with his gavel. "And I don't need a second to that—let's go home."

MARINELAND: 1430 hrs.

Winnie Greer enjoyed working at Marineland. Not that the pay was that great—75 cents a day barely made it worth her time. But the job had other benefits that were more important than money. First, she was actually treated with some measure of respect by the owners. In fact, they never once acted like she was colored—they simply gave her a job to do and left her alone to get it done. Secondly, she sometimes felt like she was working in Hollywood. Even though her work basically consisted of cleaning the bathrooms and mopping floors, she was there when movies were made.

During her morning break, she always tried to quietly go up to the platform that ran along the top of the tank where the dolphins were kept. Often there were lighting and sound technicians up there too and if they noticed her at all, they always nodded a greeting and sometimes even spoke to her just as if she were a white girl. From her lofty perch she could look down on the set below. Mostly all she ever saw was people standing around waiting for something to happen—the cameras never seemed to be rolling.

Once when she was cleaning out one of the urinals, she had heard a director shout from right outside the window; "Quiet on the set!" Then a bell rang and he shouted: "Action!" But she was too frightened to go see what was happening. She vowed the next time that happened, she was going to take a look even if she did get into trouble. If she did, Winnie felt confident that by looking completely submissive and using the phrase: "I's sorry 'bout dat. I don't know no better" she could gain forgiveness.

Sometimes Winnie felt like she was a part of the movie making process—maybe she was just a cleaning girl, but she performed a valuable function. Her confidence had gone up tremendously just a few weeks earlier when much to her amazement, Mr. Whitney had said: "Good morning Winifred." Just like that—"Good morning Winifred." She sometimes repeated that phrase just to hear the sound of it. She knew Mr. Whitney not only was one of the studio owners, but he was also the president of Pan American airlines and had worked on the production of *"Gone With the Wind"*. And just like that, he had called her by her name!

"They's late again," Rufus Pool said and brought Winnie's mental accounting of her job benefits to an end.

"Who's late? And how do you know anybody's late? You don't have a timepiece." Winnie was sorry she had spoken so harshly. Rufus shifted his weight uncomfortably and shielded his eyes from the sun's glare as he stared down the black asphalt of A1A that led south to Flagler Beach.

"Da bus is late—that's who," he said quietly. "And I don't need no watch, I kin tell time in mah haid."

"I know you can, Rufus—it must be some sort of gift you have," Winnie said as pleasantly as possible. "I'm sure the bus will be here shortly."

Rufus didn't reply. Instead, he began to sway rhythmically to sounds only he could hear. There had been a time when Winnie had thought Rufus suffered from some sort of mental illness. But over the years, she had come to the conclusion that he just thought too much about things—especially, machinery and engines. He had often repaired church members' dilapidated cars and worn out pumps and had hoped to get a job as an automobile mechanic in one of the garages in town. But no one was interested in hiring a colored boy—no matter how talented he might be.

That's why getting the job at Marineland had been such a blessing for him. Although he was primarily responsible for light maintenance tasks, painting and taking out the garbage, his supervisor had recognized Rufus' potential. He had begun to spend a few minutes each day explaining how the studio's massive pumping system operated. On some mornings, Winnie would go down to the pump room with him. The motors hummed and when she touched the huge pipes she could feel them trembling like there was something alive inside. Rufus always told her lots of details about the pumps, but the only one she could remember was that they pulled in about seven million gallons of seawater every day. She didn't know how much water that was, but guessed it must be enough to fill the huge tank where the dolphins swam and where the filmmakers shot their underwater scenes. One of her responsibilities was to clean the tank's many viewing ports and whenever she worked at that task she always paused to look inside. And while the visibility was often poor, she could sometimes see divers at work in their bulky suits with round metal helmets connected to air hoses.

But for Rufus, the best part of his job was the first scheduled task of the morning. As soon as he arrived, he would go to the pump room and open the heavy metal hatch that covered the filters beneath the floor. Then he would remove any bulky objects that had collected as a result of the night's pumping. Usually it was just beer bottles, dead fish and scraps of wood mixed in with clumps of sargassum. But sometimes he found flotsam and jetsam that he, at least, considered to be real treasurers. Included in his collection of items sucked from the sea by the massive pumps were assorted pieces of fishing gear, a folding deck chair, several unopened bottles of wine, a battered brass bugle, a hubcap from a '34 Ford, and a small rubber tire that one of the men at the studio had said must have fallen off of one of Billy Mitchell's bombers years ago. His latest find was an empty canvas mail bag marked "Aero Postale" which his mother was fashioning into a jacket for him that would have the French words emblazoned across his back. He had once told Winnie that opening that hatch made every morning seem just like Christmas.

"Now that's one fine automobile," Rufus said and Winnie turned to see a dark green Lincoln glide into the studio's parking lot. Through the open driver's window, she could see a man who seemed vaguely familiar. He had a dark complexion for a white man and as he opened the door and climbed out of the car she could see he had the features of those people from the Mediterranean— Italy perhaps. She was surprised that instead of heading for the offices, the man walked directly toward where they were waiting for the bus.

"I'll bet he's lost," Rufus said and stepped forward to meet the man. "I'm just the person he needs to help him out."

The man straightened his tie and brushed the wrinkles from his white cotton sport coat as he came toward them. Rufus met him halfway, but the man never even nodded as he brushed past him and walked right up to Winnie.

"Are you Winifred Greer?" The man's voice sounded friendly and he tipped his battered old yachtsman's cap to her—the first time, she realized, a white man had ever greeted her in that way.

"Yes, I'm Winifred Greer. Is something wrong?"

The man smiled. "No, there's nothing wrong. My name is Luigi Carbone and I'm just here to offer you an invitation?"

"An...invitation? To where?"

"Do you know Mr. Joe Miller? He owns *Uncle Sam's Bar and Pier*."

Winnie nodded.

"Well, he's heard you're quite a singer and he'd like you to come by the bar and listen to some new recordings he just got in from New York. I'm here to drive you there and I can take you home later."

"I don't know Mr. Carbone...I have to take care of things at home and...."

"Just call me Luigi, Miss Greer." The man's smile was so broad that Winnie thought it must be painful for him.

Suddenly Rufus came up behind the man.

"I know who you are," Rufus snarled—a tone of voice that Winnie had never heard him use. "You're the one who tried to scare us with your boat at the baptism yesterday!"

Winnie could see Carbone's smile fade as though a cloud had passed over the sun. He turned and fixed Rufus in a steely stare. "Listen, boy, if I were you I'd keep my mouth shut." By the time he was again facing Winnie, the cloud had passed and his smile was shining brightly once more.

"So. Are you ready to go Miss Greer?"

Up until the moment Carbone had spoken so rudely to Rufus, Winnie had seriously considered his offer. But now that incident and the realization that the man was indeed the same person who had disrupted the baptism had made her reconsider the invitation— even though the music recordings were a strong incentive to go along with him.

"I'm sorry...Mister...I mean Luigi. I told you I had things to do and I have choir practice this evening. Thanks for the invitation."

Carbone's smile remained painted on his face. "Mr. Miller thought you might say that, so he went ahead and talked to your people's preacher. What his name? Oh yes, Reverend Fulmer. He even wrote you a note." He dug into his pants pocket and came up with a tightly folded sheet of yellow notepaper that he handed to Winnie. "Here you go...you can read can't you?"

"Sure I can read...can you?" She was amazed at her brazen reply—she had to be extremely provoked to argue with people she knew, but to speak like that to a white man was something she had never done before. Winnie felt a flush of embarrassment and then a tinge of fear as she realized Luigi Carbone might very well slap her. But as she unfolded the note, the blow didn't come. She glanced up cautiously and saw that even if she had angered the man, he was apparently under orders not to do anything about it. Winnie felt an odd sense of power as she read:

Winnie:
I have spoken with Mr. Miller. I think you should hear what he has to say.
I'll check on your Granny this afternoon. You are excused from choir practice.
In His grip,
Reverend Fulmer

The reverend's words had the desired effect. Winnie's feelings of anger were immediately replaced by excited anticipation.

"Well then...Luigi...let's go," she said as she folded the note and slipped it inside the cotton flour bag that served as her purse.

Rufus couldn't believe what he was hearing.

"Winnie! You can't go with him! This man is bad...you know he is!"

"It will be all right," she said as she walked boldly toward the Lincoln. "Reverend Fulmer said I could go...and I am going."

"You better not hurt her!" Rufus shouted, but made no move toward the car. "Do you hear me Whitey!"

Carbone helped Winnie into the front seat and closed the door. As he circled around toward the driver's door, he paused just long enough to give an obscene gesture to Rufus and then out of Winnie's vision he grasped his genitals through his trousers and gave them a shake in the direction of the young black man.

As the car accelerated powerfully up A1A, Winnie glanced in the outside mirror and saw Rufus angrily kick sand in the air. Then he was gone from sight. By the time they crossed the Matanzas Inlet Bridge, Winnie had begun to appreciate the car's thick upholstery and the big band tunes coming from the radio. She couldn't help but feel she was being transported in style to a new and better world.

ANASTASIA ISLAND: 1920 hrs.

Dusk was beginning to settle over the town and the street lamps glowed warmly along the Bridge of Lions. As Bill Spencer drove the FBI-issued Chevrolet coupe across the span and on to Anastasia Island, he had to admit that even with the boring Security Council meeting, this day was the best he had ever had as a Bureau employee. The beauty of the ancient city, a sense of purpose, and the freedom to pursue his investigation without direct supervision had combined to make his job almost ...enjoyable.

"You'll need to slow down here," Michael Pomar said from the passenger's side of the Chevy. "The local police like to give speeding tickets along this stretch of A1A. Even a G-man probably couldn't talk himself out of a fine."

Spencer eased off the accelerator and downshifted to second gear. He was already glad he had decided to ask young Pomar to come with him this evening. Not only was he good company, he had a wealth of information about St. Augustine's people and places.

"Don't they make enough off tourists without setting up speed traps?"

"It's a seasonal sort of thing," Pomar explained. "The spring is a kind of in-between season. The winter visitors have left and haven't been replaced by the summer crowd so speed traps are just one way to bring in revenue during the slack periods. It's a shame people don't realize how great it is here in the spring...same as the fall. Those are the best times of the year if you ask me."

Spencer had to agree that the weather couldn't get much better. A fresh sea breeze scented with the sweet smell of wisterias in bloom drifted through the coupe's open windows. Although the

Uncle Sam's

sky was quickly fading to a deep purple, the black and white stripes on the tower of the St. Augustine lighthouse were clearly visible to his left and as he watched, a beam of light swept over their heads and out to sea.

"Yep, that's our famous lighthouse." Pomar continued his travelogue. "The Spanish built a light tower there as soon as they arrived back in 1565. They made lots of improvements to it over the next two hundred years, but it finally collapsed into the ocean. This one replaced it in 1874. They say that light can be seen nearly twenty miles away."

"And they don't think that helps the German Navy?" To Spencer, it seemed logical that the first thing a country at war would do would be to turn out the lights that might guide enemy ships to their harbors and towns.

"Well, they supposedly have dimmed the light—but I don't see any difference in it. There's also a Coast Guard lookout on duty on top of the tower at all times and I think the Navy put in some sort of radio station there—I guess so they can call for help if the Germans come ashore." Pomar shook his head in disbelief. "Maybe they know what they're doing. Joe Miller got some report from the British Coast Guard that said after they turned out their lighthouses more ships ran aground and sank than were sent to the bottom by U-boats. I think he gave everyone in town a copy."

"Miller seems to have a real interest in keeping the lights on," Spencer said. "That was pretty clear from today's meeting."

Pomar leaned forward and pointed off to their left. "See that glow? That's Joe Miller's place—our destination."

Through the windshield, Spencer could see that except for the lighthouse and the Alligator Farm across the road from it, this part of the island seemed largely uninhabited. But to the east, above the tops of the dark jungle of low lying trees and vegetation, he could see a bright patch of horizon that seemed to pulse with light. He had to admit the illumination was effective, he found himself suddenly excited about the prospects of a visit to Uncle Sam's Bar and Pier.

"Watch it!"

Pomar's warning caused Spencer to hit the brakes just in time. From their right, an Army truck came through a dark intersection and with headlights blazing went roaring past them down the road toward the beach. They could see the truck was loaded with soldiers and they could hear them singing—but the truck was going too fast for them to identify the song. Spencer eased the car forward and was about to turn left on to the beach road when he saw yet another set of headlights approaching from the right. It was another Army truck and the driver was pushing the heavy vehicle even faster than the first. As it flashed past them, they could see it too was filled with soldiers dressed in their fatigues. Wrestling seemed to be popular with this group, several were grappling in the back while their comrades cheered them on. Some of them waved at Spencer and Pomar as the car's headlights lit up the back of the truck. Then it too was nothing more than red taillights receding into the darkness.

"You can just follow them," Pomar said. "They're on their way to *Uncle Sam's*."

"I didn't know it was such a popular place—especially on Monday nights," Spencer said as he finally edged the coupe onto the beach road and slowly accelerated. He couldn't help but glance in the rear view mirror to see if another truck might be about to run over them from behind.

"Joe Miller knows how to schedule things," Pomar said. "Monday's not a big party night, but he keeps tabs on the schedule over at Camp Blanding. He probably knew some group was graduating from basic training today and invited their commanding officer to bring them over to celebrate. One night a couple of months ago, he had the entire crew of a destroyer based at Mayport down for a big bon voyage party before they left for the Pacific. He even gave them free beer! I hope I get to meet him tonight."

"He sounds like quite a guy."

The road made a turn to the right and as Spencer swept around the curve, he could see white surf splashing across rocks to his left. He could taste the salt on the breeze coming off the moonlit sea and then there was *Uncle Sam's Bar and Pier* in all its glory. He downshifted, touched the brakes and eased left into the already crowded parking lot that was lit by overhead strands of alternating red, white and blue lights. He pulled into an empty space at the end of a row of parked cars, set the brake, switched off the engine, and quickly climbed out of the Chevy.

For a moment, he and Pomar both stood looking up at the

spectacle before them and taking in the delightful scents of the sea, freshly fried onion rings and beer. Red neon on the roof spelled out the name of the establishment in letters three feet high and glowing white lights outlined a narrow porch that completely encircled the building perched on pilings that placed it ten feet above the soft sand. Warm light came from the portholes that served as windows and the sounds of loud conversations, tinkling glass, and a Duke Ellington tune on the jukebox floated on the night air. Atop one wing of the building, couples swayed slowly across a dance floor surrounded by candle lit tables while waitresses in white blouses and red shorts took drink orders and delivered fried oysters and grilled grouper to diners. From the center of the roof, a square structure like a pilot house protruded and on its top deck a rotating beacon flashed red .... white ....blue.

"Jeez, this is even better than I though it would be!" Pomar said. "Let's go!"

Spencer stopped his young companion's advance toward the bright lights with a tug on his shirt. "Wait a minute. You mean you've never been here before?"

"Not at night and even if I did show up I couldn't get in. You have to be eighteen," Pomar said as he pulled free of Spencer' grip. "But they can't keep me out with an FBI escort. Plus, I've got socks for admission. How 'bout you?"

Spencer laughed and patted the package of white cotton socks he had purchased that afternoon just for this occasion. "Got them right here...brand new too. Fresh from Woolworth's." His voice sounded serious as he added: "But one thing—don't mention that I work for the Bureau. OK? I'm supposed to remain anonymous."

"Don't worry. I'll tell everyone you're a Sunday school teacher from Savannah. That should amuse them."

A wooden ramp designed to look like a ship's gangway led Spencer and Pomar up from the dusty parking lot to the bar's main entrance where a large banner with a caricature of a stunned Fuhrer getting punched in the face with a boxing glove proclaimed "Sock it To the Nazis Night". Beneath the banner a young blonde woman in a low cut peasant blouse that revealed an ample sunburned bosom collected a pair of socks from each entering patron. Without aiming, she tossed the socks over her shoulder where they consistently smacked the wall and fell into a large cardboard box.

80

Spencer was still trying to think of something to say if she questioned Pomar's age. But as she took the boy's socks and tossed them into the waiting box, it was clear she wasn't interested in enforcing age restrictions. Instead, she had focused her entire attention on Spencer. He immediately wished he had changed into something more casual. Bureau policy mandated that he wear a coat, tie and hat. As a result, he definitely stood out in the sea of khaki uniforms and plaid shirts.

"Honey, you don't have to wrap it up for me," she said as Spencer handed her his packaged admission socks. She thrust her chest toward him and he noticed she seemed to think he would be impressed by her ability to noisily chew Juicy Fruit gum.

"Thanks," he said and hoped he wasn't blushing. "You can't be too careful these days."

She watched hungrily as Spencer faded into the bustling crowd inside. "I'd be careful with you baby," she mumbled to herself and then she was jarred out of her reverie by the next man in line who obscenely wagged his socks in front of her face. She smacked them away and cursed him under her breath. Angrily, she threw the socks into the box. "Next!" she snapped.

From his observation post in a small room directly behind the main bar, Joe Miller watched as FBI Agent Bill Spencer edged his way through a sea of laughing and loud talking customers. Miller was surprised he felt no apprehension about having an FBI agent on the premises. As he slid the viewing port closed, he smiled coldly and thought: This could be an interesting night.

"Mr. Miller are you sure I'm ready for this?"

Miller turned and gave Winifred Greer his most encouraging smile. "Of course you are! The rehearsal was great…you're gonna knock 'em dead kid!"

He could see the colored girl he intended to turn into a star might need a little more encouragement. She sat on an old wicker chair in a dusty corner and wrung her hands nervously. He had no doubts about her upcoming debut. Gloria and the other girls had done a magnificent job of turning the little black girl into a glamorous starlet. The long yellow gown complimented her figure and the large fake diamond earrings added an exciting spark each time the light glittered from their polished surfaces. He wasn't too sure about the makeup—somehow the red lipstick seemed a little much on her full lips. Miller thought it made her look a little like that watermelon-eating darky painted on the side of the truck that delivered vegetables from Jacksonville. What was it called? Oh yes, "Jig-A-Boo Produce."

"But I don't know, Mr. Miller. I've never sung before this many white folks before," Winnie looked as though she were about to cry.

"Nonsense," Miller said as he stepped toward her. For a brief moment, he considered giving her a comforting hug but quickly decided he wasn't ready for that. "Just pretend you're singing in church. These people may be white, but they will love your voice just like colored folks do. Remember, Reverend Fulmer thought this was a good idea. He wouldn't have said it was all right if he didn't think it was something you should do."

"That's right—he wouldn't have written me that note if he didn't think I should do this," Winnie said in an effort to calm her nerves. "And if he says it's OK, God must think this is where I should be."

"I'm sure He does," Miller said convincingly. Actually, he was surprised at how cooperative the reverend had been when they had met that morning. It was almost as if Fulmer had been expecting him. As the reverend had said, "Winifred has a special talent that, like we say in Sunday school, shouldn't be hidden under a basket." After getting her to the bar where she had spent most of the afternoon listening to the jukebox, Miller saw that she also had the intellect necessary for succeeding in the music business. Big band... blues... country... jazz, she had listened to them all and her questions about what she was hearing showed that she was not just some backwoods pickaninny with a marvelous voice. She had a good head on her shoulders and it would be simple for her to pick up the class to match.

"And don't forget what I told you," Miller continued. "When I lived in New York, I saw all the great ones and I'm telling you your voice is as good or better than any of them. Bessie Smith included."

Winnie's face brightened. "You really think so?"

"I'm sure of it...and in a few minutes everyone out there will know it too." Miller pulled the door open and the sound of music and laughter tumbled into the room. "Now just relax. Luigi will start the band's next set in a few minutes. After a couple of tunes,

I'll introduce you and you'll be on your way to fame and fortune."
He winked, stepped out of the room and pulled the door closed
behind him. Miller worked his way through the crowd, waving and
backslapping as he went. Despite the crush of people, it wasn't
difficult for him to locate his quarry who was edging his way
toward the open doors leading onto the rear deck.

"Agent Spencer!" Miller said. "I'm really glad you could
come!" He eased the FBI man outside onto the deck. "Sorry…it's
a little loud in there. I'll bet you don't have anything like this in
Washington."

Spencer stepped to the railing and looked out to where the
twinkling lights on the pier abruptly ended and the blackness of the
Atlantic began. "We have our watering holes there, but none of
them has an ocean as a neighbor."

"It does have its appeal," Miller said as he glanced down to
where the surf sizzled up the beach to the edge of the pilings
supporting the bar. "But I'm sure that by the time most of our
patrons head for home they might as well be in Iowa—drinking
doesn't seem to stimulate an interest in the beauty of nature.
Speaking of which…" Miller snapped his fingers and as if by
magic, an attractive waitress in a short red skirt and high-heeled
pirate's boots appeared from out of the crowd. "Maria! Please get
Agent Spencer a beer. Budweiser OK?"

Spencer nodded and Maria smiled warmly before disappearing
into the crowd.

Miller could tell Spencer was pleased with what he saw and he
filed that information for possible future use.

"I meant to tell you today that I would be happy to assist you and
the Bureau in any way possible," Miller said. "As you can see, most
of the male population of the area is here on any given night. Plus
my bartenders hear everything. So if you could tell me what you
need in terms of information, I'm sure I could help supply it."

"Thanks, but really I'm just basically visiting…trying to get
some ideas on how the Bureau might be more useful to coastal
communities," Spencer said and searched for some way to change
the subject. The problem was solved when Pomar suddenly
stepped out of the crowd with a beer in one hand and his reporter's
notebook in the other.

"Man, this is great!" The young man exclaimed and motioned

toward the mob scene behind him. "I've already got material for a couple of good stories. I'm going to have to spend more time here."

"You're not supposed to have a beer," Spencer blurted out. "What would your parents think? I can't bring a drunk home to them."

"Relax big fellow," Pomar said and stumbled slightly as he took several unsteady steps toward the railing. "I've only had one of these."

"I think one is enough," Spencer said as he deftly removed the beer bottle from Pomar's grip. "Keep it up and I'll have to arrest you for your own protection."

Before the boy could argue, Miller introduced himself.

"I'm Joe Miller, owner of this establishment. And if I'm not mistaken, you're Michael Pomar. I've read your articles in *The Record*."

Pomar seemed to be having trouble getting his eyes to focus, but he did manage to shake Miller's outstretched hand. "A fan? I've never met a fan before."

"Well you have now. I think you're a fine writer and obviously have a real nose for news."

Pomar smiled. "Well, thank you Mr. Miller. I really appreciate that. In fact, you know I was thinking that this Socks Night would make a great story—maybe even go national with it. Could I interview you right now?"

"Well, I don't know. It may not look like it, but I'm working at the moment. Maybe we could..." Miller's words were cut off by a loud train whistle triggered by one of Uncle Sam's laughing bartenders. "Well the show is starting so I can't talk to you now. I'll tell you what, why don't you come back in the morning, say around ten. We'll be packing the socks up and shipping them out— that would make quite a photo for *The Record*. Now if you'll excuse me, I have to oversee the festivities."

The train whistle sounded through the bar once more and this time it was followed by the click of Luigi Carbone's drum sticks as he counted "two...three...four" and launched *The Patriot Swing Band* into a rousing version of *Chattanooga Choo Choo*.

"Great idea Mr. Miller!" Pomar shouted. "I'll see you in the morning!" He was still beaming when he turned to Spencer and added: "He's quite a guy."

Spender merely nodded in agreement.

From the opening note, Luigi "Skinman" Carbone was in control and he savored every second of his performance. He had organized and trained the eight-piece *Patriot Swing Band*...he selected the tunes...he arranged the music...he decided if and when a band member would get a solo. Luigi even controlled the mood of the audience. He could command the band to play a blues tune that would make even the most hardhearted patrons feel a lump in their throats. Or he could select a jump tune that would have everyone's feet bouncing on the wooden decking of the dance floor. When he was behind the drums, his yacht captain's hat and less-than-clean wife-beater tee-shirt were transformed from the attire of a uneducated, New York immigrant into the trend-setting uniform of a savy, world-wise musician. When the lights were low and the music was hot, everyone knew Luigi Carbone was one Hep Cat.

A fading drum roll took them out of the *Choo-Choo* tune, but Carbone didn't bother to wait for the applause to end before slamming the band into high gear with his own version of Glenn Miller's *A-Train*. Right on cue, two of the waitresses each grabbed a soldier from the crowd and dragged their selection up onto the stage where they immediately forced their somewhat reluctant partners to dance with them. Tonight's picks were typically unpredictable. Maureen's choice, a lanky tow-headed soldier who seemed to be a walking advertisement for Indiana cornfields turned out to be an excellent dancer. The other recruit, a short dark-complexioned fellow who looked as though he worked as a delivery boy for the mob before being drafted, was in possession of the proverbial two left feet. Much to the crowd's delight, he quickly gave up on the jitterbug and settled for an off-beat but enthusiastic Charleston while little Janey danced in circles around him.

As the number headed toward its conclusion, Carbone saw Joe Miller emerge from behind the bar and make his approach to the stage. He was glad to see Joe was taking his advice. The band usually finished a set of four tunes before Miller made his welcoming remarks. But in the interest of getting the young singer up and performing before stage fright immobilized her, Carbone had recommended that she make her debut early in the evening. As the band ran through the first stanza of the catchy little "out"

Carbone had written for the tune, Miller stepped up to the microphone. The music ended with a Carbone symbol crash, the stage lights dimmed and Miller was bathed in the white light of single spotlight. Miller motioned for quiet and launched into his opening remarks:

"Ladies and gentlemen...*The Patriot Swing Band!*" The crowd roared their approval and Carbone beamed like a new father. Thanks to Miller's seemingly endless financial support, he had been able to create a really first class band whose members were paid sufficiently to allow them to practice at the club three afternoons each week. Piano, guitar, bass, trumpet, alto and tenor sax, a great trombone player and Carbone's flashy drumming has been combined into a band that could compete with the best in the country.

Miller let the applause build and then he motioned for quiet.

"I have just a couple of announcements and then we can get on with the party," Miller said and a slight feedback from the microphone caused his voice to echo briefly. Just as Carbone had taught him, Miller took a step back and the metallic hissing and echoing stopped. "First I want to thank all of you for turning out tonight. Carol tells me so far she has collected one-hundred-sixty-one pairs of socks—and who says she can't count?" Miller was pleased to hear laughter from his little joke and more laughter came when someone shouted from the rear of the crowd—"Who cares if she can count—hubba, hubba!"

"Seriously though," Miller continued. "These socks will make life a little more comfortable for the folks who are on the front line in the fight against Hitler. In fact, some of you boys here tonight might someday get to slip some of these socks onto your tired feet courtesy of the good folks of St. Augustine. Next, I'd like to make a couple of introductions. Where's Colonel Moore?" Miller shielded his eyes against the spotlight's glare and a small beam swept over the crowd before settling on a heavy-set colonel sipping a beer in a far corner of the room. "Colonel Moore brought over two companies of the Sixteenth Engineering Battalion from Camp Blanding to be with us tonight. Let's hear it for the colonel and his boys!"

"Next, we have a very special guest with us tonight. All the way from Washington, D.C. one of J. Edgar Hoover's very own G-men, Special Agent William Spencer!"

The spotlight's glare blinded Spencer as it hit him full in the face. Although he couldn't see the crowd, he sensed that everyone in the club was straining to get a look at him. "Holy Christ," he muttered, "so much for anonymity."

The applause was somewhat restrained—most people were wondering why an FBI man was in their town, a few were concerned that they might be under investigation, and one man slipped over to the payphone by the front door. He quickly called a business acquaintance and told him to move their moonshine still as far into the woods as he could take it.

"I hear Agent Spencer just solved a big case and J. Edgar sent him down here for a little vacation," Miller said. "Isn't that right?"

Spencer waved an acknowledgement and thankfully the spotlight snapped off.

"And now for a real treat," Miller said while congratulating himself for establishing the idea that he and Agent Spencer were buddies. "Tonight, we're proud to bring to you the debut of a remarkable young talent—someone from right here in St. Augustine. I'm confident she will be a big star and someday you'll tell your grandchildren you were there the first time she performed in public. Ladies and gentlemen, I give you the incredible voice of Miss Winifred Greer."

Miller stepped out of the spotlight and the welcoming applause was warm and enthusiastic until Winnie eased reluctantly into the harsh light. Everyone was anticipating the appearance of a young blonde girl. Instead, they found themselves looking at an obviously very nervous black girl. As the applause faded, Carbone could tell there was not a second to lose—he could see Winnie was about to be overcome by a major attack of stage fright.

"One...and two...and.." He launched the band into the tune they had rehearsed with Winnie earlier that evening. Unfortunately, she was too frightened to come along for the ride.

"Vamp 'til ready boys," Carbone said and to prevent the music from coming to a stuttering halt, he led them into an eight bar phrase they could repeat until Winnie could hopefully jump or stumble into the chorus.

"Oh well, at least there's still a lot of cotton that needs pickin," some hayseed shouted from the darkness and someone else responded with: "Shut up and give her a chance!"

The combination of an insult and encouragement seemed to be just what Winnie needed to snap her out of her fear-induced trance. She released her death grip on the microphone and the next time the band's now monotonous intro swung by, Winnie jumped aboard.

"All of me...... why not take all of me?
Can't you see I'm no good without you?
Take my lips, I want to lose them.
Take my arms, I'll never use them..."

Miller's song selection was perfect. The catchy lyrics were well known to everyone, but Winnie's voice made each word seem new and special. By the time she had finished the first verse, the crowd was hooked and she knew it. Winnie's frightened expression was replaced by a warm smile that seemed dazzling in the spotlight and although her stage presence was a mere shadow of what it would become, it was more than enough to energize a crowd of drunks. When the song ended and the applause billowed around her, she knew she had just taken an important step in her life--a step that could lead her to the fulfillment of dreams she had dared not mention even to her best friends.

"All right ladies and gentlemen," Miller said as he stepped into the spotlight and took the microphone from Winnie. "Didn't I tell you she was great?" Miller asked and the crowd roared its approval. "So don't forget to come back, Winifred's gonna be a regular here at *Uncle Sam's!*"

Winnie wished she had rehearsed another tune--she had not anticipated how much fun she could have singing for white folks. She smiled and waved goodbye as the band opened its next number. The spotlight followed her until she stepped off the stage and then it changed to red and swept back to the band. The happy crowd opened to let her pass through just like she was royalty, but before she could squeeze behind the bar she found her way blocked by two burly soldiers. Winnie felt the old fear returning--the two white men obviously wanted something!

"Excuse me Miss Greer," one of them said politely. "We were wondering if you'd be so kind as to give us your autograph?"

Their request was so totally unexpected that it took a couple of seconds for Winnie to react and when she did it was with gracious enthusiasm. She took the pen and signed each man's menu with a flourish.

"Gee thanks," they said humbly.

"It's my pleasure," she said as she eased past them. Carbone fired up the band again, but Winnie barely heard them. As she stepped once more into the cramped little room behind the bar and pulled the door closed, she was overwhelmed with the joy of what had just occurred. Tears began to flow down her cheeks and she raised her outstretched arms toward heaven.

"Thank you Jesus! Thank you Jesus!" Winnie was overcome by the moment and she suddenly wished more than anything in the world that her brother could be there to share her triumph.

U.S.S. LASSITER: 2210 hrs.

At that moment, Curtis Greer was unaware that his sister, or anyone else for that matter, was thinking of him. In fact, over the past few days he had convinced himself that he had been completely forgotten by his family and friends. In his mind, he felt closer to his ancestors aboard the slave ship that brought them to America than he did to the people he had known all of his life along Moses Creek. After all, he thought, I am a slave with no more chance of escape than my forefathers had when they were chained in the bowels of a rat-infested sailing ship.

This existence was not what he had anticipated when he enlisted in the Navy's special Stewards' Program six months ago. Although Curtis knew that military service that restricted him to being a seagoing servant was not exactly a career opportunity, his friend Willy Thomas had convinced him to sign up. Willy was one of twenty Negro stewards aboard a battleship in the Pacific. He told Curtis the crew treated him well and he had already visited exotic places like San Francisco and Honolulu.

Curtis, however, had been selected to participate in an experiment. Some destroyer captain had gotten the idea that he'd like to have his own personal steward, so the Navy decided they would explore the possibility of stationing a lone Negro aboard a destroyer to perform the same duties that would be expected of him on a larger warship. It only took one day for Curtis to see the experiment was a terrible failure. Unfortunately, no one ever asked his opinion about anything. As the captain had once told him: "Thinking is not part of your job."

"Hey boy!" The ship's cook stood wiping his hands on his greasy apron—the man reeked of onions and sweat. "Soon as you dump that garbage, I want you back in here on your hands and knees scrubbin' that oven. You hear me?"

"Yes," Curtis said as he began dragging the wheeled garbage can toward the hatch. He desperately needed fresh air.

"Yes? Yes what? Dumbass." The cook was advancing toward him, his muscular biceps shining in the cramped galley's harsh light. Curtis had often wondered how the man's skin could stay so white—almost like the skin on that dead man he had once seen washed up on Crescent Beach.

"Yes—sir!" Curtis said. The realization that he sounded just like some step-and-fetch-nigger made him feel dirty. He wasn't required to address the cook as a "sir," but the man had told him if he didn't, he'd "beat him into next Sunday." Curtis had no doubts that the cook meant what he said.

Curtis struggled with the bulky garbage can. The wheels helped until he had to drag them and the can over the "knee-knocker" coamings at the bottom of each hatchway. Finally, he made it to the hatch leading out to the main deck. He almost opened it without first snapping out the light in the small compartment.

"Lord only knows what they would do to me if they were to catch me violating the blackout," Curtis mumbled to himself before swinging the hatch open and stepping out on to the deck with his cargo of potato peelings, day-old grease and scraps from the last watch's dinner.

The night sky was filled with a million twinkling stars and a warm breeze whipped down the deck. As Curtis carefully wheeled the garbage toward the fantail, he couldn't help but notice the USS *Lassiter* was in a hell of a hurry. He could feel the throbbing of her engines through the deck plates and he could see her wake rushing away toward the stern. Tonight, the water boiling up from the ship's screws had that strange green glow that Curtis always enjoyed watching. Thankful for the brief entertainment provided by Mother Nature, he hurried toward the stern until he saw, to his disappointment, that he would not be alone—a dark figure stood looking over the railing. Curtis was amazed to see the man strike a match—it flared up in his cupped hands and in its glare he recognized Petty Officer Burke. The match light snapped out and was replaced by the bright orange glow of a lit cigarette.

Burke was not a happy sailor. Back in Key West, the hottest looking woman he had ever dated was now going to bed alone—at least he hoped she was alone. When it came to sex, the girl was insatiable—and her imagination knew no limits. For Burke, Marta was a fantasy come true and he had lustily accepted her offer to move his stuff into her place. After their second night of sweaty sex in her apartment, he had reported to the base only to learn that the *Lassiter* was shipping out for a new duty station in Panama. And they were getting underway as soon as possible. The captain had loaded him down with so many duties, he didn't even have time for a nooner when he picked up his seabag at her place.

After putting to sea, he had tried to find solace in the stories that spread through the ship about the sexual delights provided by the "Blue Moon Queens" waiting for them in the clubs in Colon. That therapy was just beginning to take effect when, in the late afternoon, the *Lassiter* had come about and put on flank speed back toward Key West. His hopes that it had all been some sort of mistake and that he would soon be clutching Marta's firm body were dashed at sundown as they sped past the base and took a heading that sent them racing up the Keys in pursuit of a rumored U-boat.

"Keep that garbage away from me," Burke said as he watched Curtis wrestle the can into position for dumping its contents overboard. "That shit smells like... shit."

Curtis didn't see an obvious solution to the problem. There was really only one place to dump the garbage and he certainly couldn't do anything about the wind that was carrying the ripe odor to the petty officer. He decided the best course of action was to simply get the job over with as soon as possible and get back to the galley where he would be scrubbing the oven for the next hour.

"Didn't you hear me sailor?" Petty Officer Burke was getting more irritated by the second. "I said to keep that stuff away from me."

It had been a long day for Curtis—at least that was the only excuse he could think of that would explain the reply he offered to Burke.

"If you don't like the smell…you can move! And you'd better put out that damn cigarette before the Captain finds out you're messin' with his blackout."

"What the…?" Burke sputtered. "Who the hell do you think you are?" He took a couple of steps forward. "Why it's our little nigger boy out dumpin' garbage in the moonlight!"

Curtis said nothing as he tried to think of way to do his job and get away from Burke.

"Look at me boy!" The petty officer snarled. "I said look at me!"

Curtis sat the garbage can upright. Even though a cloud slid over the moon and sent a shadow drifting over the ship, he could still the anger on Burke's face.

"Here's what I think of your advice," Burke said and the glowing ember on his cigarette changed from a warm orange to a fiery red as he took a deep puff. The wind whipped away the tobacco smoke and then he repeated the procedure. "You know, I outta just kick your black ass overboard. Nobody would care… and if they did I'd just say the poor nigger tripped."

At that moment Captain Wendell McClure had just climbed up to the four-inch gun mount located atop the fantail deckhouse. It was his habit to walk the length of his command before turning in each night and now as he walked past the gun, he affectionately stroked the cool steel of its muzzle. McClure was not the sort of man who dwelt on life's inequities. Of course, he often felt he should be commanding at least a new cruiser instead of an antiquated destroyer, but he had devoted himself to making the *Lassiter* the best old flush-deck destroyer in the navy.

He didn't care that his ship was more than twenty years old and so beat up that she hadn't even been considered worthy of going to Britain as part of the Lend-Lease program. He was determined to whip her and her crew into first class shape. So far, he felt pretty good about what he had accomplished. The Lassiter had a new paint scheme, the crew seemed to know their jobs and the recently overhauled engines were pushing them along at nearly thirty knots. As he turned and looked forward, McClure was pleased to see his blackout restrictions were working—there wasn't a light to be seen—not even a spark escaping from any of the ship's four tall funnels. The captain even allowed himself to think that although eight hours had passed between the time the U-boat had been reported off Fowey Rocks and the moment they had been ordered in pursuit, they might actually catch up with the Nazi sub by morning. Then he would show everyone what the Lassiter could do. His contentment with his ship and her crew quickly faded when he turned and looked down to see a cigarette flashing brilliantly on the stern.

"Put out that damn cigarette!" McClure's voice overcame the wind and the roar of the engines. "I want that man on report!" The captain whirled around and hurried back past the gun and down the ladder leading to the main deck.

Curtis was tempted to say: "I told you so," but the twisted smile on Burke's face as he sent his cigarette arching into the sea like a miniature flare caused him to remain silent. He was surprised that Burke didn't even seem concerned about getting caught.

"Don't worry Captain!" Burke shouted. "I've got him!"

Curtis was still clutching the garbage can when the Petty Officer's big fist caught him flush on the jaw. The night exploded in a flash of white light and then he was sinking into darkness. He was surprised at how comfortable the metal deck felt beneath his tired body. Long before he was rested, he was certain he was drowning.

"Mama!" Curtis wasn't certain he had said the word aloud until he heard laughter and saw the faces of several sailors looking down at him.

"Your mama can't help you now boy," said a sailor with a water bucket who had obviously just dumped its contents on Curtis' groggy head.

"Son, I'm really disappointed in you."

Curtis wondered how Reverend Fulmer had gotten on board the Lassiter. Slowly, he realized the fatherly voice he was hearing belonged to Captain McClure.

"Didn't you know about the blackout rules?" McClure asked. "I thought we were pretty specific about everything, especially not smoking on deck."

"Yes sir, Captain, sir," Curtis said. His voice sounded slurred from the blow he had received, but he knew everyone else who heard him would simply conclude he was dim witted. "I knowed about the blackout—it wasn't me that was smokin'."

Curtis tried to stand, but Burke suddenly reached down and shoved him roughly back to the deck. The petty officer's hand dug into the breast pocket of Curtis' now soaked blue denim work shirt and pulled out the soggy remains of an open pack of Camels.

"Well look here," Burke said as he held up the cigarette pack. "Looks like he's got enough smokes here to signal the entire German fleet."

"C'mon Burke, don't be ridiculous," said Lieutenant Rose. "He may be dumb, but he's no spy."

Curtis never thought he would be grateful to hear someone say he was dumb, but as two sailors hoisted him to his feet, he wanted to thank the lieutenant was saying something in his defense—even if it was an insult. He stood on wobbly legs and waited patiently for the captain's orders.

"Take him below, " McClure said. "Even if he didn't understand my orders, he'll have to be punished. Confine him to his quarters until I think of something more appropriate."

"Beggin' your pardon Captain, but he doesn't really have any quarters," Rose said. "We didn't feel it was right to have him bunk with white boys. He just sleeps wherever he can find a place, usually down in the engine room."

"Why didn't I know about this? I won't have a member of my crew treated like a ship's dog."

Curtis found the note of annoyance in the captain's voice to be a hopeful sign that he might be treated fairly after all.

"But sir," Burke quickly said in an effort to cut off any discussion of Curtis' accommodations. "We can't just let him roam the ship after what he did. Everybody will know about this incident by morning and it just wouldn't send the right message if the crew sees him walking around free as a bird."

"Very well then." Captain McClure sighed as he stared at Curtis. "Take him below and 'cuff him to a bulkhead—but make him comfortable. Now, I need to get back to fighting a war."

As two men led Curtis toward the hatchway, he noticed the garbage can still sitting by the railing.

"Captain McClure, sir," Curtis said loudly. "Sir, I didn't get to finish my duty. I need to empty the garbage and get the can back down to the galley."

McClure looked at him in surprise. He was impressed with the boy's sense of duty, but then he thought it might just be part of the Negro race's acceptance of the fact that they were nothing more than beasts of burden—a dumb animal's single mindedness. Born and raised in Vermont, McClure realized he had little or no experience with colored folks, certainly not enough to determine the motivation of the ship's steward.

"That's all right. We'll get someone to take care of it," he said finally and then hurried forward once more.

"I'll get it Captain," Burke said. "If I hadn't been out here, we'd have never caught him in the first place."

McClure acknowledged Burke with a waved hand and then he and the lieutenant turned the corner around the deckhouse and were gone.

"That's OK boys, I'll take care of him," Burke said and nudged aside one of Curtis' escorts. "I'm really good at taking out the garbage." He gave Curtis' arm a painful twist and tugged him toward the deckhouse where a ladder led down into the ship's darkest innards.

ANASTASIA ISLAND: 2220 hrs.

From his position hidden in a bay tree thicket across the road from *Uncle Sam's Bar and Pier,* Rufus Pool watched the comings and goings of the laughing white folks while the anger in his belly smoldered and flared. For most of the past hour, he had sat cross-legged in the darkness sipping a beer and trying to identify the bar's customers as they climbed out of their cars and hurried inside or came staggering down the gangplank. So far, he had seen several of the people who have helped insure his life had little or no purpose.

First, there had been Old Man Davis bouncing into the parking lot in his battered pickup truck. In the glare of the hanging lanterns, Rufus could see the cantankerous shrimper was wearing his bibbed overalls as though he had come to feed the hogs he kept in a pen at his place on the San Sebastian River.

"Fool don't even know how to dress to go clubbin'," Rufus had muttered while watching Davis enter the bar. He could recall with painful clarity that day more than ten years ago when Davis had given him a beating with a leather strap after catching him in the Davis boathouse. The memory of how he had pleaded with the man to stop hitting him was not only embarrassing, it reminded him of how defenseless he had been as a child. He took some comfort in the fact that he was now a man. "I ain't takin' no shit off that old bastard no more," he had proclaimed to the armadillo that went scurrying through the underbrush.

Then there was Jolene Kelly getting groped by some soldier in the front seat of her new Ford coupe. When they got out of the car, she straightened her blouse and skirt, but as Rufus watched, the man brazenly ran his hands over her breasts while he kissed her deeply. They nearly fell as they stumbled up the gangplank wrapped in each other's arms.

"Bitch!" Rufus had shouted and then ducked back into the bushes when he thought someone might have heard him. Last summer, Jolene had smiled and spoken to him at the fruit market on Route 1 where he worked part time delivering watermelons. He hadn't seen any harm in talking with her—all he had said was something about the weather, but a few minutes later two of the white boys from the high school football team had come over so one of them could tell him "if I ever catch you talkin' to a white girl again, I'll cut your balls off and hand feed 'em to the gators." Over the shortest boy's shoulder, Rufus had seen Jolene laughing. When they had finished intimidating him, she had given each of the white boys a little kiss.

But what really stoked his anger was hearing Winnie's voice coming from the bar. He didn't care how good she sounded, all Rufus could think about was how wrong it was for her to be entertaining all those white folks. As far as he was concerned, God had given her a special voice and it should be used to His glory in church, not to make a bunch of drunken rednecks feel good.

It wasn't long after she finished singing that he saw Winnie come out of the bar with the same low life he had argued with that afternoon at Marineland. Winnie looked gorgeous in a yellow gown and the man opened the door of the big sedan for her just like she was a white woman. As the car rumbled past his hiding place, Rufus had clearly seen Winnie sitting alone in the back seat with the window rolled down—just like the Queen of England. Her face was beaming with happiness in the moonlight.

Rufus drained the last drop of his beer and tossed the bottle into the thicket behind him. At that moment, he knew he was about to do something momentous… something….what was the word? Brave. He stood shakily and walked across the sandy path to where the blackness of night met the sea of colored light blazing forth from *Uncle Sam's*. The demarcation line between light and darkness was so clearly defined that Rufus amused himself by looking down at his left foot in shadows while his right foot was bathed in light. Over the noise of the jukebox, he could hear white people laughing and as he listened, the noise in his ears grew louder and louder.

"Stop it! Stop laughing at me!" Rufus shouted and banged his hand against his head until the laughter subsided to a far away ripple.

At first, he thought he would boldly walk across the parking lot—just like a white man out for a little fun. But as he watched people coming and going, he realized from past experience that there was no way he could win if he were confronted by drunken white men—his work would be over before it had begun. He edged away from the light and let the breeze coming off the Atlantic freshen his thoughts. Rufus wanted to be cunning, but the odor of fried shrimp came drifting past. His mouth watered—it had been a long day and he decided the sooner he got this over with, the sooner he would be home to some of his momma's cold corn bread.

Filled with new determination, Rufus headed south through the palmettos before stumbling to the top of the dune. From there, he could see the Atlantic spread out in all of its moonlit majesty. As he lingered there to catch his breath, he gazed at the blue-white light of a shrimp boat working two miles off the beach. He wondered what it would be like to be out there on the vast ocean, until his stomach growled and urged him onward. He staggered down the dune, flattening sea oats as he went and then he was on the firm sand of the beach.

The tide was coming in and the gentle white foam rushed up to greet Rufus, then hissed away as though trying to get him to play a game of tag. He noticed the silhouettes of two couples walking nearby, but he could see they were interested in other things so he simply put his hands in the pockets of his threadbare jacket, leaned forward like a white man and moved past them without anyone noticing his presence. Soon, he was again at the edge of the circle of light, but this time he felt no urge to enter its glare. Instead, he moved along its circumference until he reached a point where he could step unseen among the pilings supporting *Uncle Sam's*. He moved deeply into the dark forest of barnacle-encrusted timbers—their creosote smell was heavy on the damp air trapped beneath the flooring above his head. Off to his left, liquid dripped and he wished it were beer—but the smell told him it was probably a leak from one of the toilets.

Down here, the sounds of revelry above were strangely muted as though the partying were going on behind some massive wooden door. Crabs scurried away as he approached the darkest corner and then he was at his destination. He looked up and saw a narrow passageway extending upward above his head. At its opposite end, stars flickered. During the six months between the departure of the previous owner and the arrival of Joe Miller, Rufus and his friends had explored every feature of the then-deserted building. He was the one who discovered the enclosed ladder leading up to the roof. Rufus took a deep breath and reached up to grasp the slime-covered bottom rung. He began to climb.

As Joe Miller moved through the crowd, he couldn't help but feel good about how well this "Sock It to The Nazis" night had gone. In between beers, the soldiers and a smattering of sailors were happily talking about their training and upcoming deployments—some of the information was even new to Miller. Over in a corner, the G-man seemed happy. He had even been out on the dance floor a couple of times with Rita. Miller was also sure the two beers he had provided for the young reporter, combined with the attentions of Maria and Shirley, were more than enough to give the kid several months worth of warm memories about Uncle Sam's.

Best of all, Winifred Greer had been a huge success. Dozens of customers had asked him where he had found such a great new talent. Others wanted to know when she would be performing again. And when she left the bar, the crowd had parted to allow her to pass as though she were some sort of royalty. Miller couldn't help but notice how the crowd's applause had forever changed her frightened pickaninny expression into the look of a mature performer. Any concerns Miller had about her possible dilemma over having to choose between the church and Uncle Sam's were erased when Carbone returned from taking her home and reported that not only had she gladly accepted the ten dollars he had paid her for tonight's performance, she had agreed to perform again tomorrow night. In fact, Carbone said proudly, he would be picking her up at Marineland again tomorrow afternoon and bringing her to *Uncle Sam's* for rehearsal.

The jukebox suddenly went silent and Carbone launched the band into its final set for the evening. This time he opened with *"Let Yourself Go"* and the dance floor quickly filled with swinging and swaying customers. The waitresses and the handful of local girls who had come by for a drink were much in demand...some had two or even three dance partners. Everyone was laughing, the beer was flowing and as Miller checked his watch, he decided to reward himself by beginning his nightly work a little early this evening.

Miller edged away from his customers, nodded goodnight to one of the bartenders and walked quickly down the hallway to where the spiral staircase led up to his office. He glanced back once at the happy crowd and then he went up the staircase with a bounce in his step that matched the beat of the music. He twisted the key in the lock, pulled a lever and swung the hatch upward. He entered quickly, dropped the hatch in place behind him and locked it shut.

A desk lamp with a faded *SMS Nassau* lampshade provided the only light in the room. Miller liked to keep it lit this way at night—just enough to make the office look occupied, but not enough light to draw anyone's attention to his rooftop command post. The window and viewing port on the south side of the office were open and a gentle April breeze carried the sound of the band and the scent of jasmine into the room. Although he found the night air refreshing, Miller stepped over and closed and latched them both. With the room sealed off, the music below took on a throbbing beat he could feel through the soles of his shoes.

Miller felt a tingling sense of anticipation as he opened the big antique cabinet that held his *Telefunken* transmitter and receiver. A small brass swastika was mounted in the center of the control panel and as he flipped the power switch, the tuning bar lit up with a cheery glow. Although it was still more than an hour before he would send the nightly weather report, he went ahead and unlocked the drawer containing the transmitter key. Pulling the drawer open, he tapped the key lightly and the needle on one of the radio's many dials bounced in response—everything was in perfect working order.

"I don't like what you been a-doin' wid Miss Greer."

Miller could not have been more stunned if the radio had delivered a massive electrical shock through his hands. His spine seemed to lock in place and he felt the hair stand up on the back of his neck. He fought the urge to spin around and confront the intruder. Instead, he took one deep breath, forced his lips into a thin smile, and turned slowly.

"Did you hear me Whitey?"

The voice was coming from the dark form of a man sitting in the shadows in the far corner of the office. As Miller watched, the man slowly leaned forward until his large black hands entered the faint glare of the desk lamp. The right hand held a nasty-looking knife with a serrated blade.

"How did you get in here?" Miller asked the question with the same firmness he had once used with cadets aboard the *Nassau*.

"Man, I ain't answerin' no questions from you." The intruder's voice had raised several octaves. "I be tellin' you what I want you to hear." The hands and the knife disappeared into the shadows, but this time when the unannounced visitor leaned forward, there was enough light for Miller to see that the intruder was a young man, probably less than twenty-five years old. As much as he tried, Miller could find nothing about the man's face that would distinguish him from any of the hundreds of other black men he had seen working in the fields or lounging in the shade of the big live oaks along Route 1.

"And exactly what is it you want me to hear?" Miller asked and took two steps that placed him behind his desk.

"I want you to leave Miss Greer alone—she ain't got no business in a place like this and you ain't got no business bringin' her here."

"But Miss Greer is an incredible talent—she should be famous... and rich. I'm just helping her dreams come true," Miller said and eased into his leather chair behind the desk as though getting comfortable for a long conversation.

"She belongs in church, singin' for the Lord—no place else. 'Specially not over here with a bunch of sinnin' white folks. You stay away from her. You hear me?" The man moved to the edge of his seat and pointed the knife in Miller's direction.

"And if I don't? I suppose you're going to sneak in here some night and cut me with that knife?"

"You damn right I will. I'll cut you good if'n you don't stay away from her."

His threat hung in the air while the pounding of the music below seemed to get louder. Now that he had delivered his ultimatum, Miller could see the young man was at a loss as to what his next course of action should be—something dramatic like sticking the knife in the desk? Or should he just walk out? And how could he leave? He couldn't just go over and open the hatch, go down the stairs and casually walk through a crowd of drunken white people. The window through which he had obviously entered the office was now closed—did he expect Miller to help open it so he could escape? For the first time, Miller noticed the smell of sweat and old beer in the room—he knew his visitor had suddenly become very uncomfortable.

"All right, let's see if we can resolve this. How about some money? I could make a sizeable contribution to your church. Do you think that would help?" Miller spoke as if he were genuinely touched by the young man's concern about Winifred Greer's welfare. He eased the desk draw open as though he kept hundreds of dollars inside it.

"Well, maybe…that might work." The man shifted in his seat. "No. No, I don't think that will work at all," he said firmly.

Miller had never killed anyone before, but he saw no other way around the situation. Even if the boy was just another dumb nigger, Miller reasoned, he couldn't take a chance on him telling all the other darkies about the nice German radio he had seen over at *Uncle Sam's*. In one sweeping motion, he pulled the silenced Mauser out of the drawer where it had been waiting for just such an occasion.

"Whoa there boss!" The boy's eyes were suddenly so wide that the whites seemed as big as saucers. "There's no need for that. I's just tellin' you what the colored folks is sayin'. I don't want no trouble."

Miller said nothing as he cocked the pistol and pointed it directly at his uninvited guest. By now he had resolved the debate in his head over whether or not to kill the man. His problem now was deciding where to place the slugs. A head shot would be too messy—better just place them in the chest. Miller was slightly concerned about the noise. He had never fired the Mauser with the silencer in place and had no idea of how loud it might be. Suddenly, Miller realized that sheer coincidence had solved the noise problem. Downstairs, *The Patriot Swing Band* had just begun the perfect selection for his grisly task—the lyrics went "all she wants to do is dance... dance... dance!" with a Carbone rimshot to punctuate each "dance". The refrain repeated and this time, Miller squeezed the trigger in unison with each crack of the drumstick.

Pistol smoke hung in the air above the desk as Miller stood and moved quickly to stand over the crumpled figure in the corner.

"Who says white men have no sense of rhythm?" Miller asked.

TUESDAY
April 14, 1942

ANASTASIA ISLAND: 0850 hrs.

G-man Bill Spencer couldn't help but feel uncomfortable about his flagrant violation of FBI protocol. He knew he should have contacted the local law enforcement authorities upon his arrival in St. Augustine, but somehow that regulation had managed to slip his mind on Monday. He wrote it off to the sunshine and the dazzling beauty of the ancient city on the shore of Matanzas Bay--he had to keep telling himself that he wasn't on vacation. He was sure his superiors in Washington would be more than happy to remind him of his duty if they ever got a chance. Failing to check with the local sheriff was just the kind of thing that could result in a very poor performance review.

Spencer had tried to do the right thing that morning--but by the time he had finished breakfast and ambled over to the City Building, the sheriff had already gone to check on a possible murder. After listening to the deputy's explanation, Spencer decided it was his duty to offer his assistance in the investigation. Quickly getting directions, Spencer had jumped into the FBI coupe and headed south across the Bridge of Lions and on to Anastasia Island.

The morning sunlight streamed through the windshield and flashed from the chrome detailing on the instrument panel. Despite the somewhat disheartening nature of his destination, Spencer found himself singing along with "*I Don't Want to Set the World on Fire*" on the car radio.

"Yes sir," he thought, "it would be easy to get used to a place like this."

If not for the group of black folks gathered on the corner,

Spencer would have missed Old Quarry Street. He started to wave a friendly greeting to the locals gathered there, but noticed that not one of them had stopped their conversation long enough to acknowledge the presence of a shiny new Chevy. He braked, downshifted and turned off the paved road on to a sandy side street leading toward the Matanzas. Dappled sunlight filtered down through a stand of huge bay trees and then he could see the bright water directly ahead. The road suddenly widened into a clearing along the water's edge where Spencer found the sheriff's gray sedan marked with the county's logo parked in the shade to the right. The G-man pulled alongside, turned off the ignition and set the parking brake.

At first, Spencer thought the whimpering sound coming from the bushes was produced by some sort of exotic Florida creature. But as he climbed from the car and closed the door behind him, he saw several black women coming up the path that led to the water. One of them, a large woman in a red print dress had tears streaming down her ebony face. Two younger women helped support her as they headed into the clearing. Even though he stepped politely to one side to let them pass, not one of them acknowledged his presence. The trio stopped and the crying woman let out a loud moan that to Spencer seemed strangely out of place on such a beautiful morning.

The odor of rotting vegetation and the heady aroma of oysters hung heavily in the air as Spencer headed down the path where insects buzzed and the black mud sucked at his wingtip shoes. Just when he was beginning to think it might not be a bad idea to go back to the office and wait for the sheriff's return, he stepped out into the sunlight once more. Two young black boys dressed in white shirts and black trousers sat on a burned out log at the water's edge. They looked up at him with wide, soulful eyes before returning their gaze to their bare feet.

"Have you boys seen the Sheriff?" Spencer asked.

The boys continued to study their feet.

"I said, have you seen..."

"Who the hell wants to know?"

Spencer flinched at the sound of the voice, but as he turned to face Sheriff Haywood Hartson he was determined to be professional.

"Good morning Sheriff," he said politely. "I'm special agent Bill Spencer with..."

"I know who you are. You reckon I don't know when there's an FBI fella in my town?" The sheriff was visible to Spencer from only the waist up. His lower extremities were hidden from view behind the steep slope of the embankment that dropped off to the water. For some reason, Spencer had imagined the sheriff to be ponderously fat. Instead, he found himself facing a man who was so thin that he looked as though a bag of bones had been poured into his sweat-stained khaki uniform. The big Smith and Wesson revolver in its black holster looked oddly out of place on a man with such a thin frame.

"Well, yes Sheriff. I'm sure you knew I was here...I just wanted to apologize for not coming by your office yesterday," Spencer said. "There's really no excuse for it and I'm sorry I didn't meet you when I arrived."

The tension in Hartson's face relaxed slightly as his eyes took in Spencer's compact build. The last thing he had expected from a G-man was an apology---especially one delivered with a slight Southern drawl.

"It don't matter...I got too much to do than play tour guide for the Feds anyways--damn niggers been shootin' each other again." Hartson said and as he pushed up the brim of his doughboy-style hat the harsh morning sunlight revealed a badly pockmarked complexion. "They've left me a stinkin' mess here. That's for sure."

Spencer decided that the sheriff's suddenly relaxed stance was a sign that he had accepted his presence at the crime scene. In response, Spencer stepped forward, looked down at the "mess" at the sheriff's feet and immediately fought back a wave of nausea.

The wide, lifeless eyes of a black man stared up at him from the muck. The back of the head was firmly stuck in the putrid ooze, but the body lifted and fell slightly as a gentle wave lapped at the cadaver. As Spencer watched, a black fiddler crab emerged from the man's mouth and waved a large claw that held a bit of gray slime the creature had obviously torn from somewhere inside the dead man. More crabs scurried up the torso as though the piece of flesh recovered by their more adventurous companion was just the delicacy they had all been seeking. The first crab jumped down from the man's blue lips and hurried away with several of his companions in close pursuit.

"Is he....?" Spencer almost asked an extremely stupid question--it was obvious a man couldn't get more "dead" than the one at the sheriff's feet. "Is he...from around here?"

"Hell yes, he's from around here. You don't think them nigger women would be that upset about a stranger do you?" The sheriff spat in disgust and a half-dozen crabs silently raced to inspect the spittle. "His name is Pool. Grew up down around Moses Creek. As far as I recollect, he's never been in any serious trouble. I reckon his big mistake was in choosing friends."

"You think his friends left him like this?"

"I reckon so. They all come down here about every night. Build a fire, drink some homemade wine and do whatever it is buck niggers do in the dark." He lifted his boot out of the shallow water and roughly kicked away the front of the man's blood stained shirt to reveal three large and neatly rounded holes in his chest. "Don't usually find 'em with gunshot wounds though--'specially not such well-placed ones like these. Most times they just kill each other with an axe or a machete and I have to go gather up the pieces all over hell's half-acre."

Hartson sloshed over to the embankment and extended his hand. "I've had enough of this for one morning."

Spencer reached down, grasped the sheriff's hand and pulled. He was surprised at how smoothly the man came up the slippery embankment. As he released his grip, his gaze met Hartson's stare and in that brief second, Spencer realized that he was not dealing with some backwater cracker. There was obviously more to Sheriff Haywood Hartson than what was readily visible.

Hartson edged past him and walked over to where the two young black boys continued to sit on the burned out log. They looked up at him with expressions of complete submission to whatever punishment the sheriff might deem appropriate.

"So you boys swear you weren't robbin' that corpse?" Hartson asked and the boys silently shook their heads in unison. "Well, if'n you was you know you'll go straight to hell. The Lord don't put up with no messin' with the dead." He waited for his words to sink in on the boys before continuing. "All right then! Git on up the road and tell them folks they can come on back and get this corpse before the crabs eat it."

Hartson stood with his hands on his hips and smiled as he watched the two boys scramble out of sight.

"That's it?" Spencer asked. "That's the end of your investigation?"

Hartson sighed and shook his head slowly.

"Yes, I'm finished with my investigation. It don't take long when there's nothing much to investigate."

"But there's been a murder!" Spencer protested. "What about clues? What about questioning people around here to see if they heard anything? What about..."

The sheriff cut off Spencer' questions with a wave of his hand.

"Look, I know the FBI might handle this a little differently. But you're down here now and we know how much time a case like this warrants. Besides, all the so-called evidence has been tampered with. There've been niggers down here with the body half the night. Those two little boys were going through the corpse's pockets when I got here. There's nothing here worth looking for as evidence. And as far as catching the guilty party is concerned, I'll leave that up to the victim's kin."

Hartson hiked up his gun belt and started up the path toward his car.

"And what about the body?" Spencer asked quietly.

The sheriff stopped and twisted his head as though trying to work an annoying cramp from his neck. He turned halfway so that he was at least looking in Spencer's direction.

"I ain't no colored undertaker. If they want the body, they'll come and get it. If not, the tide will carry it out to the bay and the fish will get a real treat. Now if you'll excuse me, I have white folks with real problems that I have to tend to. The Widow Chapman called first thing this morning about her cat being stuck in a tree. I'm sure she's wondering where I am."

Hartson disappeared up the path leaving Spencer with the bugs, the crabs and the corpse. As the FBI agent listened to the sheriff's car start up and drive away, he suddenly felt very much alone.

MARINELAND: 0940 hrs.

By 9:30 a.m., Winnie Greer's concern about Rufus Pool's tardiness had begun to occupy her every thought. She had never known her friend to be late for work at Marineland—in fact, he sometimes arrived so early that most of his work for the day was finished by the time the staff filed through the main gate. But today, there had been no sign of him when she had arrived and in an effort to hide his absence from their employers Winnie had decided she would do his chores as well as her own.

The filter system had proved to be the biggest challenge, but she knew that if it weren't cleaned before the technicians turned on the pumps for the morning shift, Rufus' absence would be readily apparent. It wasn't until the third attempt that she was able to work the latches in the proper sequence and remove the heavy cover. Fortunately, there was very little debris in the trap—assorted beer and wine bottles, a battered wicker basket and a dead grouper. Because of its slimy texture, the fish gave her the most trouble. She had just disposed of it in the garbage bin out by the dunes when she came around the corner of the big circular oceanarium and saw her supervisor, Mr. Cleary, coming up the sidewalk with Luigi Carbone. The two of them were talking quietly and as they approached, Winnie couldn't help but notice how different these two white men were—Carbone with his dark complexion and dingy white suit looking like some Chicago mobster on vacation and Cleary in his dark blue suit, rimless spectacles and brushed back red hair that reminded Winnie of one of those---what did they call them she wondered? Altar boys.

"Good morning, Winifred," Cleary said quietly. "I believe you know Mr. Carbone?"

Winnie nodded. She couldn't imagine what could bring these two men together. Surely, Luigi Carbone was not there to study marine science.

"Well, Mr. Carbone was kind enough to come by this morning to bring us some sad news about your friend Rufus." Cleary waited to see that he had Winnie's full attention. "I'm afraid Rufus is dead."

The words were so unexpected that for an instant, Winnie hoped she had misunderstood. The early morning sunlight seemed to shift and there was a roaring in her head as the image of a smiling Rufus Pool disappeared into a bottomless pit.

"...to take you home. I think that's a good idea."

Winnie regained her focus and realized that Mr. Clearly was talking to her. She wasn't sure if his words required a response--if they did, she had no idea what to say. The horrible news about Rufus combined with the realization that two white men apparently were concerned about her welfare was too overwhelming for her to rationalize. She stood motionless and tried to concentrate on something she knew was real—the sizzle and murmur of the Atlantic behind her.

"She may be in shock," Cleary said and stared at her as though examining a dog that had just been hit by a car. "You may want to stop up at Doc Lancaster's and have him take a look at her. I, well, we can't pay for her care, but perhaps Mr. Miller would consider...."

"Of course he will," Carbone said and reached out to grasp Winnie's arm with a gloved hand. "I think we will just be going now."

Winnie felt herself stepping forward in response to Carbone's touch. She saw Cleary coming toward her as well. The man seemed to want to touch her, but she could see that physical contact with a black girl was something the office manager was not yet ready to add to his list of life's accomplishments.

"I'm fine," Winnie said firmly, but she continued to let Carbone guide her toward the walkway leading to the exit. "I'm all right Mr. Cleary. Don't you worry none. I'll be back first thing tomorrow mornin'."

Cleary smiled uneasily. "You just take care, Winifred. And I'm very sorry about Rufus. He was a good boy."

Hearing Rufus referred to in the past tense for the first time brought Winnie to a halt. She turned and stared hard at her boss.

"No sir," she said. "He was not a good boy...Rufus was a good man. And he cared about workin' here. I would just like to say thank you for giving him this job. I know he would want to thank you himself if'n he could be here."

Winnie's words made Cleary blush. He had never thought about how much an opportunity to work at Marineland must mean to poor colored folks like Winnie and Rufus. "Well, that's fine Winifred. We enjoyed having him as an employee."

"Oh and don't you worry none about them filters," Winnie said suddenly. "I cleaned them all right—just like Rufus would've done."

Cleary had already headed back toward his office, but he waved a quick goodbye without turning to face her.

Carbone tugged her arm to continue their walk and her first instinct was to pull away from him. She found his touch to be...unsettling. She didn't know much about men—especially white men. But she knew that there was something about Carbone's close proximity that made her feel dirty. At the same time, she couldn't help but feel his attentions were an obvious sign that she was moving up in society. And when Winnie realized that the other workers were staring at the two of them, she decided she liked being led by the arm out to the where the big Lincoln was parked in the shade by the front entrance.

It wasn't until they had pulled away from Marineland and turned north on A1A that Carbone finally spoke.

"I'm not takin' you home," he said matter-of-factly. "Mr. Miller thinks it would be a good idea for you to come to the club and rehearse some more. He has some new material for you to work on."

"But I think I should go see if there's anything I can do to help Rufus' family. I think they might...."

Carbone made a quick upward thrust with his right hand and Winnie flinched. "Don't you see? It don't matter what you think. It only matters what Mr. Miller thinks and he thinks you should be rehearsin'...and so do I."

Winnie didn't argue. She wanted to, but then she had to reluctantly admit that she wanted to go to Uncle Sam's. In fact, she would be willing to spend every moment there if it would somehow insure her success as a singer. In an attempt to convince herself that she had not become addicted to the idea of achieving musical fame and fortune, she tried to get the conversation back to the loss of Rufus.

"How did Rufus die?" she asked.

Carbone shifted into high gear and glanced in the rear view mirror as though checking to see if anyone were following them.

"Some nigger shot him," he said and Winnie noticed that for a brief second Carbone seemed to be smiling. "Shot him three times." And to emphasize his statement, he moved his right hand from the steering wheel, formed a fist and stuck out his index finger to serve as the barrel of a handgun. " Bang! Bang! Bang! "

Winnie stared out the car window and looked at the tranquil

waters of the Atlantic. Murder! She couldn't believe anyone could harm Rufus—and now someone had killed him. She had so many questions about what had happened to him, but by the time they rattled across the Matanzas Inlet Bridge, she was no longer thinking about Rufus. She was trying to decide which songs she should rehearse that afternoon.

ANASTASIA ISLAND: 1010 hrs.

Michael Pomar was pleased with how well his plans for the morning were working out. He had anticipated a long bike ride from downtown St. Augustine all the way out to Uncle Sam's. And although the heat of summer had not yet settled in, he knew that peddling in the thick humidity with the loaner camera from The Record would not be a pleasant experience. Fortunately, he had been sitting astride his bike at the corner of King and Cordova when Gene Sullivan's fully loaded beer truck had stopped at the light.   It was not difficult to figure out where such a massive shipment of beer was headed and Gene had quickly agreed to give him a lift. Tossing his bike on the open back of the truck, Pomar had settled into the passenger's seat to enjoy a pleasant morning ride across the sparkling waters of Matanzas Bay and out toward the beach.

His only regret so far was that he had not learned of the murder in time to cover the story. Not that there would be much to report--the murder of a colored boy was not something that got much attention in *The Record* or at the radio station. But he had hoped to get a photo of the murder scene or at least talk to some of the victim's friends and family. Even though there wasn't much money or potential fame involved, Pomar had taken it upon himself to document the lives of the colored population of St. Augustine. He didn't know why he bothered to collect photos of black people and to record some of their stories--quite possibly, he decided, it was because no one else did. And to Pomar, that continuing omission of the story of people who had called St. Augustine home for hundreds of years was simply not right.

"Hey Mike." Gene said as he downshifted to ease the truck around a corner in Davis Shores. "You know anything about that nigger they found dead over here this morning. Everybody was

111

talking about it over at the warehouse."

Pomar knew that Gene was a fine person, one of the most dependable and honest folks in the Ancient City. But his question was asked with the same enthusiasm as if he were inquiring about an unusually large jewfish someone had reeled in at the inlet. There was no hint in his voice that he was asking about the violent death of a fellow human being.

"No. Nothing other than the fact that the sheriff came over here to look at the body this morning," Pomar said. "What did you hear at the warehouse?"

The truck shook and hundreds of beer bottles rattled as Gene accelerated out of the last turn and headed up Ocean Boulevard toward the lighthouse. "Nothin'. Nobody knew anything much about it. Just somebody said they found some nigger boy floatin' over here in the Matanzas. There's a couple of colored fellas what works over there and everybody knew they was in the know about it. But they weren't talkin'-- you know how moody niggers can be sometimes."

Pomar was always amazed at how insensitive well-respected white people like Gene could be when it came to race relations.

"Yes, moody. They can be pretty moody when a member of their community has been murdered." Even though he knew prejudice would prevent Gene from having a rational opinion on the subject, he couldn't help but ask: "So, Gene, what do you think happened to the boy? You must have a theory."

Gene shifted his toothpick to the other side of his mouth and grinned.

"Of course I do--the same theory everybody else has. The nigger was stealing something from Davis Shores and drowned trying to get away with his loot."

"Gee, Gene, how did you come up with that?" Pomar asked even though he was quite familiar with the thought process that brought white people to that conclusion. "How do you know he wasn't just fishing and fell in the bay?"

Gene slowly shook his head. "And you call yourself a reporter?

Don't you know niggers don't fish after sundown? Besides, why else would he be over here? Davis Shores…new homes for wealthy white folks…easy pickn's. I can't believe you didn't figure that out for yourself."

Pomar wasn't surprised by Gene's answer--in fact, he had expected just that sort of illogical reasoning.

"You're right there Gene," Pomar said. "That just never occurred to me."

The Ford truck was now roaring down Ocean Boulevard and Pomar briefly considered engaging Gene in an in-depth discussion of race relations. But the noise of the engine would have required him to shout and besides, the warm breeze coming through the open window carried the sweet smell of Confederate jasmine. As they passed the St. Augustine Lighthouse with its white and black paint scheme gleaming in the morning light, he decided that he couldn't do anything to solve hundreds of years of racial prejudice--at least not on a beautiful morning like this one. As the truck rounded the turn into St. Augustine Beach, Pomar saw the bright blue Atlantic framed between two sabal palms jutting up from the white sand. "If God wanted a place to put injustice, He couldn't have picked a prettier setting," Pomar thought.

As usual at this time of morning, Joe Miller was out talking with the local anglers lining the railing of his pier. There was a run of whiting and several fishermen had pulled in near record catches. As a result, there was lots of good-natured banter and laughter out on the wooden pier. Miller was at the center of it for a short time, but he found his thoughts wandering to more important issues. And when he saw the beer truck pull into the parking lot, he welcomed the opportunity to excuse himself from the company of people whose intellect he secretly considered to be just slightly above that of the fish they pulled from the sea.

"Good morning Michael!" Miller shouted from the club's deck. "Glad to see you remembered your story idea."

Pomar slid out of the truck's passenger seat and pulled his backpack containing the camera down from the cab. He thought about offering to help Gene unload the beer in exchange for the ride, but the driver had already set Pomar's bike down from the truck and was busily unloading a dolly to begin his work.

Pomar started up the ramp and as he looked at Miller waiting for him at the top, he felt as though he were coming up the gangplank of an ocean liner or warship to interview its captain. Miller was dressed in a dark blue jacket with brass buttons and wore a yacht captain's hat at a jaunty angle. His arms were folded behind him and his stance was decidedly military.

"Permission to come aboard Sir?" Pomar asked and Miller responded with a flashy salute

"Permission granted, Captain Pomar," Miller said and bowed stiffly. "We have the socks in the bar. I didn't know if you wanted to do the photos outdoors or indoors. I'll leave that up to you."

Pomar couldn't help but be pleased that Miller was treating him like a professional journalist instead of a kid pretending to be a reporter.

"Oh indoors will be fine---the bar adds a nice touch and, who knows, the photo might even attract more customers."

Pomar followed Miller through the double doors and into the large room. The bright morning light created a dramatically different atmosphere than that of the night before. Instead of a romantic hideaway beneath the twinkling tropical stars, the establishment looked more like a warehouse where dozens of tables were stacked on top of each other. In a far corner, an elderly janitor moved a huge pile of peanut shells and cigarette butts with a push broom and each sweep caused more dust motes to float upward in a beam of sunlight. Even the stage where the young singer had mesmerized the audience was now just a battered-looking platform in need of a thorough scrubbing. And there was no delightful sea breeze this morning--the stench of urine and old beer wafted up through the floorboards.

"We ended up with more than two hundred pairs of socks," Miller said as he pulled the flaps back on the large cardboard box sitting on the bar. "Not as good as last month, but now that we're in the war I think more people are interested in saving socks for their own sons and brothers in the military--not in helping the English keep their feet dry and warm. My guess is that Bundles for Britain will soon fade away."

"So that's where the socks go? Bundles for Britain?" Pomar had produced his reporter's notepad and was busily writing down Miller's comments. "Where would that be exactly?"

There was a long pause and Pomar looked up to see Miller staring at him as though he had been asked something akin to 'what is the meaning of life?'

"I'm afraid I really don't know--New Jersey. I think," Miller mumbled. "My assistant takes care of the actual mailing--he even puts in a rubber liner to make sure the socks don't get wet--sends them express freight so they'll be there in just a couple of days. He's not here, but I can ask him later and give you a call."

Pomar scribbled in his notebook.

"You know, I've got a great idea," Miller said suddenly. "How about if I get one of our good looking barmaids to help with the photo? I'm sure your readers would rather see her than me."

The reporter smiled at the prospect of getting reacquainted with one of the lovely creatures who had made such an impression on him the night before.

"Sure thing!" Pomar realized his puppy-like enthusiasm was not exactly...professional. "I mean, that sounds like a good idea. We can try it and see how she works out."

"No...young man, you can try her out." Miller winked. "I'm sure you'll find she will work out, or in, just fine. I'll be right back."

Miller stepped from behind the bar and moved out of sight around the corner. As Pomar listened to the bar owner's footsteps receding down the hallway, he realized it had suddenly become very hot in the room. He repressed the image of Miller returning with a stark naked barmaid--those things don't happen in real life, he told himself. In an effort to put his mind on more wholesome topics, he moved to the bar and peeked in the box. The socks were all there--neatly folded and arranged row upon row. He absent-mindedly tucked in one of the box's flaps and noticed a white mailing label sticking out from beneath the box. He slid it free and noted the neatly lettered address:

Rabbi Jacob Levi
Beth Shalom Synagogue
4789 W. 12th Street
Camden, New Jersey

Pomar's first reaction was to show the label to Miller, but then he remembered the bar owner's suspicious response to his question about the box's destination. His reporter's instinct caused him to copy the address into his notebook and slide the label back beneath the box. He could hear a woman arguing down the hall, but a sharp command from Miller seemed to put an end to her protest. It was less than thirty seconds later that a beaming Miller appeared with the barmaid Pomar remembered as "Shirley" in tow.

"Here she is!" Miller exclaimed. "Now won't Shirley make a great picture?"

For anyone observing the moment, there was nothing remarkable about it. But for Pomar it was one of those educational events that would remain with him forever. The beautiful angel he had admired in the dim light of the bar only a few hours ago had been transformed by the harsh sunlight into a very unremarkable example of womanhood. He searched for some sign that this was indeed the woman from the night before—but then he had to admit he couldn't recall for sure whether her hair had been red, blonde, or some shade of brown. He just knew it had looked so soft, so touchable in the candlelight. But this woman's hair looked stiff and unkept—still, it was about the right length. And she was roughly the same height as the girl of his dreams. Then he noticed the small birthmark on her cheek just below her swollen left eye and her identity was confirmed. Last night, the mark had seemed exotic. This morning, it was…hideous.

"Sure, uh…it will be fine," Pomar muttered as he carefully removed the Speed Graphic camera from his backpack.

"For God's sake, you could at least comb your hair," Miller complained to Shirley. "And put on some lipstick. This could be your big break—your photo's gonna be in the newspaper."

In the few seconds it took Pomar to check the Speed Graphic, load the film, and snap a flashbulb in place, Shirley had nearly completed an impressive transformation. While looking into the mirror behind the bar, she pulled back her hair and clipped it into place with a bone-colored comb. From somewhere she produced a tube of red lipstick and with a couple of much-practiced strokes her lips blossomed like an award-winning rose. She released the top two buttons of her rumpled blouse and then pulled it from her jeans and tied the bottom of it in a knot that revealed her flat and sun-bronzed abdomen.

When she turned to face Pomar and Miller, the transformation was truly remarkable.

"My photo in the newspaper….oh my goodness, I'm really not ready for that," Shirley said and from somewhere she conjured up a smile so warm it would, to use one of Pomar's mother's favorite phrases, melt butter. She leaned in close to Miller and rested one hand on her opposite hip.

"Oh, I think you're ready for this," Pomar said as he fumbled with the camera, "but maybe I'm not."

For the next ten minutes, the camera's flashbulbs lit the bar like streaks of summer lightning as Shirley provided her interpretation of a woman's most pleasant and appealing moods— seductive...playful...curious...caring. Even though the expression on Miller's face never changed, she made him and his box of socks seem as though they were the most important objects on the planet.

"Well, I uh...I'm out of film," Pomar said reluctantly as he put down the camera and picked up his notepad. "But I do need your full name for the photo...I don't think you ever told me your last name."

"That's Hoover," Shirley said and her chest strained against the cotton blouse as she loudly sucked in air and then slowly released it, "just like the vacuum cleaner."

The innuendo wasn't wasted on Pomar. His face flushed with embarrassment and he took his time about writing her name on the pad. When he finally recovered enough composure to look up from his notes, he found Shirley staring at him with wide-eyed innocence and red lips in a full pout. A strand of blonde hair tumbled down her forehead and for some reason the way she brushed it back into place seemed incredibly sensual to him.

"All finished then?" Miller asked. "We really have a lot to do here today. Gotta get ready for another bunch of our brave boys in uniform. There's an infantry company coming over here tonight from Camp Blanding. It's their commander's birthday."

"Wow, that's really nice of you to take such good care of those fellas, " Pomar said as he finally, with great reluctance, pried his eyes away from Shirley. "I'm sure it's tough to be away from home—but you give them their own little home away from home."

"It's the least I can do," Miller said and with a nod of his head sent a now very subdued Shirley on her way back down the hallway. "Without them, I'd have to learn to speak German and the only thing on our menu would be those ugly sausages the Krauts are so fond of."

"I'll pass on that." Pomar pulled open his backpack and gently tucked the camera inside. "So you say the socks will ship out today?"

Miller swung around from behind the bar and began escorting the young reporter toward the exit.

"Yes, just as soon as my assistant gets back he'll finish packing the box and get it over to the train station. Going by express, it should get up north by tomorrow night easily." As they stepped out of the shadowy bar and on to the sunlit deck, they heard the muffled roar of an engine and the crunch of tires going through the oyster shell-coated parking lot. Slowly, a Lincoln Continental eased into view and parked in the owner's space at the bottom of the gangplank.

"There's Carbone now," Miller said. "He'll probably want to help unload the beer, but I'm going to have him take care of those socks first. No need letting them sit here when there are English lads and lassies with cold feet just waiting for new socks."

Looking down from the deck, Pomar watched as Carbone slid out of the driver's seat and hurried around to the other side of the big sedan where he opened the door for his passenger. At first, Pomar thought the black girl emerging from the vehicle was a member of the housekeeping staff. But the way Carbone seemed to hover around her made it clear that she was far more important than a domestic servant. It wasn't until she turned and started up the gangplank with Carbone's assistance that he recognized her as the girl with the incredible voice who had entertained them the previous night at this very same bar.

"Welcome Winifred," Miller said and moved down the ramp to assume a guardian position at the girl's elbow. "I'm glad you could come. Hopefully, the music will take your mind off your troubles."

The girl tried to smile, but even in the harsh sunlight Pomar could see her dark brown eyes reflected a sense of sadness and loss.

"Thank you for inviting me here, Mr. Miller, " she said quietly. "But I can't help but feel I should be helping with Rufus' family."

"Nonsense!" Miller said as they stopped at the top of the ramp. "Rufus would have wanted you to be here. I'm sure he was your biggest fan."

"I know he was, but it just don't seem right that..." Winnie's voice trailed away on the sea breeze as she suddenly noticed Pomar.

"I don't know if you've ever met Michael Pomar?" Miller said quickly. "He's a reporter with the local newspaper and radio station and I'm sure he remembers you from last night's performance."

"It's a real pleasure to meet you Miss Greer," Pomar said and gently shook the soft hand she offered to him. "You really have a remarkable voice--but then I guess you've heard that before."

"Thank you."

Pomar had never before heard those two words have such a lyrical quality.

"Miss Greer is grieving today," Miller said as he lightly touched her shoulder and guided her toward the barroom. "One of her close friends passed away last night."

"I wouldn't call it passing away," Winnie said and there was a touch of harshness in her words. "Passing away is what folks that are too old to keep on living do at the end. Rufus was just a boy and somebody murdered him for no good reason."

"Murdered?" Pomar's reporter's instincts were suddenly aroused. "You say your friend was murdered?"

"Now...now Miss Greer," Miller said and began to push firmly against her shoulder in order to hurry her inside. "That's something the sheriff will determine and I'm sure he's on the case. We really need to get started with rehearsal. There's another big crowd due here tonight."

"Well, when somebody is shot three times I think everybody knows it wasn't no accident." Winnie ignored Miller and stared directly at Pomar. "Maybe you can check that out Mr. Reporter? Tell everybody about how poor Rufus Pool got hisself shot three times and dumped in the bay."

"Yes, I will...you can count on it," Pomar said, even though he knew that the murder of a colored man was not something any of his employers would want him to spend time pursuing. "Three times? You say he was shot three times? How do you know that?"

"Well, Mr. Carbone told me so," she said firmly. "He told me all about the murder on the way up here from Marineland."

The three of them turned and looked at Carbone who acted as though he hadn't been listening to the conversation. He shifted uneasily and Pomar could see the man's Adam's apple bob as he swallowed nervously.

"Is that right? " Pomar said with ill-concealed enthusiasm. "Where did you get that information? Maybe I could go interview your source."

The silence that followed was eventually broken by the rattling of beer cases as Gene continued to unload the Budweiser from the truck down below.

"Well I'm sure Luigi was talking to those colored fishermen that were here at the crack of dawn," Miller said. "Isn't that right Luigi?" Carbone nodded, but Miller wasn't finished. "I keep telling him you can't believe a word those ol' boys tell you. The one old fuzzy-haired fellow was telling me how he caught a nine-foot hammerhead shark last week."

"Are they still here? Maybe I could talk with them...find out what they know." Pomar was beginning to think he might be on to a story after all.

"Oh hell no," Carbone said quickly. "They left by nine--they weren't about to get caught out in the heat. You know how niggers are---no offense Miss Greer."

"But do you know their names? Maybe I could interview them somewhere?"

Miller pushed the girl smoothly through the doorway and into the shadowy bar room.

"That's enough for one morning, young man. We have work to do...lots of it. So if you'll excuse us we'll get to it." Miller turned and went inside. Carbone nodded a goodbye and he too hurried inside leaving Pomar alone on the deck.

"Hey Mike!" Gene shouted and Pomar looked over the railing to see the beer truck driver standing with hands on hips in the hot sun. "I've got her all unloaded. You want a ride back into town?"

Pomar looked through the window at the three figures in the bar. He knew there was a story here--maybe two--not only a murder, but also a story of why a white man was so suddenly interested in a talented colored girl. But he also knew he would not be getting any more information from them today.

"OK Gene," he said and started down the wide wooden ramp. "I'll take you up on your generous offer."

Inside, Miller struggled to contain his anger. He suggested that Winifred go look at the dresses hanging in the women's bathroom and as soon as she left, he glared at Carbone.

"What the hell do you think you're doing telling that girl about what happened? You think that reporter won't be digging into this story now--he may be young, but he's not stupid!"

120

"Sorry boss," Carbone said quietly and tried to stare a hole through the wooden floor.

"Sorry's not enough," Miller snapped. "But the least you can do is get that box sealed up and send it on its way. You do remember how to package it up don't you?"

"Yes, boss, I remember the details," Carbone said with new enthusiasm. "In fact, I can't wait much longer."

"Good....take it on down, seal it up and get it over to the freight station. I'm anxious to get it on its way to those kind folks up in Jersey."

"Right away, boss, you can count on me!" Carbone said as he scooped up the box and packing tape. He negotiated his way around the bar, hurried out the door and down the ramp. Moving deep into the shadows among the pilings, he sat the box on the cool sand and as if on cue cats of every size and color came rushing to him and set up a cacophony of mewing as they rubbed at his trouser legs.

"All right...all right youse guys, you knew I wouldn't forget you. Here you go!" Carbone dug into his jacket pocket and came up with a grease-stained paper bag. He quickly tossed last night's leftover chicken wings among the pilings and the cats scrambled wildly after their generous meal.

Satisfied that each cat had a choice morsel, Carbone frantically unzipped his trousers, released his member and sent a noisy stream of urine into the box of clean white socks. Like a farmer watering his tomato plants, Carbone carefully directed the spray to insure even coverage throughout the socks. Finished, he let out a sigh of relief, zipped his fly and knelt in the sand. It only took a few seconds for him to tape the box shut and affix the mailing label. Satisfied with his handiwork, he glanced at his watch and to his pleasure saw that he could spend a few minutes with his feline friends and still have time to get the box into town and aboard the one o'clock express for New Jersey.

U-112 OFF BOCA RATON: 1251 hrs.

By eight that morning, U-112 had nestled herself onto the hardbottom of the narrow Atlantic shelf less than five miles offshore from Boca Raton, Florida. The previous evening had been

121

disappointing from the standpoint of serving the Fatherland. Despite prowling back and forth along the Miami shoreline throughout the night, they had spotted nothing that warranted the expenditure of a torpedo. By four in the morning, Rahn had become so convinced that no target of opportunity would present itself, he had allowed the crew to come on deck and get some air while gazing at the brightly lit hotels along Miami Beach. Earlier in the evening, a wind shift had brought with it the sound of Latin music and several of the lookouts reported the scent of frying onions. It all seemed oddly unreal, as though they were cruising the ocean of another planet rather than one that was engulfed in a world war. Americans seemed completely unaware of the horrors of war—or, Rahn thought, they really didn't care as long as they were making money.

The morning sunrise had brought with it a great photo opportunity. Every twenty seconds throughout much of the night, they had seen the brilliant white flash of the Hillsboro Inlet lighthouse just to the north of them. One of the most powerful lights on the American east coast, Rahn was determined not to miss adding its photo to his collection. With the rising sun at their stern, he had brought U-112 racing at full speed toward the spindly tower jutting upward from the dunes on the north shore of the inlet. Just as it seemed to the crew that he was going to plant the U-boat's bow on the beach, Rahn ordered full right rudder and with diesels roaring swept past the lighthouse. As he snapped the photos, Rahn was quite pleased with his timing—the rising sun gave the white paint on the lower half of the tower a warm and welcoming glow while the black upper half stood out in sharp relief against the backdrop of copper-hued cumulus clouds floating over the Everglades.

The adrenaline rush of racing along the beach combined with the warm tropical air had put the watch in a combative mood. Where were the American patrol boats? Better yet—where were the fat freighters just waiting to be sent to the bottom? Rahn continued to flaunt their presence by running in close to the palm-studded shore. They saw no one, but the look of concern on Thiele's face finally reminded Rahn of the foolishness of his action. Much to the crew's relief, he had ordered a course change to the northeast and although still within view of the shoreline had brought the U-boat to its current resting place on the seabed—a place where Rahn had allowed himself to catch up on his sleep and to dream.

No matter how often he had the dream, the setting was the same—the patio of *Der Fuhrer's* Alpine headquarters at Berchtesgaden. Admiral Dönitz, the Big Lion himself, was sitting with Hitler at an outdoor table with the snow-covered mountains as a backdrop. As Rahn approached, Dönitz always stood and said the same thing: *"Mein Fuhrer,* here he is now. I present to you our Lighthouse Ace, Teddy Rahn!" Thunderous applause came from somewhere high above and then *Der Fuhrer* was reaching out to him. "Teddy my boy, it's so good to meet you—and please let me thank you for these!" Hitler dug into his brown jacket pocket and produced a packet of photographs of Florida lighthouses. "These are just what I always wanted! You can't imagine how much these photos have lifted the spirits of the German people. You're a hero my boy and an inspiration to the Reich." Then Dönitz pulled him aside and gave him a playful hug. "That's right Teddy—a hero! A hero we can't afford to lose... not like Prien and Kretschmer. No, we learned our lesson with them. The Fatherland needs live heroes—just like you. The war is over for you...you're going to spend the rest of it writing about your experiences. I thought you could work at home...maybe even have your wife help." That's when Kat always appeared. Sometimes dressed in a white gown that clung to every curve...sometimes in a low cut red evening dress...and once wearing nothing but a smile. "Teddy, it's time to come home," she said and beckoned to him to follow her.

"Propeller noises *Herr Kaleu.*"

Rahn's eyelids snapped open and he yanked away the green curtains that provided his small, wood-paneled cabin with the only private accommodations on board. Directly across the passageway, Dahlman sat in the sound shack. Both headphones were clamped over his ears and his eyes were closed in concentration. Without looking, he reached up and adjusted the knob that controlled the orientation of the listening devices on the bow.

"Heading towards us?" Rahn asked as he swung his legs out of the bunk and sat upright. "A destroyer maybe?"

In the quiet atmosphere of the resting U-boat, Rahn's voice carried into the open bow compartment and the whispering and metallic tinkering of the torpedo men running the scheduled maintenance on one of the eels immediately stopped.

"Nein, Herr Kaleu......" Dahlman's eyelids tightened as though somehow that would improve his hearing. "Very fast screws....reciprocal engines....fading toward shore. A private fishing boat no doubt. What do they call them? Cabin cruisers?"

"Ja, that's what they call them. And judging from the advertisements in the American magazines, they always have pretty girls on board," said Timm from his seat in the adjacent radio shack. At this depth, there were no radio signals to receive so he spent his watch working crossword puzzles or increasing his already impressive collection of useless trivia.

"I think you're right," said Dahlman as he continued to listen to the hydrophones. "I hear women laughing...my English in not so great, but I think she said 'please touch my tits...oh...yes, that's sooo good.'"

Laughter rattled through the boat and someone in the bow compartment corrected Dahlman insisting that the girl was requesting that another body part be touched.

Rahn smiled and then yawned as he ran his fingers through his hair.

"That's enough, Dahlman. Please make a note of the remarkable clarity of the sound gear's reception and send it to the manufacturer. Who knows? They may give you a free hearing aid when you retire."

"Jawohl, Herr Kaleu!" Dahlman saluted with mock enthusiasm.

"And Tango," Rahn called *Funkmaat* Timm by his shipboard nickname. "How about some music? Lili Marlene would be nice...the special one dedicated to all of us poor U-boat boys, but not too loudly."

"Herr Kaleu," Timm responded and after a few seconds of fumbling through his stack of records, the clear sounds of a sultry female voice that sounded much like Marlene Dietrich whispered an undersea version of *Lili Marlene* throughout the boat.

"Auf dem Atlantik,
Auf dem weiten Meer,
Schwimmet unser U-boot

So langsam hin und her...."

For Rahn, the tune was more than a takeoff of one of the most popular songs in Germany, it was a reminder of his last night in Hamburg. As he and Kat were leaving the Officers' Club, the vocalist for the little six-piece band had provided a very credible version of *Lili Marleen zur See*. As they stood in the icy rain, the final verse had drifted through the blacked-out parking lot while he held Kat close and kissed away her tears.

Wenn wir zu Fuss nach Hause gehn,
Wie bei dir, Lili Marleen

U.S.S. LASSITER, OFF ISLAMORADA, FLORIDA: 1310 hrs.

A little more than one hundred miles to the south, Mess Steward Curtis Greer passed the time by slowly and thoroughly reviewing every pleasant memory he possessed of his family and life on Moses Creek. Despite the wide selection of happy memories available to him, he found the discomfort of his confinement to be a major distraction. Shackled to a bulkhead in a narrow compartment intended for storing potatoes, he was beginning to hallucinate about being chained in the bowels of a slave ship. The steam line passing through the space above his head created the heat of darkest Africa and the metal stool that, along with a zinc bucket substituting as a urinal, served as the compartment's only furnishings had soon become as uncomfortable as the wooden planks to which his ancestors had been chained on their voyage into servitude.

Only once in the past twelve hours had he had contact with another human---he assumed it had been around eight in the morning when a machinist's mate called "Red" handed him a sandwich and a paper cup of water. "Enjoy it, asshole," Red had muttered and then he was gone.

At first, Curtis couldn't understand Red's attitude. Although the man had never been particularly friendly, he had never displayed any hostility toward him. The only explanation for Red's anger had to be that Petty Officer Burke was taking advantage of his confinement to turn the entire crew against him. A wave of hopelessness had swept over Curtis and he had fought the despair by devouring his meager breakfast.

The heat and the gentle sway of the ship combined to rock him into a sweaty twilight world. Sometimes he dreamed he was floating in hot, stagnant green water out behind his Granny Greers' house in the marsh while snakes slithered past and their forked tongues flicked at his ears. At other times he felt himself sinking into a giant feather bed that wrapped him in cool comfort until he realized the bed was actually a bottomless pit of billowy cotton that was about to close over him and quietly suffocate the life from his tired body. Somewhere he could hear Winnie singing. Her voice was sharp and clear and the lyrics of the song spoke of a sweet redemption day. He was just about to let himself sing along with his sister when a harsh voice brought him from his stupor.

"Hey boy! I'm talkin' to you coon!"

Curtis' vision swirled and then through the sweat he could see the face of Burke staring at him through the open hatch. His personal tormenter leaned down close and Curtis could feel the man's hot breath.

"Comfy in there boy? "

Curtis could think of nothing to say in reply that would help his present situation.

"I just wanted you to know I'm checkin' on you boy," Burke snarled. "And I just wanted to remind you that you'd be wastin' your time tryin' to convince anybody it weren't you that was smokin' out there on the fantail and givin' our position away to the enemy. Ain't nobody gonna believe no nigger no how."

Curtis' tongue felt like old cardboard but he managed to reply: "That's good for you...you and your cracker friends will be able to sleep a lot better now."

He closed his eyes and waited for the blow that would send him into blessed unconsciousness. But instead of the sound of Burke's fist against his jaw, he heard voices in the passageway. When he opened his eyes his saw Petty Officer Burke standing at attention and smiling.

"Yes sir! I was just checking on our boy sir," Burke said to an officer hidden from Curtis' view by the hatch frame. "I'm sure he's learning his lesson--he won't be betraying our position again sir."

126

Curtis could hear other mumbled voices speaking.

"Yes sir, good idea sir," Burke said cheerfully and leaned down to look Curtis in the face once more. "Would you like some water Mess Steward Greer? I'd be happy to get some for you."

Before Curtis could respond, Burke was standing at upright once more.

"Yes sir, he says he could use a fresh cold drink of water and I'll make sure he gets one." Burke saluted and Curtis could hear the officers' voices fading away.

The Petty Officer's face appeared again through the hatchway and his features were twisted into a vicious mask. "I'll see you later nigger...and, by the way, I'm sure I'll forget all about that drink of cool, sweet water you was a wantin'."

Curtis tried not to think of the drink that was not to be. Instead, he concentrated on the drumming of the steel plates beneath his shoes and dreamed that the big turbines were taking him home.

ST AUGUSTINE: 1330 hrs.

Spencer was surprised by the clarity of his phone connection with Washington, D.C. He could actually hear Masterson's secretary breathing as he waited for her to connect him with his supervisor. From the window of his room at the Alhambra, Spencer could look down on the traffic moving along King Street. Although it was another sunlit afternoon, there didn't seem to be many tourists about. He saw just one family who, judging from the men's bibbed coveralls and the women's flour sack dresses, had traveled from America's heartland to visit the Ancient City. The father of the clan squinted at a tour map, but before he could get himself oriented, the mother pointed up the street and everyone except dad hurried off. Spencer was certain their destination had to be the Zorayda Castle next door—a genuine one-tenth scale version of a Spanish palace.

"Masterson."

His supervisor's voice snapped Spencer from his tourism survey.

"Yes sir. It's me, Agent Spencer, calling from Florida."

There was a brief silence before Masterson responded. "Yes, Agent Spencer, I know who you are. You see, you identified yourself to my secretary when you called and then she told me you were on the line. That's how it works in an office."

Spencer found Masterson's condescending attitude to be unusually annoying, He was about to say that he was surprised that his secretary could have successfully completed what must have been an extremely difficult task for her. Instead, he merely went on with his report.

"Yes sir. Well, I'm here at the Alhambra Hotel if you need to reach me. I've made contact with the local law enforcement authorities and managed to attend the city's Security Council meeting yesterday. There has been a murder in town and..."

"So?"

"Sir?" Spencer began mentally backpedaling in hopes of discovering what he had said to provoke Masterson.

"So have you found the Nazi transmitter?"

"Well, no sir, but I've only been here a couple of days and...."

"Listen, Agent Spencer," Masterson's voice was threatening in its tone. "The taxpayers didn't send you down there on a vacation. They expect, and J. Edgar expects, results."

Despite what he considered to be unduly harsh criticism, Spencer remained calm enough to filter a few useful nuggets from Masterson's less-that-inspiring speech.

"Then what you're saying, sir, is that there is indeed a German transmitter here in St. Augustine. Did you get a new report from the British?"

"Nothing too significant. The tracking stations did pick up a short broadcast Sunday night, but they couldn't get a fix on it. The Limeys still say the transmitter is somewhere between Daytona Beach and Jacksonville. It could be at sea or on land---no way to tell."

"Well sir, I seem to be in the right place— if there's an enemy agent here, I'll find him," Spencer said confidently.

"See that you do...we're counting on you." Masterson sounded almost supportive. "If we hear anything, someone will contact you. In the meantime, you plan on calling me back at three o'clock tomorrow. Got it?"

"Yes, sir. Three tomorrow."

"And remember what I told you—no arrests until after you clear it with me first."

"Yes, I know the procedure. I'll talk to you tomorrow."

Masterson hung up without saying good-bye—something that would have normally annoyed Spencer. But at that moment, he was too busy trying to determine where the best location for a German transmitter might be. He slowly returned the receiver to its cradle, picked his tweed jacket up from where he had tossed it on the bed and began to pull it on over his starched white shirt. At that moment, he realized the absurdity of wearing the jacket in the heat. It was time to set his own standard, he decided as he pitched the jacket over a chair, straightened his tie and placed his gray hat on his head. The shoulder holster and pistol stood out in sharp contrast to his new casual business appearance, but he reasoned that by now there probably wasn't a person in St. Johns County who didn't know there was a G-man in town. Besides, he told himself, there's a war being fought—the more weapons in sight, the better for everyone. For the first time since his arrival, Spencer felt a surge of confidence and he hurried down the stairs and out into the warm sun to take advantage of his newly found optimism before it melted in the heat.

UNCLE SAM'S: 1510 hrs.

I Hear a Rhapsody...Chattanooga Choo Choo...White Cliffs of Dover... Winnie couldn't believe that she had all the latest hit parade winners at her fingertips. Throughout much of the afternoon, she had punched the buttons on the big Wurlitzer jukebox and watched the selector arm respond to her commands by pulling the desired 78 rpm from its slot and placing it on the turntable. The dual speakers sent the selected tunes booming through the bar and out the open windows. In between tunes, the only sound was the hiss of the ocean on the beach and the occasional clinking of beer glasses being washed in the kitchen down the hall.

"Mr. Carbone," she asked as Luigi came in with a case of beer and slid it behind the bar, "what do you think of this song?"

Winnie hit D14 and the jukebox selected the requested seventy-eight and dropped it on the turntable. The needle bit and the voice of Adelaide Hall with a piano accompaniment by Fats Waller came belting out of the big speakers.

Uncle Sam's

"Oh, I saw you last night and got that old feeling.
When you came in sight, I got that old feeling.
The moment you passed by, I got a thrill,
And when you caught my eye, my heart stood still...."

Carbone listened while he tapped the bar with his bare hands to create an upbeat, bouncy rhythm.

"Not bad... but needs a beat...a little soul." He stopped drumming and disappeared beneath the bar where he began to adjust the beer taps.

When the song ended, Winnie placed her hands on the Wurlitzer's smooth glass cover and closed her eyes. Slowly, she began to sway to the beat only she could hear and then her voice, strong and vibrant, gave *That Old Feeling* a new and exciting rhythm that brought Carbone out from beneath the bar. Winnie's smile was dazzling as she finished the first chorus—she had no doubt that she had found the "signature" song she had been seeking.

"Bravo!" Miller said as he stepped into the bar and applauded what he had just heard. "That's the perfect song for Miss Greer and a valuable lesson in racial purity for you Luigi."

"Racial purity?" Winnie asked, even though she had a feeling she would be better off not knowing the answer.

"Yeah, Boss, what are you talking about?" Carbone asked. "That's a great tune and she's made it a hell of a lot better."

"Of course she has...that's my point," Miller said. "You remember the other morning when you asked my about the *untermensch?*"

Carbone nodded. "Yeah, but I don't see what this has to do with...."

'*Untermensch* -- Jews created that song---Lew Brown and Sammy Fain up in New York a few years ago," Miller said. "I used to run into them all the time up there."

"Brown and Fain?" Carbone looked confused. "That don't sound like Jew names to me."

Miller smiled. "How about Samuel Feinberg and Louis Brownstein? That's their real names. Is that Jewish enough for you? And then having Winifred, a colored girl, sing the song just the way the angels would...now doesn't that put the boot to racial purity nonsense? When it comes to music, those folks are *obermensch*--unless of course you really like to listen to polkas."

Miller could see his humor was lost on Winnie and Carbone.

"I don't know, Mr. Miller," Winnie said. "Maybe I shouldn't go messin' with songs that are already famous. I got no right to do that."

"Nonsense!" Miller walked over to her. He thought about putting his arm around the girl, but opted for just standing near her. "You don't need to apologize for being an *artiste*. You should never be shy about showing your talent."

"An *artiste?*" She looked up at Miller and her soft brown eyes begged for him to confirm that she was, even in some small way, truly special.

"Young lady, you are indeed an *artiste*," Miller said firmly. "And I know that for a fact. I've seen lots of the great ones and I can tell you that few, if any, had the talent you have when they were your age. In fact, you'd better get used to being treated like a star--I've set up an audition for you at the Cotton Club in New York for next week."

Although she never later confided it to anyone, Miller's words had brought her to nearly the same level of overwhelming emotion she had experienced at her baptism. In fact, it had many of the same trappings—a sense of floating and then sinking into a warm pool of white light. There was a roaring in her head on both occasions, but instead of collapsing into Revered Fulmer's arms and the soothing surf, this time she slid slowly to the barroom floor.

"Luigi!" Miller shouted. "Get over here—I think she's fainted. Shirley! Get some water for the girl!"

As he lifted her to the chair Carbone offered, Miller was surprised by how frail she felt in his arms. She seemed to be nothing more than skin and bones and for a moment he wondered how this child would be able to cope with going to New York for the chance of a lifetime. Shirley quickly appeared and with a damp cloth, dabbed at Winnie's face until the girl opened her eyes.

"I'm sorry...Mr. Miller," Winnie said weakly and touched the fingertips of her right hand to her temple as though trying to recall a dream. "I'm really sorry."

"No need to apologize, young lady. You've had a very trying day and I'm sure this news is a little overwhelming." Miller reached down as though he were about to pat her head, but then suddenly changed his mind and withdrew his hand as though there was a chance the contact with Winifred's skin could result in a painful burn for him. "You'll feel much better when you climb on that train to New York."

"No sir...I'm sorry, but I can't go—I just can't."

"That's crazy!" Carbone blurted out. "You can't miss an opportunity like this one."

"He's right, child," Shirley said with a motherly tone. "Mr. Miller has set up everything for you. You can't take a chance on messing it up. You want to end up cleaning other folks houses for the rest of your life?"

"But I've never been out of St. Johns County," Winnie said and her sudden need to express her feelings seemed to snap her out of her stupor. "How can I just up and go to New York? People need me here."

"Nonsense." The firmness in Miller's voice made it clear that Winnie's position was simply unacceptable. "You will go to New York and you will be a star. In fact, I want you and Shirley to go into town and get you some decent clothes for that audition." He pulled his wallet from his trouser pocket and quickly withdrew a hundred dollar bill. "Here. You and Shirley take this to town and buy whatever you need."

Winnie hesitated, but Shirley snatched the money and tucked it into her bra.

"See there," Shirley said. "You haven't even gone to that audition and you're already being treated like a queen."

"I don't know...maybe I could." Winnie was beginning to realize she might indeed be able to do this audition after all. "I would have to talk with Granny and the Reverend and...."

"Good idea," Miller said and tried to sound enthusiastic. "Why don't you talk this over with your family? I know they will want you to go. In fact, Luigi will drive you home now and you can get some rest before coming back for tonight's show."

"Thank you sir." Winnie stood shakily. "Do you think I could stop at the Pool's house for a minute? Just to give my respects to the family."

"Sure we can," Carbone said without waiting for Miller's approval. He was beginning to enjoy serving as Winnie's chauffeur—anything was better than doing the chores Miller had lined up for him this afternoon. Besides, he was certain that someday he would brag about how he knew Winifred Greer before she was a big star. He put an arm around her shoulders and guided her toward the door.

"Mr. Miller, Sir," Winnie said as she paused and gently brushed Carbone's arm away. "If I was to go on this audition, when would I be leaving St. Augustine?"

"I don't really know yet. I'll call my friend in New York on Monday and get the time and date. Cab Calloway's band will be stopping at The Cotton Club next week and that's who you will meet up there."

"Cab Calloway? You know Cab Calloway?" Winnie asked in astonishment.

"Yes," Miller said modestly. "Cab and I go back a long way together. He knows that I recognize talent when I see it. I'm sure he'll be anxious to hear you sing. In fact, when I make that call to his agent, maybe you'd like to have your family over here too. Invite the entire congregation from your church—we'll make it a real party—say five o'clock Monday evening?" Miller could see the headlines now---"Joe Miller Launches Career of Local Singer". He could even have young Pomar over to take photos for the newspaper—that kind of publicity should be great for business and even better for his reputation as a kindly American businessman.

"I'll see about that, Mr. Miller, sir," she said as she and Carbone stepped out of the bar and into the bright afternoon sunlight. Going down the ramp to the car, Winnie couldn't help but whisper "Cab Calloway!" And then she added: "Praise the Lord!"

U-112: 1610 hrs.

Oskar Beinlich grew tired of pretending he was performing complicated navigational computations. He tossed his protractor aside and pushed his pale hands into the harsh circle of light cast on the plotting table by the lamp pulled down low from the gray steel bulkhead. Sometimes he thought his skin had absorbed the whiteness of the navigation charts—even his hours on watch in the tropical sun had done nothing more than add a few red blotches to the backs of his hands. Combined with the tracings of blue veins just beneath the surface, the blotches made his hands look surprising similar to the chart of the eastern Caribbean—or were they more like the Grand Banks off Newfoundland? Annoyed at his continued procrastination, he stood slowly, took a deep breath of stale air and straightened his cap.

Beinlich gingerly worked his way forward through the dimly lit control room. All around him, crewmen took advantage of the boat's stationary position on the seabed and dozed at their duty stations like children taking their afternoon naps. In the subdued lighting, few of their features were distinguishable. But as a result of working in such close proximity for weeks on end, he could identify them just by their silhouettes or the hair on the backs of their necks. Pausing before the open hatch on the forward bulkhead, Beinlich listened to the slow drip...drip...drip of condensation falling into the bilge. For a moment, he considered asking Thiele and Lamprecht to accompany him—after all, it had been mostly their idea. *"Scheisse,"* he mumbled and bent low to move easily through the hatch.

Teddy Rahn had spent the past ten minutes contemplating the physics of time. Could it be, he had wondered, that when the boat was motionless time slowed? It certainly seemed that way. He was convinced that he had been sitting on his bunk for at least a couple of days, but when he looked at the small clock above his fold down desk, the luminous hands told him only twenty minutes had passed since his last tour of the boat. He knew he would never come up with an answer—not only was the math difficult, his mental calculations were always interrupted by wondering what Katrina would be doing at that moment. Keeping the Kriegsmarine's ships on Central European Time no matter where they operated was undoubtedly necessary for preventing confusion, but he was sure that few, if any, seaman ever looked at a timepiece without remembering that the clock in his home back in Germany showed the same time. That realization undoubtedly led to thoughts of what loved ones were doing at that very moment. Rahn was well aware that such mental diversions—even momentary ones—could lead to disaster on a U-boat.

"Herr Kaleu?"

Rahn looked up to see his navigator looking down at him with an expression of tired sadness. Such a depressed demeanor in anyone else would have been of concern to Rahn, but Beinlich's scowl was always in place. In fact, Rahn couldn't remember a single incident in which the man seemed happy.

"Hello, Cosinus," Rahn said quietly. "Doing a bit of sleep walking?"

As usual, Beinlich was taken aback by his commander's levity. He tried to form some sort of clever reply, but the effort was simply just too damned difficult.

"Uh, no *Herr Kaleu*, I was just...just..." The navigator seemed distressed. His eyes darted about nervously and when he saw Timm slumped over at the radio console, he shifted his position to shield Rahn from the *funkmaat's* view. "I, well, we wanted to talk with you about something sir."

Rahn comically tried to glance around his tall navigator. "We? And who might 'We' be and where is 'We'?"

"I'm sorry sir, I meant *Oberleutnant* Thiele and *Leutnant* Lamprecht and I wanted to talk with you. But they felt it would be better if I did the talking."

Rahn knew the routine. The other two officers had obviously convinced Beinlich to come forward and if the conversation went poorly, they would simply say the navigator had "misunderstood" them.

"All right," Rahn said as he quickly stood. "We can go back to the wardroom. It's much more comfortable there at the table--maybe we can even round up a bottle of apple juice--or even a beer."

Much to Rahn's surprise, Beinlich firmly maintained his position. "That's not necessary. Sir. This won't take long and some of the men are playing skat there. This is more...private."

Rahn was suddenly intrigued. He was certain there was no card game in the wardroom and the way Beinlich seemed determined to confine the conversation to this part of the boat showed that he wanted to limit the number of people who might overhear. His current position just inches from the navigator's nose seemed somewhat confrontational, so he took a step back and felt his mattress pressing against the back of his thighs. Returning to his seat, however, was impossible--sitting would, as they were taught in the commander's course at Danzig "allow a subordinate to assume a dominant position." Rahn smiled. Each time he recalled that phrase from the textbook, he always thought of dogs mating.

"All right then, Cosinus, what's on your mind---as well as Thiele's and Lamprecht's?"

"It's just that I, we, wanted to remind you that once we swing around Cape Canaveral, we will be on a wide and shallow coastal shelf--not like here where we can easily move just to the east and drop into deep water." Beinlich seemed relieved. He could now tell his co-conspirators that he had delivered the message just as he had agreed to do.

"Well, thank you Cosinus. And why did you and your friends feel compelled to give me this information? Did you think I had failed to notice that fact on your chart. The water depth a mile off Daytona Beach is eight meters. There, that should make you feel better--your commander knows something about how much water there will be under our keel tomorrow."

"Yes, *Herr Kaleu,* of course sir. I didn't mean to imply you were unaware of the situation, it's just that the photo-taking has...well...." Beinlich had suddenly run out of words.

"Oh, it's the photos, eh?" Rahn pushed his hat up from his forehead. "Makes you a little nervous running up on those lighthouses does it?"

"No sir...not me sir." Beinlich was far from convincing. "But some of the men think it might not be such a good idea to get that close to the enemy--even if they are only Americans."

"Well, *Oberfahnrich* Beinlich, I can assure you the photos are of the utmost importance to the Fatherland." Even in the dim light, Rahn could see the discomfort on his navigator's face. "In fact, I order you to tell every man on board about the photos. Tell them we're taking the photos for the *Fuhrer* himself."

"I'll do that right away, *Herr Kaleu,*" Beinlich said, but he made no move to leave.

"Something else Cosinus? Is there something else that is preventing you from enjoying your tropical cruise?"

Beinlich shifted uncomfortably and glanced nervously at *Funkmaat* Timm before returning his attention to U-112's commander.

"It's the music, *Herr Kaleu,*" Beinlich said quickly. "Not that I don't like music, it's just that the selection is not only questionable, many of the songs are illegal."

"So it's not just a matter of taste then…it's a matter of politics," Rahn said.

"It's simply a matter of right and wrong—jazz has been banned on German radio stations for nearly seven years, yet here on this boat it is heard almost constantly," Beinlich said with a tone of superiority that Rahn found extremely annoying. "Not only do we have to listen to Negroes like Louis Armstrong, we also are subjected to the music of Jews like that Artie Shaw and Benny Goodman. It is extremely demoralizing for the crew."

"Well, Cosinus, thank you for bringing this situation to my attention." Rahn was moving forward now and Beinlich had begun a clumsy retreat toward the hatch leading to the control room. "And please tell your friends Thiele and Lamprecht that I want them on the bridge in the morning when we photograph the Jupiter Inlet Light. Of course, you'll be there as well. You can never tell when the Americans might get smart and prepare a welcoming reception for us. And you're quite right, it would be better to have battle-tested veterans like yourselves up there instead of some of the younger boys--just in case the *Amis* get us in their gunsights."

Beinlich already had one foot through the hatch. "Jawohl, Herr Kaleu," he said as he snapped off a salute and ducked out of sight into the control room.

"*Funkmaat* Timm!" Rahn said loudly as he noticed the radioman was now sitting upright and had undoubtedly heard most of the conversation he had just had with the navigator. "Put on some music…something lively…and loud! We've been sitting here long enough---it's time to get on with the war."

"*Jawohl!*" Timm said with enthusiasm. "I've got just the thing for moments like this." He pulled a record from the rack on his right and slipped it on the turntable. In seconds, the crew was awakened from their torpor by the Andrews Sisters' *Bei Mir Bist du Schoen*. The beat was just right and the tune was infectious. Throughout the boat crewmen began to sing along with the American girls.

"I could say 'Bella Bella,' even 'Voonderbar',
Each language only helps me tell you how grand you are.
I've tried to explain, bei mir bist du schon,
So kiss me and say you understand."

Timm couldn't help but smile as he watched his happy

shipmates laughing and even taking a dance step or two. He was certain that except for Beinlich, none of them would care that the lyrics were written by three Jews named Jacobs, Cahn and Chaplin while the tune was penned by Sholom Secunda—can't get much more Jewish than that, he thought.

Rahn gave his radioman's shoulder a friendly squeeze and when the boy looked up he could tell by the smile on his commander's face that Teddy Rahn was well aware of the identity of the song's creators.

ST. AUGUSTINE: 1756 hrs.

After a long afternoon of sorting though reports in the sheriff's office, Spencer found the cooling breeze through the open window and the subdued music from the jukebox to be pleasantly relaxing. At the suggestion of the desk clerk at the Alhambra, he had selected dinner at the Neptune Grill as a peace offering to Sheriff Hartson. The FBI agent was actually a bit surprised that Hartson had accepted his invitation. In fact, he had not yet decided why the sheriff had agreed to have dinner with him. It could have been a sense of duty, curiosity about G-men, or simply because he didn't get many opportunities to enjoy a great meal at the federal government's expense.

"You have some...interesting...files in your office," Spencer said as he happily dug his fork into his stuffed flounder garnished with spicy datil peppers. "Quite a variety...rape to horse thievery. Never a dull moment around here I guess."

"Sometimes." Hartson continued to concentrate on his mashed potatoes and gravy.

"So...what would you consider to be your most interesting case?" Spencer was desperate for any sort of information that might give him a lead on possible activities by German agents. But he didn't think he could just ask -- "Got any Nazis around here?" Instead, he hoped to work his way into the subject without annoying or frightening the sheriff.

"Look," Hartson said as he put down his knife and fork. 'I don't have time to stamp what I do around here with a big red label that says 'exciting' or 'boring'. Basically, I have two goals. First, I have to maintain some level of civilized behavior on the part of the good residents of St. Augustine. Secondly, and maybe most importantly, I have to make sure I get re-elected. If it doesn't help me accomplish one of these goals, I don't have much time for it."

"And the Pool murder? Solving it doesn't fit in with your goals?" Spencer was immediately sorry he had brought up the events of the morning. The memory of the crabs...the heat...the corpse...the stench... was enough to temporarily blunt his appetite for the fish-of-the day on his plate.

"Now you've got it," the sheriff said and a smile crossed his thin face as he picked up his eating utensils and attacked his steak with enthusiasm. "The colored folk don't vote so their happiness means nothing to me in the long run. And violence, especially things like murder and rape, just come natural to them. As long as no white folks are involved...well, let's just say colored crime isn't a concern to me or most other white folks."

Spencer reluctantly concluded that his dinner companion was a small time politician first and a lawman second, or maybe third. He could now see that his impression of Hartson from the morning was correct in that there was more to the man than was obvious on his rail-thin surface. Unfortunately, the "more" was not the intellectual and moral attributes he had hoped to uncover. Frustrated, he opted for a more direct approach.

"I noticed you only had one war-related incident in your files--a German couple named Meyerhof?"

The sheriff made a noise that could have passed for a laugh or gas.

"Yeah, that was a good one." He gulped at his beer and swiped the back of his hand across his lips before continuing. "Two really stupid Krauts. Had a little motel over on the island."
Spencer felt he was finally getting somewhere. The file on the case had been very meager. Just a mention of possible espionage and a form the sheriff had signed when he turned them over to folks from the Justice Department in Atlanta.

"So you don't think they were working for the *Fuhrer* himself?" Spencer asked and this time he was sure Hartson was laughing.

"Hell no," the sheriff said. "The Germans have got to be a lot smarter than those two--but they sure looked guilty. It was kind of surprising though because they had lived over there for about five or six years and had never really bothered anybody. They weren't

139

exactly the friendliest people around, but they kept a really clean place and Mrs. Meyerhof was real popular when it came to baking contests. Her strudel won first prize a couple of times at the county fair--it would have won last year, but the judges didn't think it would be right give a prize to Kraut food what with the war and all."

"But if they were some kind of Nazis spies? What gave them away?" Spencer hated to admit that he was so short of leads that he actually hoped to get some ideas from a case in which the perpetrators seemed so harmless.

Hartson took a swig of beer and smiled as he returned the mug to the table. "Weren't nothin' to it really," he said. "I wish I could take the credit for breaking the case—that would get me some votes in the fall. But everybody knows who the real hero was in this case. I'd only look stupid if I tried to take credit for solving it."

"Sorry...I'm new here. So who was the hero?"

Sheriff Hartson rolled his eyes as though he couldn't believe a G-man would ask such a stupid question.

"Joe Miller, of course."

Spencer wasn't surprised by the sheriff's answer. Although Miller had apparently only called St. Augustine home for a couple of years, it seemed as though he had quickly become the most popular man in town. Nearly every resident Spencer had talked with had eventually mentioned something positive about Miller or at least his fishing pier or bar.

"Oh, Miller of course," Spencer said. "Entertainer... pillar of the community... generous to our boys in uniform... and now master spy catcher. How does one man do all that?"

"I don't really know, but he sure has done a lot for St. Augustine in a very short time." The sheriff paused just long enough for another swig of beer. "And who knows? Taking the Meyerhofs out of circulation could have done a lot for national security."

"So you think these two people were actual spies?"

"Look, like I said, they seemed like nice folks. No one would have thought they were spies, but when we searched their house, the evidence we found was pretty damning."

Spencer was intrigued. Maybe there was a lead here after all.

"Like what? Radio transmitters, code books or something?"

Hartson decided to savor a mouthful of steak before answering.

"No, nothing like that. Mostly Nazi propaganda stuff...pictures of Hitler and that sort of thing. A bunch of German magazines and some notes about sailing times for different ships out of Jacksonville. There was also photographs of some of our warships....looked like *Herr* Meyerhof had taken them himself. And he had a nice pair of Kraut binoculars. It was a real cozy little spy nest."

"But if these folks seemed so...nice...what tipped you off?"

"Joe Miller." The sheriff put his fist against his chest and burped loudly. "He called one evening and said he thought he'd found a couple of spies and that maybe I'd like to get a search warrant and head over to the Meyerhof's motel. He even arranged to have them to dinner at his place so they wouldn't be there when we showed up. That way, I could check out the place and see if I could find any evidence without getting anyone upset."

"And you did?"

"Yeah, like I said, it was real simple. We didn't even have to search the place. All the evidence was sitting right out in the open. They hadn't even tried to hide it."

"They don't sound like very dangerous spies to me." Spencer was beginning to think the case was irrelevant after all. "So you arrested them?"

"Yeah, I just waited until Joe Miller drove them back from his bar and then I put the 'cuffs on 'em."

"They didn't resist...didn't shout *Heil* Hitler or anything?"

"Hell no," the sheriff said smugly as though only a complete fool would try to defy his power. "They went real peaceful. In fact, they seemed stunned by all that evidence stacked up there in that room. They both said they'd never seen any of it before. You'd think they could come up with a better alibi than that."

"Well, how do you know they weren't telling the truth? Maybe somebody set them up?"

"What the hell for?" Sheriff Hartson was beginning to get annoyed. "Besides, it wasn't my job to investigate any further. I just locked them in the jail for the night and called the Feds up in Atlanta. By noon the next day, four G-men showed up to take the Meyerhofs up to the Federal pen. I ain't really heard nothin' more about it."

"And Miller? What made him think this nice couple were really Nazi spies?"

Sheriff Hartson pushed his plate back to signal he had finished his meal. 'I don't really know. He did mention something about seeing the two of them on the beach late at night with binoculars. But the reason for his suspicions wasn't important to me then...or now. So, what's Uncle Sam buying me for dessert?"

It was clear to Spencer that there would be no more discussion of German spies.

"Whatever you want Sheriff. It's the least we can do for saving us from that evil Meyerhof couple," Spencer said in jest. It was obvious the sheriff found no humor in his comment.

MOSES CREEK: 1850 hrs.

Winnie Greer felt guilty about the joy she felt in her heart when all around her people were grieving about the death of Rufus Pool. A large crowd had gathered at Moses Creek AME and she could hear wailing from the front of the church where Rufus' relatives were gathered around his plain pine coffin. She felt deeply for their loss and she knew she would miss Rufus. But at the same time, Winnie felt more like a spectator than a participant in the proceedings. In her mind, she was already singing with Cab Calloway's Orchestra.

"I'm sorry Winnie," said Reverend Fulmer as the progress of the impromptu reception line brought her to where he was standing at the foot of the casket. "I know this must be very hard for you."

"Yes Reverend....I can't believe he's gone." She wanted to be mature about the situation, but at the same time she wanted to share with him the wonderful news about her upcoming audition in New York.

"The Lord has called Rufus home... it's as simple as that and we are not worthy of questioning the Lord." The reverend always felt that "acceptance" was the only logical way to deal with life's tragedies.

"Yes of course, but still it's hard for me," Winnie said and then quickly added: "Can I talk to you about something?"

The reverend looked surprised and before he answered he wrapped his arms around a large sobbing woman dressed in a black velveteen dress and hat. "Of course child," he said quietly. "But it will have to be later."

Uncle Sam's

Winnie nodded in agreement and moved forward with the crowd. Before she was ready, she found herself standing beside the casket containing all the earthly remains of Rufus Pool. It was a closed casket and she had heard the rumors about the poor condition of Rufus' body. Thankfully, she wouldn't have to look at the twisted remains of one of her dearest friends. How could someone do this to poor Rufus? She placed her hand on the smooth wood and closed her eyes. For the next few seconds she willed her thoughts to reach Rufus. She thought of the fun they had as children and thanked him for being such a friend. Then, she silently told him about her news and in her mind she could see Rufus' broad smile. Winnie knew he would have been so happy for her!

She felt herself being pushed aside by a crush of wailing women—Rufus' sister, several cousins and Ramona, a girl who up to that moment had never given the deceased boy the time of day, despite his obvious interest in her. Winnie was happy to move aside. She took a seat at the back pew where she sat quietly observing the coming and goings of virtually every resident of Moses Creek. Of course, Granny Greer wasn't there—the tide wasn't accommodating this evening. Old Man Pell, however, had confidently predicted that tomorrow afternoon's funeral would occur during the lowest tide of the week and Bernard White had already volunteered to drive into the marsh and bring her to the church in time to pay her final respects.

When Winnie had arrived home from *Uncle Sam's*, she had rushed to tell Granny about the offer she had received. And, Winnie admitted reluctantly, she had been a bit disappointed in the reaction the news had received. The name Cab Calloway meant nothing to Granny and the fact that Winnie might be leaving for New York in a few days did not seem to make any impression on her. Instead, she seemed unusually agitated and kept mumbling about "that boy." At first, Winnie assumed that she was concerned about poor Rufus. But, as she listened, it gradually became clear to her that Granny was very worried about Curtis.

Normally, Winnie would have just written off her grandmother's ramblings as something that "old folks do". But over the years, Granny had developed quite a reputation as a person who possessed the "gift" of talking with spirits and sensing the coming of "changes" such as droughts and the Second World War.

Winnie wished there was some way to contact Curtis so he could reassure his grandmother about his welfare—but the only way to communicate with him was via letter and that could take weeks.

The church's interior was now lit by the coppery hue of the setting sun and a single beam of dying sunlight pierced a window and washed over Rufus' casket. There was a stirring among the congregation as people noticed the odd light show and responded with a scattered chorus of "Praise the Lords" and " Haleleujahs". But before Winnie had a chance to appreciate the scene, a car horn sounded outside and she knew Carbone had arrived to pick her up.

She stood quickly, eased her way toward the door and then noticed that everyone in the church was staring at her. Carbone's arrival had fatally disturbed the spirituality of the moment and Winnie felt a flush of embarrassment as she realized she was being blamed for the intrusion.

"Tell Whitey we said hello," someone shouted.

Winnie didn't know what to do in response so she simply increased her pace, pushed open the church door and stepped out into the twilight. The big Lincoln was waiting and Luigi Carbone was holding the door open for her.

"Winnie."

The voice behind her caused her to stop and turn.

Reverend Fulmer had hurried up the aisle and out the door to catch her. His eyes looked troubled, but as always there was a quiet dignity about him that made Winnie feel … secure.

"Winnie…I thought you wanted to talk about something," he said as he stepped close to her.

"Yes, but not now." She couldn't believe she was actually refusing an offer of conversation with Reverend Fulmer. "I have to go." Fulmer looked toward the car and nodded in response to Carbone's comical salute.

"I know you do child," the reverend said quietly as he watched the white man help her into the car and close the door behind her. "I know you do."

U-112: 1955 hrs.

Except for Beinlich's dour demeanor over at the navigation table, a festive atmosphere prevailed throughout U-112's steel hull.

Rahn had ordered the cook to whip up something special and within an hour the sweet smell of a chocolate cake in the oven mixed with the foul odors of sweat, urine, mold, and battery acid. To overcome the increasingly annoying smells, Rahn had taken a tour of the boat and offered each crewmember a quick splash of 4711 from his personal flask of the world famous cologne of Cologne. Its sweet mixture of sandalwood and tropical fruits was a welcome change from the lemony scent of Colibri—the most common form of personal odor control on a U-boat.

Rahn never ceased to be amazed at how quickly something as basic as a little cologne and a piece of cake could change the mood of a crew. Laughter and good-natured teasing had replaced the air of complacency and resignation that had begun to pervade the boat after sitting on the bottom for nearly twelve hours.

Even the Chief seemed to be caught up in the happy mood as he moved through the boat. His smile beamed from the depths of his beard that had reached a growth of biblical proportions. His inspection of U-112's internal organs complete, he reported the boat's status to Rahn in the control room.

"Everything in order, *Herr Kaleu!*" Chief Wieland announced and snapped off an enthusiastic naval salute.

"Very good Chief," Rahn said and gave Wieland's broad back a gentle slap. "Dahlman! Hear anything out there?"

Everyone in *Zentrale* stopped talking as though their conversation might somehow interrupt the underwater vibrations that were collected by the hydrophone sensors at the bow and then sent directly to the soundman's headphones.

"A heavy engine sound…must be a freighter…bearing one-eight-zero." In the sound shack, Dahlman adjusted the control knob and closed his eyes in concentration. "Make that one-seven-zero…range…estimate twenty miles."

"Twenty miles? Dahlman, your hearing is too good!" Rahn shouted forward through the open hatch and his light-hearted response created smiles throughout the control room. "Let me know if it gets within hailing distance!" Rahn returned his attention to the men gathered around him. "All right Chief, take her up to periscope depth. Number Two, set the watch…I want to get some more of that fresh Florida air in the boat—provided at no cost to you men, I might add, by the Fatherland."

Chief Wieland was in his element now and his orders came in a rapid fire manner: "Blow tanks....e-motors ahead one-third....bow planes up ten...stern up five..."

The rush of high-pressure air being released sounded through the boat and there was a gentle sway as U-112 freed herself from the sandy bottom. The electric motors came on and the boat slowly gained momentum. At first, the Tiefenmesser seemed stuck at forty meters, but amid the metallic pops and groans of the rising boat the needle finally began to swing upward. The Chief controlled the boat's gentle ascent and as he watched the indicator edge toward fifteen meters, he barked a series of orders. The response brought the boat steady at thirteen meters.

"Periscope depth, Herr Kaleu," Wieland announced.

"Thanks Chief. Let's take a look around," Rahn said and was pleased that he didn't have to issue an order---the periscope was already hissing up from its well. He scrambled up the ladder into the conning tower and positioned himself on the periscope's bicycle-style seat. As soon as the periscope lens broke the surface, Rahn shuffled in a circle and scanned the horizon and the sky above it with the high angle lens. He could see dusk was falling rapidly. Seaward, a towering wall of cumulus clouds rose from a deep blue base that brightened to pale lavender halfway up the sky before bursting into a tangerine summit that caught the last rays of the fading sun. The sea was already in shadow, the deep green of the afternoon's waves fading to the dark blue gray hue that was the forerunner of the nighttime sea to come. To landward, the pale sand of the beach made a clear demarcation between the dark silhouettes of the palm trees and the rolling waves of the evening Atlantic. He repeated his sweep once more and this time he could see a cluster of white lights had snapped on in a small beachside community. Satisfied that no enemy was waiting to pounce, Rahn sent the periscope back down its well.

"All clear! Surface!" He heard his orders repeated and in seconds, the boat began the brief upward surge.

"Turmluk ist frei...boot ist raus!"

With confirmation that the tower was out of the water, Rahn spun the handwheel and the heavy hatch popped open. He swallowed to equalize the pressure on his eardrums and smiled down at the helmsman coming up the ladder to take his position in the tower.

"Looks like it's going to be a fine evening," Rahn said and then bounded up the last few rungs of the ladder and on to the bridge. The helmsman's response was lost in the sudden thunder of the diesels engines coming to life as the watch scrambled up the ladder to join him on the bridge.

Lamprecht was always pleased with the diligence shown by the four men he commanded during their four-hour watch. They did their jobs well in any kind of weather—and they seemed to enjoy their assignments. Each man scanned ninety degrees of sky and horizon with his Zeiss binoculars and all of them took pride in the fact that their watch had more enemy sightings to their credit that any other aboard the *Eins-Eins-Zwei*. The five of them squeezed past Rahn as the last of the warm seawater drained away from the tower's wooden decking beneath their leather and canvas shoes.

"Number One to the bridge!" Rahn shouted down the open hatch and then returned his gaze to the twilight with special attention paid to the western horizon where more and more lights began to glow along the Florida shore. To Rahn, the lights represented the best of domestic tranquility--fathers, mothers and children gathering around the table for an evening meal. But even though the warm homes and friendly towns were less than five miles away, Rahn knew there was a very good chance that he would never get to enjoy the simple pleasures of home and hearth again. For a brief moment, he allowed himself to wonder what might happen if he merely dove into the darkening sea and swam to shore. After the war, Kat could come to America and they could, as the fairy tales say, live happily ever after. But then would she? Would the love of his life accept him if he were a traitor to the Fatherland?

"*Jawohl, Herr Kaleu!*" Thiele said as he seemed to pop through the hatch and on to the bridge.

Rahn was glad his Number One had responded so quickly to his order—now he wouldn't have to continue his mental debate over the comparative values of love and loyalty.

"Yes, now if you and *Leutnant* Lamprecht would be so kind as to join me on the balcony I think we can resolve an issue of some concern to me," Rahn said and squeezed his way past the seaman on portside watch and out on to the *wintergarten*--a railed platform that provided both a mounting for the boat's twenty-millimeter anti-aircraft cannon and a small refuge from the claustrophobic conditions inside the boat's hull. "Seaman Kunst! Keep a sharp eye out for the next few minutes—we're having a staff meeting."

The young man wedged up high on the tower lowered his glasses just long enough to nod and smile in response to his commander's order. He said something, but his words were lost in the throb of the diesels and the murmur of the wind.

"So, as I understand it from our illustrious navigator, you two have serious concerns about my ability to effectively command this boat?" Rahn decided to launch a direct assault and observe his targets' evasive maneuvers.

"Ridiculous!" Thiele seemed genuinely offended by the suggestion of disloyalty, but he avoided Rahn's eyes. Instead he concentrated on the white cover of the *Kommander's* hat. "We've been through a lot together and I've never once questioned your decisions."

Rahn noted that Lamprecht said nothing—but his Adam's apple bobbed once in the fading light as he stared at the fresh white wake U-112 was dragging across the warm sea.

"Even the lighthouse photography? You don't find my interest in photographing enemy lighthouses a bit—odd?"

"*Nein, Herr Kaleu.*" Thiele said. "It's not my job to judge your actions. Your orders are to be followed without...."

"Of course we find it odd." Lamprecht's outburst was totally unexpected. The man was not one to ruffle anyone's feathers—especially not those of a superior officer.

"Excellent!" Rahn said. "Candor is much appreciated—how can we survive if we can't say what we think?"

"Exactly!" Thiele's quick agreement made Rahn think that his Number One would some day go far in politics—if he survived the war. "That's one of the best things about serving in your command—you've always encouraged us to share our ideas."

"I'm glad to hear that, *Oberleutnant*. So then you would say you are concerned about the unnecessary risks posed by my photography." Rahn could see that Thiele was mentally drafting his response.

"Well sir, not really concerned about the risks—I'm sure you know what you're doing." Thiele glanced at Lamprecht in hopes of receiving verbal support, but the Number Two merely stared at him as though fascinated by the words coming from his mouth. "My only concern is that the crew might not meet your expectations when we run in so close to shore."

"I'm sorry, *Herr Kaleu*, but I'm confused," Lamprecht said and tugged his cap down slightly to compensate for the freshening wind blowing from the port quarter. "Our previous discussions with Cosinus led me to believe that we were indeed concerned— particularly if the photography continues after we round Cape Canaveral—the water shoals up quickly then. I guess I'm just not experienced enough to understand the situation as thoroughly as *Oberleutnant* Thiele."

Rahn stared at his two officers who were backed against the railing like misbehaving schoolboys. For a moment, he thought about telling them the whole story about his self-assigned photo mission and how he hoped that even though he didn't have a hundred thousand tons of enemy shipping to his credit, his lighthouse photos might get him a staff assignment. In fact, everyone knew that Vaddi Schultze and Lehmann-Willenbrock had just gotten staff assignments to keep them alive. He thought it might be reassuring to them to know that his plans would be useless if he didn't get them home safely. But then the chance that the crew would decide his plan was cowardly not clever was not one he wanted to take. Instead, he decided there was really no reason for that discussion—he did not have to justify his actions to anyone.

"As always, I will continue to weigh the risks against the benefits of the mission and my decisions will be based on the results of that calculation." Rahn decided to lighten the mood with a smile. "Besides, I'm not getting us killed just to get a photograph of a lighthouse."

Thiele and Lamprecht seemed relieved. They returned his smile and mumbled their support. Number One even began to move back toward the hatch as though he thought the conversation had ended.

"Oh, one other thing," Rahn added. "I assume you don't share our navigator's concern that our crew is being hopelessly corrupted by the Negro and Jew music played by *Funkmaat* Timm."

The two officers looked at each other in confusion and then both grinned.

"Corrupted?" Thiele asked. "I can't imagine that...our music

149

is the envy of the flotilla. Everyone enjoys it. Some of the boys say it reminds them of the old *Trocadero Club* in Hamburg. But then you wouldn't know anything about that place would you Herr Kaleu?" He winked and Rahn realized his interest in jazz must be common knowledge among the crew.

"I think Cosinus might have a point," Lamprecht said, "I've started having strange cravings for ham hocks and black-eyed peas. Apparently, the Negroes are far more influential than the Jews."

The three *Kriegsmarine* officers shared a laugh in the Florida twilight.

"I just wanted to make certain we were in agreement on this issue," Rahn said, "I think that when we get home, there is a good chance our navigator will inform our superiors that the racial purity of our boat has been contaminated by the music. So, should he make such an unfortunate mistake, I want to insure we maintain our solidarity on this subject. Understood?"

"*Jawohl Herr Kaleu!*" The officers saluted in unison.

"Very good then. Now let's get back to our stations and...."

"*Spritsmatzen!* Red two-ten!" The portside lookout called out the location of what could only be an enemy vessel.

Rahn and Lamprecht raised their binoculars and focused them on the now dark horizon astern. Thiele felt left out—he had failed to bring his glasses up when he had responded to the Old Man's summons to the bridge. Now he was forced to stare into the gloom in a futile attempt to locate the subject of everyone's sudden attention.

"Fine work Kovic." Rahn congratulated the lookout standing on a fold-down step attached to the inside of the tower. "Can you give me a more specific bearing."

"*Jawohl Herr Kaleu!*" There was only a short pause as the young seaman made his calculation. "Bearing is two-zero-eight."

"I see her!" Lamprecht said almost immediately. But it took Rahn several seconds to find the faint image of masts protruding above the horizon to the south. Darkness was coming on quickly now and just as he made out the shadowy lines, they faded into the gloom. He was just about to give up trying to relocate them when to his surprise, the tiny white spark of a running light appeared in his viewfinder. By the time he had adjusted the focus, he could clearly see the red and green lamps high on the mast an estimated thirteen miles away.   Whatever it was—it was big. Probably a tanker.

"I'll be damned," Lamprecht muttered as the ship's upper works came into his line of vision. "He's got all of his running lights turned on. Didn't anyone tell him there is a war?"

"We'll remind him right away!"   Thiele was practically hopping with excitement. "Should I bring up the UZO and start running a firing setup?"

Rahn was already thinking about where he wanted to be when they sent such a juicy target to the bottom. He had the perfect location in mind—it was just a matter of getting there.

"No, not yet Number One," he said finally. "No need to be in a hurry—I'm sure our target will be following along for some time. We just need the right spot to put him away."   Rahn stepped forward past the periscope housing and spoke to the helmsman through the voice tube: "Heading zero-two-zero…engines ahead two-thirds."

He listened as his orders were repeated in the Control Room and relayed through the boat. Quickly, the roar of the twin diesels rose an octave and Rahn actually had to grip the coaming around the bridge to maintain his footing.   Behind him, Thiele and Lamprecht could not believe what was happening---they were heading directly away from what could be one of the biggest targets they had ever seen. Amazingly to them, instead of turning to attack, *Eins-Eins-Zwei* seemed to be fleeing the fat merchant ship. In fact, as they watched, the running lights and mast of their quarry were now slowly sinking out of sight beneath the horizon.

"Number One, maintain this heading—I'll return shortly," Rahn said and made his way to the open hatch.

"What the hell is that all about?"   Thiele asked as soon as Rahn's white hat disappeared down the hatch. "A ten-thousand tonner running up and just asking for it and we go racing away?"

"Just relax and enjoy the ride," Lamprecht said as he watched the bow wave blossom as the U-boat's snout sliced through the warm sea. "We're in for an interesting evening."

Any concerns the crew of *Eins-Eins-Zwei* had regarding their commander's increasingly eccentric behavior soon faded as Rahn made his way through the boat. His enthusiasm for the coming encounter with the enemy vessel was infectious. He joked with the men in the forward torpedo room and asked them to make sure they picked out a couple of good eels for the coming shoot. As he passed through the galley, he helped Smutje secure some pots that were starting to roll in their racks as the boat began to sway as it raced across the surface. Amid good-natured banter and backslapping he made his way through the forward compartments and then ducked through the hatch and into *Zentrale.*

"Gentlemen!" Rahn said as he stepped over to grip the Chief's shoulder. ""We're going to score big tonight—under the Florida moon with tropical breezes blowing though our hair. A fat tanker coming up from the stern...we're getting well ahead to set up a shot. I have just the place in mind to put them in the bag...but it will take a few minutes to get there."

His enthusiasm was infectious. The Chief was beaming and even the youngest technician looked up at Rahn with a confident smile. In the back corner, Beinlich avoided looking directly at his Kommandeur, but there was a brief glimmer of a grin on his thin face as he entered the hourly position on the chart.

"Cosinus!"

Beinlich flinched. *"Jawohl, Herr Kaleu!"*

"This is such a special evening, I want you to organize some sightseeing tours topside."

Rahn's order had caught Beinlich by surprise. *"Herr Kaleu?"*

"Organize the off duty men into groups of four and take them topside—ten minutes each. This should be fun."

"Jawohl, Herr Kaleu." Beinlich pushed has navigation work aside and moved quickly forward to get the off duty men organized for a topside excursion.

"Now if you gentlemen will excuse me," Rahn said. "I'll check to see if everyone in the engine room is ready for the party—we can't really do it without them!"

The control room filled with the roar of the diesels and the smell of hot oil as Rahn opened the after hatch and ducked through it.

"I'm sure you'll find them running as smoothly as Hubelmann's sewing machines!" The Chief shouted above the clamor that was suddenly cut off by the closing hatch.

Rahn found the Chief's reference to the big Hamburg tailoring shop that catered to U-boat men to be an accurate description of what awaited him in the engine room. The two big MAN diesels were chattering with the efficiency of well-oiled sewing machines—just as they had since leaving on patrol more than six weeks ago. Over the hot roar, he shouted some compliments to the two men on duty there...asked a couple of engineering questions...and told them they would be in action soon. They happily shouted their assurances that he could depend on the engines and then he carried his personal enthusiasm into the e-motor room and then to the crews' quarters in the after torpedo room. He found Little Pete Weingarten asleep on a bunk and made everyone laugh when he woke the sleeping boy by doing an imitation of his mother urging him to get ready for school. The young seaman was startled, confused and then amused. When Rahn had their attention, he repeated his message about the impending encounter and the need for everyone to do his duty. As they proclaimed their readiness, Rahn glanced at this watch and saw that his timing was just about perfect—it had been twenty minutes since he left the bridge. It would take him ten to get back and by then it would be time for some maneuvering to get the boat into firing position. He congratulated himself on his own maneuvering – his impromptu inspection and pep talk had allowed him to avoid the second guessing and possible questions that would undoubtedly be going on up there on the bridge.

By the time he worked his way back to *Zentrale*, Beinlich's first group of tourists were coming down the ladder and the next four seamen were lined up and anxiously awaiting their turn topside. The looks on their young faces reminded Rahn of a night when he and Kat had sat on a park bench watching children ride the big ferris wheel at the Jade Park. He could almost smell the cinnamon in the air and hear her laughter.

"You first, *Herr Kaleu.*" Kreffer, the first seaman in line interrupted Rahn's reverie.

"Not tonight." Rahn said. "You boys go first...I've seen the view before."

The seamen hurried up the ladder and Rahn paused just long enough to give the Chief a wink before he too pulled himself upward into the tower and then through the hatch and on to the bridge.

"Don't bother the lookouts...stay on the *wintergarten*

only…no smoking…" Beinlich had already begun to berate the members of his latest tour group.

"Easy Cosinus," Rahn said. "You boys enjoy your visit…if you want to smoke, feel free."

It was now too dark for him to see clearly, but Rahn knew his navigator would have a disapproving scowl on his face. He could also tell by the suddenly relaxed postures of the four crewmen that they were taking his comments as an "at ease" order. One dug into his overall pocket and quickly pulled out a cigarette. There was a brief yellow glow as his lighter flashed and in seconds the man was pulling the nicotine deeply into his lungs.

"Jupiter Light *Herr Kaleu!*"

Rahn looked up just in time to see the wide beam of diffused light sweep across the velvet blackness of the night sky. He watched it race toward the horizon, its already gauzy consistency fading to a lacy filigree of light that turned away and was gone in no more than half-dozen heartbeats.

"Very good, *Matrose* Kunst!" Rahn shouted to the portside lookout. "It will be back in another thirty seconds--you can count on it!"

As Rahn edged his way over to the voice tube, he sensed the thoughts of the officers on the bridge--"another goddam lighthouse--that's the reason for running from our target" --the fact that they would have to keep their opinions to themselves, at least while he was on the bridge, struck Rahn as downright amusing.

"Engines one-third!" he shouted into the voice tube and the command echoed through the ship. A shrill buzzer sounded above the din in the engine room and the Chief saw the change ring up on the telegraph. He shouted the orders, pulled and yanked a couple of levers and the yammering of the big diesels settled down to a smooth, but powerful purr.

U-112 slowed. Her bow settled and her foaming, angry wake became a white highway across the inky blackness of the subtropical sea. The wind and noise of the snarling diesels were replaced with a gentle breeze laced with the essence of orange blossoms. Up on the bridge, the visitors from the ship's bowels and the members of the watch relaxed the rigid stances that had braced them against railings and the conning tower. It was a beautiful night there beneath the stars with the flickering lights of America clearly visible along the shore off their portside.

"Number One." Rahn shifted over to where Thiele was scanning the horizon to seaward with his binoculars.

"Yes, *Herr Kaleu?*" Thiele lowered his glasses.

"You can do the shooting on this one," Rahn said and slapped his Number One on the back. "It may be a little complicated, but I'm sure you can handle it."

"Herr Kaleu?"

Rahn was surprised by the sound of confusion in Thiele's voice--surely, he thought, they can't really believe I would simply run away from such a juicy target?

"The tanker, of course!" Rahn said and shook his head in mock astonishment. "You're such a kidder! That big-assed American tanker will be barreling down on us in..." He looked down at the luminous dial of his wristwatch ..."fourteen minutes. So what I want you to do is come abeam the lighthouse and then set up a shoot that will sink her just outside the inlet--that should get the Americans' attention."

"Jawohl, *Herr Kaleu!*" Thiele forgot all about any concerns he may have had concerning his commander's behavior. "I'm sure I can pull that off--no problem Sir!"

"*Oberfahnrich* Beinlich. I suggest that you take your tour group below. We'll have to delay the topside excursions for awhile--I think we're going to be very busy in the next few minutes."

"Jawohl Herr Kaleu."

Rahn assumed Beinlich's lack of enthusiasm was due to the fact that the navigator was silently hoping the tanker would not show up--that would more than justify his suspicions about his commander's competence.

"And Number Two," Rahn said, "go ahead and bring the UZO up and get it ready--but with Thiele on the job, we can probably do this shoot over open sights."

Lamprecht saluted and disappeared down the hatch.

For the first time in his career, Rahn stepped aside and let his subordinates set up an attack--an approach to combat that certainly wasn't prescribed in any training manual. But as he watched their enthusiastic, but professional preparations for an anticipated attack, Rahn couldn't help but think his actions were justified. The excitement and sense of total participation seemed to be just what the crew needed to snap them out of the doldrums of a long cruise. Best of all, giving Thiele a chance to demonstrate his abilities would certainly restore his Number One's sense of devotion to him. In fact, the gift of the tanker should create a sense of obligation in Thiele's mind that would silence any questions he might have about his *kommander's* competence.

Rahn stood on the *wintergarten* and watched the lights of Florida recede beyond the luminous wake that traced U-112's path in a broad arch across the warm Atlantic. Thiele's barked orders and the changing tempo of the diesels seemed to be far away as the *Kapitanleutnant* allowed himself the luxury of filling his lungs with the evening air. He released the top two buttons of his cotton shirt and breathed deeply, pushed his cap back on his head and looked up just in time to see the latest flash from atop the Jupiter Inlet lighthouse. A few stars had begun to twinkle and Orion himself hung above the horizon--a stellar appearance that Rahn took to be a indisputable sign of good hunting to come--but only if their prey cooperated. As the First Officer brought the U-boat to seaward and then ordered a sweeping turn toward the shore, Rahn quickly did the mental math once more and concluded that within five minutes, his crew would proclaim his genius or question his sanity.

Five minutes. What would he do with five minutes alone with Kat? He closed his eyes and reviewed the possibilities. Would he savor every second as he slowly stroked her golden hair and gazed into her deep green eyes before spending precious ticks of the clock pressing his lips against hers and pulling her slowly and deliciously to him? Or would he try to compress an entire night of passion into those brief minutes? Ripping apart her blouse and plunging his hands inside to caress the firm globes of her breasts while hungrily feeding at her lips and the curve of her neck....no fumbling with the always frustrating buttons and belt of her skirt, instead pulling it above her waist with one hand while the other explores the cool sensuous curves of her hips...moving past the waistband of the panties and shoving into the warm, moist recesses...

"There she is!"

The portside lookout's cry awakened Rahn from his reverie and as he moved forward past the periscope and compass housings, his thoughts of passion faded.

"Damn, *Herr Kaleu,* you couldn't have timed it any better!"

Lamprecht said as he snapped the twin eyepieces of the UZO in place and connected it to the firing computer.

"Actually, I think I made a slight miscalculation…she's about thirty seconds early." Rahn couldn't help but smile. There, through the lenses of his Zeiss binoculars, he could see the mast and running lights of the tanker above the southern horizon and as he watched, her brightly lit upper works eased into view followed by the dark bulk of her hull. "Number One!"

"Herr Kaleu?"

"Be sure to use the *Atos*. No need to waste the electrics," Rahn said without lowering his glasses.

"Already got them ready Sir---it won't matter if they leave a wake," Thiele said. "At this range, they won't be able to escape even if we send up a flare to let them know the eels are on their way."

"Good work," Rahn said and he gave his Number One's broad shoulders a friendly pat as he squeezed past the UZO. "It's your show."

During the next few minutes, Rahn was treated to a performance that left little doubt that the untold hours of training he had given this crew had been time well spent in the service of the Fatherland. It was a tricky situation. The boat had to be held perpendicular to the edge of the northward flowing Gulf Stream while their target continued to steam toward a crossing of their bow. Thiele jockeyed U-112 into position so that the forward torpedo tubes pointed directly toward the line of dark water that formed the mouth of the Loxahatchee River at Jupiter Inlet. The towering lighthouse on the north bank and a cluster of lighted buildings on the south side clearly marked the narrow inlet's location.

"Target speed twelve knots…range eleven hundred meters…Helmsman, come to two-six-five…engines one-half…open bow caps one and two," Thiele called out the data and orders as he gazed through the UZO and fixed his target's doom with mathematical certainty. "Range one thousand now…angle on the bow twelve Red. Track!"

In the conning tower, Lamprecht entered the tracking information in the Siemens targeting computer and a light on the control panel blinked on to confirm the information from the UZO was being fed accurately down to the forward torpedo room.

"Track!

He shouted up the ladder to the bridge. A few seconds later, the loudspeaker crackled with "Track!" as the torpedo mate confirmed that the data had been successfully fed into the gyroscope humming inside the torpedo sealed in tube one.

"Depth three!" Thiele ordered and the torpedo mate manually entered the setting that would insure the torpedo would strike the tanker's hull just short of ten feet below the waterline.

Thiele watched the glowing pip in the UZO's viewfinder move past the tanker's bow and punched the firing button. *"Torpedo los! Ready number two!"*

"Running time forty-seven seconds!" Lamprecht reported.

"Torpedo los!" Thiele shouted and heard a confirmation from the torpedo room. He looked up the UZO and saluted. *"Herr Kaleu,* the torpedoes are on their way."

Rahn had plenty of time to adjust the aperture of his Leica to take maximum advantage of the faint available light. Through the camera lens, he composed the image he wanted to capture...the dark phallic symbol of the lighthouse with it's glowing head....the tanker, lit up like a cruise ship on Christmas Eve, approaching from the left side of the frame....

"Ten seconds," Lamprecht announced from his new position back on the bridge.

Rahn's forefinger rested on the shutter release button...four...three...two...

The first torpedo smacked the thin hull of the tanker just aft of the foremast and sent a towering column of white water erupting upward where Rahn caught it on film just as it reached its apex and hung for a split second before collapsing. The thump of the explosion echoed across the water and Rahn cranked frantically against the film advance lever, but by the time he had re-focused the water and debris from the second hit was already raining on the tanker's deck amidships. He pressed the shutter release and at that instant the tanker's cargo ignited in a fireball that roared toward the stars.

"Gott im Himmel!" a lookout exclaimed as they watched the fiery spectacle unfold and then a wave of heat tinged with the harsh scent of petroleum swept over them. In seconds, the darkness that had hidden them in its velvet folds was ripped away as though the

door to hell had been suddenly opened.

"Engines astern one-third!" Rahn ordered and everyone on the bridge was relieved as the screws bit and began pulling them away from the flames and toward the darkness of the far horizon. Although he was tempted to increase the speed of their withdrawal, Rahn didn't want to miss what he considered to be the ultimate photo opportunity of his patrol and quite possibly his career. The tanker had slowed to a halt, flames roiling upward with sporadic whorls of blue fire vomiting from its shattered hull. Just beyond the hellish spectacle, the Jupiter lighthouse stood firmly, its brick tower bathed in the fiery glow. Rahn snapped frame after frame.

Down in the radio shack, Timm quickly tuned to the six-hundred-kilocycle band and listened for the tanker's distress signal. From past experience, he knew the radio operator on the doomed ship would do everything possible to send a message—on the open sea, what little chance of survival the crew might have was largely dependent upon the bravery of the man tapping out a signal. Even here, close to shore, one last transmission might make all the difference between life and death.

"*Dit..dit..dit.....dit..dit..dit.....dit..dit..dit.*" Timm smiled as he heard the letter S repeated three times---the Allied code that meant "attacked by submarine" – at least they knew what had hit them. The signal came three more times and then the courageous radio operator working in the midst of an inferno, sent out a burst of information that Timm expertly intercepted and noted.

"She's the *Texaco Zephyr!*" Timm shouted into the control room and heard his words repeated to the bridge.

At the chart table, Beinlich quickly flipped through the boat's copy of Lloyd's Registry until he found the appropriate page. He ran his finger down a column, noted the relevant details and shouted them up the ladder.

"A ten-thousand tonner, *Herr Kaleu!* Less than two years old!"

"Such a short life," Rahn said and although he was referring to the *Texaco Zephyr's* abbreviated career, his comments could just have easily applied to the young sailor he saw running frantically across the tanker's burning forecastle. Halfway to the bow, he was engulfed in a sudden burst of bright flame that sent his blazing body spinning over the railing. When he hit the water, his flaming clothes ignited a patch of floating oil that flared and bubbled like molten lava.

Except for the watch on the bridge, U-112's crewmembers were unaware of the hellish scenes their handiwork had created. All they knew for sure was that they had scored a victory—one that was considerably more important than the sinking of some tramp steamer. As a result, the confines of the boat's hull suddenly seemed much like the post game locker room of a winning *fussball* team.

The laughing, joking and backslapping became so loud that Timm nearly missed the new series of dits and dahs echoing in his headphones. It only took him a few seconds to realize the new message on the six hundred meter band was intended to be a reply to the American tanker's distress call. The message was repeated and he jotted it down with one hand while with the other he made several adjustments to his receiver in hopes of determining the bearing and range of the transmitter. He quickly reviewed the message, made sure his translation was accurate, yanked off his headphones and scrambled through the hatch and into the control room.

"*Herr Kaleu!*" Timm tried to remain calm, but it was obvious to everyone in the control room that something out of the ordinary and something possibly quite dangerous had occurred. "*Herr Kaleu...*another ship has responded to the tanker's radio broadcast!" He looked up the aluminum ladder and saw Rahn's face framed by the open hatch leading on to the bridge. "It's an American destroyer...broadcasting in the clear and very close. They told the tanker they should arrive in twenty minutes!"

"Very good *Funkmatt!* Keep me informed." Rahn took one more look at the burning tanker through his binoculars and as he watched a small group of men struggling with a lifeboat swinging from its davits on the stern, he made his decision. "Gentlemen, let's take her down and prepare a welcome for the *Amis*."

In less than three minutes, the sleek U-boat slid out of sight beneath the flame-tinged waters.

U.S.S. LASSITER   2050 hrs.

The atmosphere on the bridge of the *USS Lassiter* was a mixture of thinly veiled excitement and quiet confidence. Although not one of the officers had ever seen combat, they looked at the glow of the burning *Texaco Zephyr* just beyond the horizon and told themselves that all of their training was about to pay off—they were going to kill a German U-boat. No doubt about it.

"Excuse me sir," said the young lieutenant standing next to the helmsman. "The radio shack reports that transmissions from the tanker have stopped."

Captain McClure nodded in response and quickly raised his binoculars to get a magnified view of the fiery furnace just over the horizon. He wondered if it was his imagination or did the intensity of the fire seem to increase with each passing second?

"Captain," came another voice from the far side of the blacked out bridge. "Moon rise will occur in approximately one hour."

McClure lowered his glasses and turned to face his assembled officers.

"Gentlemen, our time has come," he said gravely. "The enemy is within striking distance and I know you share my determination to strike a blow for the good guys. We've trained hard and we're ready---I've been preparing for this moment for more than twenty years and I, for one, intend to make the very best of the next hour. We can't save the *Texaco Zephyr*, but we sure as hell can make certain those Krauts don't get another chance at a defenseless American ship."

To the young officers, McClure's appearance was not unlike that of some biblical prophet. His commanding physical presence was backlit by the tanker's glowing funeral pyre and in the dim lighting of the bridge, his mature countenance expressed a sense of solidity that his crew found both comforting and inspiring. Few of the men under his command had even the slightest inkling that their captain had already exceeded his intellectual capacity for waging modern warfare. Instead of collecting data, analyzing it and formulating a tactical plan, McClure was visualizing a U-boat being torn apart by the guns under his command. He couldn't decide whether to have the German boat explode or simply let it sink under his *Lassiter's* pounding.

"Sir, a question if I may."

McClure was always happy to share his genius with his subordinates, but when he realized the question would be coming from Ensign Deane, his enthusiasm quickly faded. Ever since

Deane had attended a British training course up in St. Johns, the man had been a constant source of annoying questions and suggestions.

"Go ahead Ensign...but make it quick. We're all about to become very busy."

"Yes sir...well sir, I just wanted to say the British instructors went over a situation just like this and they maintained that the best course of action would be to approach cautiously and allow our sonar, or asdic as they call it, to determine the U-boat's location. Once we get a hard contact, then we can move in with depth charges."

"That's what the Brits suggest is it?" McClure made a snorting sound that indicated his contempt for anything and everything British. "Did it ever occur to you Ensign Deane, that if the limey's were any good at this sort of thing, we wouldn't have American seamen being incinerated off the coast of Florida?"

Deane had to admit that he had not, in fact, ever considered anything quite so ridiculous. "But sir, they've had lots of experience in these sorts of situations and..."

"Ensign Deane!" McClure's voice boomed. "What we need is more speed. Report to the engine room and see if you can't find some way to squeeze another knot out of those turbines."

"Yes sir," Deane saluted and backed away. He had no intention of pursuing any sort of reasonable conversation with a man he was convinced was a complete lunatic.

McClure smiled and shook his head as though he had just shooed away an enthusiastic child. He was pleased to see several other young officers shaking their heads in agreement as Deane left the bridge. When they returned their gaze to the Florida night, they could see flames flaring up from the shattered tanker dead ahead and as they watched, the flash of the Jupiter Inlet light seemed to be saying one thing---hurry!

During the next ten minutes, the *Lassiter* behaved like a ship less than half her twenty-four years in age. She steamed smoothly across the dark sea, her bow cleaving the tepid waters, her guns loaded and their crews at the ready. There was no trace of the engine troubles that had slowed her progress up the east coast. In fact, the old destroyer's engineering personnel were well pleased with the way her turbines were humming. Several of the engine room veterans remarked that they had never heard them in such fine form.

A slight course change to starboard brought them into the glow of the burning oil that lit the old destroyer's upper works with an eerie orange tint. Seeing debris and a body swishing past to port, McClure finally ordered the helmsman to ring up one-third ahead. As the ship slowed, the *Lassiter's* twin searchlights began sweeping across the carnage bobbing in the oily water.

At that moment, the only piece of the *Lassiter's* gear that wasn't working at peak efficiency was her sonar system. Installing the sensitive equipment had been a difficult chore—the designers of the flush deck destroyer had never considered that a sophisticated listening device would someday be a necessary addition. Training had been less than complete and the two seaman assigned to the unit had been keeping a list of questions they hoped someone would someday answer. They had just jotted down question 19— "How do you keep the recording paper straight?" – when Seaman First Class Dunn slipped on the headphones and flicked the series of switches that activated the sonar system.

At first, he thought the high pitched whine in his ears was some sort of malfunction, but a quick check of the dials and indicators showed that for once, everything was working perfectly. He was wondering if the sound was coming from some sort of marine life, when suddenly he knew exactly what was causing the noise that was now quickly increasing in volume.

"Torpedoes coming in!" Dunn yanked the headphones off in one motion and bounded out the hatch. "Torpedoes!" He shouted at the top of his lungs and ran toward the ladder leading up to the starboard bridge wing.

The awesome spectacle of the blazing tanker had momentarily distracted everyone on the bridge from his goal of catching a U-boat on the surface. The idea that they could be under attack was so foreign to them that even when they heard the shouted warning about torpedoes, only one young officer turned around in time to see the twin wakes rushing toward them just beneath the surface of the oil-stained sea.

"Captain! Tor...." The blast cut his words short, drove the air from his lungs and thrust him into the air where his spine was snapped by the impact with the overhead. For a split second, the men on the bridge bounced up as though they had been dropped on a trampoline. Before they crashed to the deck, the magazines erupted in a shattering explosion that sheared off the bow and sent the forward superstructure, including Captain Wendell McClure shooting upward toward the stars.

In the forward engine room, Ensign Deane was trying to stand up after having his legs kicked out from under him by the blast. He had just regained his footing when the U-112's second torpedo detonated against the hull less than ten feet from where he was standing. The blast turned Deane from a living, breathing human into nothing more than a large smear of bone fragments and viscera along the opposite bulkhead. Seawater rushed in to fill the vacuum created by the blast and swept the hot protoplasm that had been Ensign Deane downward past the ship's shattered keel and into the darkness of the Atlantic.

Even with the forward third of her hull vaporized, the *Lassiter* continued to slide forward, her stern rising out of the water and her big screws churning uselessly. Finally convinced her days were over, she settled forward, the sea edging up to the first funnel.

For those crewmen who had survived the blasts, sheer terror had gradually been replaced by mindless panic. In an effort to get as far away from danger as possible, they had instinctively gathered like sheep on the *Lassiter's* fantail. Although there was some moaning and a few sobs, no one spoke. Instead, they listened to the hellish roar of the flames from the burning tanker less than half-mile away and waited for someone to come to his senses and lead them to safety.

Petty Officer Burke wasn't stunned--he was angry, but not with the Germans who had destroyed his ship--he had never cared much for the Lassiter in the first place. His fury had resulted from the realization that not only had life's circumstances placed him in the "goddamn Navy", they had also conspired in an attempt to kill him. As a result, when he came through the hatch and stepped on the destroyer's angled deck he was pissed.

"What the hell are you doing?" He yelled at his cowering shipmates and advanced on them as though he intended to work his way through the crowd kicking and punching each survivor. "Are you just gonna stand there and wait for this bucket to go under?"

Although he would have gladly left them to drown, Burke knew he would need help to launch a lifeboat to save himself--and he did intend to survive. He had things to do with his life and they didn't include dying in the service of the U.S. Navy.

"Get to those lifeboats and prepare to lower away---or do you want to die?" When it became obvious that these men needed more motivation, Burke reached out and grabbed a young sailor by the throat. In the reflected glow of the burning tanker, the boy's eyes were wide with terror.

"Get over there and unshackle that boat!" Burke shoved the sailor toward the portside lifeboat and delivered a swift kick to the seat of his pants. "Move it!"

The Petty Officer's violence seemed to have the desired effect on the others and they began to move--some even worked their way down the slanted deck in an effort to release a large life raft affixed to the deckhouse.

Burke carefully inspected the lifeboat to insure it was sufficiently intact to carry him to safety. Convinced that its wooden hull had not been pierced, he was about to order it lowered into the water when his work was interrupted.

"Petty Officer Burke. Sir."

Burke turned angrily to see Seaman Barton from the machine shop staring at him.

"What the hell do you want sailor?" he snarled.

"What about Greer, Sir?"

"Who?"

Barton's calm expression never changed as he tried to maintain a semblance of military dignity while chaos surged around him.

"Greer. You remember, the sailor you have chained up below decks."

"Oh, the nigger!" Burke smiled and returned to his inspection of the lifeboat's keel. "He's dead."

"Begging your pardon sir, but I don't think he is...I heard him calling out. You can't just leave him down there to drown."

"Don't tell me what I can and can't do, sailor!" Burke would have planted his fist firmly in the boy's face, but by now several other men had stopped working long enough to observe the encounter. "If you're so concerned about that coon, you can go check on him!"

"Yes sir, I would do that sir, but you have the key to the

handcuffs. Without it, I can't get him out of there."

Frustrated, Burke probed his trouser pocket with his right hand while keeping Barton fixed in an angry glare. He felt the small brass key and by the time he had pulled it from his pocket, he had decided what he had to do.

"You're right Barton. I'm responsible for Greer. I should be the one to free him--if he's still alive. You men get this boat in the water and wait for me—I'll check below for more survivors."

Burke forced his way through the crowd and with one hand against a bulkhead to balance his descent down the sloping deck he stepped through the hatch and into the ship's darkness. Groping along the corridor, he went down a short ladder and was surprised to suddenly splash into ankle-deep water. The remains of the *Lassiter* were going down more quickly than he had thought. Time to get out, he decided.

"Is someone there? Sweet Jesus! Get me out of here!"

Son...of...a...bitch Burke thought as he slogged forward through the slowly rising water until he found the opening to the narrow compartment.

"Oh thank the Lord!" Curtis Greer said as he realized someone had reached his improvised prison cell. "I didn't think anyone would come for me!"

Burke realized that even if he had wanted to, it would have been extremely difficult to unlock the handcuffs in the darkness. Fortunately, it only took him a second to find just what he needed---a heavy pipe wrench was lying on the workbench that ran the length of the bulkhead. He picked it up with his right hand and leaned inside the locker. Although he found the thought of touching Greer repulsive, he had no choice. He reached forward with his left hand until he touched warm flesh.

"I've got you," Curtis Greer said as he frantically grabbed Burke's hand and guided it downward in the darkness. "Them handcuffs are fastened down here somewhere. I can feel the lock ...I'll help you with the key...just don't drop it."

Burke yanked his hand away and then swatted in the darkness until he felt Greer's tightly curled hair. He locked his fingers in the strands and pulled.

"Hey! That's my head!" Greer shouted. "The handcuffs are down..."

Burke brought the wrench down with all his force and felt Curtis Greer's skull crack like an eggshell under the impact. Just to make sure, he swung once more and this time the wrench sank into the dying man's head.

The ship groaned and water sloshed as the Lassiter rolled ten degrees to starboard. For the first time in his life, Burke fought against panic that threatened to swallow him as he scrambled, crawled and clawed his way upward and out of the steel tomb. Much of the deck was now under water and the survivors were piling into the lifeboat and the raft, both of which were now bobbing in the oily sea.

"C'mon sir! She's going down!" A sailor called to Burke and reached out to pull him from the deck and into the lifeboat. In the darkness, no one noticed his blood splattered uniform.

UNCLE SAM'S: 2145 hrs.

"Miss Greer. Could I please have your autograph?"

Winnie was startled by the question. She was leaning on the railing that ran along the rear deck of Uncle Sam's in hopes that the late night sea breeze would cool her off. She had put her heart and soul into the last set and when she had finished, the cheering, the cigarette smoke, and the red stage lighting had suddenly seemed stifling. The dimly lit deck and the fresh breeze offered salvation.

"I don't want to bother you none, but I reckon this might be the only chance I'll ever have to meet an honest to God star."

A white girl was asking for her autograph! For a moment, Winnie hesitated. Not that she would have denied the girl's request—it was just that this moment was so totally unanticipated that it took a few seconds for her to get past the significance of the event and move on to an appropriate response.

"Of course...it's no bother at all." Winnie smiled as she accepted the pencil and scrap of paper from the girl's outstretched hand. "What's your name?"

"Lenora. I'm Lenora Ledbetter from over toward Palatka."

"Oh, you must have come over on the bus tonight." Winnie wondered what kind of girl would take advantage of Joe Miller's special round trip bus service that provided free transportation to girls who wanted to visit his bar on Tuesday nights. Now that she could see one up close, Winnie was surprised that Lenora looked perfectly…wholesome.   She had that pale, delicate look that Winnie thought all Southern white girls seemed so pleased to have—not that any of them she had ever met could be described as delicate.

"Yes, me and Retha Ann rode over here. It wasn't a bad trip at all and Mr. Miller promised the bus would have us home by eleven—I'll just tell Ma and Pa that we was at choir practice."

Winnie placed the paper on the railing and signed it with a flourish: To Lenora.
All the Best! Winifred Greer.

"You know it's a sin to lie to your parents," Winnie said as she handed back the pencil and paper.

"Well, I reckon that if they know'd I was here, it would worry them," Lenora smiled broadly and Winnie could see one of the girl's front teeth was missing. "So I'm doin' them a favor by lettin' em think I'm at church."

Winnie wanted to quote scripture, Exodus 20:12 "honor they father and thy mother" came to mind, but instead she allowed herself to savor this moment—the first one in her life when she not only felt equal to, but downright superior to a white girl.

"Well, Lenora, I hope you enjoyed your visit…come back real soon. Oh and what about Retha Ann? Does she want an autograph too?"

Lenora had already turned and headed back toward the bar, clutching the autograph to her chest. "No, that's all right," she said. "Her daddy don't allow her to talk to no nig…I mean, colored folk." She pulled open the door and the sounds of the jukebox playing "String of Pearls" escaped from the bar. She gave Winnie a wave and then stepped inside where she was swallowed by the crowd.

Winnie felt embarrassed that for a moment she had allowed herself to think she had become something more than a nigger in the eyes of a white girl from Palatka. Then she was angry…angry at herself and angry at a world where stupid, no talent rednecks could make her feel so badly. She stamped her foot in frustration and turned to face the sea breeze once more.

Suddenly, she felt an icy chill pass through her body and for a brief second she sensed that something was horribly wrong with Curtis. All of her thoughts of anger faded as she hurriedly prayed that God would look after her brother.   She was still a long way from "Amen" when Luigi Carbone rushed out of the bar to hurry her back inside for the next set. As Winnie stepped through the door a splatter of applause and whistles welcomed her. She should have been thrilled by the spontaneous response of the crowd, but instead she stole a look over her shoulder to where the moon was rising out of the placid Atlantic. A cold hollowness formed deep in her stomach as she whispered one word: "Curtis."

Uncle Sam's

WEDNESDAY
April 15, 1942

UNCLE SAM'S: 0435 hrs.

Over the years, Miller's dream had evolved from an anger-inspired delusion into a full-blown horror story with a cast of thousands. Not that it was a complete fantasy. In fact, the dream had been inspired by an actual event twenty years ago when he had been sent by the impotent *Weimar* Government to check on the status of *SMS Nassau*. Given as a war prize to the Japanese, his old ship had been consigned to a Dutch shipyard and finally sold by its Oriental owners to a British salvage company.

Even though he knew her fate could be ignominious, nothing had prepared him for the scene that awaited him on that warm summer day. His heart was beating with excitement as he approached the yard--he couldn't wait to see her again. But when he turned the corner and was confronted by the hard reality of her fate, something deep inside had broken. *Nassau* was being slowly butchered. Her once pale gray paint was filthy and rust-stained and as he watched, steam-powered cranes dipped inside her hull and removed her innards dumping them in filthy heaps on the dock. Cutting torches flared and to Miller the workers seemed overjoyed at their success in tearing apart the only thing he had truly loved.

As the years had passed, that incident had repeated itself hundreds of times in the form of a dream that seemed determined to test his sanity. In the latest version, the shipyard workers had been transformed into thousands of Japanese each dressed in baggy trousers, white blouse and wide brimmed rickshaw hat. They marched in an endless single file over the *Nassau,* pausing every few steps in response to an unheard command, kneeling in unison and ripping apart the ship's steel plates with their teeth. In his dream, the ship's cries of agony caused him to toss and turn in a sweaty, but vain attempt to ease her pain.

"*...dash-dash...dot-dot-dash*"

The chattering of the radio receiver roused Miller from his dream. Even before he came fully awake, his brain had automatically begun to decode the dots and dashes---K—T—M—U. KTMU! Heart pounding at the realization that he was receiving a personal message, Miller rolled from his bed, stumbled over a chair and hurried into his office.

The big *Telefunken* radio seemed to be alive—its dials glowing in the darkness and his repeated call sign crackling from the loudspeaker. Fumbling at his desk, Miller flicked on the lamp, set up the transmitter and slipped on the headphones. Within seconds he was sending his acknowledgement flashing through the ether above the Atlantic and deep into Germany. Then, he waited. In order to lessen the anxiety of whether or not a response would come, he busied himself with arranging his message pad, making sure he had two sharpened pencils....

The message came rushing in and Miller was ready to receive. He was proud of his abilities and when he was convinced he had copied the entire missive after only hearing it twice, he quickly sent an acknowledgement. The German transmitter sent a signoff signal and the receiver fell silent.

Miller moved quickly to obtain the decrypt. Removing the top secret *Enigma* from a wall safe, he placed it on his desk in the circle of light provided by the lamp and carefully opened its polished wooden cover. The first few times he had operated the Third Reich's most valuable code machine, Miller had moved with the careful deliberation of a craftsman adjusting a rare timepiece. But now the technical intricacies of the device were well known to him and his hands rapidly prepared the *Enigma* for use. Checking the coded entry in tonight's message, he consulted his outdated and dog-eared key to determine the corresponding rotor settings and plug-ins. When at last everything was ready, he began typing in the coded text and copying the solution that lit up on the Enigma's panel. After only the first few letters were entered, Miller could see all the settings were correct—the coded dots and dashes he had received were slowly being transformed into words and sentences.

By the time the far horizon above the dark Atlantic began to brighten with the first hints of dawn, Miller had read the message so many times he had committed it to memory. Standing by the open window and breathing deeply from the fresh sea air of morning, he smiled at the knowledge that although he was thousands of miles from home, the Fatherland considered him to be an important part of Germany's *Kriegsmarine*. So important, he proudly told himself, that within two days' time he would be hosting the crew of one of Hitler's gray wolves of the deep—a U-boat was coming to *Uncle Sam's!*

ST. AUGUSTINE: 0658 hrs.

FBI Agent Bill Spencer was awakened by the metallic jangling of the telephone beside his bed. Fumbling in the darkness, he managed to remove the receiver and mumble a sleep-laden hello.

"Agent Spencer! You won't believe what's happened!"

Spencer continued to hold his eyes closed as his brain labored to match the voice with a name and a face.

"Is that you Scoop?"

"Of course it's me—I'm a newsman—who else would be callin' with news this early in the morning?" Michael Pomar was excited—and he quickly explained to Spencer that he had just gotten off the phone with the AP office in Jacksonville and they had assured him they would file his story regionally, if not nationally. They had even asked how to spell his name!

"OK. Calm down…what's so newsworthy? FDR coming to town?"

"No…but that U-boat you were looking for might just very well be. It might already be here!"

Spencer' eyes snapped wide open and in the dim light he tried to focus on the slowly turning blades of the ceiling fan.

"A U-boat? Where? When?" The news was like a caffeine rush that propelled him out of bed and left him standing in the middle of the room in his undershorts.

"I can't talk now…I've got to get down to the marina. If you want to know the details meet me there in ten minutes. Gotta go."

The line clicked dead and Spencer rattled the receiver into place before stumbling over to the window. He released the shade and it snapped noisily upward on its roller to reveal the radiant sunrise warming the Moorish towers of the Ponce de Leon across the street. The view was so much like what he had imagined Tripoli or Algiers to be that he half-expected a muezzin to step out on to one of the ornate balconies and call the believers to morning prayer. Instead, he heard the clock tower chiming the hour and he was surprised when it struck six and then seven.

"Jesus!" he exclaimed as he looked across the room and saw that the clock on the nightstand was in total agreement with the tolling bells. "Must be the sea air!" he said as an answer to his mental question about the lateness of his sleep here in the Ancient City.

As he splashed water on his face, ran a comb through his sandy blonde hair and pulled on his clothes, he couldn't help but think that having a teenager set the place and time for a meeting with a G-man was a bit unprofessional. He told himself to slow down, but he couldn't—after years of sorting and filing, he suddenly found this FBI stuff to be terribly exciting.

0720 hrs.

By the time Spencer arrived, the normally quiet St. Augustine City Marina was bustling with activity. Fishermen, boat owners, two milkmen in their white uniforms, even the bums who had spent the night sleeping on the benches in the plaza were all there talking excitedly and hurrying up and down the dock for no apparent reason. Spencer looked down on the excitement from the marina office patio and wiped perspiration from his face with his handkerchief. Although the walk from the Alhambra Hotel had only been four blocks, the pace he had set and the morning heat made his heart pound.

The pistol tucked into the shoulder holster beneath his armpit seemed to weigh a ton and as he reached to loosen the strap, he saw a man pushing the marina's fish cart through the arched corridor leading from the street. Two young boys hurried along on each side as escorts and as the cart swung around the corner and headed down to the dock, several men gathered around it and joined in the procession. The battered old metal cart had often drawn a crowd as it carried the carcass of a record-breaking kingfish or the bloody remains of a shark in the opposite direction, but this was the first time it had attracted such attention on its way to the boats. As it passed down the ramp, Spencer leaned over the railing and got a good look at its contents. At first, he thought the metallic cylinder in the cart was part of an ice cream churn—but then he recognized what was causing all the excitement. The cart was carrying a brand new .30 caliber Browning machine gun!

When Spencer turned the corner in pursuit of the cart, he saw Michael Pomar standing in the corridor where he was engaged in a heated argument with a man dressed in an expensive-looking gray suit and a matching fedora. It was obvious from the way the man was shaking his finger in young Pomar's face that the conversation wasn't going well for the cub reporter. Spencer slowed his pace just enough to allow the man to finish the conversation and head for the street before he walked up to Pomar.

"So Scoop, what's the story?" Spencer asked cheerfully.

"There is no story," Pomar said dejectedly. "There was a story—a great one—but that stuffed shirt killed it."

"Who's the stuffed shirt?"

Pomar glared at the well-dressed man who was now climbing into a new Ford parked at the curb on *Avenida Menendez*. "That would be Mr. K.T. Jeffers, editor and publisher of the St. Augustine *Record*."

Spencer let out a low whistle and smiled. "The big man himself...that must be some story you've got if he wants you to keep it quiet. What's it about?"

"Oh that's right!" Pomar's demeanor suddenly seemed much brighter. "You don't know what happened? You may be the only man in a hundred miles who doesn't know what happened---and you call yourself a G-man."

"Ok...I give up...you're the newsman, give me some news."

"Last night, about two hundred miles south of here right outside of Jupiter Inlet, a U-boat blew up a big tanker and then sank the destroyer that was its escort---lots of casualties."

Spencer was stunned by the news. Up until that moment, his assignment had seemed more like some sort of scavenger hunt, but now there were dead Americans in the equation. "But how could...? I mean surely they must have known there was a German submarine out there. Why didn't they do something?"

Pomar shrugged. "How do I know? Maybe they were trying

to do something when they got themselves killed. All I know for sure is that my story is going nowhere."

"But if everyone already knows about the attack, what good was your story anyway? There must have been reporters down that way who have the story—maybe even photos of the sinking."

"I'm sure they do," Pomar said with a touch of annoyance, "but they won't be filing one either---there's a doggone blackout of every story dealing with U-boats. Unless, of course, it's one put out by the Navy...like the one a couple of weeks ago where Admiral King announced that we'd sunk a couple of dozen U-boats. Now a story like that can get published—even if it is a bunch of lies."

Spencer started to point out that Florida teenagers probably weren't qualified to question the veracity of the Navy admiral defending America's eastern shoreline. But it only took a second for him to recall that lying to the public was an essential part of the federal government's daily operations. Regrettably, he had to admit that the "official" number of sunken U-boats was probably greatly inflated.

"But surely you weren't the only one to report the U-boat attack last night," Spencer said. "You might be a phenomenal reporter, but I don't think you'd get the inside story on something that happened a couple of hundred miles away."

Pomar rolled his eyes in exasperation. "Of course not. My story wasn't about the sinking. It was all about the reaction of the St. Augustine Security Council. It's a story of brave men boldly taking the defense of America's oldest city into their own hands."

"Brave men? You must be talking about a different group of men than the ones I saw in that meeting the other day. What are they going to do? Kill the Nazis with boredom?"

"For a government agent, you don't seem very patriotic." Pomar smiled and motioned for Spencer to follow. "Come with me—I'll show you what it's all about. But I can assure you my story was much more...inspiring...than what you're about to see."

The reporter headed down the steps to the dock with the G-man close behind. They walked past a wide assortment of moored boats ranging from a large three-masted schooner to a mullet boat with its outboard motor mounted in the center of the hull so the stern would be clear for deploying nets. But it was the big Chris Craft cabin cruiser at the end of the dock that had drawn all the attention this morning. A large American flag hung from the staff at the stern and as a slight breeze ruffled it, Spencer could see the boat's name in gold letters emblazoned across the stern *"Naughty Boy – St. Augustine, Fla."* Judging from the boat's girth and the way it settled sluggishly in the oil-stained water, Spencer couldn't help but think that "Dirty Old Man" would be a more accurate moniker.

A crowd had gathered to watch several men struggle to load supplies aboard the boat and as Pomar and Spencer approached, they could see two dockworkers lifting the new Browning out of the fish cart. They gingerly passed it over the boat's gunwale to two shabbily dressed men Spencer had seen begging in the Plaza the day before.

"Careful with that baby!" Hank Duke shouted down from the cabin cruiser's bridge where, dressed in a blue yachtsman's blazer and a captain's cap, he commanded the operation below. "That's our stinger!"

"Stinger? That's a good one!" said Joe Miller from where he and Carbone stood apart from the crowd near the boat's bow. "All you've got is a stinger and every U-boat has a swatter that will splatter you and this boat like you were a palmetto bug!"

The popular bar owner's comment sent a ripple of laughter through the crowd. The other Security Council members, however, were not amused.

"That's defeatist talk and I won't tolerate it!" Council chairman Homer Cooper shouted as he stepped out of the boat's cabin and then puffed out his chest to display his old Army tunic with the double row of campaign ribbons attesting to his visits to supply depots in far corners of the world. Much to the crowd's amusement, Cooper was wearing his ancient Army-issued jodhpurs and shiny black cavalry boots.

"And just what are you going to do about it Homer? Smack me with that little stick of yours?" This time Miller's comment brought outright laughter from the crowd.

"Why I outta..." Cooper stepped forward menacingly, but then stopped as he slowly realized that perhaps the riding crop he was clutching in his hand might indeed be a bit out of place...and maybe the boots weren't exactly standard issue for an ocean cruise. He blushed, but he wasn't sure whether it was caused by anger or embarrassment.

"Hey Joe! How do you know how big of a stick Homer has?" The question was shouted from the crowd that had now lost the solemnity of the moment. Instead of gathering to see their leading citizens off to battle, the folks on the dock now seemed to be there to say a fond farewell to local comedians on their way to try there luck in the big city.

"Mirrors!" Miller shouted. "Haven't you ever noticed the mirrors above the urinals at my place? We had to get a special magnifying one for Homer!"

County Commissioner Jerry Strickland had never anticipated that their patriotic actions would be turned into a circus sideshow. "That's enough!" He shouted and the laughter quickly faded to a few barely disguised snickers. "That U-boat could be right outside the inlet and until the Navy gets here, we're the only defense available. So I'm sorry you all find this so damn funny, we're just risking our lives to save yours and your property. I don't see the humor in that."

"That U-boat's nowhere near here," Miller lectured. "At least not yet anyway. I don't think the Germans would be foolish enough to be running on the surface in daylight so that means they could have only made it up the coast to somewhere near...."

"We can do the math," Strickland snapped. "We even use secret Navy information only we have...isn't that right Jeremy?"

From his position on a crate in the stern, the council's resident bookkeeper was dreamily contemplating the possibilities posed by the mirrors above the urinals at *Uncle Sam's* bar. The commissioner's question caught him off guard, but he quickly recovered.

"Yes...yes, we have the numbers," Jeremy Coleman stammered before mentally coming up with the numbers he had calculated late the previous night. "Allowing for the one hour the Navy says U-boats usually spend in the vicinity of their victim, we can anticipate that they traveled on the surface until dawn at a speed of fifteen knots. Shortly before dawn, they probably dived and have been headed toward us submerged for the past two hours at a speed of three knots. That means they should arrive at the inlet in about another ninety minutes. Oh, by the way, the Nazis call them U-boats because that's short for *unterseeboot* – which means underwater boat."

"That's brilliant," Miller said sarcastically. "I don't believe a word of it, but it sounds good and that's what's important. And Jeremy, on behalf of our enemies, I'd like to thank you for sharing the Navy's secret information with the couple of hundred people who are standing here."

"Now just you wait a minute there Miller," Strickland scolded. "We don't have time for this---are you coming with us or not?"

"Not on that boat. I told you I was working on the paperwork to get us an honest to God patrol boat down here from Charleston---I'll even get one with some proper weapons on board."

"We've got weapons—just look at this Browning—she's a real beauty!" Cooper leaned down to give the machine gun an affectionate pat.

"But it doesn't have the hitting power needed to discourage a U-boat.... If you see a U-boat, and that doesn't sound likely, you'd better not take a shot at him with that pathetic little garden sprayer—it will just encourage them to blow you out of the water." Miller's patience was quickly fading.

"Well, we've already asked Camp Blanding for depth charges," Coleman said in his squeaky voice. "I'll bet they'll deliver them today."

"I don't think so...Blanding is an Army facility. As a rule of thumb, the Army doesn't stock depth charges. You should have called Mayport, they probably have lots of depth charges lying around that naval base—they don't seem too interested in using them." Miller's voice reflected his annoyance with the other council members. "Besides, you have no racks for dropping them and I doubt that boat could hold more than one depth charge."

"So you're not going with us?" Hank Duke was obviously itching to get started. He had primed the engines and his finger was resting on the starter switch.

"Of course not...you're just wasting fuel," Miller said as he and Carbone began walking away.

"That's all right Hank, we don't need a coward on board anyway," Homer Cooper shouted from where he was trying to attach a belt of gleaming ammo to the Browning that now sat on the boat's deck.

Miller stopped and turned slowly. He could feel the eyes of the crowd on him as they waited for his reply. He considered several options—defiance, anger—he even briefly considered going with them. But in the end, he came up with what he thought would be the perfect answer.

"No, you don't need me," Miller said loudly. "But I'll give you some good advice."

"And what might that be?" Cooper said defiantly. His old Army uniform gave him a sense of authority he hadn't felt since he last ordered supply clerks around up at Fort Eustis.

Miller pointed at the Browning. "The ammo feed is on the other side of the breach...that's where the ammo belt goes. Colonel."

Homer Cooper glanced down and saw the obvious error he was making. When he tried to quickly follow Miller's advice, he painfully scraped his hand on the gun and dropped the ammo belt.

The crowd's laughter was drowned by the *Naughty Boy's* engine as it roared to life at Duke's command and sent a cloud of blue exhaust smoke billowing across the dock. He was so anxious to get away that he quickly gunned the engine and swung the wheel to head them away from the dock. Fortunately, several townspeople noticed the defenders of their community had neglected to cast off. Just before the boat edged away, they hurried forward to undo the lines around the dock cleats and tossed them aboard the boat.

In the excitement of the boat's departure, Spencer temporarily lost sight of Miller and Carbone. When the crowd and the smoke began to clear, he finally saw them climbing aboard a sleek triple cockpit Chris Craft at the far end of the dock. By the time he caught up with them, Carbone had already cast off and he and Miller were in the cockpit. The *Lady Liberty's* engine was gurgling happily.

"Mr. Miller! Joe!" Spencer called as he hurried toward them. He saw Miller motion for Carbone to hold the boat at the dock.

"Special Agent Spencer!" Miller said as though he were truly pleased to see the G-man. "I hope you aren't going to arrest me for abandoning my duties with the Security Council."

"Not at all," Spencer said as he stopped to catch his breath. When he placed his hands on his hips, he couldn't help but notice Carbone staring at the pistol holstered beneath his armpit. "I don't think they will be contributing much to the war effort—even if you went with them. I just wanted to ask you a question."

"Fire away," Miller said good-naturedly. "Or maybe that's not the right choice of words."

"Don't worry. I was just wondering how you happened to know the Meyerhof couple were spying for Hitler?"

Spencer noticed that his question had caused Miller's happy demeanor to fade.

"The Meyerhofs?" Miller struggled to return a smile to his face.

"You know, the German spies over at the beach. Sheriff Hartson told me all about how you arranged their capture."

"Oh there was nothing to that…I just happened to notice that every time a big freighter or one of our warships passed by, Herr Meyerhof was out on the beach taking photos of it. I just thought there was a chance he might be doing it for some reason other than a hobby so I mentioned it to the sheriff."

"And as it turned out, he was collecting photos for the Nazis?"

"Yeah, he and his missus were running a regular spy nest right under our noses," Miller said and he motioned for Carbone to get underway. "Now, if you'll excuse us, we've got work to do."

Spencer gave the speedboat a casual salute as it pulled away from the dock. In seconds it was speeding across Matanzas Bay and as Spencer watched, it cut across the *Naughty Boy's* bow and flashed beneath the imposing Mediterranean architecture of the Bridge of Lions.

"There goes my story," Michael Pomar said as he walked up behind Spencer.

"I don't think it was censored because of the U-boat attack," Spencer said. "I think your story was killed to prevent East Coast residents from finding out they are being defended by idiots."

U-112: 0810 hrs.

Despite the previous night's victories, U-112's *kommandeur* was feeling a bit depressed this morning. His crew was still excited and it showed in their enthusiasm for even the most mundane duties. But he couldn't help but feel his successes in sinking the enemy had seriously hindered his ability to complete his collection of lighthouse photos. The problem had become apparent just before dawn. After running on the surface all night, he had positioned the boat exactly where he wanted to be so he could get a photo of the Cape Canaveral light just as the rising sun lit the black and white bands encircling its tower. Much to his amazement, a twin-engined airplane had suddenly appeared and before he and the watch members could clear the tower the American bomber had roared directly over them. They were helpless and as they slid down the ladder to the cacophony of the alarm bell each of them expected a bomb to follow them into the control room. By the time the U-boat had leveled off at a depth of a mere twenty-five meters with the keel skimming over the sandy bottom, it had become apparent that they were not under attack— miraculously, the bomber's crew had failed to see them. Within minutes, the enlisted men aboard the U-112 were laughing and joking again. If anything, the close encounter with the enemy had made their successes a few hours earlier seem even more breathtaking. After all, they reasoned, the Americans weren't totally inept—at least they had forced them to make an actual emergency combat dive for the first time since leaving the Caribbean.

For the officers, the near miss was much more ominous. As they sat with Rahn in the cramped wardroom, they were all thinking that if the same thing had happened a few minutes later or after they had rounded the Cape, the water would have been too shallow to dive. The only alternative, if the Americans had spotted them, would have been to try to shoot it out on the surface—something that was extremely risky, if not suicidal. Rahn decided the best tactic now, would be to put their minds on something else.

"*Funkmaat* Timm received this message about twenty minutes after transmitting our victory report last night. Of course I thought it was some sort of congratulatory message from Dönitz, but when I ran it through the Enigma...well here's the result," Rahn said as he slid the decoded message across the table. "What do you make of it?"

Thiele pulled it toward him while Lamprecht inched in to read it. Sitting beside Rahn, the Chief had to lean forward and read it upside down. Although he didn't plan it that way, Rahn was silently pleased that Beinlich had to stand and squeeze his way halfway around the narrow table in order to see the text. Skipping the technicalities of the message header, each went directly to the main text.

Offizier:
To: Rahn
Rendezvous with KTMU at Dora Bruno 9992 at 0700 hours 104X
Exchange package stowed at Fr.23a1 for package at KTMU pier.X
Beacon on 700 meter band 0600-0700 hoursX
Landing point is white over redX
Recognition signal is AntonX
Report resultsX
(signed) Hugo. 40 Heilbrunner Strasse.

"Which *milchkuh* is KTMU? Isn't that Weber's boat?" asked Lamprecht.

"No, I think KTMU is Biermann's boat," said Thiele. "Remember, we saw it being overhauled in Lorient just before we sailed."

"Sure I remember!" The Chief never forgot a boat. "That was one broad-assed *milchkuh*. She's sure to be stuffed with eels, fuel and food. Maybe even mail from home....just the kind of package we need."

"Strange." Beinlich said and as he stood erect his upper torso disappeared into the darkness above the glare of the shaded lamp above the table. His voice seemed to come from a headless body. "I don't recall KTMU on the list of boats....and those coordinates are not too far south from here—Bahamas I would guess. We would never be sent to meet a supply sub so near the coastline. But why would they use the word 'pier'?"

"Cosinus is correct," Rahn said and he was glad he couldn't see the smirk on Beinlich's face. The man had apparently memorized the call signs of more than 100 U-boats—a feat that left Rahn feeling uneasy. "As you may have noticed, the security status of this message is of the highest level and, I think I can tell you, that means there are some special codes included by the Big Lion himself. The 40 in the signature address means that should be subtracted from the coordinates in the message that now become *Dora Bruno* five-nine-nine-two. And before Cosinus gives himself a headache trying to visualize the chart, I'll tell you where this message sends us—to a rendezvous at a pier jutting out into the Atlantic just south of St. Augustine, Florida."

"*Mein Gott!*" Thiele exclaimed. "A landing on the Florida shore! Now that's just the kind of..."

"*Herr Kaleu,*" Lamprecht interrupted. "I'd like to volunteer to lead the landing party on this hazardous mission."

"But you can't! I'm the Number One...I'm the logical choice for this mission." Thiele's matter-of-fact tone left little doubt about who he expected to be in charge.

"What about the package?" The Chief asked with childish enthusiasm that seemed oddly out of place coming from someone with such a luxuriant beard. He studied the message looking for a clue. "This notation looks like... *Ja!* It's a frame number, back in engineering." The Chief suddenly rose from the table and squeezed past Rahn. "I'll be right back--- hopefully, with our gift for KTMU."

"Good work Chief!" Rahn shouted as Wieland disappeared through the hatch and headed back toward the engine room.. "It's bad manners to show up without a gift."

"But *Herr Kaleu,*" Thiele said. "How could we not know what we're supposed to deliver?"

Rahn smiled at his officers gathered around the table. "I don't know... this is something completely new to me. In fact, if the Chief doesn't come up with something I'll have to embarrass myself and radio BdU for clarification. I'm sure that would make them question the ability of *Eins-eins-zwei* to complete the mission."

"But what will we get in return?" Lamprecht asked.. "It must be something pretty special or the Big Lion would never authorize such a risky mission."

"I don't know what we'll get...that's part of the excitement isn't it? You never know what might be behind all that wrapping paper." Rahn grinned. "But I do know that you're right about Admiral Dönitz—he would never put us in such danger if the mission were not vitally important. That's why we'll have to do everything possible to take the 'risk', as our Number Two calls it, out of this operation. We have approximately forty hours to get prepared. During that time, I'm certain the Americans will be making an effort to find us. I don't think that aircraft this morning was an accident. Even the *Amis* can't ignore getting a warship and a tanker blown to hell right on their doorstep."

"Maybe they can, *Herr Kaleu,*" Thiele said. "We could not make ourselves more... available to the Americans, yet they seem to ignore us. That patrol plane this morning had us cold...no doubt about it... yet they either didn't see us or thought we were friendly. Even the Poles put up a much better defense and we took them and their antiquated military by complete surprise. The Americans have had nearly three years to get ready, they possess some of the most advanced technology in the world and yet they are apparently impotent."

"I think you underestimate them," Beinlich said and edged his way into the seat vacated by the Chief. "You see, for Americans it is a matter of money. Always money. When they determine how to make a profit from fighting us, then we will all be in trouble. My father toured the States several times, from Atlantic to Pacific. When he would come home, I always wanted to hear about red Indians and cowboys, but all he talked about was the factories...the biggest he had ever seen and they have hundreds of them. It's just a matter of time until they start making destroyers instead of washing machines—then we'll be in real trouble."

"*Mein Gott! Herr Kaleu,* we have a defeatist for a navigator!" Lamprecht blurted out.

"*Ja,* I thought you were some kind of National Socialist poster boy," Thiele said. "But you sound more like a communist!"

"Communist!" Beinlich was more agitated than anyone had ever seen him. "Communist? You wouldn't know a communist if you saw one...I don't think you even know what...."

"Enough!" Rahn cut off the conversation as quickly as possible—he was surprised by the rancor in his officers' voices. "We're not hear to discuss politics—politics are of no interest to *Kriegsmarine* officers. We have one task—to serve the Fatherland."

Rahn paused for his words to take effect. As he glanced from face to face of the men gathered around the table, he could see that Lamprecht and Thiele seemed to have quickly gotten over the dispute. Beinlich, however, continued to glare at his two fellow officers.

"From this moment," Rahn said, "I want all of us to behave as though we are sailing along the English coastline and that the Royal

Navy is out there in full force. That should keep everyone alert and ready for action. Agreed?"

"*Ja, Herr Kaleu,*" the three officers answered in unison.

"Just one question sir," Lamprecht said. "What about the sunshine and the palm trees? I don't know if I can convince myself that such a bright and beautiful place is really cold and gray England."

"You convinced yourself that the little redheaded barmaid at Kranzl's wanted you," Thiele said teasingly. "If you believed that...you should have no problem deluding yourself into believing that Florida is England."

All of them laughed at Thiele's little joke—even Beinlich seemed amused. Rahn wanted to say something witty to prolong the feeling of camaraderie that had just been kindled, but all he could think of was the mission to come. Fortunately, the sound of the Chief coming back through the control room was more than enough to maintain the light-hearted mood.

"I've found it!" The Chief said proudly as he came through the hatch and placed a box enshrouded in black rubber on the table in front of them. Water dripped down its sides and there was an oily sheen on its surfaces. "I couldn't believe it... it was right there all along. Just beneath the floor plates at the base of frame twenty-three between the diesels and the e-motors—right where the message said it would be. I can't believe we didn't notice it. And how did it get there? That's the real mystery."

"I'm afraid I don't know who stowed it onboard, Chief," Rahn said. "I guess we'll never know how it...."

"*Abwehr,*" Beinlich said suddenly and everyone turned to face the navigator. "I know of one other instance like this."

"Well, are you going to share the details with us?" Thiele said when Beinlich seemed to hesitate. "Spit it out man or... do you think we can't be trusted?"

"Oh, I trust you, but it's obvious the agents working in the *Abwehr* believe it is best not to inform us of the details of our mission," Beinlich said smugly. "It was the same with Hartwig's boat in the Med. They were on their way back to La Spezia one night when they got a message that told them to deliver a package that had been taped to the top of the loudspeaker in the aft torpedo room. Sure enough, it was just where they had been told they would find it. They next thing they knew, they were paddling ashore to deliver it to some Arab camel jockey waiting on the Coast Road eight miles behind the English lines."

"But why hide it from the crew?" The Chief obviously was uncomfortable with the idea that after all his years of service to the *Kriegsmarine,* someone felt he might be a security risk.

"To keep it quiet, Chief, at least that's my guess," Rahn said reassuringly. "It's not that we can't be trusted. It's just that once a delivery like this is made, someone is going to talk about it. If the crew was briefed about it in advance and then, for some reason, the mission couldn't be completed, *Abwehr* couldn't try it again because of the possibility that some of the crew would talk about the details after returning home. This way, no one knows anything until the mission is about to be underway. Then, even if someone talks about it later, the mission had already been completed--no harm done."

"You mean if someone like Beinlich talks?" Thiele asked.

"What's the harm in it after the mission has been completed," Beinlich said. "In fact, I had two crewmen off Hartwig's boat tell me all about it."

"So what was the big secret?" Thiele obviously wanted all the details. "What did they deliver?"

"Nobody knows...at least no one on the boat," Beinlich said. "They never opened the package. Speculation was that it contained some kind of drugs or medicine. Maybe we were trying to impress the Arabs by saving a sick child while showing our contempt for the English. None of them ever knew the true purpose of their mission."

"We won't make that mistake. Will we *Herr Kaleu?*" Lamprecht asked. "We need to know what's in there. It's essential for the success of the mission. Don't you agree? Can we open it now?"

Rahn was surprised at how quickly he had been put in a difficult position. It was bad enough that he had suddenly been saddled with a dangerous and somewhat complicated mission. But now he would have to choose between divulging information that should probably be kept secret or telling his officers it would be best if none of them knew the contents of the package. All of them were now looking at him expectantly and he was sure he saw

Lamprecht lick his lips as though he were certain the mysterious box was filled with gourmet food.

"You can do the honors, Chief," Rahn said and his response created smiles around the table. "There is nothing in the message that tells us not to open it--and you're right, knowing the contents might actually improve the chances that we'll deliver it successfully."

The Chief moved quickly and after a short struggle with the fasteners, he removed the rubber wrapping to reveal a highly waxed, but otherwise nondescript wooden box about two feet square and one foot high. He released the double latches, reached inside and removed a waterproof folder, a small wooden box marked with an eagle and swastika and a larger box that all of them had seen before--a container for an *Enigma*.

"That's all? Are you sure there's nothing else in there Chief?" Lamprecht said and his disappointment was obvious.

"What were you expecting?" The Chief said as he tilted the box forward so everyone could see it was empty. "Fairies perhaps? Or maybe a nice little miniature woman... one-fifth scale, but fully functional?"

"She'd be just the right size for him," Thiele joked and added in his best female falsetto: 'Oh, *Leutnant* Lamprecht, it's so small.... we were made for each other!"

While the laughter and kidding continued, Rahn opened the folder just enough to see it contained several sheets of water soluble keys for decoding messages for the next couple of months. He snapped it closed and lifted the lid on the *Enigma* to reveal a brand-new four-rotor model for use in communicating with the new Triton code. Finally, he picked up the small box and released the single spring-loaded latch designed to keep it watertight.

"*Mein Gott!*" Lamprecht exclaimed. "There must be a fortune there... are we supposed to buy Florida real estate with that?"

Rahn pulled the wrinkled and used American currency from the box and spread it fan-like across the table. Although the money was far from fresh, it was arranged in an orderly fashion—at least fifty five-hundred dollar bills and what Rahn guessed to be twice as many one hundred dollar bills! Nearly 150,000 *Reichsmarks*— a veritable fortune by anyone's calculation.

"Our friend in Florida must have some very expensive tastes,"

Rahn said, but no one responded—they seemed stunned by the presence of so much cash. "Well, now we know what we're delivering. Obviously, the recipient is someone the *Abwehr* and *BdU* consider to be extremely valuable."

"It looks like a lot of money," Beinlich said, "but not enough to make me take a chance on putting my neck in a noose."

"But this guy is in America," Lamprecht countered. "He could just take the cash and run... maybe buy his own place, nice clothes, women...whatever he wants."

"I think we can assume this fellow has a sense of loyalty to the Fatherland... otherwise such an investment would not be made to continue his work," Rahn said as he quickly gathered up the cash and returned it to its container. He suddenly felt guilty about exposing the contents of the box--it seemed as though they had done something disloyal. "So, let's get this sealed tightly, just like we found it. And Chief, get us out to where we have at least fifty meters under our keel. We'll put her on the bottom and spend the quiet time working on the details. Dismissed."

Rahn's officers jumped to their feet with the enthusiasm of a soccer team heading out for the big match.

"Herr Kaleu," Thiele said as he followed the other conference attendees toward the hatch leading to the control room. "The entire crew regrets that you couldn't get your photo of the lighthouse this morning. We might not know why you want them...but if it's important to you, it's important to all of us."

"Thank you Number One. It's good to hear I have my crew's support." Rahn immediately regretted his sarcasm. It was obvious that Thiele was sincere. "Well, at least it sounds like we all may get a very close look at the St. Augustine lighthouse." He winked at his First Officer.

"I'm looking forward to it," Thiele said as he ducked through the hatch.

ST. AUGUSTINE: 0840 hrs.

As his speedboat raced past the *Naughty Boy*, Miller was tempted to give his fellow Security Council members an obscene gesture. But instead, he stood erect in the cockpit and presented them with his best *Kriegsmarine* salute. Over the past couple of weeks, he had grown so contemptuous of them that the possibility they would think there was something un-American about his salute was of no concern to him. In fact, he was thinking of wearing his old Imperial Navy tunic the next time he and Luigi went for a little cruise—he seriously doubted anyone would recognize it and if asked, he decided he would just say he used to be a bellman at the Ritz Carlton. He smiled at the mental image of the Security Council members nodding in agreement as he explained how rare and valuable such a bellman's uniform could become.

"Fools!" Miller shouted and the wind whipped away the sound of his voice.

Carbone throttled back as the *Lady Liberty* rounded the north end of Anastasia Island and encountered the choppy water coming through the inlet. The boat bobbed and rocked as he jockeyed it around a stretch of shallow water where a dark patch of sea grass danced just beneath the surface. Free of the shoal, he gunned the engine and the boat came up on plane once more, its bow cleaving the rollers that were struggling against the outgoing tide. He concentrated on thinking the boat through the turbulent water and only took a quick glance to the left to get a mental fix on Porpoise Point and the little hamlet of Vilano Beach. To his right, Davis Shores with its unfinished "planned community" was beginning to pass behind his right shoulder while straight ahead he could see the metallic framework of the channel marker buoy. For him, this was always the trickiest part of his and Miller's voyages to and from town. The buoy was notorious for shifting with the tide. On an incoming tide, the channel might be to the right of the buoy. An outgoing tide could put the channel on the opposite side. The big dredging project the Army was undertaking had so far failed to alleviate the guessing game that confronted the captain of every vessel coming through the inlet. He stood in hopes of getting a better view, his right hand reached down to grasp the wheel while his left kept his grimy yachtsman's hat pinned to the top of his head.

Miller, however, was looking over the stern where, in the distance, he could see the *Naughty Boy* coming on hard. Although they were too far back for Miller to see them clearly, he imagined that Cooper, Strickland and probably even the effeminate Coleman were crowded around Hank Duke at the heavy boat's controls.

Miller smiled as a plan worthy of Admiral Scheer suddenly formed in the military part of his brain—a sector that he hoped to exercise to its fullest during the next couple of days.

"Carbone! Full throttle!" Miller shouted. "Pass this side of the buoy!"

"I don't know....I can't see the channel there.... It might be too shallow!" Carbone hesitated—something that Miller had decided he would not tolerate.

"That's an order! I don't care what you think!" Miller's blue eyes flashed and his jaw jutted out defiantly.

Carbone could see there was no need to debate the issue. He dropped into his seat, slammed the throttle forward and lined up the jackstaff on the bow with the big buoy. In mere seconds, he closed the gap to the point that he could see the slimy barnacles clinging to the buoy's battered metal surface. Carbone felt that the boat was running out from under him and he pulled the wheel to the right just to see if the rudder would respond. When it did, he decided the new course was more to his liking.

"Closer! You idiot...you're going to run us aground!" Miller leaned over and shoved the wheel to the left.

"Shi.iii... tt!" Carbone yelled. He could count the rust-stained rivets on the buoy and then he closed his eyes. When the pain of being smashed against a metal wall didn't come...he slowly opened them and was relieved to see the open Atlantic directly ahead. Behind them, the big buoy bobbed in their wake.

"Nice work *Matrose* Carbone, Miller said. "Throttle back...we're in no hurry."

Carbone complied and the boat settled into a gentle chop beyond the inlet's churning waters. He took up a southerly heading toward home, but surprisingly, Miller told him to make a wide circle to the left. Back in the inlet, they could see the *Naughty Boy* slow as Duke considered the best course across the sandbar. Just as Miller had predicted, the captain of the *Naughty Boy* made one of the basic mistakes of the inexperienced sailor—he opted to abandon any attempt at nautical competence and instead, simply followed the same course as the boat in front of him. Carbone was surprised...Miller was simply amused as they watched the cabin cruiser swing toward the buoy and then come to a shuddering halt, firmly grounded in the shallows.

"That should keep them out of trouble for several hours," Miller said and Carbone swung the bow of their Chris Craft southward and advanced the throttle until the boat was skimming along just outside the breakers.

"Are those fellas idiots or just incompetent?" Carbone shouted above the roar of the engine and the wind.

"Both!" Miller answered. "But more importantly, they're irrelevant!"

ALHAMBRA HOTEL: 0855 hrs.

It only took Bill Spencer one phone call to the FBI office in Atlanta to get the information he wanted. The agent assigned to the Meyerhof case was refreshingly candid about the two prisoners being held in the Federal penitentiary: *Herr und Frau* Meyerhof were as innocent as new born babes—and everyone there knew it. Unfortunately, the folks at FBI headquarters in D.C. weren't about to let any judge turn them loose—the positive PR for the Bureau had been tremendous when the couple had been arrested. J. Edgar and his boys were not about to admit they had made a mistake. What was particularly galling to this agent was the fact that the Meyerhof's only son had been beaten to death by four Nazi brownshirts because he was dating a Jewish girl. That was why they had left Germany to live in the United States.

"Ain't that a killer?" the agent had asked and Spencer had to admit the irony was indeed in the "killer" category.

By the time he finished dialing the number for Deputy Director Frank Masterson, Spencer had finalized his plan for the coming evening. Unfortunately, he had to endure a lengthy period of ranting and raving before he could put it into action. "Yes sir...yes, sir...no sir," had been the sum total of his response to Masterson's thinly veiled threats about what would happen if the story of the Nazi agent were not confirmed one way or the other---especially now that an American destroyer and tanker had been sent to the bottom "right in your backyard" as he had phrased it.

"Sir...." Spencer finally tried to interrupt Masterson's tirade. "Didn't you tell me the problem with getting a fix on the transmitter's position was the fact the messages sent from it were so short?"

There was silence on the other end of the line and then Spencer could hear his supervisor grumbling to someone in the office. He couldn't make out the exact words, but Spencer guessed the man was complaining about the quality of the car washing he received from the elderly colored fellow. Or else he was ordering his secretary to remove the rest of her clothes.

"Yes, that's it basically," Masterson said finally, "The Brits say the broadcasts are short, coded snippets—probably a weather forecast. They need to get at least two fixes to locate the transmitter and so far the messages have been far too short for that to happen."

"So can you get a message to British intelligence to have their stations listen for a longer broadcast?" Spencer asked. "I mean, do we have that kind of relationship with them?"

This time the silence was total as Masterson considered all the implications of Spencer's request.

"Well, yes, I think so. But I would need some more information. I just can't order all the British spies to stop what they're doing because some junior G-man has a hunch. So Agent Spencer, what have you got?"

To Spencer, there was something in Masterson's tone of voice when he asked the question that made it suddenly seem that both of them were playing on the same team. Although he found it oddly disturbing, he decided had no other choice but to provide the information.

"I don't really have much to go on, but if it's anyone I've met so far, I'd have to vote for a man named Miller. He owns a bar and fishing pier just outside of town—*Uncle Sam's*—perfect cover don't you think?"

Masterson ignored the question. "So you don't have anything more than a hunch? That's not much to go on when we would be asking the British to spend some time looking for a secret transmitter instead of tracking U-boats and protecting their ships. I don't know if they'd go for that."

"Sorry, I don't have much more than that—at least not right now. But if they do pick up a longer transmission, I think it would just about nail the door shut on this case."

"Ok, I'll see what I can do—but I can't promise anything."

"That's all I ask," Spencer said. "In the meantime, I'll see what more I can dig up here."

"Fine," Masterson said. "And just when do you want the British to put their radio tracking stations to work for you?"

Spencer paused for only a second before giving his answer. "Tonight."

MARINELAND: 1110 hrs.

At first, Winnie tried not to listen to the talk going on among the staff at Marineland. As she had for the past two mornings, she performed Rufus' chores of cleaning the big filter in the pump house and making sure the rest rooms had toilet paper and towels. Mr. Whitney had told her again that she didn't need to do such a big job, but Winnie had insisted that it was not that much additional work and that it seemed to her that was the least she could do until a replacement was found for him. She didn't tell the facility's manager that deep down inside, she knew the work was also her way of belatedly repaying poor Rufus for being a good friend.

But it wasn't until mid-morning when she was cleaning the viewing ports on the beach side of the oceanarium that she finally realized what all the white folks seemed so excited about. She was working on the row of portholes on the second level when most of the staff came in and gathered around one of the picnic tables in the courtyard. Mr. Whitney said that in the interest of getting people's minds on their work and to end all the rumors that were going around, he would have Roy Tynes and Richard Campbell tell everyone what they had seen last night.

Winnie continued her work cleaning the thick glass. Directly below, she could see Roy and Richard seated on top of the table. She had never liked Roy, mainly because he frightened her. A big, muscular man from over in the Panhandle, Roy seemed to make a point of ordering her around at every opportunity. She wasn't sure about the details, but he had made some sort of discovery about jellyfish that seemed to impress all the other researchers. Richard, on the other hand, was a shy young man from somewhere up north whose approach to her had always been to act as though she were invisible.

As she continued to scrub, she listened as they told how they had gone all the way to Jupiter Inlet in hopes of catching a big hammerhead shark some fisherman had told them had been seen nearly every evening around dusk just outside the mouth of the inlet. Richard had started to explain why they needed a hammerhead for their shark repellent study, but Roy interrupted by saying "nobody's interested in that stuff." In his slow Southern draw, Roy then described how they had waited 'til dark for the shark to appear, but when it didn't they turned their boat around to head back into the inlet. That's when they heard "this hellacious explosion" and a big tanker went up like "every Fourth of July you ever saw all rolled into one." Richard took over the narrative and described how they had headed toward the flaming ship, but the heat was too much and the flaming oil was beginning to spread toward them. And then Roy described how a "big-assed" destroyer had arrived and how just a few minutes later, it also got hit by a torpedo and the "whole bow and bridge disappeared in one big flash"..

"We tried to get in close and pick up survivors," Richard said. "There was one man floating nearby, but we couldn't get him in the boat."

"That fellow was plum dead—no doubt about it." Roy added. "I reached down and got him by the arm, but when I pulled, all the flesh came off in my hands—nothin' left but a bone shinin' in the firelight just like peelin' meat off'n them ribs over at the Pork Pit."

"Roy!" Mr. Whitney shouted. "Show a little respect—that poor man died defending all of us. You could at least give his death some dignity."

Winnie decided she had heard enough. She started humming a tune and applying even more pressure to the rag as she scrubbed. The thought that something horrible like that could happen to Curtis was more than she could bear.

"*Lassiter.* That's what they told us. *U.S.S. Lassiter.*"

Winnie wasn't sure who had spoken, but there was no mistaking the words. For a moment, she thought she was going to faint. But the idea of collapsing in front of all those white people was so appalling that she struggled to retain consciousness.

"Sweet Jesus!" she blurted out and as she grabbed the stair railing to maintain her balance, she found herself looking down into a sea of white faces. "My brother's on the *Lassiter.*"

She started down the stairs, her knees suddenly shaking.

"Oh don't you worry none, there ain't no nig....I mean

coloreds... on the *Lassiter*," Roy said knowingly. "Them colored boys are only on battleships and aircraft carriers. You're just confused."

Winnie's despair turned to such intense anger that by the time she reached the bottom stair she was gripping the railing to keep from springing forward to rip the insolent smile off of Roy's face.

"I'm sorry, Mr. Tynes," Winnie said coldly. "But my brother is a Mess Steward second class, assigned to the *U.S.S. Lassiter*, a destroyer that's commanded by Captain McClure. You're the one who is confused."

Her comments shocked the crowd into silence. Some were stunned to hear a black girl put a white man, even a pain in the ass like Roy, in his place. Others were simply amazed that a black girl could express herself in perfect English.

"I wouldn't worry too much...miss," Richard Campbell said quietly. "We saw lots of lifeboats with survivors. In fact, I didn't know there were so many men on a destroyer until I saw all those lifeboats and life rafts."

"Thanks for reassuring me, Mr. Campbell," Winnie said with perfect composure, "but I'm sure you can understand how upsetting it is to think...to think...your brother may...be in trouble." She felt her determination not to cry slowly slipping away.

"Winifred," Mr. Whitney said in an obvious attempt to try to reassert some control over what had become a very awkward situation for him and his employees. "Maybe it would be best if you went home...maybe you can find out something about your brother's welfare. If you want, I can have someone drive you there."

Winnie quickly reviewed her options. It was an hour until the next bus... she could call the church and hope the reverend could come and get her...or she could take Mr. Whitney up on his offer, but then everyone at Marineland might find out she lived way out in the marsh. But when she suddenly remembered the unsettling thoughts she had experienced the previous night concerning Curtis' welfare, she knew pride had to take second place.

"Well thank you, sir. That would be wonderful if someone could drive me."

Mr. Whitney nodded and turned to face the crowd. For one awful second she thought he was going to tell Roy to drive her home, but then she was relieved when he selected Richard Campbell.

"Richard can drive you. He might be able to answer some of your questions about the sinking."

"That would be great," Winnie said. "I thank all of you for your concern."

As she walked toward the front gate with Campbell close behind, several people shouted encouragement. Winnie had to admit, that except for Roy Tynes, the employees of Marineland were pretty good people to be around.

MOSES CREEK: 1320 hrs.

Winnie would have been frantic if not for the calming influence of Reverend Fulmer. Instead of going home and burdening Granny Greer with the rumor that Curtis' ship had gone to the bottom of the sea, she had asked Richard Campbell to drop her off at the church. At first, she had been very brave about the whole thing. She had told Reverend Fulmer about what she had heard at Marineland and even added the part about her premonition that something had happened to Curtis. But after more than an hour of futile phone calls to Navy authorities, Winnie had suddenly burst into tears.

It wasn't until the reverend wrapped her in his arms in a reassuring embrace that she was able to stop sobbing. For a long moment, she clutched at him and for one of the few times in her life she felt completely safe and secure. Reluctantly, she pulled away from him and hoped that God would not punish her or Curtis because she had allowed herself to enjoy the reverend's touch.

"I...I wouldn't worry about it," Reverend Fulmer said. He tried to maintain his composure, but it was obviously a struggle.

Winnie couldn't tell whether he meant for her not to worry about Curtis or not to be concerned about what they had felt during their brief embrace.

"I'm sorry," she muttered and like a child, wiped a tear away from her finely chiseled cheek with the back of her hand.

Now it was his turn to be confused. Was she apologizing for her tearful outburst? Or, he dared to hope, was she apologizing for her feelings toward him? He wanted to ask her exactly what she meant, but knew he wasn't ready for the answer. It suddenly seemed to have become very warm in his small office at the back of the church.

"Well, let's keep working and see what we can find out about Curtis," Reverend Fulmer said and both of them seemed relieved to abandon their unspoken questions and to move on to something more tangible. "Unfortunately, the Navy won't help us with this. They wouldn't tell us anything even if we were white—they probably won't even admit the ship was lost. Are you sure those Marineland boys know what they're talking about?"

"They wouldn't have any reason to lie...and they were there when it happened." Winnie felt her anxiety returning. "One of them can be a disgusting redneck, but both of them agree they saw survivors who said they were from the *Lassiter.* I believe them."

"All right then, I'll make some more calls...maybe the minister of the AME church down at Melbourne knows something about it. In the meantime, you might want to go on home and check on your Granny."

"Yes, maybe you're right—Curtis is probably fine." Winnie tried to smile. "But I do really appreciate all your help Reverend Fulmer. I know you've got lots of work with Rufus' funeral tomorrow...prayer meeting tonight and all."

"That's all right Winnie. Rufus' service has been changed to Friday morning to give his father time to get here from up in the Carolinas. His mama wants a sunrise service down by the beach just like we did last Sunday and then we'll drive back here for the burial. It's a lot of effort, but that's the least we can do for them."

"I can sing at the funeral, I mean if you want me to...I didn't have time to prepare anything Sunday. But I will for Rufus, if you want."

"I'm sure his family would appreciate it...we all would. Maybe we could rehearse something tonight after prayer meeting," the reverend said hopefully and then realized she might have other plans. "Sorry...you're probably performing tonight at Uncle Sam's. You'll be working tomorrow...so it will have to be tomorrow night I guess."

Winnie could see the look of disappointment on the reverend's handsome face. She was pleasantly surprised that he was so familiar with her daily schedule.

"No, I think I'll be at prayer meeting tonight. We can rehearse afterwards." She immediately wondered what the consequences of not performing for Joe Miller might be—but the way the reverend's face brightened convinced her she had made the right decision. Besides, she needed the Lord's help to find Curtis and she was not yet convinced that singing in a bar was something that He would approve—at least not completely.

"Good, I'll see you tonight then." Fulmer said and stepped toward her once more, but this time Winnie backed reluctantly out the door and into the sanctuary. "And Winnie, when we're working alone like this I think it would be all right for you to call me Amos. That 'Reverend Fulmer' seems awfully formal."

Winnie wiped away one last tear and she wondered if it was produced by concern, relief or joy. "I'll try to do that Reverend...I mean...Amos."

As the Reverend Amos Fulmer watched the slim figure of Winnie Greer move down the aisle and disappear through the front door, he felt compelled to offer a prayer of thanks to the Good Lord who had brought this woman into his life. As an afterthought, he added a plea for forgiveness if his feelings toward her were improper or impure.

UNCLE SAM'S: 1440 hrs

Luigi Carbone was thankful that Joe Miller had opened the portholes and sliding glass windows of his office to take advantage of the soft sea breeze that gently rattled the papers on his boss' desk. Carbone enjoyed springtime days like this when the sun was bright and warm and the sea took on a sparkling blueness that reminded him of the only pleasant days of his youth that he could recall—days spent at the beach at Coney Island. Down below, the fishing pier stretched out lazily in the warmth, its sun-bleached wooden railing lined with anglers of all ages hoping to snag a redfish.

"Is that the last of it? Did you bring it all up?" Miller asked from his seat behind the big wooden desk.

"Yes, boss. I got it all." Carbone nodded toward the stack of boxes and canisters he had carried up from the storage room behind the bar. "That's the jugs of seawater...the sand...everything you asked for."

Miller stood and walked over to join Carbone at the big, open window. He breathed deeply and tasted the saltiness of the sea on his tongue. Yes, he had to admit, the office had never seemed more like the bridge of the old *SMS Nassau*—opening the ports had given it just the atmosphere he had wanted—he even allowed himself to pretend the pier was the forecastle of the battleship. The only thing missing was the massive Anton turret that housed the big eleven-inch guns. Despite the mental imagery he conjured up, he couldn't prevent the intrusion of the painful truth—that his beautiful old ship had been given to the Japanese and torn apart for scrap twenty years ago. The fact the she didn't even get an opportunity to scuttle herself with her sister ships at Scapa Flow was, for Miller, the ultimate indignity and another sin for which the cowardly Bolsheviks would have to some day pay.

"Here, I have another assignment for you," Miller said and thrust a piece of paper at Carbone. "I want you to secure these supplies immediately."

Carbone glanced down at the paper and saw that it contained one of Miller's detailed shopping lists. Each item was followed by an exact quantity by number, weight or volume: Grape juice (12 cans); sugar (10 pounds); coffee (5 pounds); flour (10 pounds); evaporated milk (24 cans). It was a long list with one extremely unusual item at the bottom – men's undershorts (60 pair, assorted sizes).

"Well, I can probably come up with the groceries, but I don't know about this last thing—sixty pairs of underwear?" Carbone pushed up the bill of his battered old cap and shook his head in disbelief. "Is there something you haven't told me about?"

"We need them for a special promotion I'm planning—I'll tell you about it soon." Miller said, but he wasn't very convincing. "If you have to go to several stores to get them, then do it. In fact, for the groceries, I want you to divide the list between the Quality Food Store and the City Gates Market."

Carbone rubbed his cheek as he studied the list.

"There's no time to waste on this." Miller said sharply and Carbone looked at him in surprise. "I want you back here in plenty of time for tonight's show—no socializing...just get the stuff and get back here. Understand?"

"Sure...sure, I understand. I ain't no dummy." Carbone had

never seen Miller in such a demanding mood. "It might take me a awhile to round up your underwear, but I'll be back as soon as I can."

"Please do." Miller watched as Carbone jammed the list into his pocket and stepped over to the open hatch in the middle of the floor. He could tell his subordinate was not happy. "Trust me, this is an important...mission. Our most important mission."

Carbone paused part way down the circular stairs, his head protruding through the hatch. "I'd say our mission is pretty damn obvious. I'd say we're having guests—lots of them."

"You could say that...but don't," Miller said, "some people might get the wrong impression."

"Aye, aye Cap'n," Carbone said as he snapped off a comical salute. "You can count on me."

"I know I can!" Miller shouted as Carbone disappeared down the ladder. He had wondered just what role, if any, he should plan for his assistant over the next two days. Now he knew the answer— Carbone would be a full partner in the endeavor.

With clipboard in hand, Miller walked over to the items Carbone had carefully brought up from the storage area to add to the collection of materials that had been locked away in the office. Prior to Germany's December declaration of war against the United States, Miller had been able to make monthly deliveries of intelligence data to the German consulate in Miami. But after its closure, he had been forced to stockpile the results of his ambitious espionage activities.

At first glance, the collection of cartons, bottles and cans looked much like what would be left on the street corner after a weekend of attic cleaning. There was the complete set of Army drawings for the St. Augustine Inlet dredging project—probably the easiest acquisition in his collection. A corrugated cardboard carton held carefully labeled bottles, each with a sample of sand taken from beaches stretching from the Georgia line to Daytona—the samples would provide valuable information for *Kriegsmarine* planners if an invasion force ever needed to be landed on the Florida shore. Stuffed with cotton padding, another box held a selection of American ammunition acquired during the Security Council's visit to Camp Blanding. There was also a technical manual on torpedoes he had stolen from an American destroyer during an "open house" at Mayport.

He was particularly pleased with the quality of his photo albums. In addition to a collection of warship photos, he had a complete set of images depicting the dock facilities, repair capabilities and weapons storage areas at the naval base. He also had taken photos of a new type of American tank that he had seen running around a test track at Camp Blanding. As he flipped through one album devoted to the various types of aircraft he had photographed at the Daytona Beach airfield, he couldn't help but smile at how anxious the owner of the local photo shop had been to process and print the photos for the Security Council. He had even thrown in an extra set for Miller at no charge!

The canisters of water he and Carbone had collected from the offshore Crescent Beach springs were a cause for concern--they were heavier than he had anticipated. But for some reason unknown to him, the water samples had been specifically requested by the *BdU* -- he had no choice about making the delivery. As an added bonus, Miller tossed into one box a set of tourist guides to the 17th century fortress *Castillo de San Marcos* that had guarded St. Augustine and its inlet for nearly 300 years.

As Miller looked over the results of his labors during the past four months, he couldn't help but feel he had indeed done something positive for the Fatherland and something befitting an officer in the *Kaiserlichemarine*.

1520 hrs.

FBI Special Agent Bill Spencer downshifted as he turned the FBI-issue coupe into the parking lot at *Uncle Sam's*. Just as he had hoped, there didn't seem to be any customers around. In fact, he had his choice of any parking space in the lot so he swerved into the opening at the base of the gangplank.

"OK, Scoop, you've got your story. Right?" Spencer switched off the engine and pulled on the parking brake. "We can't take a chance on scaring him off."

"Sure, Mr. G-man, it's a good story—and easy to remember," Pomar said as he opened the passenger's door and slid out of his seat. "And as far as I'm concerned, it's all true—it makes sense to me. Let's get started."

"Hey, calm down…there's no rush," Spencer said. "We'll just go in and calmly tell our story and leave. I'll set it up and all you have to do is follow my lead. Got it?"

"Got it, Chief. Let's go---but calmly."

The warm afternoon sun beat down on them as the walked across the parking lot and up the gangway leading to the bar. The door was open so they let themselves in and waited patiently among the overturned chairs stacked on the tables throughout the bar.

"Anybody home?" Spencer shouted, but the only response was the laugh of a gull and the sizzle of the surf just below the open windows.

"Not much security," Pomar said and walked over to the bar where freshly washed beer mugs were lined up to dry. "Maybe they all went fishing."

Spencer moved to the center of the large room and stood waiting for some sign that he was actually in a Nazi spy nest. But there was nothing out of the ordinary to see, hear or touch.

"Hello my friends! It's good to see you again!"

Miller's voice startled Spencer and Pomar. They had just come to the conclusion that they were alone in the building when its owner had suddenly and silently appeared. Spencer assumed the man had come from just down the hallway behind the bar, but admitted Miller could just have easily materialized out of thin air. In fact, Miller's long sleeved white shirt and black trousers gave the man a spiritual look—for a moment he reminded Spencer of the snake handling minister he had once seen preach up on Paint Creek.

"Hello Joe," Spencer said affably and reached out to shake Miller's hand. "We were just beginning to think we had this place all to ourselves. So where is everyone? Did you give them the day off?"

Miller's thin lips stretched into something vaguely resembling a smile. "Not at all. They won't report for duty for another half hour and Carbone is off gathering some supplies. Now…what can I do for the federal government?"

"Actually, I'm just serving as Scoop's driver. He's on the trail of a great story and I'm just trying to help him out."

"I can't imagine what kind of story would bring him here. Believe it or not, even music and partying can get a little boring at times."

Pomar didn't need a cue from the FBI man to know the time had come to dangle the bait in front of Joe Miller.

"Well, it won't be boring on Saturday--not with the entire Atlantic Fleet sailing past your pier!" Pomar said and he could see Miller's jaw tighten and a shadow seemed to pass over his face.

"I...I think you must be mistaken," Miller said and he placed one hand on the bar to steady himself. "Surely the Security Council would be informed before such a major operation would be launched. The Navy wouldn't just come steaming into town without letting us know they were coming."

"Oh, but they did...sort of," Spencer said quickly. "Show it to him Scoop."

"We got this over at the radio station this morning via good 'ol Western Union," Pomar said as he offered Miller the telegram. "I was going to call the chairman of your Security Council, but he and his friends are out chasing U-boats all day."

"Well thank you, gentlemen," Miller said as he slowly scanned the telegram. "You've certainly done the right thing in bringing this to my attention. I'll get this information to them as soon as they return—whenever that might be. I'm not sure where they were headed. Probably going down to...." His voice trailed off to silence as he read the note.

That moment was the most difficult one for Spencer and Pomar as they both struggled to keep from laughing at the look of concern on Miller's face. Originally, Pomar had drafted a short telegram that included numbers like '10 B-17's, 6 PBYs, 2 cruisers and 4 destroyers.' But Spencer said that although he couldn't tell Pomar the reason, the idea was to have as many letters as possible squeezed into the message. It only took a few minutes to make the required changes. The B-17s became Flying Fortresses, of course, and the PBYs were listed as Catalinas. But it was the names of the ships that gave them their greatest satisfaction. There was the *Chattanooga*, the *Minneapolis*, a destroyer called the *Malcomb McGillicutty*, the battleships *Mississippi* and *Tennessee*, and as an special bonus, Spencer had included an exiled Polish destroyer, the *Wzynilowsky* commanded by Admiral Sebastian Szerchikowitsky. Satisfied with the draft, Pomar had simply typed it on a blank telegraph form. After adding some Naval-looking acronyms and some references to security, they had an "official" telegram from the Office of the Secretary of the Navy.

"Yes, I see...." Miller said as he completed reading the telegram and handed it back to the reporter. "This is really important information. I'll have to copy this and get it to the council members immediately upon their return."

It was clear that something much more important was on Miller's mind and the distraction of the message was enough to make him forget about maintaining his Pennsylvania Dutch accent. His choice of words and the inflection in his voice convinced Spencer that the man might be speaking English, but he was thinking in the German tongue. As their eyes met, Spencer suddenly had the uncomfortable feeling that Miller was somehow reading his thoughts.

"Nah, you just go ahead and keep that one," Pomar said.

"Hell, yes!" Miller said with an enthusiasm that seemed oddly out of place. "We better get ready to welcome our guests! I know they can't get a battleship into Matanzas Bay, but every ship will be sending their captain's launch to pay their respects and pick up some beer."

"I don't know about that," Spencer said quickly. "But I do know we have to go. I have to meet Sheriff Hartson in a few minutes. He wants to show me around Lincolnville--wants me to compare his colored district with what I'm familiar with up in D.C." He glanced at Miller and was relieved to see that although the man was looking at them, his thoughts were obviously elsewhere. Berlin maybe? It wasn't until his guests began moving toward the door that Miller seemed to notice them again.

"Thank you boys from coming by...that's really good news!" Miller escorted them out on to the deck and herded them toward the ramp leading down to the parking lot. "I tell you, it makes you proud to be an American just to know that fleet is coming down. It's about time they ran those U-boats away."

"U-boats?" Spencer said jokingly. "I thought there was only one. Are you Security Council guys keeping information from the FBI?"

"Of course not," Miller said and mechanically gave Spencer' shoulder a squeeze. "But you know how those goddamn Krauts are...those bastards are bound to have several subs out there—but that just means more targets for our fleet when it gets here."

"Damn right!" Scoop said.

"Hey, does your mama know you use that kind of language?" Spencer asked and then turned to Miller. "I can't take him anywhere. See you later Joe."

When they reached their car, Spencer and Pomar looked up to see Joe Miller give them a quick wave and then hurry inside.

"Jeez," Pomar said. "Do you still think he swallowed our story?"

Spencer glanced up to where the huge American flag snapped in the springtime breeze and smiled. "Hook...line...and sinker."

U-112: 1550 hrs.

The news that U-112 would be making actual physical contact with the American mainland sent a wave of excitement through the boat. Coming on top of the sinking of the tanker and destroyer, the realization that they had been selected for such an important undertaking was just what was needed to delay the increasingly evident conclusion among the crew that it was time to go home. All that was needed was the official recall message from Dönitz and they would be on their way to Lorient and then a train ride to Germany—a destination each man on board had begun to believe only existed in his dreams.

"So, that's it then," Rahn said as he leaned back against the wood paneled bulkhead, stretched his arms, flexed his fingers and stifled a yawn. "Any questions?"

The boat's officers looked down at the charts and notes scattered on the wardroom table among their coffee-stained mugs and several now-empty sardine cans. They had spent more than two hours discussing and planning the landing operation. Except for Thiele, who was openly disappointed he would not lead the landing party, everyone seemed pleased with the results.

"*Nein, Herr Kaleu,*" said Beinlich. "I think we have done an excellent job of planning. There should be no problems."

Rahn acknowledged his navigator's comment with a glance— nothing more. It was obvious to him that Beinlich was now trying to be more...agreeable. Probably, Rahn thought, because a return to home and the filing of reports on crewmembers' performance were not far away. Rahn had already decided this would be his last

206

patrol with Beinlich. It wasn't that the man was a failure as a navigator... far from it. For Rahn, the problem was that Beinlich's presence was an irritant, like having something stuck in a tooth and to put up with that sort of irritation for weeks on end was simply...unbearable. For a brief moment, he allowed himself to fantasize about Beinlich alone with a gun to his head and Rahn's performance evaluation in his hand. But then he realized that his navigator was not someone who would take his own life over a bad report. More likely, the man would launch some sort of appeal and a counterattack that would claim that Rahn had endangered the crew with his picture taking. So be it, Rahn thought, it will be worth it to be rid of this jackass.

"All right then," Rahn said. "We'll meet at the same time tomorrow to finalize everything. It should be a simple task...get in there, exchange goods and get out. Simple. Right?"

"*Jawohl, Herr Kaleu*....no problems...a simple job..." A chorus of positive comments came from U-112's officers as they took Rahn's cue that the meeting was over and headed back to their duty stations.

"Hey Thiele!" Lamprecht shouted as he headed down the passageway to the control room. "Don't look so glum...I'll bring you some fresh oranges. I'll pick them myself!"

"Kiss my ass." Thiele's response was good-natured, despite his disappointment.

"You won't find any oranges on the trees," Beinlich stated flatly. "The harvest was over two months ago."

"All right then, I'll just go to the market and buy some," Lamprecht responded in a cheerful voice. "And while I'm at it...I'll pick up a personality for you—maybe a good American one. No need to thank me."

Laughter rattled through the boat at Beinlich's expense.

Only the Chief remained at the table with Rahn. It was obvious from the thoughtful way that Augie Wieland stroked his beard that something was troubling him.

"A flaw in our plan Chief?" Rahn asked.

Wieland shifted his seat and his mouth formed a reassuring grin. "No...no flaws. As usual, you have everything under control. It's another message that I'm concerned about...one that will soon be overdue."

"The rendezvous message? Where to meet the *milchkuh?*"

Wieland's face brightened as he realized that the seeds he had planted in Rahn's brain concerning their supply situation had apparently taken root.

"Precisely, *Herr Kaleu.* Our fuel reserves are down to eighty tons and although Smutje is doing a good job of covering it up, he tells me that in about three more days, we will have nothing but canned goods for food. There's only a little flour left...the few remaining lemons are covered with a gray, fuzzy mold...a completely different strain than we found on the bread."

"OK, Chief...I understand...and I have faith that BdU is aware of our situation and have sent a supply boat for us. It's just a matter of time...we'll get the recall message any day now."

"But our current operations along the coast, *Herr Kaleu*, are not conducive to conserving...."

Rahn cut him off with a wave of his hand. "I know that Chief. I'm changing our tactics. Tonight, we'll run at slow speed away from the coast charging batteries as we go. I don't think the Amis will have any patrols out more than few miles offshore—if at all. Tomorrow we'll stay on top as long as possible, then run in close and put her on the bottom in a position where we can easily surface and make the run into St. Augustine after nightfall. Close to shore we'll be using the e-motors—no need waking up Americans with the sound of diesels."

"But the lighthouses... no more high speed cruising to get a good lighthouse photo?"

Now it was Rahn's turn to smile. "Just one more...the St. Augustine lighthouse tomorrow night. And I won't even need the telephoto lens for that one Chief."

"That's good. We were burning up a lot of fuel for those photos," Wieland said with obvious relief in his voice. "Not that I question your lighthouse photography mission. I'm sure it was well worth the effort."

"Not if I don't get home with the photos," Rahn said quietly. "And I can assure you, I intend to get us home."

"I'm sure you will sir." The Chief gave a nod and a casual salute before heading for the control room.

Rahn twisted his neck and could feel the vertebrae grinding. A massage, he thought, that's what I need. He glanced up at the clock on the bulkhead and noted the time—a little before ten in Germany. Kat would be in bed now, curled up tightly in the old pink quilt her grandmother had given her for her sixteenth birthday. As he closed his eyes and tried to remember the fresh, intoxicating scent of her hair, Rahn knew that if given the chance he would gladly exchange all of the money intended for the Florida spy for just one minute beneath that old blanket with her.

NAUGHTY BOY: 1945 hrs.

Sundown found the *Naughty Boy* drifting at the edge of one of the many giant eddies created by the northward surge of the Gulf Stream. For the boat's intrepid crew, the day had been one of embarrassing and unsettling contrasts. For the first three hours of their cruise, everyone on board had been painfully aware of their exact position stuck firmly on the bar at St. Augustine Inlet. Even if the amateur crew had been struck blind, they would have still known their position—it seemed as though the town's entire population had come by in small boats or at least visited the sand spit just a few yards away to remind them that "you're stuck on the bar!" Fortunately, they couldn't hear the laughter their inept boat handling had sent rippling through the streets of the nation's oldest city.

Finally freed from the clinging mud and sand, they had spent the next few hours restoring their self-image of seagoing warriors as they cruised southward within plain sight of beach goers and the traffic along A1A. Turning at Marineland, they took up a northward heading that slowly carried them further from shore with each passing minute. By the time they had finished their late lunch, the reassuring gleam of the Florida coastline was far over the horizon and continuing to pull away from them. It was Jeremy Coleman who first suggested that perhaps they should return to within sight of land. Even though some of his shipmates had come to the same conclusion, none of them wanted to follow the suggestion of someone whose masculinity was so suspect.

At last, after another thirty minutes of northward cruising, Hank Duke put the wheel over to head for shore. It was at that exact moment that the engine had coughed twice, backfired and quit. Since that moment of sudden silence, no amount of tinkering, pleading or cursing had coaxed the reluctant engine back to life. The *Naughty Boy's* condition was now in sharp contrast to the first hours of their patrol—now none of her crew had the slightest idea of what their position might be.

"What now? Captain," Cooper said in a voice filled with sarcasm. "It'll be dark soon, we're lost and I don't see any way we're gonna get that engine going again."

Duke looked up at the gathering twilight and closed his eyes. After a long afternoon of almost constant bickering, the gentle sway of the boat and seemingly happy splish-splash of wavelets breaking against the hull seemed oddly relaxing. For one brief moment, he let his cares drift away and be replaced with....

"Didn't you hear me?" Cooper was now beginning to sound belligerent. "What are we going to do now?"

"Well Homer," Duke said slowly and opened his eyes to fix Cooper in a cool stare. "I reckon we could radio the Coast Guard station over at the lighthouse and tell them we need help."

"Sounds good to me!" The chairman of the Security Council pushed his way toward the radio mounted in the boat's cockpit. "Show me how to use this thing and I'll get us some help."

"He's right Hank," said Commissioner Strickland as he climbed the aluminum ladder leading from the deck to the boat's small bridge. "It'll be dark in just a few minutes. We've got no time to waste."

"And what happens if we radio for help? How long do you think it will take for them to find us in the dark?" Duke had had enough of babying his fellow members of the St. Augustine Security Council. "Besides, I think the last thing we need is to be picked up and towed in—we'd be the laughing stock of the whole town—if we're not already."

"I don't know about you Hank, but I'd rather be embarrassed than dead," Strickland said. "We can't just go drifting all night out here in the middle of nowhere."

"Of course we can—and we will," Duke said confidently. "It's going to be a clear night with no storms to worry about. The Gulf Stream will carry us north and by morning we'll be in the middle of the shipping lanes."

"Then what?" Cooper was unconvinced of the wisdom of Duke's attitude. "We'll still have to be picked up and how will you explain why we didn't radio for help sooner?"

"Simple. The radio will be ready for emergencies until just before we're picked up, then I'll disable it. We can all swear it didn't work all night. And we'll drain our fuel tanks dry as well. Our story will be that we ran out of gas chasing a U-boat all night." Twilight had slipped so far into darkness that none of them could see the smile on Duke's face. "Just think of the votes you'll get Jerry. I can see the headlines now— 'Commissioner Cheats Death Defending St. Johns County'. And think about it Homer, people will be lining up to enlist in the Defense League. The Navy will probably give a real fighting man like you your very own patrol boat."

Cooper and Strickland were silent as they both came to the conclusion that Duke's plan seemed perfectly logical.

"I'm cold...that wind is going to be chilly tonight," Coleman said from his seat in the stern. "I didn't dress to spend the night out here."

Duke couldn't think of anything Coleman would get out of this caper, but he was sure by morning he would come up with something. Otherwise, there would always be a chance the Chamber of Commerce's representative would squeal on them.

"Don't worry Jeremy," Duke said with more warmth than anyone on the Council had ever shown toward Coleman. "There are plenty of blankets in the cabin—and there's beer in the refrigerator. Why don't you help yourself to both and get comfortable? It's going to be a long night."

Coleman reluctantly stood and shuffled toward the cabin hatch.

"*Naughty Boy* from Coast Guard St. Augustine...Coast Guard calling *Naughty Boy*...over." The radio crackled to life and everyone on board stared at Duke in anticipation of his response. "Come in *Naughty Boy*."

Hank Duke leaned forward in his captain's seat and flicked the radio switch to the OFF position.

"We can't be bothered with that," he said loudly. "We're busy chasing one of Hitler's U-boats."

UNCLE SAM'S: 2155 hrs.

Tonight, Joe Miller had been far too busy to meet and greet his customers. As he worked at his desk, he could hear the music and laughter coming through the floor and when the Patriot Band launched into its final set for the evening, he could feel the vibrations through the soles of his shoes. He did allow himself to smile when he heard the protests over the early closing—it was always a good sign when customers had to be forced to leave. His orders to Carbone had been to have the customers out by ten and as usual, the little Italian diligently performed his duty. By five after the hour, the bar noises had been replaced with the noise of cars pulling out of the parking lot. It suddenly became very quiet in Miller's office—the only sound came from the radio in the corner that was tuned to WFOY. As it did every weeknight at ten, the station was broadcasting a 15-minute selection from the Glenn Miller Orchestra.

He took his time in setting up the *Enigma* for coding the message he intended to send this evening. First, there was the selection of the proper three rotors as prescribed in the monthly indicators book. Unfortunately, the formal declaration of war against the United States had put an end to the delivery of the books to the consulate in Miami. As a result, the monthly visit of the kindly German "tourists" who came up from South Florida to secretly deliver his copies had ended. He was therefore, left with no choice but to use the settings for January 1942 over and over again. Although he knew that such a practice made it increasingly simple for the code to be broken if his messages were intercepted, he had no choice—at least not until he got a new set of books. Hopefully, he thought, they would come in the materials to be delivered by the U-boat.

After completing the proper rotor setting and installing them in the *Enigma*, Miller had begun the lengthy process of configuring, selecting codes, adding a randomly determined security identifier and then determining the proper broadcast frequency. The tedious work complete, he then began typing in the text of his message one letter at a time and noting the corresponding coded letter that appeared on the *Enigma's* illuminated panel. He had only finished the first line of text when he heard a knock on the office hatch.

"Permission to come aboard sir?" Carbone's question was the same he always used to gain entry when Miller was working behind locked doors.

Miller carefully marked his place on his message coding before moving over to the hatch and unlatching its lock.

"Another busy night!" Carbone said as he came through the hatch and then helped Miller lower and lock it in place. "I love making money."

"What about the crowd? Did anyone ask about my talented new discovery?"

"Oh sure boss—lots of 'em." Carbone walked over and dropped heavily into the leather sofa. "Just two nights here and she's turned into a singing sensation. I've never seen so many white men interested in a little colored girl. She's on her way to fame and fortune, that's for sure."

"What I can't understand is why she didn't call today to let us know she wouldn't be here tonight," Miller said. "I'm giving her the opportunity of a lifetime—you'd think she would show me a little more...respect."

Carbone shrugged. "That's niggers for you. You want me to go look for her? I think I can track her down...but don't ask me to go over in that swamp where she lives. That place gives me the heebie-jeebies in daylight. I sure as hell don't want to go in there after dark."

"Don't worry...I have far more important things for you to do." Miller returned to his desk and prepared to continue his encryption. "This is the longest message we've ever sent and it has to be right. I want to transmit as soon as possible after I finish with it. How long 'til everyone will be gone?"

"The band's gone...went drinkin' in town. Sylvia and Marta are still washing some dishes, but they should be gone soon. That's everybody." Carbone yawned and displayed the results of a lifetime of poor dental hygiene.

"All right, first I want you to pull the last few sightings reports we've made. Then, I want you to get downstairs and make sure everyone is off the pier and on their way home. Then make sure the staff is gone. Tell them they can finish up tomorrow—kill all the exterior lights. That should convince everyone we're closed." Carbone didn't move as quickly as Miller desired. "Get off your can now! Get the reports, make sure it's all clear and then run up the antennae!"

"Yes sir!" Carbone said as he struggled to his feet. "I didn't know you were in such a hurry."

"Listen, Luigi, the next couple of days are critical for us," Miller said and his voice showed that he was struggling to regain his composure. "We can't take a chance on failure."

Carbone had never before heard his boss use such a life-and-death tone of voice.

"Sure boss, you know you can count on me. I don't suppose you want to tell me what 's so impor..."

Miller silenced his subordinate with a raised hand as he tried to hear the news bulletin on the radio. Without having to be told, Carbone stepped over and turned up the radio's volume.

"...We repeat, WFOY has learned from the Coast Guard that the boat carrying Security Council members Homer Cooper, Jerry Strickland, Henry Duke and Jeremy Coleman is overdue and is presumed missing. The boat, the *Naughty Boy*, was due back by four this afternoon after patrolling for enemy submarines. The local Coast Guard office will be organizing a search effort in the morning at the City Marina. Boat owners are encouraged to assist."

"Congratulations Boss!" Carbone said gleefully and he turned down the radio's volume. "It sounds like you may be the only remaining member of the Security Council—now we can really get to work."

"No such luck-- they'll be back," Miller said. "They're too stupid to know how to use the radio and probably got themselves lost as well. They'll show up tomorrow—if not, we'll just have to carry on the Council's work. I'll be the chairman, of course, and you can be my vice chairman."

"I'm the man for that job," Carbone said proudly. "When it comes to vice, I'm the world's leading authority."

ANASTASIA ISLAND: 2230 hrs.

The Reverend Amos Fulmer never expected to be parked in the dark across the road from *Uncle Sam's*. But then he had never dreamed a girl could possess him the way that Winnie Greer had— he seemed helpless to her every suggestion. Prayer meeting had gone fine that evening and afterwards when they had picked out two songs for poor Rufus' funeral, Winnie had seemed so mature... so self-controlled. But in the middle of rehearsing *Rock of Ages,* she had burst into tears and for a long while he felt he might never see her smile again. Despite his best efforts to console her, she had wept uncontrollably and even now he wasn't certain whether her tears were shed because of the uncertainty about her brother or the fact the she may have jeopardized her career by not performing at *Uncle Sam's* –or both.

The only thing that seemed to bring her any comfort was his decision to drive her over to the bar so she could personally apologize to Joe Miller for her absence. His plan had been to simply pull into the establishment's brightly lit parking lot. Then he would escort Winnie through the sea of drunken white folks and up to Joe Miller's office where she would apologize. But during the drive from Moses Creek, he decided that approach was not going to work. There was a growing animosity against Joe Miller among members of his congregation, and he had to admit, he could easily understand their intense dislike for the man. Trying to explain why he was at *Uncle Sam's* or why the church's 1931 Ford was in the parking lot would be…impossible. So instead of the bold entrance he had imagined, he was parked in the dark like a common criminal while Winnie had gone on her own to make amends with the only man who could giver her a chance at true stardom.

When Winnie saw *Uncle Sam's* bright lights go out, she nearly panicked. What if they had closed because she had not shown up? What if Mr. Miller had lost a lot of money because of her? Would he be angry…or understanding? Would he just tell her to forget about auditioning for Cab Calloway? All these questions were swirling through her mind as she hurried up the gangplank only to find the doors to the now-darkened bar firmly locked. Determined to get in, she worked her way around the boardwalk in hopes of finding an unlocked door or some member of the staff to let her in. When that failed, she stepped back and looked up to where she could see light coming from the windows of Joe Miller's rooftop office. For a moment, she considered shouting at the top of her lungs in hopes he would hear her, but somehow that approach seemed a bit –unrefined. Of course, she could always go back to the church and call him on the telephone to say she was sorry. But that seemed too impersonal. She needed to see Miller in person and as she stared up at his office, Winnie suddenly realized she did indeed have access to the roof.

Uncle Sam's

The tide was coming in and the crash of the waves seemed much louder there beneath the boardwalk and up among the pilings supporting Uncle Sam's. Winnie wished she had a light of some sort, but she forged ahead in the darkness and forced her brain to filter out the sounds of nocturnal scurrying and splashing she caused with each step. Actually, she was surprised at how easy it was to find the piling with the metal ladder rungs nailed in place. Up she went, pulling her way up one rung at a time while focusing her full attention on the two faint stars framed by the open top of the access shaft. Halfway to the top, she had to rest and to take her mind off the disturbing feeling that the shaft was suddenly becoming much more narrow. She tried to remember every detail of the day Rufus had shown her how this climb led to the roof of what was then an abandoned restaurant.

When she finally emerged, Winnie took a moment to straighten her dress and push the cobwebs out of her hair before stepping gingerly over to the exterior wall of the office. It had never occurred to her that there wouldn't be a door—at least not one that she could easily find. Moving along the wall, she came to a narrow window that was tilted outward just enough to let in the breeze coming off the sea and which gave her an unobstructed view of the office's interior.

Winnie was just about to tap on the glass to get Miller and Carbone's attention when a sudden feeling of danger stopped her. She couldn't explain the sensation, but it was just like the time she was out in Granny's smokehouse fumbling in the dark for a can of beans. Although she had been sure she could eventually find them, something made her stop and light a candle and in its glow she saw the cottonmouth poised to strike from the very spot where she would have placed her hand in search of the beans. She still shivered each time she remembered the dry, rustling sound made by the snake as it slithered through a rough hole in the wooden slats.

Although there was no poisonous snake here, Winnie had no doubt that she was in the presence of something deadly. At first glance, it appeared that the two men were busily engaged in routine office work. But then she saw the long-range transmitter exposed by the opened doors of its storage cabinet. Several indicator lights and various meters glowed and even from her vantage point outside the window, she could clearly see the brass *swastika* affixed to the top of the control panel. Mr. Miller was hunched forward working with some sort of small keyboard attached to a lighted panel. Before she could study it in detail, Carbone stood suddenly and walked directly toward her!

Winnie turned away from the window and pressed her back against the wall. She could feel her heart pounding as the footsteps came closer.

"So how many U-boats do you think will show up?" Carbone's voice came from just inside the window, but Miller's response was muted by the wall. "That many! Hell, that's enough to sink the entire American fleet. You'll probably get a medal from Hitler himself." She could hear him shuffling papers on a desk that was obviously just beneath the window. "Do you think you could get Mussolini to give me some little reward? You know…maybe a billion gadzillion lira or something?" Miller's response was indistinct, but Winnie could tell he was angry and she heard Carbone mumble as his footsteps shuffled away from the window, "Yes sir, I'll have the antennae up and ready for you to send in the next twenty minutes."

Spies! Mr. Miller and that sleazy Carbone are German spies! For Winnie, the revelation was one that at first seemed simply surprising. But as she took several deep breaths to try to calm her nerves, the ramifications beyond the threat to America became clear—the two men on the opposite side of the wall were working to hurt Curtis if, please God, he were still alive. And what about her chances for a singing career? She felt ashamed for asking herself the last question—it seemed so selfish—and stupid when she realized her life was in immediate and serious danger.

Winnie waited until a wandering cloud drifted across the quarter moon before making her move. She pushed herself away from the security of the wall and hurried toward the opening in the roof that offered her only escape route. Halfway to safety, she tripped over an old tar bucket and fell heavily, the abrasive roofing digging into the palms of her hands and her bare knees. Worse, the bucket rattled across the roof and banged against the office wall.

"What the hell was that?" Miller stopped encoding his message and Carbone scrambled over to the window. For a moment, he thought he saw movement--a shadow absorbed by the darkness. But as moonlight washed across the roof, he saw nothing.

"Just a bunch of roof rats looking for a nest, Boss. Nothing to worry about," Carbone said, but he reminded himself that tomorrow--or at least the day after, he would have to check out that strange passage from the roof to the sand beneath *Uncle Sam's*.

ANASTASIA ISLAND: 2238 hrs.

Bill Spencer had assigned himself to stakeout duty tonight. He had pulled off the road just south of *Uncle Sam's* where he could get a good view of the parking lot, as well as the ocean. He sat with the windows rolled down and savored the sea breeze, the moonlight on the water and, until ten, the sounds of the *Patriot Swing Band* drifting on the wind. Shortly thereafter, the parking lot had quickly emptied as cars and pickup trucks headed north and south along the coast road. Left alone, he wondered why he had even come over here. What was it that he expected or even hoped to see? Even if Miller did transmit a message to Nazi Germany, he wouldn't be able to see it flashing into the ether. A few minutes later, the carnival-like lighting had snapped off and as his eyes adjusted to the absence of the dazzling light show, he had seen the girl come out of the undergrowth, cross the road and walk alone up the gangplank to *Uncle Sam's* front door. Spencer had watched her unsuccessful attempt to gain entry and then she had retraced her steps down the gangplank and disappeared into the darkness beneath the boardwalk.

The girl's appearance was a mystery, but not one that immediately indicated some sort of criminal activity. Because she didn't have a car, he guessed she was someone Miller had hired to clean up each night. Or maybe she was Miller's or Carbone's girlfriend—or both, for that matter. Whoever she was, Spencer decided to wait only until eleven-thirty for something to happen— then he was leaving. Fifteen minutes later, he saw the girl again, this time she was running and the fact that she was hugging the shadows at the edge of the parking lot meant she was trying to get away without being seen.

When she ran across the road and plunged in among the palmettos, Spencer decided to act. He climbed out of the car and walked down the road toward the spot where he had last seen her. The sound of a car engine starting caused him to break into a jog on the pavement and then with a grinding of gears and spinning tires, the Ford burst out of the woods and turned south, its headlights trapping the G-man in their glare. Spencer waved his arms in a futile attempt to stop the car and got a brief glimpse of the driver before he was forced to jump and roll into the ditch to keep from being run down.

As Spencer sat in the sand and watched the fleeing car's taillights fade from view down the long stretch of black pavement, he decided that the Reverend Amos Fulmer and Winifred Greer had a lot of explaining to do.

GEORGETOWN, GUYANA: 2310 hrs

Bill Spencer was not the only one on stakeout duty that night. Although they had been extremely skeptical of the American request to monitor the frequency used by a mysterious German transmitter, the staff of the Submarine Tracking Room had decided to comply. It was a scramble, but by 2200 GMT the request had been transmitted from their bombproof Operational Intelligence Centre in the Admiralty Building's Citadel in London to their network of direction finding stations. As a result, as Miller keyed in his message and sent it flying toward the big German Navy receiver at Nauen, it was intercepted not once, but three times.

The first to eavesdrop on Miller's wireless dots and dashes was the British Direction Finding station at Georgetown, Guyana. Elizabeth Price, the Women's Reserve Naval Service operator on duty there was the granddaughter of one of the original British traders working that part of South America. When her husband had gone on active duty two years ago as an officer aboard *HMS Ajax*, she was left with the choice of walking the seawall and waiting for his return or getting involved in the war effort. Enlisting in the WRENs, she had been selected for duty in Naval Intelligence and after a two-month training course in England, she had returned to her hometown as a section leader in the new Radio Direction Finding station at the old fortress.

On this night, the onset of the heat and humidity had kept her tossing and turning in her lonely bed and by ten-thirty she had decided to go to the station early. After a strong cup of Colombian coffee and a quick review of the evening's intercepts and directives, including a priority alert requesting the monitoring of an unusual frequency, she had relieved another WREN at the listening post an hour early. The girl, who was four months pregnant, gladly gave up her headphones to Elizabeth and headed out into the warm dampness of the equatorial night.

Elizabeth seated herself at the desk in front of the DF unit, slipped on the headphones and heard the usual hum and crackle. Checking several common frequencies, she remembered the Admiralty's alert. She flipped the tuner to the designated frequency and immediately her ears were flooded with the rapid beep-dit-dit-beep of a transmission that made the glowing green line on the cathode ray dial jump and dance.

"Intercept on three-one-seven!" She shouted into the telephone speaker in hopes that other DF operators would hear and be able to get a bearing as well. "Intercept on three-one-seven!"

She watched the circular cathode ray tube glow brightly as the antennae searched far out over the Atlantic to lock on to the signal at its strongest point. When it did, a single shimmering line suddenly bisected the screen. Immediately, Elizabeth rotated the glass cover until the thin metal wire embedded in it lined up perfectly over the bright line on the screen. Magically, one half of the line disappeared, leaving the remainder to point like an accusing finger in the direction of the transmitter. Quickly, she read the number off the scale on the outside edge of the glass cover.

"Got it!" Elizabeth exclaimed as she wrote down the azimuth. Based on past experience, she expected to have only a few seconds to complete the process. But this time the message was lengthy. She had time to double and triple check her numbers before the unknown transmitter operator decided his task was complete.

NOVA SCOTIA: 2311 hrs.

A similar process was underway at the DF Station at Hartlen Point, Nova Scotia, where the intercepted broadcast was judged to be the longest intercept in the station's history. The message's unusual length and the speculation about its source were topics that helped the staff forget about the snow squall blowing outside and the fact that they had now gone six days without once seeing a blue sky.

BERMUDA: 2312 hrs. (local time 0012 hrs. Thursday)

The third intercept occurred at the Royal Navy Dockyard in Bermuda where the technicians on duty actually cheered when the azimuth of the message was logged. There was no doubt that this transmitter was the same that had teased them for months with short broadcasts, usually not more than eight to twelve letters.

Despite their best efforts, they had never been able to get a good fix due to the brevity of the transmissions--all they had been able to determine was that the source was somewhere off to the southwest...somewhere between North Carolina and Venezuela. But now they were confident their reading, compared with those from other stations in the network, could easily identify the location of the phantom transmitter.

LONDON: 2355 hrs. (Local time 0455 hrs. Thursday)

Within the hour, the teleprinter in the Admiralty's Submarine Tracking Room in London had chattered out the bearings received from each station and these had been passed to the watch officer in the DF Section. Despite the technological sophistication of the DF system, the plotting of the results was decidedly low-tech. In one corner of the room, a large chart of the North Atlantic had been mounted on a wooden backing and the location of each DF tracking station was indicated by a small hole encircled by a compass. Whenever an intercept was made, a piece of black string was pulled from the appropriate hole and stretched across the chart at the bearing reported by the station. Where the strings intersected was, theoretically, the location of the transmitter.

It was all quite simple. The thread from Guyana was lined up on the bearing reported by the station and then stretched northward past the Windward Islands, over Hispanola, and up the Bahamas before crossing the Florida coast. The Nova Scotia thread ran down the board along the Atlantic coast, skirted the Outer Banks, and crossed the Guyana thread on Florida's northeast coast. When the Bermuda thread was pulled across the map on the reported bearing, its intersection with its companions left no doubt about the location of the source of the radio transmission.

"And the winner is...." The watch officer announced as he

leaned over to get a better look at the chart. "Saint Augustine, Florida. Could someone please call the mayor and let him know there appears to be a U-boat docked in his city marina?"

His comments added a bit of much-needed humor to the morning tea. The location of the "fix" was passed on up the line of command until it came to the office of the director of the Operational Intelligence Centre. After a brief discussion among the officers on duty there, the fix was sent to the folks who had requested it—the FBI in Washington, D.C.

THURSDAY
April 16, 1942

NAUGHTY BOY: 0215 hrs.

"What time is it?" Coleman's voice sounded childlike in the darkness.

No one was in a mood to talk, but Cooper glanced at the luminous glow of his watch in an effort to keep Coleman quiet at least for a few more minutes.

"Two-fifteen."

The crew of the *Naughty Boy* had been drifting in silence since WFOY had gone off the air at eleven. There had been nothing to discuss except argue about Hank Duke's decision not to radio for help and it had quickly become obvious that nothing they could say was going to change his mind. For a while, they had amused themselves with speculation about how the good people of St. Augustine would react to the news that nearly their entire Security Council was missing. But as time went by, the enormity of the sea and the smallness of their boat had drained the humor from all of them.

"What's that noise?" This time, Coleman had come out of the cabin to ask his question. His three shipmates had all elected to remain on deck rather than take a chance on being the butt of jokes about sharing sleeping quarters with the Chamber of Commerce's representative on the Council.

"I don't hear anything," Cooper grumbled. "Can't you shut the hell up? I was just falling asleep."

"He's right," Jerry Strickland said from the stern. "I hear it too---a rumbling sound."

"Diesels. Big ones," Hank Duke said from his perch in the captain's chair. "I've been listening to them for the past ten minutes. They're getting closer."

"Where's the flare gun," Homer Cooper said as he rose from his seat like an old bear coming out of hibernation. "Hank, you may be the captain of this boat, but I'm the chairman of the Security Council and I say we've had enough of this. Get our lights on…send up a flare…do something to get us picked up before it's too late."

"Or get run over!" Jerry Strickland shouted. "They're headed straight for us!" In the darkness, it was hard to make out details of the darkened ship bearing down on them from astern. She showed no lights and only her white bow wave made her visible until she came close enough for them to pick out the deck gun, the conning tower…

"Jesus! It's a goddam U-boat!" Hank Duke exclaimed.

U-112:   0220 hrs.

The American cabin cruiser had appeared out of nowhere. At first, there had been an argument on the U-boat's bridge about the identity of the white object drifting in the darkness directly ahead. By the time they had confirmed that they were looking at a pleasure boat bobbing helplessly, it was too late for U-112 to alter her course.

"Lamprecht! Get up here! *Schnell!*" Rahn shouted down the tower hatch and someone grabbed the second watch officer and dragged him from his bunk. By the time, he reached the bridge the twenty-millimeter guns were manned and ready.

"Engines all stop!" Rahn shouted and the roar of the diesels fell away to a faint gurgle. "Hit them with the light!"

"Number Two, tell them not to use the radio," he said and thrust the megaphone at Lamprecht. "Tell them if they use the radio, we will kill them."

The U-boat's searchlight sent a finger of brilliant white light to split the darkness. It swung wildly and then locked the cabin cruiser it its glare. They could see four men standing helplessly on the pleasure boat's rear deck.

Lamprecht's English was impeccable as he shouted out Rahn's warning about the radio. As an afterthought, he added a hearty "Hands up!"

Uncle Sam's

The four Americans now stood shoulder to shoulder, their arms stretched toward the stars. As they squinted their eyes against the intensity of the searchlight, it was easy for the U-boat men to see the *Naughty Boy*'s crew posed little, if any, threat to them.

"Number Two, take a boarding party over there—six men only. Thiele! You have the con…takes us along side," Rahn ordered and dropped down the ladder into the control room with Lamprecht close behind. He hurried forward to his quarters and quickly retrieved his pistol and stuck it in the pocket of his trousers.

"You have them *Funker*?" He asked the radio operator as he headed back to the control room.

"*Jawohl, Herr Kaleu*," Timm said. "Even if they just switch on their transmitter I'll know it."

"If they try anything, tell the bridge immediately," Rahn said and stepped back into the control room where the Chief had opened the weapons locker. There was a commotion as Lamprecht came through the engine room hatch with Seaman Kroll and Boegnik close behind. Chief Weiland took an MP-40 from the locker and handed the machine gun to Lamprecht who put the strap over his shoulder. Kroll got the next MP-40 and as he did he stroked its smooth surface and smiled like a kid who had just received the best Christmas gift of his life. He also took a Mauser carbine. Boegnik looked less than thrilled as he was handed two rifles and then they were hurrying forward after the boat's Number Two.

"Paulson, Meinhoff, and Weber get your asses in here!" Lamprecht yelled into the bow compartment. "Somebody crack this hatch we're going up."

Rahn was impressed. Lamprecht had done his homework—he had picked all four of the boat's fluent English speakers and the other two men were from the nine rated as "basic speakers".

"How big is she?" Augie Wieland asked as Rahn started to ascend the ladder once more.

"Not much bigger than a rowboat Chief. Come on up and take a look" he said cheerfully. "You too Beinlich—but first compute a dead reckoning course for St. Augustine."

One of the diesels began to throb as Lamprecht jockeyed the big *Atlantik*-class U-boat alongside the cabin cruiser.

NAUGHTY BOY: 0232 hrs.

"Are they going to kill us?" Coleman asked and when he received no answer he repeated his question. "Are they going to kill us? For God's sake somebody say something?"

"I don't want to die," Homer Cooper muttered. "I want to see Maude again."

"Shut the hell up! Both of you!" Hank Duke growled. As he stared into the blinding light, he was reminded of the redfish they often caught at night from the Matanzas Inlet bridge. It was basically the same process, shine a light on the water and blind them, then spear them while they were helpless. He tried not to think of what it must feel like to be punctured by cold steel.

The U-boat was so close they could smell its exhaust and hear shouted orders in German. Shadows darted on the edge of the light and there was a crash as a grappling hook landed on *Naughty Boy's* foredeck. They could feel themselves being dragged toward the steel monster.

Suddenly, the light flashed out and left them in complete darkness. Boots thudded on to the deck and as the boat rocked from the added weight of six U-boatmen, the four temporarily blinded Americans grabbed each other for support. Rough hands patted at them for weapons and someone who smelled of lemons and damp wool yanked Duke's .45 from his holster.

"Good evening gentlemen!"

Freed from the harsh glare, the members of the Security Council slowly regained their vision and saw that they were being greeted by a German naval officer. At least they assumed he was an officer, there was nothing about his appearance to suggest he held any special rank, but the way he stood with hands on hips and boots widely spaced on the swaying deck made him look like some modern day buccaneer—a man who was definitely accustomed to giving orders. He wore some sort of unbuttoned gray-green leather jacket over a black t-shirt and his baggy trousers were cinched tightly around his narrow waist by a brown leather belt. His dark blue peaked hat was tilted at a jaunty angle above a face that sported a scraggly black beard and a wide smile. He was flanked by two seamen armed with submachine guns and who looked at them with a mixture of curiosity and disappointment. The one wearing a blue and yellow plaid shirt nodded a greeting while his companion dressed in black overalls simply stared at them as though they were some sort of exotic insects.

"Perhaps you didn't hear me," the officer said. "Good evening." He held one hand up to his ear to indicate he was waiting to hear something from them. Frustrated, he rolled his eyes, held out his arms and like a symphony conductor, made a sweeping motion with his hands to draw a response from them.

"Good evening," the Americans mumbled in response to his coaxing.

"Now we're cookin'," the officer said. "It's so important to break the ice with a friendly greeting whenever you're visiting strangers. So now that the preliminaries are out of the way, would you mind telling me what the hell you're doing out here?"

"Fishing," Homer Cooper said quickly. "We're out here fishing for grouper."

"Ah, fishing are you?" The officer said in a mocking tone. "Well, where is your gear? I don't see any fishing gear. Hey, Pete! Do you see any fishing poles up there?"

"No, *Herr Leutnant*, no poles... no tackle...no bait," a voice from near the bow answered.

"So... you are telling a little fib now aren't you?" The officer wagged his finger as though chastising children. "You better tell the truth, or someone will have to be punished."

"Ok, you've got us," Hank Duke said good-naturedly. "We were really just out sightseeing and drinking when the damn engine broke. We've been drifting ever since."

"Now that's a little better," the German officer said. "I don't really believe you, but I can tell we're getting closer to the truth. Bob," he said to the seaman in the black overalls, "go check out their engine. Maybe we'll find out if they are telling the truth."

As the sailor squeezed past, they heard a crash come from the cabin. They turned in that direction and could see at least two of crewman from the U-boat rummaging through the boat's interior.

"What are they looking for?" Duke said. "Maybe we could help them find it."

The officer stroked his cheek with one hand. "I don't know. This is so embarrassing! I can't take them anywhere without them getting into some kind of trouble. Steve! What in the hell are you looking for in there?"

"Pin ups, *Herr Leutnant.* Especially Betty Grable—what a babe!"

"And you Darrell! What is the goal of your quest!"

"Nothing now, sir," the sailor said as he stumbled through the hatch clutching a wide selection of scotch, rum and bourbon bottles to his chest. "I've found just what we need!"

"Excellent!" He motioned toward the sub and the sailor known as Darrell began tossing the liquor bottles up to the waiting hands of the crewmen lining the U-boat's deck. "I hope you don't mind.... we're going flat out for home, but it will be another six days before we pull into port. The boys could really use a little liquid libation to speed us on our way."

"Consider it a gift," Jerry Strickland said.

"That's the spirit! Or should I say spirits? Damn! I should be a comedian," the German officer said with a happy chuckle.

Their conversation was interrupted by the grinding of the boat's starter. And then silence returned.

"Well, at least you weren't lying—that engine sounds terrible! It's lucky for you boys that we found you," the officer said.

"You Nazis think you're pretty clever," Homer Cooper blurted out suddenly.

"Now...now... old man. Don't you know better than to bring politics into a conversation with someone you barely know. That's definitely not a good way to start a meaningful relationship."

"Relationship? We're at war—we're enemies you idiot." Cooper spat the words out.

"Oh well, I'm sorry you feel that way old man," the officer said sadly. "And I thought we were going to be such great friends. That's really too bad."

"*Herr Leutnant!*" Pete shouted. "I think you'd better take a look at this!"

"Excuse me gentlemen," the officer said and stepped around his captives to where the sailor known as Pete had pulled back a sheet of canvas to reveal the .30 caliber machine gun and its ammunition lying on the deck.

"Oh dear Lord, we're in big trouble now," Coleman muttered.

"Shut up you little faggot!" Cooper hissed.

"Gentlemen...gentlemen," the *Leutnant* said as he shook his head sadly and looked down at the new Browning. "I'm afraid this changes everything! Here I was about to believe you were simply adrift, but now I find you are on a warlike mission—and with no uniforms, it appears to me you might all be spies. You named this boat correctly, you guys really are naughty boys."

"We're no spies..." Duke said. "We were just out for a little cruise...the gun is just for...for target practice."

The *Leutnant* ignored Duke's explanation.

"Normally, this situation would be simple to resolve—I would simply have you shot and then dump your bodies overboard for the sharks to chew," the officer said and shook his head slowly. "But damn it, I like you fellows. I know we've only known each other a few minutes, but, well, I felt something special from the first time I saw you guys and I can tell you feel the same way about my boys. So, I'm gonna take this up with our captain. Maybe you've heard of him—*Grosse Admiral* Ludwig von Harddick? He's quite famous—sunk more than a million tons of enemy shipping. No? Well that's him up there on the bridge. How about a wave?"

The four members of the St. Augustine Security Council found themselves inexplicably looking up and waving toward the big U-boat's conning tower. They could see an officer in a white hat wave in return.

"That's good— now that he sees how friendly you guys are, maybe I can convince him to at least let you try to swim for shore," the *Leutnant* said seriously. "Hey boys! Keep an eye on these friendly Americans for a few minutes – I'll be right back!"

A crewman on the U-boat's deck reached down and grabbed the *Leutnant's* outstretched hand and as the *Naughty Boy* rose slightly on the next swell, pulled him easily on board.

"Have a seat," the U-boat man known as Pete said and pointed toward the transom with the muzzle of his rifle.

The Americans sat on the wooden stern and each of them was left to contemplate the fact that his life could soon end.

"Where did you boys learn to speak such good English?" Jerry Strickland asked in an effort to break the painful silence.

"New Jersey," Pete said. "We all went to high school together in Teaneck."

The answer was so mind-boggling that, combined with the very real prospect of dying in a few minutes, the prisoners lapsed into silence. The sea rocked them gently and each American savored every second of life.

"Attention!" Pete shouted and the Americans struggled to their feet just as the *Leutnant* dropped expertly from the U-boat to the deck of the *Naughty Boy.*

"Hey, Bob! Any luck with that engine?"

"We'll see *Herr Leutnant,*" said the crewman in the overalls as he leaned forward and turned the key in the ignition. There was a rattle...a bang...and with a quick jockey of the throttle by Bob...the engine caught and began to purr happily.

"All right toss the popgun," the *Leutnant* said.

Steve and Darrell wasted no time in picking up the Browning and heaving it over the side where it sent water splashing over the gunwale.

"All right my friends, I did my very best but I'm afraid his mind is made up on this matter," the *Leutnant* said with deep sadness.

"Oh Lord no!" Coleman shrieked.

"That's right!" *The Leutnant* was now beaming. "We're gonna let you live!" He stepped over to Duke and handed him a small, folded piece of paper. "Here's a heading back to St. Augustine— our navigator is a pain in the ass, but he knows his stuff. He says you should be there by daylight."

Duke was stunned and could only mumble "Thank you" as he watched the German sailors scramble back on board the U-boat.

He moved forward with Cooper and Strickland close behind. Coleman was too overcome by the events to function—he clung to the flagstaff at the stern for support.

As a final act, the *Leutnant* stepped to the stern and with one quick jerk removed the American flag and its jackstaff from both Coleman's hand and its mounting.

"Just a souvenir—I hope you don't mind," he said.

"Well, actually I do mind," Coleman said defiantly and to everyone's surprise, reached out to reclaim the national ensign. "Give it back!"

"You sonofabitch!" Cooper roared and charged toward the German officer like an angry bear until the *Leutnant* stopped him in his tracks by raising his Luger and pointing it directly at the center of the council chairman's forehead.

"Old Man, I've had enough of your attitude, you tried to spoil our little party and that's well.... that's rude!" He shifted his aim three inches to the right, squeezed the trigger and fired. The blast sent Cooper stumbling away gripping his burned face and the radio transmitter sparked and blazed briefly from the direct hit from the 8 mm bullet. "Sorry, but we can't have you telling anyone about us."

The muzzle blast just inches from his ear was enough to stun Coleman into releasing his grip on the jackstaff. With the American flag over his shoulder, the *Leutnant* once more climbed aboard the U-boat. "We're going home now!" he shouted as the U-boat's diesels thundered. "Y'all be careful now you heah!"

Less than ten minutes later, the U-boat had disappeared heading due east into the darkness.

PARIS: 0300 hrs. (0900 hrs. local time)

As he did every morning, *Admiral* Karl Dönitz, commander in chief of U-boat operations, listened patiently to the reports presented by the six staff officers assigned to the Situation Room within his spacious new headquarters in an apartment building on the *Avenue Marechal Maunoury*. He was not happy with his new location. The old chateau at Kernevel had put him on the water with his men—he could see the boats under his command coming and going. Best of all, there had been almost daily opportunities to interact with the crews. But now he was stuck in Paris and all because of the damn British commandos who had raided St. Nazaire six weeks ago. Reluctantly, he had to admit that an enemy that bold would eventually find a way to strike the chateaux. BdU had no choice but to relocate. Regrettably, he had found the beauty of Paris in April to be no substitute for the sea and the U-boats he loved.

To add to his annoyance this morning, he saw that *Major* Schade, the *Abwehr* officer who had visited them on Monday, had returned -- the covert operations specialist was sitting on a folding chair in a far corner of the briefing room.

Dönitz's first impulse was to ask Schade to wait outside until the briefing was completed— allowing the man to sit in on what the *Admiral* considered to be a "family" meeting made him uncomfortable. However, that course of action would undoubtedly label him as "uncooperative" -- a designation that could have a serious impact on the longevity of one's military career. Next, he considered whether or not to let the outsider speak first and then simply excuse him from the room when he finished. While that approach had a certain appeal, Dönitz decided that appearing to give *Abwehr* priority status would just further contribute to the air of smug superiority that oozed from the man. Frustrated by the realization that he was wasting valuable time on a political problem, the *Admiral* simply waved his hand to indicate it was time to begin.

"*Danke, Herr Admiral*," said *Kapitan zur See* Godt, *BdU* Chief of Operations. He quickly arranged some briefing papers and then launched into his summary of the previous night's activities.

"Contact with the enemy during the past twelve hours has resulted in the sinking of two freighters from a small convoy north of Spitsbergen that is bound for Murmansk—the ice is breaking up nicely, Herr Admiral. We have twenty-two boats in the Atlantic, eight in the Med and three in the Baltic. No losses reported. Three boats are being withdrawn due to various mechanical problems and, I'm afraid, the supply needs of two boats operating in American waters will soon reach a critical stage. A-1, your report please."

The First Operations Officer provided the details on each of Godt's comments and then followed up with a discussion of the location of all known Allied convoys and their relation to existing U-boat Wolfpacks. He completed his ten-minute presentation with a summary of the current situation at each of the French bases and a quick review of boats that were returning and those departing for action.

The A-2 had an annoying habit of giving far more detail to his report than was necessary. Responsible for U-boat escorts, minefields and other support services, he seemed compelled to spice up his somewhat mundane subject matter with details that were obviously selected on the basis of their human interest content rather than their overall use in assessing and planning future strategy. When he finally finished, it was the Intelligence Officer's turn and as the young officer rose to speak, Dönitz noticed the man from *Abwehr* shifted uncomfortably in his seat.

"*Herr Admiral*, if you don't mind, I would like to change the order of my presentation somewhat this morning," *Oberleutnant der* See Bergmann said and adjusted his wire-rimmed spectacles. "I have the report on suspected sabotage by French workers for you to review, but I would like to discuss a rather remarkable message received last night from the agent we discussed on Monday—the one in Florida."

Dönitz nodded his assent and the officer removed a yellow message sheet from a folder before continuing.

"Sir, this agent reports that a major American fleet movement will take place tomorrow along the East Coast of the United States," he paused briefly for effect. "According to him, there will be several battleships passing the Florida coast, as well as a large number of aircraft and...let's see, oh yes, the Polish destroyer *Wzynilowsky*, commanded by an admiral named...excuse me..." Bergmann said and flipped through his notes. "Ah, yes, here it is... *Admiral* Szerchikkowitsky, first name Sebastian."

"Remarkable," Dönitz said. "Is this information reliable?"

"I can answer that," Schade said from his seat in the corner. "*Abwehr* has the utmost confidence in this agent. As I mentioned in our previous meeting, his reports have always proved to be correct and..."

"I can assure you this report is horribly flawed," the intelligence officer said with poorly concealed glee. "In fact, it is pure fantasy."

"I beg to differ, our Florida agent is always right." The major's retort was delivered with arrogant conviction. "I would have to say your analysis is in error."

"Error? I suppose we are to believe the American battleship *Tennessee* will somehow lift herself out of the mud at Pearl Harbor where she was put by our Japanese friends and steam ten thousand miles to Florida by tomorrow afternoon?" Bergmann smiled crookedly. "Or perhaps, you think we should get ready to attack the cruiser *Piscattaway*—a ship, that according to our records, has never existed."

"Well, perhaps your records need a little updating, *Leutnant*." Schade remained convinced of the accuracy of the message. "Our agent may have the wrong names for these ships, but there is no doubt about the basics of his message."

"And the Polish destroyer, the…" the *Leutnant* had to check the name from the message before continuing. "…the *Wzynilowsky*--a ship that is unknown in the Polish Navy as is its commander, the man Szerchikkowitsky. We have all the Polish Navy's records…as well as all of their surviving officers…and not one of them has ever heard of this ship or its captain. In fact, we have a Polish-speaking officer on our staff and he says there are no names like those in their language. He suggests someone with no real knowledge of Polish simply made them up."

"But such a lengthy message, he would not have sent a message of that length had he not been certain of the facts." For the first time, Schade seemed to have lost some of his self-confidence.

Kramer, the communications officer, could no longer watch the dispute from the sidelines. "Perhaps the message was a ruse. It may have been planted in order to see what he would do with it. It's not unlikely that an English tracking station was somehow waiting and listening for the message just to see if he would send it."

"And this is the agent that *Eins-eins-zwei* is scheduled to contact tonight?" Dönitz asked and everyone in the room nodded an affirmative.

"*Jawohl, Herr Admiral*," Bergmann said. "That is our concern. If this message is some sort of …plant … it could mean the Americans have identified the agent and they are trying to lure our boats into a trap."

"But if the message is accurate as we believe it to be," Schade said, "you will be missing an important opportunity to strike a blow for the Fatherland."

"And, Herr Admiral, may I remind you of our current situation," Bergmann interjected. "U-112 is already positioned to make the rendezvous. We have them ready to make the run in to St. Augustine tonight."

The implications were immediately apparent to Dönitz—risk the lives of a crew and a valuable boat by sending them into a possible trap or decline an opportunity to pick up unique intelligence information that could lead to more victories and even help save other crews.

"*Major* Schade," Dönitz said. "Perhaps you could tell us what is so important about what this agent has to offer. And don't bother being evasive like you were the last time I asked this question. I have to have a good reason to risk the lives of one or my crews."

"*Herr Admiral*, our agent has always provided us with remarkably accurate and valuable information about American military preparations on their southeastern coast, as well as weather bulletins that have proven to be essential for long range forecasting in the North Atlantic." Schade paused long enough to see that Dönitz had not yet been firmly convinced of the agent's value. "He has a number of documents and items that we can only obtain through direct contact, plus there are two canisters requested by the *Kriegsmarine's* very own research section."

"Canisters?" Dönitz asked. "Containing what?"

"Seawater." Schade's reply caused a moment of incredulous silence around the conference table.

"Seawater? Seawater?" Dönitz said. "In case you haven't noticed, there are oceans full of seawater—we can get that anywhere. What makes this seawater so special?"

"I'm not privy to that information, but I can assure..."

"*Herr Admiral*, I believe the seawater is undoubtedly part of *Project Aquarius*," Bergmann said, " – an effort to provide hiding places where U-boats would be undetected by enemy listening devices. Something like the salinity layers our boats use to slip past Gibraltar."

Dönitz was surprised he had not heard more about the project, but then realized that because of operational demands on his command he had abandoned his weekly research briefings months ago. He had ordered that the staff was to only inform him when a new development was ready to be tested at sea—not while it was being studied. Obviously, *Project Aquarius* had not advanced to that stage.

"And what is it we are offering in exchange for this miraculous seawater?"

"*Enigma* keys for one," Schade said and then stood slowly as though he intended to take over the briefing. "When we declared war on America, we were no longer able to send him the monthly keys. As a result, he is using the same keys over and over again. The security measures we have in place ensure the code cannot be broken, especially with the new four-rotor model. But if he keeps transmitting with the same code, even the Americans will be able to solve it. Plus, without the four-rotor, he cannot transmit or receive our new *Triton* code. And of course, *Herr Admiral*, there is the money."

"Money? We are running a banking service?" Dönitz asked.

"We provide the American currency needed to operate his business, purchase information, whatever needs to be done."

"But counterfeit money will eventually be discovered and it will be traced to our man—what's the point in that?" Dönitz suddenly realized there was much to this spy business that he didn't know about.

"That's not a problem, *Herr Admiral*, the money is genuine," Schade said proudly. "We have a virtually endless supply of good ol' Uncle Sam's currency. It is made available through the German subsidiaries of major American corporations. You'd be amazed at how profitable American businesses can be here in Germany—even in the midst of a war."

Dönitz knew he had the facts and the decision on whether or not the rendezvous would take place would be his alone to make. All the pieces were already in place and although he did not have time to study the details of the benefits to be achieved by making contact with this agent, he had to accept the fact that if it were not vitally important it would not have come this close to fruition.

"All right then," he said quietly. "What are the risks to Teddy Rahn and his crew?"

"I'll answer that one," Bergmann said. "The American defenses are virtually non-existent. And even if by some miracle the agent's report on the approaching American fleet is correct, U-112 should be in and out hours before they arrive—or Teddy Rahn can wait and take a shot at them."

Dönitz knew the success of the mission was dependent on more factors than simply avoiding an enemy fleet. There could be navigation problems, U-112 could run aground or the Americans could capture the landing party. But, he thought, the odds of any of those events taking place would be greatly increased if the right person were in charge of U-112 and as far as he knew, Teddy Rahn was just the level-headed no -nonsense kind of man who could pull it off.

"Excuse me, *Herr Admiral*," said Kramer. "But it has been *Kapitanleutnant* Rahn's habit in recent days to dive just after sunrise and spend the day on the bottom. I feel certain that will be his tactic today—put her on the bottom somewhere near St. Augustine. If we are to contact him, we should do it quickly before he gets to a depth that even the *Goliath* cannot reach."

"If I might add one more bit of information, *Herr Admiral,*" Schade said, "the agent in Florida is a former *Kaiserlichemarine* officer. He served on the *Nassau* throughout the war and his motivation for his work seems to be based on his continued loyalty to the old Imperial Navy. I am not authorized to do so, but I will tell you his name is Joachim Mueller. Perhaps you knew him?"

"No, but then I didn't know many surface ship officers," Dönitz said, "but I can understand his affection for the Kaiser's Navy. Back then, our role was much easier to define and politicians stayed where they belonged." Suddenly aware that he had probably said too much, Dönitz sighed. "All right then, we'll let Rahn make the rendezvous, but let him know of the possibility of an approaching American fleet. He can use his own discretion in the matter, but it's time for U-112 to be thinking of home."

"*Jawohl, Herr Admiral.* I will write and transmit the message personally—and I'll include your personal best wishes," Kramer said.

U-112: 0430 hrs.

Kat's soft, golden tresses were spread fan-like across the blue silk pillowcase and her exquisite face looked up at him with an expression of barely controlled passion. Her green eyes seemed to glow in expectation and her full lips formed words he could not hear. He moved closer and her eyes seemed to be pleading for him to join her. Her naked arms reached out to him…he could feel her touching his shoulder. What was she saying? What was it that she….

"*Herr Kaleu. Herr Kaleu*…sir."

Rahn's eyes snapped open and he found himself staring directly into the face of his alarm clock whose luminous hands had arranged themselves to indicate 1030 a.m. Berlin time.

"Sorry, *Herr Kaleu,* but you said to wake you if something important came in."

Rahn suddenly realized the fingers probing his shoulder belonged not to Kat, but to *Funkmatt* Timm.

"Yes, I'm awake," Rahn mumbled without moving from his fetal position facing the small section of wood paneling affixed to the bulkhead in his tiny cabin. "What is it?"

"An officer-grade message sent directly to us from *BdU*— perhaps it is information that you need right away?"

"Yes, perhaps so," Rahn said as he slowly moved to a sitting position on the bunk and rubbed the back of his neck with one hand as he tried to make the transition from dream land to reality. "Do you have the *Enigma* set up?"

"*Jawohl, Herr Kaleu,* whenever you are ready."

"Very good." Rahn said. "I'll be right with you."

Timm backed awkwardly out of the cabin and let the privacy curtain fall back into place.

Rahn punched the off button on the alarm clock to prevent it from ringing in another hour and then took a brief moment to gather his thoughts. The perpetual throb of the diesels helped ease him into motion and the gentle sway of the boat set the rhythm for the coming morning. Swinging his legs over the edge of the bunk, he slid forward and his feet tucked into his waiting deck shoes. He pushed his hair back with both hands before turning on the faucet of his washbasin and splashing his face with cold saltwater. The shaving mirror revealed an old, tired man...a man he barely recognized.

"*Mein Gott,*" Rahn muttered, "I need to go home to my wife." Picking up his officer's key book from his desk, he slid the curtain wide and stepped across the passageway to where Timm sat reading a paperback that featured a colorful depiction of a cowboy gun duel on its cover. The funkmaat had adjusted his headphones so that one ear was uncovered to hear orders and gossip from within the boat while listening for messages from *BdU* with the other.

"Good morning, *Herr Kaleu!*" Timm said cheerfully as he looked up from his reading. "Here's the message pad and I've already set up the *Enigma* for today—just enter your key. How about some coffee sir? I think Smutje has a fresh pot ready."

"Thanks. Coffee would be perfect."

Timm stood, squeezed past Rahn and headed forward to the galley. "I'll be right back, *Herr Kaleu.*"

Rahn settled into the radio operator's warm seat and placed his officer's key next to the *Enigma*. Checking the key for the day, he dialed in the proper settings and inserted the designated plugs. He quickly began entering the coded message from the *funkmaat's* pad and writing down the solution as each de-coded letter lit up on the machine's display panel.

By the time Timm had returned with the mug of steaming coffee, he had completed about one-third of the decoding of the go-ahead message for the visit to Florida. He took a sip of the coffee and without saying a word returned to de-coding process.

It was a short message with a warning that Rahn intended to keep in mind:

Offizier
To: RAHN
Rendezvous confirmedX
American battle fleet may arrive in area afternoon 17.4X

"Good news Sir?" Timm asked.

Rahn looked up and smiled at the radio operator who had followed up his question with a look of innocent curiosity. He knew the young man wanted desperately to be the messenger who delivered the latest news to the rest of the crew.

"I don't know if it's good or not," Rahn said. "But I think you can safely say that we are off to a big adventure. I'll give the crew the final details later today."

"*Jawohl, Herr Kaleu...* that's exciting news," Timm said with ill-concealed excitement. "Well, I'll let you get back to the message. If you need more coffee, just let me know sir."

"Thanks. I'm fine." Rahn shook his head and grinned as he realized the *funkmatt* had already headed forward to the crew's quarters to inform them they were indeed going to have some excitement.

It only took a couple of minutes to complete the decrypt :

God Speed to You and U-112X
Signed: Dönitz

Rahn grinned. He had already decided that he had no intention of running into an American fleet--it was time to go home. Thankfully, the Big Lion's closing had implied his support for such a decision. Not a warlike "Good Hunting" but instead a message of closure... "God Speed"--coming home.

ST. AUGUSTINE: 0505 hrs.

The tide was running high and despite the pre-dawn darkness, Hank Duke had no trouble bringing the *Naughty Boy* through the inlet. It was just a few minutes past five in the morning when he edged up to slip number eight in the city marina. As soon as Jerry Strickland and Jeremy Coleman hopped down to the dock and tied them off, Duke shut down the engine. For the four men, the sudden silence seemed deafening.

"Where's our Welcome Home banner?" Coleman joked as he quickly gathered up his gear and prepared to head up the marina's gangway. "I thought they would at least have the high school band out here to welcome us home."

"I don't know about the rest of you fellas, but I don't need an audience," said Jerry Strickland. "I just want to get home and get a hot bath. Then I'll draft up a statement and get back down here to meet the press—how about nine o'clock? Is that OK with the rest of you?"

"I don't give a damn what you do Jerry," Homer Cooper muttered as he eased his way down from the *Naughty Boy* to the dock. "I've had all the combat I can handle for one day—or even one year. I just want to go home and climb in my own bed."

"And just what is it you plan to put in that statement Jerry?" Duke asked loudly from the boat's cockpit where his bulk seemed to have found a permanent resting spot on the captain's chair. "Something about how you single-handedly sank one of Hitler's U-boats?"

"Of course not," Strickland said. "This isn't about votes—it's about our town's security. We need to let the Navy know what we saw. We have to tell the truth about it."

"The truth?" Duke asked. "The truth is some German U-boat surprised us and part of the crew came onboard the *Naughty Boy*. They made us cower like a bunch of schoolgirls while they searched us. Then they tossed our new machine gun overboard, put a bullet through our radio and to make things worse, stole our flag."

"Yep, we're all a bunch of heroes," Coleman said as he slung his backpack over his shoulder.

"But Hank, we need to tell the military," Cooper pleaded. "Maybe the Army or Navy can send a patrol plane out and catch that U-boat on the surface."

Duke had spent the last couple of hours reviewing his answer to that question as well as several others he thought sure he would be asked. It had not taken him long to realize that the U-boat's presence so close to St. Augustine was bound to stir up overwhelming support for blackout measures—so much support that it would be impossible to prevent them from being implemented. And that would mean the photos would go to his wife and he would be ruined financially. He was not about to let that happen.

"Look, that U-boat is well on its way home by now—let's see, how fast can they go on the surface? Twenty-five knots? That would put them seventy-five miles further east than where we saw them and we were probably fifty miles out," Duke lectured them like a math professor. "By the time we can get the Navy or somebody to put a plane in the air, another couple of hours will have gone by then they're more than one hundred-fifty miles offshore and probably not even on the surface any more. If nobody sighted them when they were cruising just off our beaches, they're sure as hell not gonna find them all the way out there."

"But Hank, we have to report this—even if nobody can find them. The Navy needs to know about it," Strickland said.

"Needs to know what?" Duke's voice now had an edge to it as though he were looking for a fight. "That we're all a bunch of cowards? And even more importantly, what will tourists think if they hear about a U-boat cruising just outside the city limits? People don't take vacations to be close to the war—they take them to get away from the war. It will be worse than that summer two years ago when we had that shark problem—a couple of days after that announcement was made, the hotels were deserted. Can you imagine what it will be like if everyone thinks there is a big metal shark filled with Nazis cruising just off the beach?"

"So...you want us to just keep our mouths shut?" Cooper asked. "I don't know if I can keep something like this just to myself."

"Do you want that Navy patrol boat you've been promised?"

Duke asked and when Cooper nodded in agreement, Duke continued.

"Do you really think they'd put a patrol boat under your command if they ever found out what happened out there last night?"

"Well, no, I guess not," Cooper said.

"And you Jerry," Duke continued. "How many votes do you think you'll get if anyone finds out the details of our little outing? You'll look ridiculous and then two months from now people will remember your name in connection with the fact that tourism is dead in St. Augustine because of that U-boat. You won't be able to get elected dogcatcher. And you Coleman, you probably aren't that concerned about whether or not people think you are a coward. But if tourists stay away, there will be no need for a Chamber of Commerce."

"I don't care about tourists or the damn Chamber," Coleman said and his voice had a hard edge to it that none of them had heard before. "But I do care about myself as a person and as a member of this community. You won't hear me talk about this incident – I wouldn't want anyone to know I had anything to do with this cowardly bunch. Those Germans took our nation's flag and you did nothing to stop them. Hank Duke, you make me sick."

The other members of the Security Council would have found it difficult to choose what had been the most unexpected event of the past twenty-four hours – encountering a German U-boat or being shamed into silence by Jeremy Coleman.

Last night, Michael Pomar had just settled into bed at his home on San Marco Avenue when he heard the news broadcast about the missing members of the Security Council. It only took a few minutes for the feeling he liked to think of as "reporter's instinct" to kick in and tell him there was a story here—maybe a big one. He had waited until he was certain his parents were asleep and then he had sneaked out his bedroom window and headed for the marina where he felt certain something momentous was going to soon happen. After spending the night huddled on the wooden bench outside the closed marina office, Pomar was beginning to question the accuracy of his "instinct". But any doubts he had about his ability to predict where and when news was about to be made disappeared as he watched the *Naughty Boy* appear out of the darkness and dock quietly just beyond the warm glow of the marina's shaded streetlamps.

Pomar's first instinct was to rush down to the dock and start asking questions. But as he watched the men aboard the overdue cabin cruiser, he could tell there was an important conversation underway—one that, judging from their body language, was not about where they were going for breakfast. He waited patiently until they seemed to have reached some sort of agreement before walking the final fifty yards of planking leading to the *Naughty Boy.*

"Good morning gentlemen!" Pomar said in his friendliest tone while still several paces away from the boat. He couldn't help but remember his mother's warning about walking up to stray dogs—he smiled as he wondered if he should take her advice and let them smell his hand before talking to them. "So, those that were lost now are found."

"Lost? We weren't lost," Duke grumbled. "What makes you think we were lost?"

"Oh, I don't know, maybe the Coast Guard's announcement that you were missing," Pomar said. "Or the fact that you have fuel for about four, maybe five hours of cruising and right now it's been about sixteen hours since you left out of here. So... where have you been?"

"We're not talking to reporters," Coleman said as he pushed his way past Pomar and headed for the marina office.

The old "not talking" phrase alerted Pomar to the fact that there was definitely a story here—he'd just have to find it.

"But Commissioner Strickland, you must have something to say about your adventure last night," Pomar said. "Your supporters are concerned about your welfare—can't you tell them about last night?"

Strickland hesitated. Force of habit made him want to make a statement, but they had agreed to keep quiet. "No, I don't think so," he said quietly. "Maybe later. It has been a very long night for me."

"What about you Mr. Cooper? Can't you give me a story—I know our readers would appreciate learning about what happened. Can't you just..." Pomar pleaded until he saw the mark on Cooper's cheek. "Jeez, Mr. Cooper, what in the world happened to your face?"

The chairman of the council raised his hand to cover the bright red burn on his cheek and said nothing. To Pomar, the man seemed to have slipped into senility during this boat trip. There was none of the cantankerous attitude that he so often displayed. Instead, he seemed like he just waiting for someone to admit him to the old folks home.

"It's nothing," Duke answered for him. "Homer was trying to fix the radio in the dark with a screwdriver—you should have seen the sparks fly! Hurts like hell, but he'll be fine. You're OK aren't you Homer?"

Cooper gave a half-hearted wave and continued his slow pace toward the street beyond the marina office.

"Well, Mr. Duke, you all sure had a lot of folks worried." Pomar said. "Why didn't you radio in from time to time?"

"Radio went out as soon as we cleared the inlet—I think a tube or something got broken when we ran aground."

"But that's not when you lost Old Glory is it? I mean I'm sure she was flapping in the breeze when you finally got off that sandbar. What happened to her?"

Hank Duke was growing more annoyed by the second. "I don't know what happened to the flag—it was awfully dark out there. I think Homer must have broke it off trying not to fall overboard when he burned his face."

"That could be…" Pomar said as he studied the *Naughty Boy's* transom. "But where's the broken shaft for the flag? It just seems to me that the broken stub would have still been stickin' up—but it isn't."

"Goddam it boy," Duke said as he slowly descended the ladder to the main deck. "You ask way too many questions so just get out of my way. It has been a long night –a hell of a long night."

"Certainly sir," Pomar said as stepped aside. The boat rocked once on its moorings as Hank Duke disembarked. "I'm sorry to have troubled you."

UNCLE SAM'S: 0700 hrs.

For Joe Miller, the message he had received from *BdU* was far more than just an announcement of an upcoming adventure– it confirmed that he and his work were indeed important to the

Fatherland. If not, he told a sleepy-eyed Carbone, they would never risk having a U-boat run in this close to the enemy shore, let alone make actual physical contact with them by sending in a landing party.

"So, my friend," Miller said, "we have a busy day ahead. First, we must make certain we have the designated signal lights on the pier and that they are working properly. The local yokels will be showing up soon to go fishing...so take care of that task first. If the early risers ask questions...well, I'm sure you can make up a believable story about what you are doing."

"Yes, sir," Carbone said quietly. His stomach was churning with the remnants of last night's beer drinking binge and he was not pleased at being awake so early. To make matters worse, he had been counting on a leisurely breakfast of ham, eggs and lots of coffee to cure his hangover. Now it looked like that was not going to happen.

"More supplies...that's what the boys on that U-boat need," Miller said thoughtfully as he scribbled on the notepad on his desk. "Go into town and get fresh fruit... bananas, oranges, whatever you can find. And Spam—a couple of cases. And take the *Lady Liberty* and top off her tank at the marina—we may need her tonight."

"Yes sir," Carbone said and began shuffling toward the office hatch.

"Just a second, matrose," Miller said and the harshness of his tone stopped Carbone in his tracks. "I cannot stress enough the need to say nothing about this to anyone. This is a serious game now...it can be a matter of life or death for us as well as the men who are coming here tonight. Any questions?"

"Just one...why do you call me a 'mattress'?"

"Mattress? Not a mattress...a *'matrose'*—a sailor in der Kaiserliche Marine—the old navy of Imperial Germany. That is now what you have become and I expect you to act accordingly. In fact, before our guests arrive, I want you to bathe, shave and put on some clean clothes."

"Aye-aye Sir!" Carbone said and made a feeble attempt at a salute.

"*Nein*," Miller snapped. "The proper response to my orders will be – '*Zu Befehl, Herr Kapitan*' and if you don't understand the order you will say: '*Wie Befehlen, Herr Kapitan?*' Understood?"

Carbone looked confused. "Yes...sir...I mean... Zoo biffle."

"We'll work on that," Miller said and saluted smartly. "Now... Get busy,"

Carbone half-waved, half-saluted and headed down the spiral staircase. By the time he had reached the bar, he had convinced himself that his boss was flirting with insanity.

ST. AUGUSTINE: 0720 hrs.

Sunrise flooded through St. Augustine's *Plaza de la Constitucion* and gave the ancient plastered exterior of the cathedral an ethereal glow. Spanning Matanzas Bay, the Bridge of Lions looked as though it were waiting for one of the European masters to capture its graceful curves and sunlit towers on canvas. Even the usually brooding gray coquina walls of the *Castillo de San Marcos* seemed to shine with a happy brilliance that signaled the beginning of another warm, spring day.

Down at the marina, the large crowd of sailors, fishermen, Coast Guardsmen and gawking onlookers were completely oblivious to the natural beauty unfolding around them. Instead, their attention was focused on a battered and tired-looking cabin cruiser that had been hastily moored to the dock.

"I'll be damned!" Walter Thomas, the town's oldest and often most annoying retiree summed up everyone's thoughts. "Frank, how the hell did they get in here without anybody seein' 'em. Was you asleep?"

Frank Arredondo served as the harbormaster for the city and as such was expected to keep track of the arrival and departure of boats docking at the marina. He was also the frequent target of Thomas' ire both in person and through letters published in *The Record.*

"Hell yes I was asleep—at home in my own bed," Arredondo said and thrust his chin forward as though challenging Thomas. "I only get paid until midnight—then I'm finished for the day. I've thought about staying all night and donating my time to the city, but then when I think of how ungrateful and undeserving you and your friends are, I don't waste my time."

"Wasting time? I'll tell you about wasting time," said Lucas Holt, one of St. Augustine's most successful commercial fishermen.

"Me and my crew could have still been out there chasing shrimp, but instead we came in last night to see if we could help find this here...missing...boat. Those sons of bitches cost me money—I should have known better—there's no sense in worrying about no politicians."

"I can't believe nobody in this whole town saw them come in," old man Thomas ranted.

"I saw them," Michael Pomar said and pushed his way forward through the crowd.

"You saw 'em?" Thomas said with a snarl of disdain. "I doubt that boy. I'll bet your momma don't let you out of the house after six in the evening."

"Listen, old man, do you want to hear about it or not?" Pomar couldn't believe he had taken that tone with an elder—it must he lack of sleep, he reasoned.

"Why you little whippersnapper!" Thomas got his shaky frame in motion toward Pomar.

"Shut up Frank and let him talk!" Someone shouted. "That's right old man! Keep quiet—we didn't come out here to listen to you cackle."

The crowd grew quiet as they waited for Pomar to speak.

"Well, actually, there's not much to tell," he began and realized his audience was expecting something...dramatic. "They came cruising in here just as pretty as you please about five a.m. Tied up, gathered up their gear and said they were going home."

"And you didn't ask where in the hell they had been?" asked Holt. "I thought you were supposed to be some kind of junior reporter or sumptin'. You sure ain't gonna win no journalism awards if you don't do a better job than that of gettin' the facts."

"I asked questions," Pomar said defensively, "they just didn't give me any good answers. I think Mr. Duke told them not to say anything."

"That sounds just like ol' Hank Duke," said Thomas who had obviously restrained himself for as long as possible. "We all outta go over to his big ol' house and drag his sorry..."

"Excuse me son."

Pomar turned at the sound of the voice and saw a Coast Guard lieutenant looking at him from the deck of the *Naughty Boy*. The man's dark blue uniform and brass buttons were enough to quiet

247

even Old Man Thomas.

"You say you saw the men from this boat this morning?" the officer asked.

"Yes sir," Pomar said. "All four of them—they're members of the Security Council you know."

"And they didn't tell you why they never radioed their position or responded to our calls to them?"

"No sir...they said their radio got busted when they ran aground at the inlet yesterday morning."

"I see," the officer said and took another glance around the deck. "And their Browning machine gun? Did they take that home with them?"

"No...I'm sure I would have noticed that."

"Very good then," the officer said as he gracefully stepped over the boat's gunwale and on to the dock. "I think I'm finished here. You two men!" He motioned to two Coast Guardsmen who were standing at the edge of the crowd. "I want a security cordon around this boat—nobody is to board her.   Not even the owners. Understood?"

"Aye-aye Sir!" They responded in unison and flashed their best salutes.

"The rest of you Guardsmen!" The officer shouted. "I want you to go up to the hotel, check out side arms and rifles and get back down here.   You are to guard this boat and if anyone tries to board, you have my permission to shoot them."

A chorus of "Aye-ayes" came from the crowd and at least a half-dozen young guardsmen went racing up the dock like children. Two others, in an effort to display their maturity, walked—but at a pace that was just short of a jog.

"Now, if you will excuse me," the officer said and as he stepped forward the crowd gave way.

"Wait a minute!" Thomas croaked. "You can't just leave us with no information. We came out here first thing in the morning to go and try to save these men—who obviously didn't need our help. We deserve some answers."

The Coast Guard officer stopped and for a moment, everyone thought he might have Old Man Thomas locked up.

"Well, you know, I think you're right," he said finally. "Unfortunately, I don't have any answers, but I do have several questions. In fact, if you see the men from this boat, you might want to ask them. One, who ransacked the cabin?" He ticked the questions of on his fingers. "Two, what happened to the Browning machine gun entrusted to them by the U.S. Government? Three, how did they manage to stay at sea for sixteen or more hours on one tank of fuel? Four, who put the bullet hole in the middle of their radio?"

The last question caused a murmur from the crowd.

"Sir," Pomar said. "The flag too. They might want to ask what happened to the *Naughty Boy's* flag."

The Coast Guard officer smiled and nodded. "Yes, that's another very good question."

MARINELAND: 0945 hrs

Warm sunshine and hard work had helped Winnie Greer get through the morning without having to agonize over the dilemmas that had kept her awake through much of the previous night. She had mopped the pump room and emptied the filter and her cleaning of the viewing ports on the oceanarium had been completed in record time. But no matter how hard she scrubbed, the same questions kept nagging at her: "Is Curtis all right? Should I tell the FBI man what I saw in Mr. Miller's office? Is my career as a professional singer over before it even started? Does the Reverend Amos Fulmer feel the same way about me as I feel about him?"

And although the staff at Marineland thought her only worry was the welfare of her brother, they had been more than supportive of her request to leave early and come to work late the next day after Rufus Pool's funeral. In fact, Mr. Whitney had even allowed her to use the telephone on his desk to call Reverend Fulmer to ask if he could come pick her up. That call had been particularly stressful for her—she worried that asking a favor like that might seem like she was being too aggressive and at the same time she couldn't help but worry that he would say no to her. But he had seemed genuinely happy to comply with her request and now as she watched the church's old black Ford sedan turn into the Marineland parking lot, she couldn't help but notice that the Reverend Fulmer had wasted no time in getting there. Winnie felt good to know she was one of his priorities.

"Good morning Miss Greer!" Reverend Fulmer said and smiled broadly through the Ford's open window. "Your limousine has arrived."

"Thanks for coming for me, Reverend Fulmer," Winnie said as she stepped up to the car. "I hope I'm not being a burden for you."

"Burden? Girl, you'd never be a burden for me," Fulmer said and his big toothy grin made Winnie smile. "Climb on in—the day's a-wastin'."

Winnie hurried around the front of the Ford and as Fulmer leaned over to open the door, she saw the big, green Lincoln turn off the road and come barreling through the parking lot directly toward them.

"Oh Dear Lord!" she said as settled into her seat and slammed the door.

"What does he want?" Fulmer asked and he tried not to sound nervous as he watched Joe Miller's car come to a halt right in front of his car, blocking any sort of exit for them.

"I don't know!" Winnie said and forced herself to sit upright instead of giving into her fears and hiding under the dashboard. "Oh Dear God! What if he knows I was on that roof last night? What if he saw me?"

"Just try to relax—if you look scared, he'll know something is going on. He didn't see you," Fulmer said in a tone that was not nearly as reassuring as he had hoped.

Carbone was out of his car quickly and it only took him a few brief seconds to reach the reverend's open window.

"Good mornin' folks," Carbone said and doffed his grungy yachtsman's cap. "Where you all off to on such a fine day?"

"We're on church business, sir, and I'm sure that's certainly none of your business," the reverend said firmly.

"Hey, I've been to church a few times—I was almost an altar boy until I found out there was no money in it," Carbone said as he leaned forward to rest his forearms on the car door. For a moment, Winnie thought he was going to thrust his entire head through the open window—thankfully, he kept his pockmarked face outside the car, but it was still close enough to Amos Fulmer to make the reverend very uncomfortable. "Just relax there Rev., I ain't really interested in where you're going anyways. I just wanted to deliver a message to your passenger there."

When Carbone's large, bloodshot eyes locked Winnie in their gaze she thought she knew how a mouse would feel when it looked into the eyes of the snake that was just about to swallow him.

"And what message would that be, Mr. Carbone?" she asked politely.

"I was told to tell you that Mr. Miller expects you to sing tonight—we were a little disappointed that you didn't let us know you weren't coming by last night." Carbone waited for an apology, but when he realized that wouldn't be coming, he resumed his assignment. "So Mr. Miller says you should be there at six...we'll do a little run through on a couple of numbers and then we'll start the first set around seven. Sound good to you?"

"Yes, that's fine with me...please tell Mr. Miller I'll be there," Winnie said quietly. "And I'm sorry I wasn't there yesterday. I came by to tell you last night, but I..." Her voiced trailed off as she realized she had just said far more than she had intended.

"You were there last night?" Carbone suddenly seemed extremely interested in what she had just said. "What time was that? I know I didn't see you there."

"Oh, it was early... but too late to go on stage." Winnie tried to sound as though she were just making friendly conversation when in fact she was desperately trying to talk her way out of any possible suspicion. "When I saw all those cars in the parking lot, it didn't seem like you needed me much anyway."

"Cars huh? Well, yes you're right. We did have a nice crowd for a Wednesday." Carbone looked down the road as though he were giving something a great deal of thought. When he turned back to face them, the pensive expression on his face looked oddly out of place. "Well, Mr. Miller just wanted to make sure you didn't forget about the opportunity he is offering you."

"I won't forget. How could I? It's just about the most wonder..."

"Listen, Mr. Carbone," Reverend Fulmer said suddenly, "do you reckon you could move that car so we could be on our way? We have a very busy schedule."

"Oh, by all means Reverend," Carbone said as he backed away from the car, he held his hands up, the palms facing them as though surrendering. "See you this evening then Miss Greer."

Carbone hurried to his car and instead of merely backing up a few feet, he swung the big Lincoln in a half circle and accelerated out of the parking lot and up A1A leaving behind a cloud of dust that drifted just above the hot pavement.

"He wouldn't be so arrogant if he knew we were on to him and his boss," Fulmer said as he let out the clutch and the Ford shuddered as though shaking itself loose from the sand.

"No, he would probably just kill us both," Winnie said as she struggled to control the fear she felt rushing over her. "Just like he killed poor Rufus…I just know he and Mr. Miller had something to do with his killing."

Fulmer shifted into third and reached over to gently squeeze her hand.

"Then why don't you tell what you saw? You can't let them get away with it." He pulled his hand away to shift and then wrapped her hand in his once more. "What did your granny say when you told her?"

"I didn't…I couldn't." Winnie looked out to where the bright blue Atlantic glistened in the sun. "But I have to tell her and then I'll do whatever she thinks is right. I should do—well, that's what I'll do."

"Well, I think she'll want you to put Miller away for good," Fulmer said and waved at a group of black men and women who were fishing from the Matanzas Inlet bridge. "It probably wouldn't do no good to talk to the Sheriff—that dumb redneck would probably say he couldn't arrest Miller because if'n he did, Miller would have to close *Uncle Sam's* and that would be just too hard on the town's morale. But I'll bet that young G-man could help—he'd know just what to do."

"Yes, I know I have to tell that FBI man," Winnie sighed. "But it's gonna be a hard thing—it's gonna be the end of my dream when they come to lock up Mr. Miller."

"You don't know that for sure," Fulmer said. "It could put you on the right path to an even bigger dream. You won't be punished for doing the right thing—the Lord will take care of you and His countenance will smile down upon you."

Winnie wasn't too sure of the value of having the Lord smiling at her. What she needed was for the Lord to get her an audition with Cab Calloway.

ST. AUGUSTINE: 0950 hrs.

Michael Pomar was surprised that Special Agent Bill Spencer didn't show more interest in his story about the safe return of the St. Augustine Security Council. He had been waiting for Spencer in the lobby of the Alhambra when the G-man came down for breakfast. Together, they had walked down to the marina where they got a good look at the *Naughty Boy.* But instead of being intrigued by all the possibilities regarding the mysterious disappearance and re-appearance of the St. Augustine Security Council, Spencer seemed to spend most of his time glancing at his watch and pacing nervously along the dock.

"OK, I give up," Pomar said in frustration. "What do I have to do to get you to track down the clowns who were on this boat last night and get some answers from them?"

"Sorry, but I don't see these gentlemen's little outing as something affecting national security." Spencer slipped off his jacket, swung it over his shoulder and allowed one thumb to serve as a coat hanger. Sweat stains were starting to form in the armpits of his freshly laundered white shirt and he could feel the warm dampness beneath his leather shoulder holster. "They probably just got lost or... something."

"So, you think they just happened to drop their machine gun overboard and one of them accidentally shot a hole in the middle of their radio?"

"I admit those questions need answers, but right now I'm more interested in catching our spy with his radio transmitter." Spencer looked at his watch again and saw that it was five minutes later than the last time he checked. "Aren't you anxious to see what we caught with that bait we put out last night? We might be right on the verge of cracking this case."

"Sure, but..."

"Look, we can follow up on them later," Spencer said. "They aren't going anywhere... but in a few minutes, I have to call Washington and if I'm lucky, today could be the day we make an arrest. You're welcome to come back to the hotel—someday when you write your memoirs you'll want to devote a chapter to the day you helped catch a Nazi spy."

Pomar hesitated. People he had known all his life and who had never struck him as anything more than vaguely interesting now seemed somehow...vital. The mystery of the *Naughty Boy* had swept through town and everyone suddenly had an opinion that they were anxious to share. The forlorn cabin cruiser guarded by armed sailors was the focus of interest for every St. Augustinian and he was reluctant to leave the marina to watch someone make a phone call, but in the end, he decided the G-man was right.

"Let's go," Pomar said reluctantly and hurried to catch up with Spencer who was already setting a good pace toward the marina office. By the time they turned west up King Street toward the Alhambra Hotel, Pomar was beginning to feel the same sense of anticipation that had obviously infected the young FBI agent who, despite his hurried gait, still found time to nod or doff his hat as a pleasant morning greeting to everyone he passed.

WASHINGTON, DC: 1005 hrs.

Deputy Director Frank Masterson was, quite frankly, amazed at the thoroughness of the report that had rattled off the teleprinter shortly after his arrival at FBI headquarters that morning. At best, he had expected the British Admiralty to confirm that they had indeed intercepted an unusually lengthy message sent on the frequency used primarily by the German *Kriegsmarine*. Much to his surprise, the British intelligence gathering capabilities were far more advanced than he had imagined. If everything in the report were true, the Bureau's skills looked positively juvenile by comparison. He was equally impressed by the Brits' genuine interest in sharing the information—as long as he had anything to do with setting policies, he intended to insure that America never willingly shared the results of their intelligence gathering with foreigners.

First, the teletype gave the results of the High Frequency Direction Finding effort. Three stations had picked up the transmission and due to its length their operators had been able to at last get a firm fix on the source—somewhere within an eight-mile radius of St. Augustine, Florida. Even though the electronic eavesdropping and tracking were impressive, Masterson couldn't help but admire what the Brits had done with good ol' fashioned research. For the first time, they had been able to copy a complete transmission from the mystery station, including a call sign – KTMU. Nothing resembling it appeared in their constantly expanding catalog of letter designators assigned to ships of Hitler's Kriegsmarine. But it was indeed the call sign assigned to one of the Kaiser's First World War battle cruisers–the *SMS Nassau*. Checking their records of German Navy personnel dating from the early 1900's, they discovered that the Nassau's last communications officer was a man named Joachim Mueller—a man who had headed to the States in 1922 and, to the best of their knowledge, had never returned to Germany. The final bit of information contained in the telefax was labeled "speculation," but it said there was strong evidence that Joachim Mueller had Americanized his name to "Joseph Miller" and was working in the music business in New York.

Based on the report, it only took Masterson a few minutes to come up with a plan. The purpose of the meeting he had convened in his conference room was to put the plan into action.

"Keane, what was the name of the suspect Agent Spencer reported the other day?" Masterson asked even though he already knew the answer. The son of Pennsylvania Senator Walter Keane, young Patrick had been assigned to Masterson's staff one Tuesday afternoon on the basis of a telephone call from J. Edgar Hoover. The Director had simply said the Senator needed some help with his son and that was all the direction Masterson needed. He didn't ask the nature of the young man's problem—but it didn't take him long to assume it had something to do with Patrick Keane's limited intellect.

"I don't know…" Keane answered brightly, but then returned to fiddling with the keys to the new Ford sedan his father had given to him the previous Sunday.

"Miller? Wasn't that his name?" Masterson asked quickly. He liked to give Keane a chance to answer simple questions. Unfortunately, the boy usually failed miserably.

"Yes, I think it was Miller." Keane mumbled.

"You're right! Miller…Joe Miller," Masterson said with relief that he had done his part to include the Senator's son in the meeting's deliberations. "Good lad." Masterson now felt he could move on with what he liked to term "an operational meeting."

"Gentlemen, you've read the telefax and the accompanying

notes. I think it's clear that we have all the evidence we need to act—the sooner the better. Let's start with you Burt."

Burt Logan was an Agency legend. As far back as Prohibition, he had successfully put together special operations teams that had moved quickly to make arrests, break up counterfeiting operations, shut down illegal gaming houses and even, it was widely believed, assassinate gang leaders. Now in his mid-50's and suffering from chronic alcoholism, his florid complexion and pot belly struggling to burst through his blue satin vest seemed out of place for a man who once epitomized the glamorous G-man mystique.

"No problem here Chief," Logan said quickly and squeezed one fist with a pink, chubby hand until the knuckles cracked loudly. "I got three boys here all ready to go—they're real anxious to get down to that Florida sunshine."

"Good work," Masterson said. "Make sure they go loaded for bear— I want everybody packin' a Tommy gun. It'll look good in the newspapers. Which bring us to you George. We want this to get maximum coverage—The Director himself wants to get in on this."

George Watts merely nodded and continued to scribble furiously on his yellow legal pad. A compact man with dark brown hair that was perpetually plastered to his skull with a pomade whose identity was known only to him, Watts had parlayed a career as the editor of a small town daily in Alton, Illinois, into a position as the FBI's chief press spokesman. Actually, the transformation had been quite simple. He merely traded the Alton Clarion's one-hundred-plus years of journalistic integrity for the re-election of a Congressman whose ineptness was about to be punished by the voters of his district. But thanks to the smear campaign conducted against his opponent in the pages of the Clarion, the incumbent retained his seat and rewarded Watts with an appointment to the press officer job for the FBI in Washington. Although on the surface the appointment seemed to be merely a case of political payoff, the fact was that Watts was the prefect choice for the job. It had always been a dream of his to write fiction and now he was getting a chance to do just that—at a salary more than four times what he had earned as a newspaperman.

"I've already drafted up a press release—I'll give it to you for review when we finish here," Watts said as he glanced up from behind his frameless spectacles. "And I've got Doug Whitehall over at the Post all lined up for an exclusive. He's ready to go and, as usual, he'll write whatever we tell him to…he'll be bringing a photographer with him too."

"Good work," Masterson said, "make sure you've got the radio networks covered. This is just the kind of good news the Bureau needs—we should be able to have this wrapped up and ready for broadcast by noon tomorrow. Now, our flight out of here will be ready to go by five and we'll…"

Masterson was interrupted by his secretary as she opened the conference room door and stepped inside.

"Sorry to barge in," she said, "but Agent Spencer is calling from Florida—I thought you'd want to talk to him as soon as possible."

Masterson leaned forward and picked up the receiver of the telephone on the conference room table. Before speaking, he placed a finger in front of his lips to signal his wish that everyone remain silent.

"Agent Spencer! Good to hear from you," Masterson said cheerfully. "What's new?"

Masterson rolled his eyes and nodded his head impatiently as he listened to Spencer's telephoned report.

"Well, I'm sorry Agent Spencer, but I'm afraid the Brits couldn't come up with anything at all last night…either you're looking at the wrong man or he just didn't get around to transmitting," Masterson said smilingly and gave his guests an exaggerated wink. He waited for Spencer to finish before answering: "Yes, I know you're frustrated, but we can't do anything based solely on your gut instincts. So here's what I suggest. Keep a close watch on this…what's his name? Right. Miller. But whatever you do, don't scare him off. Got it?"

The FBI supervisor held the receiver away from his ear and the men seated around the table could hear the scratchy, indistinct sound of Spencer's voice on the line. Speaking once more into the receiver, Masterson wrapped up the conversation.

"No… under no circumstances should you make an arrest—you have no evidence. Even if you do come up with something, you check with me first. Who knows? He might try to transmit tonight and we'll be ready to intercept it. So just sit tight. Give me a call again on Monday. OK?" Spencer's reply was obviously very brief. "Good boy, that's the kind of commitment I like to hear. Take care and I'll talk to you in a few days. Goodbye."

Masterson replaced the telephone receiver and shook his head. "Young Spencer is doing some good work down there... he has set it up nicely for us and he doesn't even know it yet."

"And you're not going to tell him?" Watts asked.

"Sure...I'll tell him in person tonight," Masterson laughed. "Which brings me to the final details. I want you all at National tonight at five....at Hangar Six...you know the one. I'd like to get started earlier, but the Director's briefing isn't until three and I want him to have all the details in advance. He's going to like this one. Questions? No? Good. See you this evening and Watts, leave that draft behind and I'll give it a look."

"Sure thing Boss, I'll think you'll enjoy it. Thanks to young Spencer's work and the report from the Brits it was easy to put together." The press officer slid his latest creation across the table and then followed Logan's hefty backsides out of the office. Realizing the meeting was over, Keane scrambled after them.

Masterson picked up the handwritten draft news release in anticipation of another of Watts' masterpieces. He read:

NAZI SPY NABBED BY FBI IN FLORIDA

WASHINGTON, DC, April 17 – Moving swiftly in the dead of night, FBI agents descended on America's oldest city to arrest one of the Nazi's most dangerous spies. Disguised as a nightclub owner in St. Augustine, Florida, the enemy agent operated a secret communications system and was in direct contact with German U-boats and Hitler's naval headquarters.

"This is another example of the Bureau's relentless war against the enemies of Democracy," said FBI Director J. Edgar Hoover. "Our sophisticated technology combined with the courage of our agents has created an unbeatable weapon for ridding our shores of Axis spies."

As a result of their unmatched surveillance skills, FBI agents discovered that the spy, Joe Miller, was actually one Joachim Mueller who served as a high-ranking officer in the Kaiser's Navy during the First World War. A popular member of the local business community, Miller had set up a powerful radio transmitter for communicating with his Nazi masters. Fortunately, using technology developed by the Bureau's scientists, Miller's very first transmission was intercepted by FBI agents and his fate was quickly sealed.

Hoover credited the success of the operation to the outstanding work of FBI Deputy Director Frank Masterson who single-handedly coordinated the operation and was present   to put the handcuffs on the Nazi spy who was immediately transported to the federal penitentiary in Atlanta.

Masterson had to admit that when it came to telling the FBI's story, there was no one better than Watts. Planting the idea that in addition to heroic G-men, the FBI also had scientists working to defend the Nation was a stroke of genius. He read through the draft once more and with his pen, changed the last sentence to read: "Special Agent Patrick Keane, son of Pennsylvania Senator Walter Keane, was present to put the handcuffs on the Nazi spy who was immediately transported to the federal penitentiary in Atlanta."

Satisfied with his editing, Masterson folded the release neatly and tucked it inside his suit jacket. He was already mentally compiling a list of what he would need to take with him on a late night trip to the Sunshine State.

ST. AUGUSTINE: 1040 hrs.

Special Agent Bill Spencer found it hard to believe that he could have been wrong about Joe Miller. All that was needed to make an arrest was some sort of tangible evidence and he was certain that Miller would have been unable to resist transmitting the "secret" information that he and Pomar had passed on to him.

Even more disturbing was the lack of support he had received from the Bureau in Washington. Of course, he had not expected Masterson to be his personal cheerleader, but the man had seemed genuinely interested in the effort to trap Miller into sending a traceable broadcast. Now, Masterson seemed unconcerned about the lack of success. Instead, he seemed perfectly happy with the news—almost as though he had long since moved on to a bigger and more important project. The worst part for Spencer was the demeaning assignment he had been given. Instead of cracking a major espionage case, he had been ordered to simply keep an eye on Miller. And Masterson had left no doubt that even if Miller goose-stepped down King Street while shouting *Sieg Heil* to everyone in town, he was not to be arrested.

"I'm sorry about not catching Miller red-handed," Pomar said from his seat by the window in Spencer's hotel room. "Maybe he'll send the message tonight. Surely the monitoring stations will be listening."

"I don't know," Spencer said quietly. "I was certain they would find him wearing his finger out sending that message we gave him. And I was sure you would be in on one of the biggest scoops of all time—just sitting here when I got the word by phone to go arrest the biggest spy master ever to operate in this part of the world."

"Don't worry about it, Mr. G-man," Pomar said brightly. "I've got plenty of other stories to follow up on—the mystery of the Security Council's little boat trip for one. Maybe I could sell that one to Abbott and Costello. And then I've got one of those 'feel good' stories to complete. What about you? What's next?"

"I don't really know." Spencer moved over to the window and looked down on the traffic moving slowly along King Street. "My only assignment for the moment is to keep tabs on Joe Miller. Maybe I'll start on that at sundown—in the meantime, I guess I'll just do some sightseeing."

"Sounds good to me," Pomar said and as he moved toward the door it was easy to see he was anxious to get on with gathering background for new stories. "You could use some relaxation. I'll catch up with you later and see what we've been able to come up with—who knows we might find the spy after all. I'll check back with you around five this evening."

Although the young reporter didn't seem to need any encouragement, Spencer motioned for Pomar to move on. "Five it is then...I'll meet you in the Plaza."

ST. AUGUSTINE: 1120 hrs.

"Yes, I'm sorry about this...you know I am," Hank Duke said and banged his heavy forearms on the top of his desk. "What more do you want me to say? We're incompetent? We look like idiots?

Guilty as charged."

Coast Guard Lieutenant Tom Boyd sat in the uncomfortable chair Duke reserved for his most annoying guests. It was obvious to him that Hank Duke was either not telling the truth or was omitting some very relevant facts from his story. He had been questioning the man for nearly thirty minutes and so far the results had been far from encouraging.

"So...you say the machine gun was lost overboard," the lieutenant said as he flipped back through the pages of his notepad. "And how did that happen again?"

"Look, I know you want to keep asking hoping I'll change my story, but it's like I already told you," Duke sounded as though he were pleading not to have to repeat his account of what happened. "We propped it up on the foredeck just to see what it would be like to fire it, but we didn't brace the tripod. When we squeezed off a burst, it went sliding along and over the side. It dragged the ammo with it. Big splash...no gun...simple as that."

Boyd drew a line through one of his notes. "And you say your engine broke down and you drifted for... let's see, some ten hours, and then the engine miraculously repaired itself."

"Well, I wouldn't say it fixed itself...that's not exactly true," Duke said and suddenly realized just how exhausted he was and how much he was looking forward to a nap on the big leather sofa over in the corner. "We banged around on it for hours. I guess we finally jarred loose something that was blocking the fuel line. After that, she purred like a kitten."

"I see. And the radio...you say it just quit working?"

"Yep, never had a minute's trouble with it before we ran aground." Duke sighed and stared up at the slowly turning blades of the big ceiling fan that kept his office cool even in summer. He couldn't help but notice that the pattern of shadows created by the sunlight coming through the office window's louvered shutters looked ominously like the bars of a jail cell. "After we hit the sandbar, all we could pick up was static."

"So you shot it? Just to put it out of its misery. Correct?" Boyd noticed that the more times he repeated Duke's answers, the less preposterous they seemed.

"Well, maybe not to put it out of its misery... it was more like to put us out of our misery. There was constant griping about the radio and then Homer Cooper decided he'd fix it by jamming a screwdriver inside it," Duke said and rolled his eyes in disbelief. "The next thing I know, there's this bright flash and Homer is clutching his burned face. That's when I walked over and put a bullet right through the front of it—the radio that is. A little dramatic maybe, but it sure got quiet after that."

Boyd made a final entry in his notebook, folded it closed and tucked it inside his jacket pocket. "Very good then," he said. "I suppose your fellow shipmates can confirm everything you have told me?"

"I don't know…you'll have to ask them," Duke said in a voice that reflected his frustration and exhaustion. "Frankly, I don't really care what they say. It will be a long time before I can stand to hear their voices again."

The lieutenant stood and gently placed his officer's hat on his head with obvious concern about its potential impact on his carefully combed blonde hair. "Well, Mr. Duke, believe it or not the Coast Guard has more important things to do than go around listening to tales of incompetence from would-be war heroes. My orders were to find out why we had to waste time worrying about your boat's whereabouts and to confirm what happened to the missing machine gun that was entrusted into your care by the taxpayers." Boyd frowned and shook his head in disappointment. "I consider this sad case to be closed."

Hank Duke could feel his heart take a happy leap, but years of practice allowed him to maintain a poker face. "Again, I'm sorry for all the trouble and if you want to go ask the rest of them what happened I'm sure they would tell you the same thing. We may be fools sometimes, but we're not liars."

"That won't be necessary," Boyd said as he turned to go and then stopped suddenly. He turned to face Duke once more with a quizzical expression on his face. "What about the flag? I noticed it was missing from the boat. What happened to it?"

Duke had somehow failed to anticipate that question, but he had learned long ago that in situations like this, the best course of action was to plead ignorance. "I don't know," he said quietly.

"Don't know? You don't know what happened to our national ensign?" Boyd sounded indignant. "You mean to tell me you simply lost a symbol that brave men have given their lives to defend?"

"I don't know...Strickland and that Coleman boy were wrestling around back there. They must have knocked it overboard," Duke said and bowed his head. "I'm ashamed of all of us."

"You very well should be," the lieutenant said in a tone that any school principal would have admired. "And I would suggest that until this war is ended, every time you hear a radio broadcast about the struggles of America's fighting men, you should think of how shabbily you have treated the banner that inspires their courage. Good day to you sir."

Duke looked up just in time to see that as the lieutenant pulled the door closed behind him, he was delicately gripping the doorknob with his fingertips as though he felt it was coated in some sort of disgusting substance.

ST. AUGUSTINE: 1420 hrs.

Michael Pomar couldn't help but feel that when it came to being a big time reporter, he was on the verge of striking out. Strike one had been having his story about the Security Council's efforts killed by *The Record's* owner. Strike Two had to have been the "non-story" that occurred when the FBI told Spencer that he was after the wrong man. Not getting the inside story on the Council's adventure last night had been a hard fast one just enough outside the strike zone. He decided that the best cure for being way behind in the count was to do something positive—lay down a bunt and beat it out to first..

Even though it was one of those "feel good" stories that he generally avoided, he couldn't help but think this one might get him the national recognition he craved. After all, it had everything that America wanted—servicemen and merchants working together to provide a basic comfort to those in need – warm, dry socks. The "Sock it to the Nazis" theme was perfect and the photos he had gotten of Miss Shirley Hoover and Joe Miller had turned out even better than he had hoped. She really was a looker in one of the photos—the way her white blouse had gapped open was a classic. And having her posed with Joe Miller, bar owner, complete with bottles of booze in the background, seemed to say that in this world war against evil, even sinners were doing their part for the good guys.

Uncle Sam's

It was a little difficult making the connection through the long distance operator, but finally he heard the ring on the other end— all the way up in New Jersey. Pomar was wondering what he would do if they answered in Yiddish when, on the third ring, someone picked up the receiver.

"Temple Beth Shalom."

"Hi...I mean shalom," Pomar said. "I'm a reporter down here in St. Augustine, Florida, following up on a story. Our town sent a box up there to you fellows a couple of days ago and we were just wondering if you got it yet. If you did, I'd like to get your reaction. I'm sure our readers would be interested in knowing what you thought of it."

Pomar had pinned the receiver between his jaw and shoulder in true reporter fashion and was poised to jot down the response in the notebook he held in his left hand. He was tempted to go ahead and draft a response, the words "touching gesture" and "thoughtful gift in our time of need" came to mind—he had seen enough of those kinds of stories to know what the response would be. Surprisingly, there's was no response. Just silence on the line and then the sounds of two men speaking loudly in what he assumed was Yiddish. He was surprised there was so much anger in their voices.

"This is Rabbi Levi. What do you want with us?"

The commanding tone and ill-concealed irritation in this new voice made Pomar conjure up images of some Old Testament prophet with fiery eyes, a beard blowing in the wind and lightning flashing in an angry sky.

"Oh...uh, good morning sir.... I mean rabbi, sir," Pomar said hesitantly. "I'm a reporter in St. Augustine and I was calling to see if you had received a box we shipped to you. It was sent as an expression of our support for...."

"We received the package."

Pomar waited for some elaboration, but it became apparent it wouldn't be coming without some prompting on his part.

"And what did you think? Were you surprised?"

"Surprised? Yes, Mr. Reporter. For us, it was a surprise. We never expected to receive such a...*frassk.* Especially from total strangers."

"*Frassk?*" Pomar asked as he struggled to spell the word, scratching out two attempts. "Is that like a gift or something?"

"A *frassk,* my ignorant friend, is an insult...a slap in the face...often painfully delivered without warning."

Pomar was confused. An insult? What could be insulting about socks? He knew Jews didn't like pork, but did they have some sort of religious aversion to cotton... or socks? Surely, Jews wear socks.

"I am sorry sir. I'm sure we meant no disrespect... if you were offended it must be because we didn't know any better."

"A box of socks soaked in urine. You didn't think we would be offended by the piss of your townspeople? I will, however, give you credit for imagination. I don't think even the Nazis have come up with that insult yet."

"Urine? I don't know what you mean? There was no urine... the socks were collected as a gift. I don't know how they could have...."

"I am a busy man," the rabbi said firmly. "If you want to know what we think of the people of St. Augustine, you could say that, as fellow human beings, we consider them to be a *shandeh un a charpeh.*"

"A *shandeh*...do you spell that with c or an s?" Pomar asked.

"Do you have any of God's chosen people in St. Augustine? I'm talking about Jews, of course."

Pomar was already trying to get out of this conversation and get busy finding out the identity of the culprit he had already dubbed "the phantom pisser." Even though there was a synagogue across from *The Record* building,, he couldn't really think of any Jews except for old Herman Cohen and he was a Presbyterian.

"Yes, I'm sure there are Jews in St. Augustine." Pomar said.

"Well, my idea was for you to assemble all of your townspeople and have a Jew translate *shandeh un a charpeh* for them...but I can see that will not happen. So...I will translate for you. It means we think you and your community are a shame and a disgrace."

The line clicked dead and left Pomar with a mystery to solve.

MOSES CREEK: 1610 hrs.

Granny Greer seemed to be listening to voices only she could hear. All through the long afternoon, she had sat on the front porch in her wheelchair facing out to where the deep blue of the Matanzas mixed with the vivid green of the salt marsh. White-feathered egrets sailed in on the warm breeze to wade silently in the shallows until with one sudden thrust of their beaks they would snare their lunch from among the sea trout fingerlings flashing in the tidal pools. But for her, the day was marked by a passing of light and dark-- the beauty of the marsh hidden behind the cataracts that robbed her of her sight.

"Are you thinking about Curtis?" Winnie asked, but she already knew the answer.

"Yes, child, your brother is lyin' heavy on my mind today." Granny Greer spoke without moving her head to look in Winnie's direction. "I've asked the Lord to tell me if he's all right or not, but I haven't heard a thing. He must be busy with the war or something. But I ain't gonna rush Him none—patience is a virtue, sayeth the Lord. I got no right to hurry Him."

Winnie continued to fold the freshly washed and dried clothing she had brought in from the clothesline in the backyard. She had waited all afternoon for the right moment to begin a conversation that, to her, could change her life forever. There was no need to wait any longer, she decided, there would be no perfect time to decide her fate.

"Granny, do you think those German people are evil?"

Granny Greer shifted uneasily in her wheelchair. Winnie was relieved that the answer didn't come right away—it obviously required some thought.

"Well, child I reckon it would depend on what kind of evil you was talkin' about." There was an unusual enthusiasm in Granny's voice as though she welcomed an opportunity to discuss the subject. "If you was asking if them Germans are Satan's disciplines you might get one answer. If you wanted to know if'n I thought they was as mean as some of the folks in this town you might get another."

For Winnie, her question had quickly become much more complicated. What she really wanted to know was Granny's opinion on whether or not she should tell anyone what she had seen in Mr. Miller's office. But she just couldn't be that blunt—not when the answer was so important to her future.

"Well, what I mean is..." Winnie set aside the stack of bed

linens she had just folded. "Well, some of us were talking the other day about the fact that these Germans we're supposed to be hatin' are Christians just like us."

"That's sho 'nuf true," Granny said brightly. "That Martin Luther fellah was a German and anybody who knows anything about church history can tell you he was mighty important to Christians."

"And, well, we was thinkin' about how America had slaves and still don't treat us so good just because we're colored," Winnie said. "And before that the British had all the slaves here and still make lots of trouble for colored folks in Africa and India, but America is doing everything it can to help the British. But then those Germans never had any slaves and as far as I know they never hurt any colored people anywhere...but our government says we're supposed to hate them. It gets kind of confusin' for colored folks."

"Well, I ain't no expert on history," Granny said, "but I do know something about people—white people that is. It has been my experience that white people just can't help treatin' us bad—it just comes natural as the sunrise. I remember when I was a girl some white folks came down here from New York to help us out—least that's what they said and we believed them because they was from up north. Two weeks later they was bossin' us around worse than some big old plantation owner. So I reckon if the Germans ain't done nothin' bad to no colored folks, I'd say it's just because they ain't had the opportunity."

"So then you'd say that they ain't any worse than the white people in this county?" Winnie asked.

This new question was one that obviously caused Granny Greer much thought. In fact, her answer was so long in coming that Winnie was about to ask the question again.

"Well, child, I have to say there are some fine white people living in St. Johns County—people that I will always feel happy to have known. But there are also some ornery white folks around here who don't have the sense that God gave a goose. I doubt there's been a week go by in my eighty years that they haven't tried to embarrass me."

Winnie could tell this conversation was beginning to drift away from her original intent. Somehow she needed to get it back on track.

"But the Germans, Granny, they've never done anything to

us—not like the white people in this country. But now there's a war going on and there are Negro boys like Curtis fighting for America—but this country will always treat us like we ain't good as white folks."

Granny Greer tilted her head back and closed her eyes as though she were listening to voices that had been carried into the marsh by the sea breeze many long years ago. Slowly, she turned to face Winnie and when she opened her eyes it seemed for one brief moment that her vision had been restored.

"Winnie, I know these things have been troubling you for some time now. It's only natural that by the time you get to be your age you finally have to see the world as it really is," she said slowly as though composing and reviewing each phrase before speaking. "When it comes to the way things are between colored folks and white folks, I can't tell you everything that has happened in my lifetime—but you've heard the stories and you know how some of those cracker boys treat you. And then sometimes, white folks just ignore you as though they can't see you at all. That's probably the worst part when they act like you don't even exist. That's the way it was with me and if'n that's how it is with you then things ain't changed that much. And yes, Negro boys fight and die for this country—but that's because it's our country just as much as it is the white man's. We built it. Yes indeed, it was our labor, our sweat, our tears—and if the truth be known, our brains that built this here civilization. And even if white folks don't never give us no credit for it, we know that we have helped build this country and we are proud. It's something worth fightin' for—even if it ain't perfect."

For a moment, Winnie felt as though she were being lectured. But as she listened, it became clear that Granny Greer was only trying to share something important...something she wanted her granddaughter to remember. All she could say in reply was a simple "Yes m'am."

"And them Germans?" Granny said quickly. "Well, I reckon they's like having a water moccasin or rattler under the front porch. It's just their nature to defend themselves by bitin' anyone who gets too close. And child, I know if they had the chance they would kill Curtis just as quick as they would kill a white boy—at least in their eyes, we're all equal."

Winnie knew she had the answer to her question and for a

moment the image of Joe Miller's office filled with rattlesnakes each marked with a swastika seemed very real.

ANASTASIA ISLAND: 2150 hrs.

Special Agent Bill Spencer could not remember when he had spent a more frustrating afternoon. Even though he often questioned the value of his work in the bowels of the FBI building in Washington, at the end of the day he at least had the satisfaction of having a stack of processed paperwork to attest to his productivity. Today, he had little or nothing to show for his efforts.

After the apparent failure of his scheme to trap Joe Miller by convincing the Nazi spy suspect into sending a bogus radio message, Spencer had suddenly realized he really had no backup plan. A careful review of what little evidence he had accumulated, followed by a leisurely stroll through the ancient streets of St. Augustine did nothing to lessen his conviction that Joe Miller was a spy—and a dangerous one at that.

Unfortunately, nothing he could say would convince Sheriff Haywood Hartson that Joe Miller was anything other than a pillar of the community. His first attempt had come in mid-afternoon when he tracked down the sheriff who was busy running off a couple of elderly colored men who were fishing just a little too close to Mrs. O'Malley's property over by Oyster Creek. Spencer had politely summarized the case for the sheriff and asked if maybe he could get some help staking out Uncle Sam's in compliance with his orders from Washington. In response, Hartson had laid out the facts of his office—one deputy to watch over several hundred rowdy troops coming in from Camp Blanding, one deputy off duty because he and his wife would be having a baby in the next few hours, the remaining deputy on duty at the jail, and a sheriff who had already worked twelve hours "at low pay and few benefits."

His next try at what the FBI manual called "securing local investment" occurred in Hartson's office at the end of his workday. Spencer had excitedly presented the sheriff with Pomar's freshly-told tale of the arrival of the urine-soaked socks at the New Jersey synagogue. After Hartson stopped laughing, the sheriff had suggested that Spencer should take his case to the Health Department—there was probably some statute prohibiting

269

interstate "trafficking of piss". As a last resort, Spencer had tried the same sort of bribery that had gotten him his first off duty meeting with the sheriff. It was apparently an offer Sheriff Hartson found impossible to refuse.

"Man, this barbecued chicken is the best," Hartson said from the cramped rear seat of Spencer's coupe. "I think it's that hickory smoke that makes all the difference. You boys want a piece? I think there's a couple of wings down in the bottom of the bucket. I don't care much for wings—too much work and not enough reward if you know what I mean."

Spencer and Michael Pomar both mumbled a "no thank you" from the front seat without taking their eyes off *Uncle Sam's*. Not that there was much to see. It was just that turning around to see the sheriff sprawled across the rear seat with the cardboard bucket of chicken in his lap and a film of grease glistening on his chin was just too...unsettling.

"If you boys don't mind, I think I'll take a little nap," the sheriff announced. "Y'all let me know if Mr. Hitler shows up. I wouldn't mind meetin' that crazy sonofabitch."

Spencer and Pomar said nothing as they continued to watch the bar and its parking lot where a sea of cars stretched out beneath the gaily-lit lanterns. Spencer did notice that the floodlight illumination for the flags seemed unusually bright tonight. Even though their car was parked a hundred yards south of the bar, the lights were so brilliant that the stars overhead were lost in the loam.

Sheriff Hartson began to snore. At first it was just an occasional gurgle, but as he slipped deeper into his slumber the snore became an annoying rasp and rattle. The night was hot and even with the windows down the smells of fried chicken, Hartson's sweat and the warm beer oozing from the sheriff's pores soon created a suffocating aroma that was determined to remain inside the car's warm darkness.

"I think I'll leave this part out of my story," Pomar said quietly.

"I think I'll leave it out of my memory," Spencer added and shifted his weight in another futile attempt to get comfortable beneath the steering wheel.

Both found themselves gazing up at the brightly lit windows of the bar as they tried to recognize the tune drifting faintly on the breeze. Spencer wondered how much longer he should continue to watch for something he might not recognize when and if he saw it.

UNCLE SAM'S: 2210 HRS.

As Winifred Greer finished her last set, even the most intoxicated patrons of *Uncle Sam's* could easily recognize what they were seeing—talent...incredible talent. When she departed the stage to a standing ovation, catcalls and whistles dozens of young white men suddenly realized something that just an hour earlier they would have believed impossible—they had found a colored girl to be sexually desirable. For some of the boys from Dixie, the physical evidence of the impression she had made on them was both wondrous and darkly disturbing.

"You knocked 'em dead kid!" Carbone exclaimed as he rushed from behind his drum set and opened the door to her makeshift dressing room behind the bar. "Damn, you're gonna be famous—don't forget me when you make the big time baby."

"Oh Luigi," she bubbled. "I know I'll never...never forget you." She leaned heavily against the door and forced it closed despite Carbone's obvious interest in joining her. "How could I ever forget such an ugly face...or evil soul," she muttered and instantly heard the voice of Granny Greer somewhere within her subconscious – "Judge not lest ye be judged."

When she turned, she found herself looking at her image in the makeshift dressing room's mirror. She could scarcely believe the transformation that had taken place in just a few days time. Just last week, she had been a simple colored girl with a voice that entertained the poor, but honest members of Moses Creek AME. Today, she was decked out in a dress that she would guess cost more than all of the clothes worn by the church's entire congregation—and the jewelry she wore was undoubtedly more valuable than her home. She touched one of the diamond-pendant earrings and watched as the light flashed and glittered in the mirror. Winnie's hand brushed over the gold necklace and noticed how bright the metal seemed against her dark skin...just like some Nubian princess she thought. And now all that would be gone just as soon as Mr. Joe Miller was led away in handcuffs and, for all she knew, hanged for treason. For a moment, it all seemed so unfair that she would have burst into tears if not for the knock on the door.

Uncle Sam's

"Winifred...may I come in please?" Joe Miller asked with a politeness that, to Winnie, seemed oddly out of place.

She stepped across the cramped room and when she opened the door the sound of complaining customers rushed in along with Miller dressed in his best pin-striped gray suit and blue satin shirt. His black fedora was cocked at a jaunty angle and his burgundy silk tie glistened in the harsh light. Closing the door behind him, the voices in the bar became a soft murmur.

"Winifred, I just wanted to say that was one of the most magnificent performances I have ever seen," Miller said. "When I heard you sing a few nights ago, I was sure you were a good as it gets. Tonight you proved me wrong."

"Well, thank you Mr. Miller. That's kind of you to say so," she said and noticed that his taunt skin was definitely more pale than usual and there seemed to be a nervous twitch beneath his left eye.

"You probably heard some of the folks outside don't want to leave—but we need to close up a few minutes early tonight. It's not like it's a weekend or something and ten is late enough for these boys on a Thursday night."

"Yes sir, they did seem a bit rowdy tonight," Winnie said. "And I really have to be getting along too. I'm singing at poor Rufus Pool's funeral service on the beach in the morning at sunrise. Awfully early, but that's the way Rufus' momma wanted it."

"Good!" Miller said. "I mean, not about the funeral. It's just that it's good you need to get home. I just wanted to tell you how great you sounded. Oh, and I just about forgot." Miller reached into his coat pocket and pulled out a fat white envelope with her name on it. "Here's your pay for tonight—you earned every cent of it."

Winnie took the envelope and immediately knew that even if it were stuffed with only one dollar bills, she was suddenly wealthy.

"Go ahead and open it if you want," Miller said proudly. "But if you don't, I'll just tell you there's a hundred and ten dollars in there."

Winnie felt her knees go weak. "Oh Mr. Miller...that...that can't be right. That's way too much money for just one night of singing."

"Nonsense young lady," Miller scolded. "You're a star...just a small star now, but in a few months everyone in America will be talking about you. Just wait and see how much you earn this weekend."

Winnie's mind was reeling. She had never considered the money during her agonizing over whether or not to tell what she had seen in Miller's office—she had only considered the loss of an opportunity of a lifetime. Now, with cash in hand, she couldn't help but think it might not be a bad idea to wait at least until Monday to talk to the FBI.

"Boss!" Carbone shoved the door open and struck Miller with the doorknob—there was no way he could squeeze into the room. "Sorry...but I was just talking to one of those Navy guys—he says there's no way our visitors will show up tomorrow!"

"What do you mean?" Miller asked with obvious concern in his voice. He glanced over at Winnie and then said quickly to Carbone: "We'll talk about this after you get everybody out of here. Hurry it up."

"Right boss, right away," Carbone said as he stepped back and pulled the door closed again.

"I'm sorry Winifred...but we were expecting a large contingent of sailors to arrive tomorrow," Miller said anxiously. "I have to make some other arrangements so as soon as you get ready you can head on home. The reverend is picking you up?"

Winnie nodded.

"Good, so I'll see you tomorrow evening. The show was aces."

As Miller backed through the door, Winnie saw her opportunity slipping away.

"Mr. Miller!" Winnie said much louder than she had intended, but she managed to stop his exit. "I was just wondering. We're still going to meet Mr. Cab Calloway next week aren't we?"

"Sure we are. All the arrangements have been made. Looks like we'll be leaving Monday morning. But I'll give you all the details sometime this weekend. Now, you hurry on home," Miller said and pulled the door nearly closed before she could stop him again.

"Mr. Miller!" Winnie said and this time *Uncle Sam's* owner looked annoyed when he stepped back inside the room. "I know you're awful busy...so I was just wondering if you might rather me go up and meet Mr. Calloway on my own. You could give me all the information right now and I could...."

"That's out of the question," Miller said and his good mood quickly faded. "I'll take you there personally. Besides, I can't wait to see the look on his face when he hears you sing."

"But my granny and Reverend Fulmer both wanted to know where we would be meeting Mr. Calloway…where we're going to be staying and…."

"We're closing in ten minutes," Miller snapped. "I expect you to be out of here in five minutes." He stepped outside and slammed the door angrily.

"Yes sir," Winnie said as she latched the door. She knew her attempt at finding enough details to get to her audition without Miller had been a feeble one and as she quickly undressed, she couldn't help but think this would be the last time she would touch such elegant clothes. Tomorrow, she decided, she would go to the FBI.

2225 hrs.

"And so this Navy guy says: '*Tennessee*? Are you nuts? The Japs bombed the hell out of her at Pearl Harbor. She's sittin' on her bottom in the mud out there.'"

Carbone retold his conversation with the sailors in the bar to Miller who sat behind his desk and took notes on everything his assistant said.

"So then," he continued. "I thought maybe I had made a mistake about the name of the ship. But I was sure about the name of that cruiser, the *Pauxatawney*, but when I said that they both started laughing—said something about there not being a ship named that, but if there was they'd be usin' it to haul ground hogs."

"I see," Miller said as he removed a copy of the message they had sent the previous evening from his desk drawer. He quickly took it to the table by the window where he opened his copy of the 1940 edition of Jane's Warships of the World and began searching for the names in the message among the listing of hundreds of U.S. Navy warships. There was no *Malcomb McGillicutty*, no *East Mifflenberg* and no *West Tolomotomy*. Flipping to the index for the Polish Navy he quickly discovered there was apparently no ship named the *Wzynilosky*.

Caught! The word exploded in Miller's brain and then it

echoed away as he immediately began to consider his plan for damage control. The first step had to be damage assessment. Miller closed his eyes in thought as he reviewed what had happened. He had broadcast a fictitious message given to him by that FBI agent and his kid sidekick. And they had seemed so...harmless. And why? Perhaps they could intercept his message and then compare it against the text they had given him as a means of creating a key for breaking the naval code. Not likely-- he was certain the code was unbreakable even if the Allies had the type of primitive key the message could provide. Were they trying to lure U-boats into a trap by announcing the arrival of an American fleet? Miller quickly ruled out that possibility. If they were smart enough to come up with a plan like this, they would have created more attractive bait such as a convoy of merchant ships. Surely, they must know that U-boats would be more likely to avoid a confrontation with a battle fleet. So what's left? The most likely answer came to him quickly. Direction finding. That's what they were up to. Get him to broadcast a long message and let the direction finding stations home in on the transmitter.

"So… Boss. What's the deal?" Carbone asked.

"It means, my friend, that our young FBI acquaintance and his pet reporter tricked us into sending a false message." Miller said quietly.

"And...I'm sorry if I ain't so bright...but what's the bottom line?"

"The bottom line is there is a good chance they know we have a transmitter here."

The color drained from Carbone's face and he leaned forward to brace himself with his hands on the desk as though his knees had suddenly turned to jelly. "But if they know, why haven't they come to arrest us? You sent that message last night."

"A good question," Miller said. "Perhaps it takes several days for them to calculate our position. Maybe they're waiting for reinforcements.... or maybe they failed to get a fix on us. Who knows? Maybe it's just some sort of FBI joke."

Carbone's demeanor quickly brightened. "Yeah! I'll bet that's it. Those two are a couple of real cut ups. That kid probably thought this whole thing up--it sounds like something he'd think was real funny."

"We have no choice but to proceed with our plans--it's far too late to cancel the invitation we have made to our guests," Miller said firmly. "They will be arriving soon. So we must be at our best. Are you ready to do your duty *Matrose* Carbone?"

Carbone did his best impression of a sailor at attention. "Yes Boss... I mean, yes sir!"

"Very good then," Miller said, took a deep breath and let it out slowly. "I want you to make certain the pier is deserted and the gate is locked—we don't want any surprise guests. Then, come back here and we'll take our cargo down to the far end of the pier—no need to make our guests come up here to carry it. You have the signal lights burning out there don't you?"

"Yes, sir, just like you said...a white light above a red one out at the end of the pier," Carbone said proudly.

"*Sehr gut, Matrose* Carbone," said Miller. "Carry on with your duties."

Carbone tried to remember the correct response, but gave up quickly. He merely saluted and scrambled over to the wooden hatch. He quickly swung the door upward and then disappeared down the spiral staircase as he pulled the hatch closed behind him.

Alone, Miller reviewed the checklist he had prepared weeks ago just in case a night like this one ever developed. Satisfied that everything was in order, he went over to the battered sea trunk that he kept lodged in a corner of the office. Since moving in two years ago, he had limited his access to the trunk to nights when the yellow moon hung full above the ocean. Not that he couldn't open the old Navy lock anytime he wished—he had simply imposed the "full moon only" rule in order to give himself something to look forward to with keen anticipation at least once each month.

But tonight was an exception to the rule—a special occasion that called for something truly out of the ordinary. As he twisted the heavy brass key and pulled the lock open, Miller couldn't help but feel an unusual sense of elation. On some nights, the monthly opening of the trunk had produced an almost overwhelming nostalgia that was so unsettling that he looked forward to closing up his collection of memorabilia from a previous life and putting aside the trunk for another lunar cycle. On other nights, especially when the opening was preceded by the ingestion of a strong shot of schnapps, Miller felt a warm affection for the relics contained within the cedar-scented trunk.

This time, he barely paused as he shoved aside the photos of *SMS Nassau* steaming though the Baltic, or the group photo of her officers wearing tropical uniforms and squinting against the harsh light of the African sun. He removed the ship's diary he had kept whenever he was aboard the battleship and paused just long enough to briefly admire the photo of his Uncle Karl von Muller, captain of the famed raider *SMS Emden.* As always, the photo reminded him of a captain's devotion to the welfare of his crew. One of Germany's true heroes, his uncle had spent his pension taking care of the men who had served under him during their extraordinary adventures in the Pacific and Indian Oceans. And when influenza claimed his life within a few short years of the armistice, the final words he gasped were inquiries about the needs of his former crewmembers. Although he only possessed one subordinate, Miller was determined that tonight he would model his behavior toward *Matrose* Carbone after that of his illustrious uncle.

At last, he reached the paper-wrapped package that occupied the bottom third of the trunk. Carefully removing it and placing it on the table by the window, Miller folded back the paper covering to reveal his most prized possession—the uniform of an *Oberleutnant zur See* in the Fatherland's *Kaiserlichemarine.* He wriggled out of his gray suit coat and replaced it with the dark blue jacket with brass buttons he had last worn on active duty more than 20 years ago. Tossing aside his stylish fedora, he placed the peaked officer's hat on his head and set it at a jaunty angle.

Miller was pleased with the image that stared back at him from the mirror on the far wall. He allowed himself the luxury of admiring his appearance and recalling a few of the happier moments he has spent while wearing this uniform from the Kaiser's Navy. He remembered a bright summer day when a young girl in an Adriatic port had shyly asked if she could touch his hat. But before he could positively recall the color of her eyes, a gust of night air came through the open window and disrupted his reverie.

"Enough," Miller said aloud and rubbed his eyes with one hand as though erasing the images from his past. He knew he had one more task to perform—a job he had first anticipated two years ago when he had begun supplying military intelligence to *BdU.* Miller walked across his office to the far wall where he carefully removed an inexpensive painting of a sailing ship to reveal a large wall safe.

Quickly working the combination, Miller pulled the door open and with both hands reached far into its dark recesses. He withdrew a wooden box and gingerly carried it over and placed it in the center of his desk. Taking a deep breath, he slowly removed the cover to reveal its contents—twelve sticks of dynamite, each individually wrapped in plain red paper. Thoughtfully included in the box was a pre-wired detonator and a choice of a timer or a push button trigger.

It was a simple matter to prepare the explosives and when finished, Miller couldn't help but smile at the results of his handiwork. He felt a great sense of relief in knowing that this time, no matter what happened, *Uncle Sam's* would not suffer the same humiliating fate as his beloved *SMS Nassau.*

FRIDAY
April 17, 1942

U-112: 0015 hrs.

Through Teddy Rahn's binoculars, the city of St. Augustine glowed like the Hamburg waterfront on Christmas Eve. The towering twin spires of the old Ponce de Leon Hotel were clearly visible as was the well-lit, burnished copper dome of a church to its right. As the U-112 completed her leisurely turn onto a southerly heading, he could see the bright headlights of cars crossing the Bridge of Lions as they made their way to and from the mainland and Anastasia Island. Then, as though the city was a theatrical prop mounted on wheels, St. Augustine seemed to slide away and out of sight behind the dark silhouette of the island where a few scattered lights could be seen just beyond the white line of breaking surf.

Just to the south, the St. Augustine Lighthouse sent a powerful beam of light streaking overhead every thirty seconds. For Rahn, the lighthouse served as the perfect waypoint for his run toward the shore and as U-112 came abreast of the tower, he gave a final course correction to the helmsman:

"Come to course one-nine-zero," Rahn ordered. "Ahead one-third."

The bow of the U-boat swung slowly to starboard and settled on a course that carried them past a long stretch of dark and apparently unoccupied beach that led to a glowing smear of light directly ahead. Within minutes, the brightly lit fishing pier and carnival-like setting of *Uncle Sam's* came clearly into view.

"Gentlemen, our destination," Rahn said matter-of-factly. "Course one-nine-five and diesels all stop. Go to e-motors and give me red in the boat."

Uncle Sam's

The big diesels shuddered as the Chief shut them down and their roar and vibration were replaced by the gentle swish and slap of the warm sea as it caressed the hull. Powered by the electric motors, the big *Type IX Atlantik* boat edged closer to the Florida shore.

Down in the control room, the keen sense of anticipation created by the unusual switch to the e-motors on the surface was heightened by the sudden change in lighting. In compliance with Rahn's orders, the primary lighting system had been extinguished and replaced by a red glow that both improved the landing party's night vision and reminded many of the crew of the pleasures they would find in Lorient's brothels when they returned.

"Ready Paulson?" Leutnant Lamprecht asked and wondered why the switch to red light always seemed to make everyone on board suddenly speak in whispers. Paulson was no exception— Lamprecht could barely hear the man's muted response and at once he began to second-guess his choice of companions for this mission. Maybe Paulson wasn't really up for this, he thought. After all, the man had a wife and two kids in Wilhelmshafen. Maybe his English language skills weren't that necessary... maybe it would be better to have someone who was more skilled with an MP-40—especially if they ran into trouble.

"I'm ready *Herr Leutnant*," Matrose Weber said enthusiastically. The young U-boatman leaned against the ladder leading up to the conning tower and cleaned his fingernails with an enormous *Kriegsmarine* dagger. "Do you think we'll get a warm welcome?"

Lamprecht wasn't sure whether Weber meant an enthusiastic greeting or one in which they found themselves staring into American machine guns. He couldn't help but feel that Weber would find this little side trip to be a major disappointment if he didn't get a chance to kill someone.

"I really don't know...but I would be happy with just a welcome...warm or cold," Lamprecht said and noticed that Weber's expression of childish good humor remained unchanged. The man seemed to be an ideal candidate for a hit man for some Chicago mob, but Lamprecht refrained from suggesting that career option to the sailor. "Where's Stranzl?"

Weber shrugged, but to Lamprecht's relief, Paulson suddenly

280

seemed interested in the mission.

"He's up forward, *Herr Leutnant.* I think he's getting something to eat... said he didn't know if there would be any restaurants open this late in Florida."

Lamprecht smiled. At least he was certain his choice of the big Silesian farm boy for this mission had been correct. Stranzl was so strong that half the crew believed his claim that he could sit in a basket and lift himself off the deck. He was confident he could handle whatever package was waiting for them in Florida and his English was passable, even if he had his mother's Scottish accent.

"Number Two to the bridge!" Rahn's order was shouted down the open tower hatch and seemed much too loud for the now quiet boat.

"Coming up, *Herr Kaleu!*" Lamprecht responded, but before he headed up the ladder, he gave Paulson and Weber their orders. "First, find Stranzl and then wait up by the forward hatch until we're ready to go. Paulson, sidearms for you and Stranzl. Weber, bring along an MP. And all of you, put on your night goggles and keep them on until you go topside."

"*Ja, Herr Leutnant,*" the two men responded and pulled the smoked lens goggles up from around their necks and adjusted the elastic bands to hold them snuggly over their eyes while their pupils adjusted to the lack of light. Lamprecht gave them an encouraging smile and then he hurried up the aluminum ladder.

On the bridge, the watch allowed themselves to believe that the silence of the engines had transformed the U-112 into a sailing ship. And as they edged toward the unknown Florida shore, the more imaginative of the group couldn't help but think of the bold Spanish explorers who had first come ashore here nearly 400 years ago.

"Tide is running in, *Herr Kaleu,*" Thiele said. "That should help them get ashore."

"Personally, I would be more concerned with getting back out here. Especially if I had the *Amis* on my tail," Rahn said as he lowered his binoculars. Seeing Lamprecht standing there, he suddenly displayed a confident smile. "But that's not going to happen. Is it Number Two?"

"Of course not *Herr Kaleu,*" Lamprecht said. "It will be just like my first visit to the whorehouse—in and out quickly and quietly."

The commander of U-112 reached out and gave his Number Two Watch Officer's shoulder a firm squeeze. "All set then?"

"Everything is ready *Herr Kaleu.*"

Rahn released his grip, winked and then looked up into the night sky for a long moment as though considering variables known only to him. Satisfied that the moment had arrived, he leaned over and shouted down the open hatch.

"Engines all stop! Landing party topside!"

Without the engines and the wind, the men on the bridge could clearly hear their commander's orders being repeated through the boat.

"This is as close as we get," Rahn said to Lamprecht. "Another fifty meters and we'll be dragging our keel. So just get in there, make the trade and get out. We can't afford to linger."

"*Jawohl, Herr Kaleu,*" Lamprecht replied and snapped off his very best naval salute. He waited for Rahn's less-than-regulation reply and then descended from the bridge by way of the outside handholds on the tower.

By the time Lamprecht reached the deck, the landing party had already come through the forward hatch and with the help of four other crewmen was busily removing the wooden decking that covered the inflatable. Despite the darkness, they quickly removed it from the storage area and released the restraining latches. Compressed air began to hiss and the black rubber cube seemed to come alive as it unfolded and slowly transformed itself into a very utilitarian-looking raft.

Nearly a mile away, the lights of *Uncle Sam's* glared brightly and while the crewmen struggled with getting the inflatable over the side, Lamprecht studied their objective. Even without binoculars, he could now see the single red and white lights burning at the end of the pier. The bar seemed empty, but just beyond it two small spotlights were holding a gigantic American flag in their determined grip. Lamprecht found it difficult to believe that within the next thirty minutes he would be walking along the pier that at the moment seemed to be part of an alien world.

"*Herr Leutnant,* we're ready to cast off!"

Lamprecht turned his attention to U-112's starboard side where the inflatable had been lowered into the water. It was so close alongside that the boat was hidden behind the curve of the big saddle tank, but Weber, Paulson, and Stranzl had taken their seats in the inflatable and could be seen rising and falling in response to the gentle swell. Lamprecht carried the shoulder satchel containing the *Enigma* and the cash over to the side and with the help of two crewmembers, edged down the sloping hull and handed the package to Paulson who quickly stowed it in the middle of the inflatable. Lamprecht waited for the next wave to lift the rubber boat and when it did, he stepped into the inflatable and tumbled into his position in the stern.

"Good luck to you!" A crewman said and tossed the mooring line into the inflatable. "We'll see you in a couple of hours."

Lamprecht waved an acknowledgement and then lifted his oar from the boat's surprisingly sturdy bottom.

"All right gentlemen, all together please," Lamprecht said as he dug his oar into the warm waters of the Atlantic. After only three strokes, the four of them had agreed on a rhythm that quickly pulled them away from U-112.

"Aircraft approaching!" The starboard lookout's warning caught everyone by surprise.

"Shit!" Rahn exclaimed as he turned to face the U-boat's stern. "Good work Kovic. Where is the bastard?"

"Green one-three-five. *Herr Kaleu.* Coming directly toward us."

Through his binoculars, Rahn quickly picked out a slow moving white light from among the hundreds of stars above the northern horizon. Focusing, the plane's red and green navigation lights came clearly into view.

"I see him," Rahn announced. "Looks big...probably twin-engined."

The drone of the plane's engines was now clearly audible and even without lowering his binoculars Rahn could sense the sudden tenseness of everyone gathered around him on the U-boat's bridge. He would have to decide on a course of action...and quickly.

"*Herr Kaleu!* Do we keep going?" Lamprecht's voice rang out and Rahn turned to see the inflatable bobbing gently on the dark sea. "What should we do?"

Rahn mentally reviewed his very short list of options. Dive? Out of the question—not deep enough to even put the deck under water. Run for deep water? The diesels would betray their position and Lamprecht and his landing party would have to be abandoned to their fate. Shoot it out with the aircraft? The noise and the tracers would jar everyone in St. Augustine out of their beds....firing would definitely show the enemy aircrew the U-boat's exact position... and there was a good chance they would lose the duel to the aircraft's bombs or depth charges.

"Sit quietly!" Rahn shouted. "They won't see you!"

"But *Herr Kaleu*," Lamprecht protested. "How can they miss us?"

"Maybe it's the same crew that flew over us in broad daylight the other morning—if they didn't see us then....they sure as hell won't see us in the dark," Rahn said as he focused his binoculars on the approaching aircraft. "Number One, tell the Chief to stand by to start the diesels...just in case we have to get out of here."

"Chief!" Thiele shouted down the hatch and the tone of his voice bordered between urgency and panic. "Get ready to start the diesels!"

"He's diving," the lookout said with the kind of matter-of-fact approach to his job that Rahn thought would be more appropriate for his Number One.

It was clear that the enemy aircraft was descending quickly and Rahn suddenly wondered if the Americans had some sort of detection device on board that had picked them out of the inky black sea. If they did, Rahn realized he and his crew would probably be dead within the next few minutes. He knew that he should be doing something to save them, but now the only option left was to pray. Instead, he chose to concentrate on Kat. She would be just waking now, he thought, and he remembered how delicious she had looked one warm morning when the sun's early light had picked out her figure through her blue nightgown as she stood in front of the bedroom window.

"He's turning...he's turning *Herr Kaleu*."

The lookout's report brought Rahn back to reality and he watched the lights of the American aircraft fade to the brief red glimmer of the port wingtip light and then disappear as it descended into the glow above the town. He tried to sound calm as he realized the immediate threat of violent death had gone.

"Landing at the local airport, no doubt about it," Rahn announced to those on the bridge before shouting out to Lamprecht:

"All clear! Have a good vacation in Florida!"

Lamprecht waved and the paddles splashed as the inflatable resumed its journey toward the bright lights of *Uncle Sam's.*

FBI CHARTER DC-3: 0035 hrs

The pilot and co-pilot of the DC-3 flying down from Washington, D.C. had no idea that they had nearly flown directly over one of Hitler's finest U-boats. They were much too busy preparing to land at the St. Johns County airport. For some odd reason, the FBI agent in charge had refused to allow them to contact the airport until they had it in sight—by then, the one man on duty in the operations office was sound asleep and it was only a frantic radio call after they had entered the landing pattern that roused him from his slumber and resulted in the runway lights coming on.

The sudden appearance of the lights had come as a great relief to the pilot who had become uncomfortable with his approach from the sea. Flying across the blackness of the ocean to land on a brightly lit shoreline was not something he had previously experienced, but he quickly made the appropriate corrections and the big tires kissed the tarmac sweetly.

"We're here!" FBI Deputy Director Frank Masterson shouted and jumped up from his seat in the DC-3's cabin as soon as the plane's tail wheel touched down. Bracing himself against the sway of the taxiing aircraft by gripping a seatback, he reached down with his other hand and lifted his new hat from the empty seat. Made of a deep burgundy felt with an unusually wide brim, the fedora sported a gold hatband—a color combination that matched the uniforms of the Washington Redskins. Although he had never been an avid football fan, he had selected this particular chapeau because it was distinctively Washington. And that's what he needed, he had decided, a symbol or icon that would help make G-Man Masterson a household word throughout America.

"OK, Burt are you and your boys ready?" Masterson asked as he pulled the brim of his new hat down until it hid one eye.

From his window seat three rows back, Burt Logan tried to shift his bulk but had to settle for a slight rotation of his upper torso. After the long flight, he could no longer feel his legs. But when he glanced down to confirm they were still attached to his body, all he

285

could see was the top of his beer gut straining against the cloth of his favorite green satin shirt.

"Sure Chief, we're ready....aren't we boys?" He twisted his head in a failed attempt to see the rear of the cabin where his three trigger men had spent the flight napping in separate seats. In response to a wave from Logan's chubby hand, one of the agents made a motion as though swatting a fly. The other two merely straightened their shirts and ties without saying a word. "Hey Chief," Logan said, "this was a damn long flight and I'm ready for a drink. Do you think we can pick up some hooch when we get to that bar?"

"No problem there Burt," Masterson said as he reached into his briefcase and pulled out a pearl-handled .38 which he slipped into his shoulder holster. "After we get the cuffs on this Nazi, you can have the whole bar if you want. What is that old saying? To the victor belongs the spoils. In fact, as soon as this job is over all of you boys get two days off in the Florida sun. Doug, you don't have to put that in your story."

Doug Whitehall, the *Washington Post* reporter, seemed to be growing more nervous by the minute and when Logan's three gunmen stood and pulled their Tommy guns out of their cases, the color drained from his face. To Masterson, the reporter looked like a man in charge of the reference desk at an all-night library.

"Don't worry Mr. Masterson, I'm sure I'll have plenty of other exciting things to write about," Whitehall said. "This is all quite a....a... thrill for me."

"I'm glad you're enjoying it Doug...I'm sure the Director will be anxious to read your story," Masterson said and gave George Watts, the FBI press officer, a wink that said—thanks for getting us such a compliant reporter, let's insure we make the best possible use of him.

On the other hand, he wasn't so sure about *the Post's* photographer. He seemed like a surly young man who was skeptical of everything he heard. As he gathered up his camera, Masterson decided he didn't care about the man's attitude—just as long as he took photos that showed his best side. Getting his photo in the Post was bound to help with the ladies. And if he didn't, Masterson decided he would arrange for the photographer to go to work immediately for *Stars and Stripes* where his first assignment would be a photo essay titled "The War in Siberia."

The pilot throttled back on the starboard engine and gunned the port Wright-Cyclone to turn the plane in front of the operations office. A slight touch of the brakes brought them to a halt and the engines popped and gurgled as they were shut down.

"Who says Southern boys are lazy?" Masterson said as he leaned down to look out a cabin window. He could clearly see the four cars he had requested from the Jacksonville FBI office sitting at the edge of the taxiway with their lights on, engines idling and drivers waiting behind the steering wheels. "All right then, any last minute questions?"

Except for young Patrick Keane, all the passengers were scrambling to gather up their gear and some had already pressed toward the rear cabin door that was being opened by the co-pilot. The son of Senator Walter Keane, however, seemed a bit confused by this first FBI mission.

"Mr. Masterson, sir, " he asked from his seat in the front row. "What about our agent here in St. Augustine? Remember Agent Spencer? What's his assignment going to be when we get there?"

"Hurry up Keane," Masterson said as he stepped aside to allow Burt Logan to squeeze out the door. "And don't worry about Spencer— if we run into him, I'll put him to work parking our cars."

ANASTASIA ISLAND: 0115 hrs.

Bill Spencer was about to call it a night. The sheriff had finally wakened from his demonstration of all the unusual sounds the human body can make while asleep and had wandered off somewhere to relieve himself. The thrill of the stakeout had eventually faded for Scoop Pomar and the boy now slept peacefully tucked in a fetal position against the opposite door of the Chevy coupe. As he looked at the sleeping boy, Spencer decided that as soon as the sheriff returned, they would head home. It was obvious to him that nothing was going to happen, the least he could do would be to return Pomar to the safety of his room—although the wasn't sure how he would explain the situation to Mrs. Pomar.

He was still trying to come up with a believable alibi for Scoop when the headlights of an approaching car glared in his rearview mirror. Spencer expected the car to speed on by up the coast road, but when it pulled in behind him and the mysterious driver switched off his lights, the G-man had no choice but to draw his pistol from its holster and step out of his car to confront the new arrival.

"Good evening...or should I say good morning Agent Spencer," Reverend Amos Fulmer said as he slowly got out of the church's battered Ford and closed the door behind him.

"Hello Reverend," Spencer said and sheepishly returned his pistol to its holster. "I'm sorry about the heater...I had no idea it was you."

"Now don't you fret none about that gun...you was just doin' your job and I don't blame you none either. A man can't be too careful out here this late at night...some of us can't always rely on the Lord's protection," Fulmer said and even in the darkness, Spencer could see the man's smile.

"Well, I would say you can certainly rely on the Lord, but I unfortunately have to rely on Smith and Wesson," Spencer said. "What brings you out so late?"

"Looking for you actually." Fulmer walked around the front of the car and Spencer could see he had a passenger in the front seat. "I came by here earlier to pick up Winifred Greer and I don't know if you were trying to hide out or not, but your car was pretty easy to see. I just hoped you would still be here."

"Another few minutes and I would have been gone. I think my work here for tonight is finished," Spencer said. "So what can I do for you?"

"Well, it's not me that wants to see you. It's Winifred Greer who needs to tell you something," Fulmer said as he opened the Ford's passenger door. "Winifred, you go ahead and talk to Agent Spencer. There's no reason to be shy."

Winfred Greer stepped from the car and straightened her dress. Spencer noticed that even on a dark night, there was something...what was the word? Elegant. There was something elegant about Winifred Greer.

"I just wanted to tell you what I saw the other night."

Her voice was strained and as Spencer looked at her sad face, he could tell she had been crying.

"I should have told you right away," she continued. "I wanted to, but …well, you probably wouldn't understand anyway. So now I feel like it's the only thing to do because, well I, just think it's the right thing to do."

"That's all right Winifred," Spencer said and for some reason felt compelled to do whatever he could to ease her obvious discomfort. "Just take your time and tell me what you saw."

"That's right Winifred. Don't hold nothin' back," Reverend Fulmer said.

"Well," she said, then took a deep breath and let it out slowly. "Last night I had to come back to *Uncle Sam's* to talk to Mr. Miller after it was closed. The door was locked so I climbed up on the roof through a passage not many people know about. I was going to peck on the office window to get them to let me in and, well, that's when I saw it."

Spencer knew the evidence he needed was about to be given to him. He didn't even have to ask her to continue. Winifred seemed anxious to tell him her story.

"Mr. Miller had that big closet-like cabinet of his open and he and Mr. Carbone were working on something that looked like a radio. Mr. Miller was typing on some kind of keyboard and lights were coming on every time he pressed a key. I could hear them talking about ships and things. First, I thought maybe they were working for the Coast Guard or somethin', but then I saw those German things like you see in the newspapers — you know, them hex signs or something…."

"*Swastika,*" Fulmer said.

"Yes, that's it," Winnie continued. "There was one of them on the front of his radio and I could just tell that the two of them were up to no good."

"I'll be damned!" Spencer blurted out. "Sorry Reverend. But that's the evidence I needed. I was sent down here to find a Nazi spy and I thought it was Miller, but I just couldn't prove it…. not until now anyway. Miss Greer, you've performed a valuable service for the American people."

"It was the right thing for me to do," Winnie said quietly. "The right thing for my country." She could feel her composure breaking and the tears were welling up from deep inside. Without another word, she returned to her seat in the car and pulled the door closed. "You can't imagine what this has cost her," Reverend Fulmer said as he stepped around the car and paused by the open driver-side door. "Miller was her ticket to the big time...now he's going to the big house."

"I'm not sure I understand," said Spencer, "but maybe there's something we can do at the Bureau to help her out. I'm not sure what it would be, but...what the hell is that?"

Four FBI sedans roared into the parking light with red lights flashing. They came to a stop in a cloud of dust and sand at the bottom of the gangplank leading up to *Uncle Sam's*. When Reverend Fulmer saw what had to be at least a dozen white men pouring out of the vehicles, some armed with submachine guns, he knew it was time to go.

"Good luck to you Agent Spencer," Fulmer said as he fired up the old Ford and began backing away.

Spencer never even bothered to wave goodbye. Instead, he hurried toward the crowd of heavily armed men who appeared to be about ready to launch a raid on *Uncle Sam's Bar and Pier.*

UNCLE SAM'S: 0120 hrs.

For *Leutnant* Lamprecht, his excursion to Florida had been far different than he had imagined. Paddling the inflatable had been hard work for muscles that had spent weeks in the cramped confines of U-112 and the heat had made the trip even more draining. By the time they reached the shadows cast by the pilings supporting the pier, all four of them felt as though they had been on a ten- mile hike with full packs. Sweaty and breathless, they wanted to rest, but instead found themselves struggling to secure the inflatable so that the gentle rollers that rocked them did not rupture its thin skin on the barnacle-encrusted pier.

It wasn't until they had finally scrambled up a rope ladder to the pier's main deck and met their hosts, that Lamprecht's pre-conceived notion of his Florida vacation completely collapsed. He couldn't help but be reminded of a story he had once read about an explorer who had spent years preparing to encounter a primitive tribe in the jungle. When the big moment finally came, the explorer was so overcome by the odors, the appearance of the savages, and the sudden contact with an alien world that he had vomited on the chief's bare feet and fainted. Lamprecht had not been nauseous, but the smell of rotting fish and the sudden firmness of his footing after weeks of being tossed about at sea had been unsettling. But it was the appearance of their contact that Lamprecht had found to be most disturbing—he had never expected to meet someone dressed in the full uniform of an officer in the Kaiser's old navy. Introducing himself as *Leutnant zur Zee* Joachim Mueller, the man said everyone called him Joe Miller. He then insisted on following the same protocol for bringing them aboard his fishing pier as was used to bring an admiral aboard a battlecruiser of the old High Seas Fleet. To make the situation even more bizarre, the man commanded a crew of one consisting of a gnome-like fellow who seemed compelled to obey every command—even ones that made no sense whatsoever.

By the time Lamprecht had walked the length of the pier with Mueller and the little man, he had decided he had made a mistake in accepting the old officer's invitation to see his "command center". By the time he had climbed up the spiral staircase, through the hatch and into the office, he had decided to concentrate on getting away as soon as possible.

"So, *Leutnant*, what do you think of my quarters here on the bridge of *Uncle Sam's?*" Miller asked in perfect German with a Prussian accent.

"Very nice, sir," Lamprecht said. "You have a great view here--must be wonderful to be permanently stationed here in Florida." Miller completely missed the U-boatman's attempt at levity.

"It's difficult, of course, I should be at sea--that's the place for a naval officer," Miller said as he moved to his desk, opened a drawer and produced a bottle of schnapps. "But we have made the best of it in an effort to serve the Fatherland."

"I'm sure you're doing good work here, sir," Lamprecht said and stepped over to one of the windows in hopes of seeing the landing party at the end of the pier or in the inflatable. Surely, they had loaded Miller's cargo and were ready to go. Seeing nothing he turned to find Miller pouring schnapps into three shot glasses. "Sir, really I must go. Our boat is waiting. Here is the package we were to deliver." He pulled the satchel from his shoulder and placed it on Miller's desk.

"Nonsense!" Miller snapped and pushed a glass of schnapps toward Lamprecht. "We'll open the package, then I will show you around. I think you'll be impressed with our transmitter. It's a two hundred watt *Telefunken.*" He handed Carbone a shot glass and motioned for Lamprecht to pick up his drink. "Gentlemen... *prost!*"

Lamprecht had to admit that the fiery liquid helped settle his nerves. But at the same time, it sharpened his senses as he searched for the answer to an important question: What am I doing here?

"Now, let's just see what we have received," Miller said as he put down his glass and unfastened the satchel. He pulled out the polished wooden box containing the new four-rotor *Enigma*. Placing it carefully in the center of his desk, he reached inside the satchel once more and withdrew the cash box. His pale hands moved over the woodwork slowly and then he unlatched it and lifted the top.

"Jesus! Look at the size of that wad!" Carbone blurted out and Miller gave him a disapproving look before carefully closing the box.

"Yes, that seems to be adequate funding for keeping us afloat," Miller said. "If you would be so kind, *Herr Leutnant*, as to convey our thanks to the High Command."

"Of course, now if you'll excuse me, my men are waiting." Lamprecht had taken only one step toward the hatch when the sound of car engines, screeching brakes, and headlights sweeping across the windows stopped him in his tracks.

"What the hell--don't those Army idiots know we're closed?" Carbone said and shoved past Lamprecht giving the U-boat officer a strong whiff of garlic and sweat on his way to the window overlooking the parking lot. "Shit! It's the FBI! A dozen of them--we're dead men."

Lamprecht knew he had to get away, but at the same time, duty compelled him to at least offer these people who were risking their lives for Germany a chance to escape what was probably a death sentence.

"Come on! Come with me," Lamprecht said as he paused at the open hatch. "If you hurry, we can all make it to the boat."

"We have our duty and you have yours," Miller said firmly. "I have made my arrangements for just such a situation." He leaned over his desk and scribbled something on a note card. "But if you could please arrange to bring your U-boat past these coordinates at dawn, we would be most appreciative."

"Of course, we'll do what we can," Lamprecht grabbed the card and started down the staircase. "Good luck to both of you."

"Boss! Let's get out of here!" Carbone pleaded. "Those G-men will be here any second!"

"Secure the hatch, *Matrose* Carbone," Miller said. "That's an order."

Lamprecht only went circling down a few steps before jumping over the railing and landing with a thud on the barroom floor. He could hear the FBI agents coming up the gangplank and as he ran around the corner at the end of the hallway, he heard breaking glass and splintering wood as the G-men came crashing through the front door. He stumbled as *Uncle Sam's* suddenly plunged into darkness.

"Deputy Director Masterson! It's me!" Bill Spencer shouted as he rushed up the entry ramp to where Masterson and a group of people he took to be reporters were watching through the shattered door while three burly G-men lumbered through the dark interior of the bar leaving a path of destruction in their wake. "What are you doing?"

"Ah, young Spencer...good to see you," Masterson said as he turned away from the bar to face his subordinate. "And in answer to your question, what we are doing is arresting one of Hitler's most dangerous spies."

"So my plan did work, you were able to trace the radio transmission!" Spencer exclaimed. "But why didn't you call me? I could have made the arrest for you."

"Look, son," Masterson said as he pulled him away from the reporter who suddenly seemed interested in what they were saying. "This is big...bigger than you would ever know. This is a real feather in the Bureau's cap---arresting a Nazi spy. We even brought that reporter over there along with us from the *Washington Post*. How was I to know some local telephone operator wouldn't be listening in to let Miller know we were coming. We couldn't take that chance."

"I don't think there was much chance of that," Spencer said just as one of the G-men inside smashed the big mirror behind the bar. "Hey, I don't know what they're doing in there, but they're not gonna find Miller by busting up everything. He's bound to be up there in his little fortress on the roof and you can only get there by going up a small spiral staircase and through a hatch in the ceiling. C'mon, I'll show you."

Spencer took only one step toward the door when Masterson reached out and grabbed him roughly by his jacket

"You just don't get it do you kid?" Masterson snarled in a way that reminded Spencer of the rabid dog that had attacked his grandpa's cows nearly twenty years ago. "This is my show... I'm in charge and I'm telling you to get down to that parking lot and stay out of the way. If you get in the way, I'll make sure you spend the rest of your career in that basement cubicle of yours. Understand?"

All the pieces had not fallen into place for Spencer, but it was clear that he had somehow been used as a pawn in a game that was apparently designed by Masterson to increase his stature with the Director.

"I understand," he said and shoved Masterson's hand away, "and I can assure you I will stay as far as possible away from you." He headed quickly down the gangplank to where Pomar was looking up at him with a puzzled expression.

"All right fellas," Masterson said. "I've got a hunch our spy is in that upstairs office and we'll have to climb a ladder to get to him. Let's just go see if I'm right."

Masterson stepped into the bar with public relations man George Watts and Agent Keane close behind. *The Post* photographer entered more cautiously and the reporter, Doug Whitehall, walked gingerly as though he were certain the glass shards covering the floor could easily penetrate his shoes and his feet.

"Burt!" Masterson shouted at the burly G-man who seemed to be deciding whether or not to smash the beautiful Wurlitzer jukebox. "Come with me. I think we've treed our spy. All we have to do is go up and shake him out."

With Masterson in the lead, the entire FBI party trooped down the hallway that was now lit only by the faint moonlight coming through the windows. Even in the darkness, it didn't take long to discover the spiral staircase.

"Here we go boys," Masterson said proudly. "Just like I predicted. Now if one of you boys would be so kind as to open that hatch, I think we can arrest our spy pretty quickly."

One of Burt Logan's men shoved his way forward and handed his Tommy gun to Masterson. He looked upward for a couple of seconds and then went charging up the ladder until his shoulder made contact with the hatch. Instead of resisting, the hatch bounced open.

"A piece of cake sir," the G-man said. "Not even locked."

The sounds of music drifted down from the open hatch and the subdued lighting visible through the opening in the ceiling gave the impression that the upstairs office was someone's cozy living room.

"Mr. Masterson, sir, I'm sure you'll want to go first," the G-man said as he began backing down the ladder.

"Uh, no that's OK…you're already up there," Masterson said and gingerly handed the agent the Tommy gun. "Wait 'til I give you the word and I'll be right behind you."

Masterson looked at the crowd of expectant faces gathered around him in the faint light. It only took him a few seconds to decide who would be immortalized in the history of the FBI.

"All right now listen up," Masterson said and stroked his chin as he thoughtfully made his selection. "I'm going in and I want you, Mr. Photographer, right behind me. Next, I want another man with a Tommy. That would be you." He pointed to the agent wearing a bright red tie and the man nodded in agreement. "Burt, you're next and then Keane. You got that Keane?"

Young Keane stood at the edge of crowd as though he were more of a spectator than a participant. "Yes sir, I understand."

"Do you have your heater with you?" Masterson asked.

"Heater?" Keane looked confused. "Oh. You mean my gun. Yes, I've got a gun."

"Good. I want you to take it out of its holster and when you come through that hatch I want you to look like you mean business. Understood?"

The young man nodded and Masterson hoped he could follow those directions. He had spent a lot of time trying to make sure they got just the right photos of Senator Keane's son in action—photos that would undoubtedly help gain Congressional support for increased appropriations for the Bureau.

"All right. The rest of you wait down here until I give the all clear. You with the other submachine gun-- you stay down here and cover our backs the whole time. This man might have friends. We can't be too careful."

Ready at last, Masterson straightened his tie, tilted his new hat at a jaunty angle and pulled his .38 out of his shoulder holster.

"Joe Miller! This is the FBI!" Masterson shouted up through the hatch. "We're coming up!"

In response to Masterson's nod, the agent at the top of the ladder went scrambling through the hatch. Masterson was close behind followed by the Post's photographer and another Tommy-gun toting G-man.

When the FBI arrived out front, Joe Miller thought he would be hard pressed to complete all the needed preparations in time. As it turned out, their bull-in-a-china-shop approach to their work had given him plenty of time to finish the small tasks he had scheduled for just such an occasion. In fact, he had time to re-start the record he had placed on the phonograph before coming back to his desk and checking to make sure the new Enigma machine was leaning against the bottom drawer. Satisfied with the arrangements, he stood at attention and awaited his fate.

The first G-man popped through the hatch and quickly pointed his submachine gun at Miller. Masterson's entrance was a bit less dignified.

"Joe Miller, you're under..." Masterson said as he tripped and sprawled face down on the floor. Scrambling to his feet, he awkwardly straightened his hat with the muzzle of this pistol. "Joe Miller. You're under arrest for treason against the United States."

The photographer and the other FBI gunman hurried into the office and all four of Miller's guests gazed at their host in surprise. None had expected the evidence of Miller's guilt to be on display, but to their amazement Miller was in full uniform and behind him the dials and indicator lights on the transmitter's control panel glowed brightly. A gentle breeze came through an open window at the rear of the office and stirred papers that Masterson was certain contained all the written evidence he would need for a conviction.

"Technically, Mr. FBI Agent, you're incorrect," Miller said. "Treason can only be committed by a citizen against his own country. Because I obtained my citizenship through false representation, I am not actually a citizen. Therefore, it would be impossible for me to commit an act of treason against the United States."

296

"Hands up Mr. Smart Guy," Masterson ordered. "Nice uniform—but I don't recognize it as one of the more popular Nazi outfits. Is it just for spies?"

"This is the uniform of an officer in the Kaiser's Navy—the *Kaiserlichemarine*. It has nothing to do with the Nazi Party. I'm surprised you weren't better schooled by your employers."

"We don't waste time studying losers' uniforms," Masterson said. "Search him—he might be armed."

The first G-man to enter the room, put down his Tommy gun, stepped forward and began patting down Miller.

"I can assure you I'm unarmed." Miller said pleasantly. "My only weapon is right there on the desk."

Satisfied that Miller was telling the truth, the agent picked up the heavy Luger. "Nice piece," he said as he tucked it into the waistband of his pants. He looked at Miller and with a crooked smile on his face, reached over and yanked one of the brass buttons from the officer's jacket. "Just a souvenir---hope you don't mind."

Miller's jaw stiffened and his composure began slipping as he was reminded of the stripping of his beloved *Nassau* so long ago. No respect for the ship....no respect for the uniform.... any compassion he felt for these men quickly faded as he realized they more than deserved what he was about to give them.

"Can somebody give me a hand?" Burt Logan said. He was stuck tightly in the hatchway and it wasn't until one of his subordinates gave him a tug that he was able to squeeze through and stand shakily in the office. The distraction the incident caused gave Miller an opportunity to lower his hands and rest one finger lightly on the small push button switch on the edge of his desk.

"Maybe you'd like to sit down sir," Miller said pleasantly and motioned toward the leather sofa with his left hand. "You don't look so well."

Logan's face was bright red and his breath came in short gasps. He nodded in agreement and sat heavily on the sofa.

"All right Keane! Your turn!" Masterson shouted and said to the photographer: "Get a shot of him coming through the hatch—you know what I'm looking for—'Senator's son smashes Nazi spy nest'."

"Whatever you say Boss." The photographer knelt just a few feet from the hatch and waited until Keane had emerged halfway before focusing the camera. The flash bulb's ignition was a total surprise for the young man. Temporarily blinded, he nearly fell backwards through the hatch before catching his balance and stumbling into the room. He staggered sideways before Masterson grabbed him.

"Christ!" Masterson snarled at the photographer. "Are you trying to blind him? George! You and your reporter friend get up here—you're missing the best part!"

As Miller watched two more men in suits and ties come through the open hatch, he couldn't help but be amazed that his neatly arranged and smoothly running espionage operation was about to be terminated by such bumbling idiots.

Sheriff Haywood Hartson was zipping his fly after relieving himself in the dunes when the lights went out. Mumbling to himself about the "goddam electric company," he waited for his eyes to adjust to the darkness before starting his trek back toward *Uncle Sam's*. He had not intended to wander so far away from the parking lot, but the stakeout with the FBI agent and the kid reporter had been just too boring for him to endure any longer. He figured that a nice ten minute stroll up the beach and back would give them just enough time to decide it was quitting time.

The undulating dunes, sea oats and sandspurs stretching between him and the FBI coupe seemed much more challenging in the darkness than they had been when bathed in .garish light. Taking a much easier route, he slid down the foredune and began walking along the beach's hard packed sand. It wasn't until he had reached the forest of dark pilings supporting the bar that he first looked out to sea where to his amazement, he could see a small inflatable boat bobbing at the end of the pier. In the moonlight, he could see it was occupied by three men and, as he watched, a fourth shadowy figure scurried down a rope ladder to join his companions in the boat.

"Hey! What the hell are y'all doin' out there!" There was very little wind, but the sound of the surf was enough to keep Hartson's words from being heard by the inflatable's crew.

Hartson stepped down to the water's edge in hopes that getting five feet closer would make it easier to be heard. But before he shouted again, he saw a white light flash twice aboard the little boat. A single answering flash came from out near the horizon where the sheriff could see the dark silhouette of a submarine. Although he had not bothered to study the Coast Guard-issued flash cards showing the outline of enemy vessels, he knew at once that he was looking at a German U-boat.

"Sonofabitch!" Hartson said as he nervously fumbled with the snap button on his holster. Pulling out the big revolver, he steadied it with both hands and took careful aim at the inflatable. He knew his target was nearly out of range, so he raised the muzzle just a hair in hopes of dropping a .44 caliber slug in the middle of the nearest man's back. His thumb began pulling back the hammer, but before could get it cocked an intense pain shot up the back of his neck and set off a fireworks display in his brain. As he fell, his last conscious thought was how nice the wet sand would feel against his hot skull.

Luigi Carbone tossed away his driftwood club and reached down to retrieve the sheriff's pistol. He brushed the sand away from the gun before jamming it down into the leather satchel the U-boat man had brought to the office. He swung the satchel over his shoulder and paused just long enough to give Sheriff Hartson's unconscious form a swift kick in the backsides. Hurrying back into the darkness beneath *Uncle Sam's*, Carbone resumed his task of frantically pitching as many mewing cats as possible into the cockpit of the *Lady Liberty*.

For Miller, events were unfolding as if in a dream. Images of his childhood flashed through his subconscious, his mother's voice called to him, there was his father and a day or rowing on the Weser, a long line of Kaiserlichemarine cadets marched past in the summer sun, the *Nassau* in gleaming white paint formed the backdrop as the Kaiser's yacht sailed across the harbor, guns flashed at Jutland, he could feel the grinding of the *Nassau's* hull as she rammed a British destroyer, a funeral in the rain...

"Keane! Get over here and stand next to our Nazi spy."

Masterson's words jarred Miller back into reality and he realized that the FBI was using him as a prop for some sort of propaganda photo. Masterson was at his side with a revolver pointed at his ribs while the young agent who seemed so clumsy on his feet now sheepishly took up a position on his other side. The photographer was directly in front of him, focusing his camera on the trio while the other intruders stood in the background. They looked amused by the proceedings.

"OK, I think that's it—FBI agents Masterson and Keane, son of Senator Walter Keane, capture Hitler's most dangerous spy—I like it!"

As the photographer shifted to get them all in the frame, the last lines of the old German Empire's *Deutsches Flaggenlied* came from the phonograph --- *"Ich starb den Ehretod fur Deutschlands heiligstes Panier, die Flagge Schwarz-weiss-rot. Hurrah!"*

Miller's finger pressed the button on his desk at the same moment the photographer triggered his flashbulb and for everyone in the room the final electrical impulses in their brains confirmed that the blinding light had not captured them on film—it had transported them to eternity.

FBI Agent Bill Spencer lay on his back in *Uncle Sam's* parking lot and gasped for air to fill his empty lungs. As he stared up into the night sky, it slowly dawned on him that his belief that he had been hit by a truck was incorrect—his current situation had been caused by a tremendous explosion. As the numbness in his body faded, the stars were replaced by the dust covered, but smiling face of Scoop Pomar staring down at him. The young man's lips were moving, but Spencer couldn't make out the words until Pomar helped him stagger to his feet.

"I've got a hell of a story this time!" Scoop shouted. "Man, you should have seen that poor bastard come falling out of the sky!"

Spencer looked in the direction Scoop had nodded and saw a smoking carcass of a man sprawled across the hood of one of the FBI cars. Except for one black and white saddle oxford attached to a twisted leg, the charred corpse was completely naked. He shifted his gaze upward to where *Uncle Sam's* had been turned into a roaring volcano belching flames into the night sky as debris continued to drop around them.

"Look! Someone survived!" Pomar shouted and pointed to the left of the blazing building where flames glistened from the polished woodwork and brass of a speedboat as it accelerated out of the canal and disappeared into the darkness as it headed seaward. "Aren't you going after him?"

Spencer grinned and shook his head. "Nope. My orders were

to stay out of the way and that's what I intend to do. Right now, I think we need to get you to a telephone so you can phone your story in to the *Washington Post.* I'm sure they'll be interested when I vouch for everything you say—especially since I'm pretty certain their reporter won't be filing a story."

Something dark came spinning down out of the darkness and landed in the dust at their feet. When Spencer realized it was a new, but badly battered burgundy fedora with a gold hatband, he stepped forward and ground it beneath his shoe.

"*Herr Kaleu!* There's a speedboat pulling away from shore!"

The lookout's warning caused Rahn to swing his binoculars away from the approaching inflatable that was now backlit by the towering flames flaring upward from the shattered remains of *Uncle Sam's.* He focused on the dark form of the boat which was kicking up a rooster tail of white spray as it shot out of the fire's glare and into the darkness. Just as he prepared to order the gunner manning the twenty-millimeter cannon on the wintergarten to open fire, the boat swerved away and headed north with its engine screaming at full throttle.

"Relax, he's pulling away," Rahn said and shifted his glasses back to the rubber boat silhouetted against the flames on shore. Its four occupants were paddling frantically but seemed to be making little progress against the tide and a current that was carrying them northward. He estimated that it would take at least twenty minutes for them to reach the U-112—much too long under the circumstances.

"Number One!" Rahn ordered. "Go to diesels…quickly."

"But sir, the enemy is bound to hear our engines this close to shore," Thiele protested. "Our position…"

"Our position is already clearly visible to everyone!" Rahn shoved past Thiele and shouted through the open hatch. "Chief! Diesels…quickly! We need them now!"

Rahn could hear Chief Wieland shouting his orders to the engine room where a flurry of activity accompanied the transition from electric to diesel propulsion. In less than thirty seconds, a loud bang jarred them as the portside diesel came to life followed seconds later by its mate. U-112 vibrated with power and Rahn ordered her directly toward the Florida shore at flank speed.

"Number One!" Rahn shouted above the roar of the engines.

"*Herr Kaleu!*" Thiele said and uncharacteristically snapped to attention in an obvious attempt to make amends for his questioning of his commander's decision to start the diesels.

"Go below and get a recovery party topside. We have no time to waste—just get the landing party aboard and get out of here," Rahn said.

"*Jawohl Herr Kaleu!*" Thiele dropped into the hatch and slid down the ladder.

"And send Beinlich up here!" Rahn shouted after him.

The gap between the U-boat and the inflatable closed quickly, but with each passing second everyone knew the hard-packed seafloor was coming closer to their fragile keel.

"Engines back two-thirds," Rahn ordered and the roar of the diesels fell an octave but the bow continued to slice toward the shallow waters directly ahead.

"Yes, *Herr Kaleu?*" Beinlich said as he arrived on the bridge. The navigator looked as though he had just awakened from a nap.

"Cosinus, you've undoubtedly spent hours studying the chart of these waters," Rahn said. "So tell us, when do we turn to avoid running aground?"

Beinlich glanced at the approaching shoreline and then looked southward to where the beach turned out to sea in a crescent. If not for the darkness, the men on the bridge would have seen the fear on his face.

"Now! *Herr Kaleu!* We must turn now!"

"Course zero-zero-zero! Emergency turn!" Rahn shouted into the voicetube, but it seemed to take ages before the U-boat's bow began to turn away from the oncoming beach. As it settled on a new course, the inflatable came clearly into view off the port bow and Thiele emerged from the forward hatch followed by a dozen crewmen carrying ropes and a couple of boat hooks. Just as he lined them up shoulder-to-shoulder, the U-112 slid across a sandbar. The collision vibrated every frame in the boat and sent the recovery team sprawling across the deck.

"Full right rudder! Port diesel flank speed! Starboard reverse!"

The screws bit into the sand and churned it to the surface in a foaming patch of frothing water, but after much scraping and rattling, Rahn's orders succeeded in bringing the boat off the bar. A minute later, Thiele's team had secured the inflatable alongside and dragged its exhausted occupants and their cargo on board.

As the U-112 pulled away from shore, Rahn focused his Leica on the black and white striped tower of the St. Augustine Lighthouse that was glowing in the reflected light of the blazing remains of *Uncle Sam's*. As he snapped off the last exposures on his roll of film, he couldn't help but think these photos would be the best in his collection. The only detail he couldn't see was the two Coast Guard lookouts atop the tower who were now frantically reporting the U-boat's presence to the Gulf District's headquarters in Key West.

0545 hrs.

Although Luigi Carbone was grateful he had escaped both the explosion that shattered *Uncle Sam's* and arrest by the FBI, he couldn't help but wish he had thought to bring along a cold beer-- or even water. Stretched out in the *Lady Liberty's* cockpit, he looked up at the stars and watched the lighthouse's beam sweep over every thirty seconds.

"Damn it's dry!" Carbone said aloud and to confirm his analysis, he reached over and snapped a branch from a bay tree that helped shield the boat from prying eyes. A long winter without rain had left the vegetation tinder-dry and just waiting for summer lightning to set it ablaze.

Despite his thirst, Carbone was pleased with the temporary sanctuary he had found hidden away on the south side of a small creek just two miles north of the blazing remains of *Uncle Sam's*. Actually, he had to credit the cats for the discovery of the ideal hiding place. Concerned about where to put them ashore, he had suddenly remembered the *Oyster Bucket* restaurant and the dozens of cats who seemed to live happily beneath its dilapidated front porch. Judging from the rotund bodies of the restaurant's resident felines, it was apparent that food was in plentiful supply—a few more cats sharing the bounty wouldn't shortchange any of them.

Although his position hid him from view, the fire that continued to devour *Uncle Sam's* created an odd orange glow in the night sky and its reflection sometimes flickered and danced in the waters around the grounded boat. As Carbone watched the strange light show, he couldn't help but be amazed at how quickly his life had changed --- and how narrowly he had escaped death.

When the FBI arrived in the parking lot, it was if time itself had been accelerated. He had felt helpless, but fortunately, Joe Miller had already thought of everything. The instant the U-boat sailor had disappeared down the office hatch, Miller had begun scrambling to prepare a greeting for the G-men. Papers got rearranged, the volume was turned up on the transmitter, both the old and the new *Enigma* machines were stacked beneath his desk and he had placed a special record on the phonograph.

Carbone had felt incapable of helping and in response to his "What do you want me to do Boss?" Miller had said simply: "Survive."

In less than a minute, Miller had given him his instructions for a rendezvous with the U-boat, scribbled out the name and address of "someone who will help you" in Germany and without fanfare had handed him the wooden box containing the money delivered a few minutes earlier by the young U-boat officer. It had been obvious that Miller had no intention of fleeing with him, but Carbone had felt compelled to ask "you're not coming?"

"The *Kapitan's* duty is to provide for the safety of his crew and to remain faithful to his ship even unto death," Miller had said. "That was not done aboard *SMS Nassau*—this is my opportunity to make amends for that failure."

There was nothing more to say—a quick handshake and Carbone was out the window and on to the roof. By the time he had begun descending the passageway leading down to the beach, he could hear the FBI agents smashing through the bar.

Carbone tried not to think about the events of the past few hours—Miller's obvious death and his own lucky escape from both the explosion and a date with an executioner were not memories that he found inspiring. He glanced down at the luminous hands on his watch and saw that it was time to get started on a new life.

"All right fellas, it's time to go," he announced loudly.

Carbone reached down into the cockpit floor and came up with a male calico who seemed quite content to be set over the side in the shallow water. There were a couple of gentle splashes and then he saw the cat scurrying up the muddy bank to disappear among the bay trees. Next, came a big, black tomcat with white feet followed by a yellow tabby with a cropped tail. He felt beneath the seat until his hands touched the kittens intertwined and sleeping peacefully on the wooden floorboards. Somehow it just seemed too cruel to put such peaceful critters into the water—it may have been only a few inches deep, but for a kitten it would be terrifying, especially after having been frightened by a bomb blast only a couple of hours earlier. He picked them up in a mass of warm fur that shifted and nuzzled against him as he swung one leg over the side of the boat. He was surprised at how warm the water felt as it flooded into his shoes.

Setting the now helplessly mewing kittens on the muddy shore, Carbone splashed back the *Lady Liberty,* shoved her bow off the sandbar and as she wallowed in the three-foot deep water, he noisily swung himself back aboard. Firing up the Chrysler engine, he eased the boat back down the creek until he saw the feathery white line of surf coming in to meet him. As a final preparation, Carbone picked up the cash box, stuffed it into the waistband of his trousers and firmly tightened his belt until he was satisfied that the money was not going to become separated from him no matter how rough the seas might become. Standing in the cockpit, he jockeyed the boat through the shallows until at last he could see the open waters of the Atlantic dead ahead. He opened the throttle and pointed the bow toward the faint glow that was beginning to brighten the far horizon.

BUTLER BEACH: 0615 hrs.

Even from where she stood on Butler Beach three miles away from *Uncle Sam's,* Winnie Greer found it impossible to divert her gaze from the pall of smoke that now hung motionless above the burned out remains of the nightclub. In the pale light of another spring dawn, the smoke had taken on the form of a gigantic question mark whose coloring ranged from inky black on its open western side to a purplish-gray on its curved and dimpled eastern face. The more she stared at it, the more solid and permanent it appeared to be—as though some giant sculptor had carved it in stone during the night and placed it where it would forever serve as a reminder of the question she knew she would never be able to answer -- Why? Why had she given away her future by revealing Mr. Miller's secret? Why had Curtis joined the white man's navy? Why did Reverend Fulmer's touch make her tremble with joy and fear?

Winnie felt guilty when she realized she actually welcomed Mrs. Pool's sobbing—the woman's grief helped her forget about her own troubles.

"That's it Mary, let it all out," Reverend Fulmer said as he wrapped an arm around the sobbing woman's shoulders. "The Lord will hear your grief and will hasten to your side—a healing presence that will ease your pain." The reverend motioned for help with his other arm and two women Winnie didn't recognize hurried over to help support Rufus' distraught mother.

Although the crowd was not as large as it had been at Sunday morning's baptism, Winnie was impressed that so many members of the community had turned out so early to say goodbye to Rufus Pool. There was, of course, a large contingent from the Moses Creek congregation. But there were also several young men known more for their brushes with the law than their church attendance. Two of them stood atop the dune behind her and while one puffed on a cigarette, the other took an occasional swig from a beer bottle. It was obvious that the church-goers found the presence of these men distasteful, but Winnie couldn't help but believe Rufus would have been pleased to see them. He had spent much of his young life trying to make friends or at least fit in somewhere—apparently, he had somehow made a positive impression on these men who represented their race's defiance to the white man's world.

"My baby! Lord.... Lord! My baby!" Mrs. Pool's wailing became uncontrollable as Bernard White's old flat bed truck pulled through the gap in the dunes and turned up the beach toward the crowd. The pine casket strapped to the truck's open rear frame seemed much more primitive than it had in the church where it had been surrounded with flowers.

"Winnie get ready to sing," Reverend Fulmer whispered. "I don't think her heart can take a long service." As he stepped out of the crowd and raised his arms to show Bernard where to bring the truck to a halt, the first ray of sunlight on this day struck the Bible he held in his left hand and created a golden halo around the word of God.

Gears rattled and the truck's big tires spun as it shuddered to a halt. In the sudden silence that followed, the distant hum of a powerboat's engine could be clearly heard. For many in the crowd, there was a genuine sense of apprehension that their tormenters from last Sunday had returned. For Winnie, the approaching boat offered hope that all was not lost—if Mr. Miller were at the controls, there was a chance that her dreams of musical stardom might still be alive.

But to the funeral crowd's relief and Winnie's disappointment, the *Lady Liberty* was on a course that was quickly taking the boat away from the beach and toward deep water. Silhouetted against the fiery orb of the sun rising out of the Atlantic, the boat seemed to be racing toward an unseen destination. In the glare of the early morning light, few people noticed the Coast Guard cutter heading directly toward them in an effort to intercept the powerboat. Even fewer eyes saw the flash of the cutter's four-inch gun, but everyone heard the screeching whine of the incoming shell just before it burst with a thunderous thump on the beach and sent shrapnel flying. White's vehicle took the main impact--the windshield exploded and coffin splinters danced into the air before its punctured tires deflated and the loyal old truck collapsed like a dying mule.

Pandemonium broke out on the beach as people scrambled over the dunes for cover. Winnie began to run, but stopped when she looked back to see Mrs. Pool clinging to the remains of the truck.

"I can't leave my baby!" she shrieked, but Reverend Fulmer managed to pry her loose and lead her toward the dunes. Winnie moved to help him when, to her horror, she saw two children just down the beach. The little boy sat sobbing in the sand while the girl stood looking down at him.

As Winnie began to run toward them, she said a silent prayer that the next shell would not rip them apart. Her bare feet pounded in the sand and as she approached, she recognized the children as little TJ Rivers and his sister Cici--Winnie couldn't imagine where their mother was at that moment. She scooped the crying TJ up with one arm and yanked Cici toward safety—the child's little legs churning as she tried to keep up with Winnie without falling or having her shoulder disconnected from her body.

It wasn't until their feet hit the hard-packed sand of the roadway through the dunes that Winnie realized her choice of escape route may have been faulty. On both sides of them, people from the church were now shielded by the towering foredune, but the cut for the roadway left her and the children totally exposed to the firing from the sea.

"Run Cici! Run!" Winnie shouted and they rushed across the paved Ocean Highway and plunged into the thicket just as the next shell kicked sand from the top of the dune, skipped across the road and burst with a sharp crack somewhere in the underbrush. As Winnie clutched TJ to her chest and pulled Cici deeper into the jungle of tangled brush and bay trees, she suddenly heard flames crackling hotly behind her.

U.S. COAST GUARD CUTTER POLARIS: 0618 hrs.

"Goddam it Huffman! Florida's on our side--you're supposed to hit that boat not set the Sunshine State on fire!" The old chief in charge of the cutter's big gun couldn't believe how poorly the four-incher was being handled.

"But Chief, I've never fired this thing when we're underway," Huffman said while keeping his eyes pressed against the padded gunsight. "It's not so easy when the damn gun and the target are bouncin' up and down."

Everyone on board was excited about the prospect of getting into a fight. They had come up the coast flat out since five that morning when they had first received the message from Key West telling them to intercept and destroy a U-boat and an enemy agent trying to escape by sea from the St. Augustine area. They had all expected something bigger than a speedboat as their target—after all there was supposed to be a U-boat in the area. Another shell was passed forward by the handlers and the breech clanked shut behind it.

"Locked and loaded Mister Huffman," a gunner's mate shouted. "Give 'em hell!"

The cutter's captain turned the ship to port and the gun crew braced themselves as the bow swung sharply away from the approaching coastline. Spray cascaded down on the deck and splattered across the lens of the gun sight. When it dripped away, Huffman realized the captain had put him in an ideal shooting position. The target was dead ahead—zero deflection—and now that they were both running in the troughs between the gentle green swells, the up and down pitching of the boat had been considerably diminished. The target was continuing to pull away as it fled at high speed, but the cutter was still close enough that Huffman could see the Chris Craft's waxed woodwork and polished brass glistening in the early morning sun. Such a pretty little boat, Huffman thought, as the crosshairs settled on the center of its open cockpit. He squeezed the trigger and with a bone-jarring blast, the gun sent thirteen pounds of high explosives streaking toward the *Lady Liberty*.

Carbone was more concerned with finding the rendezvous point than he was about the pursuing Coast Guard cutter. Without Miller to guide him, he had to rely on memory and sense of smell to find the springs—any second now he expected to get the whiff of rotting eggs that would tell him he had arrived. Hopefully, the U-boat would be waiting to take him aboard—but so far there was no sign of his ride to Germany.

He glanced over his shoulder once and saw the cutter was still behind him, but the *Lady Liberty's* big Chrysler engine at full throttle was clearly pulling him away from his pursuers. He turned the wheel just a little more to the left and the boat sent a rooster tail of spray into the bright morning air. Just as he settled on a new course, Carbone sensed a change in air pressure as though something big were about to run over him. The next instant he was flying through a sea of flames. His last thought was: "Is this hell?" And then there was darkness.

U-112: 0622 hrs.

Even before their sound gear had picked up the throb of the American patrol boat's engines, Rahn had decided that there was little chance that they would be picking up passengers this morning. It was only because of Lamprecht's insistence and the fact that, thanks to the mysterious agent's generosity, each crewmember was wearing new, clean underwear, that he had even brought U-112 to the coordinates scribbled on the piece of paper by the German spy. If conditions were perfect... perhaps he would try to bring them aboard. But under no circumstances was he about to endanger the lives of his crew to save a spy, especially when they already possessed his complete collection of intelligence information and materials.

Through the periscope, he could see the situation was far from perfect. The speedboat coming on....the American gunboat doggedly in pursuit. For a moment, Rahn considered a torpedo attack on the gunboat—but quickly dismissed the idea. At periscope depth, they now had only twenty feet of water beneath their keel. If their attack failed, there could be no escape from the American depth charges. And then, the situation resolved itself in an instant. The speedboat disappeared in a bright flash and then a fireball erupted upward as its fuel tanks exploded. As debris tumbled out of the sky, a bright ring of flame spread across the water.

"Course one-zero-zero," Rahn barked. "All ahead full." As U-112 turned toward deep water, he guided the periscope around to maintain a careful watch on the gunboat until, much to his relief, he saw it come to a halt at the edge of the burning fuel that was now sending a towering column of oily black smoke soaring skyward.

"Number One, maintain this heading for the next hour and get us down to one hundred meters as soon as possible," Rahn ordered as he sent the periscope hissing into its well.

"*Jawohl, Herr Kaleu,*" Thiele said quietly.

As Rahn descended the ladder from his perch at the periscope in the conning tower, he slowly realized every man in the control room was staring at him in expectation of what was to come next. He took a deep breath of air that was thick with the smell of mold, rot, sweat, and assorted pungent gasses. Rahn smiled.

"Home, gentlemen. Let's go home."

His command was greeted with cheers, laughter, and a little singing and dancing that quickly swept throughout *Kreigsmarine unterseeboote* U-112.

Five miles to the west, Winnie Greer was rapidly coming to the conclusion that she might not live to see home again. Each way she turned, flames and choking white smoke swirled. Sometimes the smoke billowed up in clouds that blocked out the sky and left her and the children stumbling blindly down a seemingly endless series of dead end paths.

"Mama! I want my mama!" Little TJ stopped and refused to

budge. Tears streamed down his smoke-stained face and he yanked away from Winnie. She frantically regained a grip on his small hand—the smoke had become so thick that she knew if she let go of either child she might never find them alive again.

"Winnie, please, what you gonna do?" Cici asked. Up until that moment, she had never questioned Winnie's judgment. She had allowed herself to be tugged across the beach and through the burning woods without complaint. But now her faith had begun to fade.

"Don't worry, I'll get us out of here," Winnie said and knew she had to save them somehow—she had promised them salvation too many times during the past twenty minutes to fail them now.

A sudden gust of wind caused a clump of dead palmetto leaves to burst into flame—its withering heat forced Winnie and the children to back away.

"Hold on to me! Don't you let go," Winnie pleaded as she got down on her hands and knees. The two children grabbed her red leather belt and she crawled painfully through the hot sand. Down low, the air was a little better and she could see a few yards ahead. Finally, through a break in the smoke, she could see a black line of pavement directly ahead. Coughing and wheezing, she picked up TJ once more and with a firm grip on Cici she stumbled onto the coastal highway.

Flames were now jumping on both sides of the road and the crackling roar of the fire grew louder. To Winnie, it seemed as though her feet had sunk into the warm pavement. She had only two directions of escape to chose from—either up or down the road, but she couldn't force herself to move either way. She knelt in the middle of the highway and pulled the two children close— and the only positive thing she could think of was the fact that if they died here, it would much easier to find their bodies in the road than in the burned out marsh. Winnie hugged TJ and Cici and when she looked up she saw two bright lights coming toward her through the smoke. At first, she thought they might be angels coming to take them all to heaven...but then the screeching of brakes told her she was staring into the headlights of a truck.

"Oh my God! I almost didn't see you!" A man's voice boomed out of the smoke and then he was lifting the children up into the cab of his truck. "C'mon let's get out of here!" he said as he practically threw Winnie up into the seat. He slammed the door behind them before hurrying around the front of the truck and climbing into the cab.

"I told your people I'd drive through here and look for y'all...but I was beginning to think you wuz goners!" He shifted gears and the truck lurched forward, picking up speed until it burst from the smoke and into the clear, bright sunlight.

"I found 'em!" He shouted. "I didn't think I would...but I found 'em!"

Winnie couldn't stop the tears as she looked down from the truck at the sea of happy black faces staring up at her. She had never seen the congregation of the Moses Creek A.M.E. church look so joyful as they did at that moment gathered around Gene Sullivan's Budweiser beer truck.

Winnie climbed down from the truck's cab and as the happy throng flooded around her, she reached up and helped Cici down. The crowd parted just enough for the children's mother to push her way through to the truck.

"Cici! TJ!" she shouted. "Praise the Lord! Praise His righteous name!"

TJ seemed reluctant to leave the truck and when Winnie reached in to lift him down, he backed away from her and looked up to focus his big brown eyes on the driver.

"Thank you Mister White Man," TJ said quietly.

Sullivan's weather-beaten face took on a look of surprise that soon relaxed into a warm smile.

"You're welcome boy," he said and then with a chuckle he amended his statement. "I mean, you're welcome...son."

MONDAY
April 20, 1942

MARINELAND: 0715 hrs.

Winnie had decided to take Granny Greer's advice. Not that she had spent a lot of time debating the issue—she was too emotionally distraught for rational thought. First, there had been the end of Mr. Miller and his promise to get her auditions with the biggest bands in show business. That dream died on Friday and on Saturday she had learned that her brother was also dead.

Winnie could remember thanking that young FBI agent for coming all the way out into the salt marsh with Reverend Fulmer to tell her about Curtis. He had insisted that no thanks were necessary, and added that as far as he was concerned, after what she had given up to help arrest Joe Miller, she at least deserved to know her brother's fate. Using what influence he had as an FBI agent, he had managed to get the list of the *Lassiter's* dead from the Navy. When he found Curtis' name on it, he knew he had to bring her the horrible news.

Reverend Fulmer had wrapped her in his powerful arms and while she sobbed hysterically, he prayed aloud for God's help in bringing her and her family the strength they would need to face a future without Curtis. For Winnie, the next twenty-four hours had passed as though she were in a dream. People came and went at the house and she could hear their voices and sometimes crying, although she wasn't certain whether the sound came from her own sobs or from those of visitors. At times, she could hear herself responding to people who had come to pay their respects—but she was never sure of the words she was speaking.

By late Sunday night, reality began to return and although the pain in her heart remained, Winnie had slowly come to accept the truth that her life had to continue. But where and how it was to continue remained a mystery until Granny Greer gave her some guidance.

"Child, Lord knows you're feeling hurt—everyone who ever knew Curtis is suffering right now," Granny had told her while they sat on the porch in the lantern's light. "But you've got to be strong... you can't just quit and let grief take over. So in the morning, you go to your job and you do your work and hold your head up high. The Lord will guide you and watch over you. You'll see, something good will come of this."

And so, Winnie had left her tear-stained pillow behind and well before dawn had walked out to the highway where she flagged down the bus headed south on the Coast Highway. By seven, she was walking through the unattended gates of Marineland.

It always seemed so peaceful at this time of day hours before the first tourists would arrive to gawk at the sea life in the oceanarium or applaud as the dolphins went through their routines. She took a deep breath of sea air and headed for the closet containing the cleaning supplies. Winnie was halfway there when she noticed that the hum coming from the pump room was a couple of octaves higher than usual. Hurrying across the courtyard she opened the pump room door and hurried down the stairs.

When she saw the glowing red warning light on the control panel, she knew at once that something had jammed the filtration system. Winnie's first thought was to open the filter cover and try to pry loose whatever had jammed itself in the system. But then she remembered her emergency training. Going over to the far wall, she opened a control panel and quickly pulled the two red-handled levers. Winnie waited patiently for the sound of the straining pumps to fade away before cautiously sliding the big filter cover aside.

Even to Winnie's untrained eye, the problem was obvious—a small, flat wooden box was jammed tightly against the filter's opening. She knelt on the floor and tried to pull it loose, but enough pressure remained in the line to keep it pinned against the opening. But by shoving downward, she was able to rotate the box a couple of inches before it was forced up against the metal opening once more. Looking down at the box, she could tell if it were rotated just enough, she could pull it from the filter pipe. Winnie

314

pushed the box below the water surface and it turned a few inches. Another push and the corners of the box swiveled a few more inches. At the third push, the box shot skyward on a fountain of seawater, just missing Winnie's face as it smashed against the pump room roof and scattered one hundred dollar bills in all directions. The spraying water suddenly stopped as the filter was jammed once more—this time by the charred head and upper torso of Luigi Carbone!

Winnie scrambled away in horror and for one brief moment she thought the blackened corpse was trying to crawl through the opening and into the room with her. Her back was flat against the wall –there was no place to go as one lifeless eye stared out from the blackened face and locked her in its gaze. Slowly, the pressure in the line escaped and the remains of Luigi Carbone slid inch by inch downward and out of sight.

Winnie's first instinct was to run for help, but then she realized none of the other employees and staff would arrive for another thirty minutes. As the pounding of her heart slowed to a normal pace, Winnie realized she had better get started if she wanted the pump room to be clean and presentable.

"Thank you Jesus!" Winnie's voice was choked with tears as she began gathering up thousands of dollars worth of soggy, wrinkled money and stuffing it in her apron pockets. "Thank you Jesus!"

Uncle Sam's

EPILOGUE

Las Vegas
March 6, 2002

"And that's how it happened? I mean, you took the money from the Germans and started your career?" Rachel Rubinstein could barely contain her excitement—Marty Edelmann was going to be blown away by this story. "This is so cool!"

Winifred Greer was exhausted. Telling the story of that one week of her life had been far more demanding than she had anticipated and to now realize that it had been largely wasted on the vapid, shallow young lady seated across the table from her was extremely annoying.

"So...you think that's what happened do you? That I just up and took all that money and somehow bought myself a career?"

Rachel was confused. Apparently, she had said something that annoyed Miss Greer, but she had no clue as to what it might be. She was pretty sure, however, that antagonizing the subject of an interview was not a good thing.

"No...I mean, of course not, I didn't mean to imply that...," Rachel said as she searched for some sort of peace offering. "I mean that, well, today all the big stars get created when some wealthy person or company decides it would be good business for them to own a superstar. It's just business, that's all. You can't be a singing sensation without the money to market yourself."

"Well, things were a lot different back then. We didn't have public relations firms to make something out of nothing or advertising agencies selling entertainers like they were washing machines or fly swatters," Winnie said. "Back then, you had to have something called talent. Without talent, all the money in the world couldn't get people to turn out to see or hear you perform."

"Oh, I'm sure that's true, I've heard my grandparents say the same thing." Rachel decided that appeasement might be the best approach. It always seemed to work for her when talking with the elderly. "It's just that all that money... I mean that must have been a fortune back then."

Winnie realized that the young lady would never understand—her life experience was so different from that of a black girl from the coastal marshes of Florida that they might as well have been from different planets. But she had gone this far with her story, Winnie decided she should finish it so she'd never have to mention it again. She took a deep drink from the glass of mineral water on the table.

"Yes, the money. I took the money and never thought twice about it. In fact, for a long time I had nightmares about that burned and hideous corpse of Luigi Carbone popping up like that.... it made me think of poor Curtis out there beneath the sea somewhere." Winnie paused and looked out across the balcony to where the city of Las Vegas now glittered with its nightly display of neon in all its varied shapes and colors. She swallowed back the tears and sighed at the thought of her lost brother. "But then, I finally got over the bad dreams by deciding that ugly little man was giving me the money— the way it shot up in the air and he just jumped right up all burnt like toast, well I decided he was bringing me that money just because he liked the way I could sing."

"I'll bet you bought some bitchin' clothes with it---I've seen the way women dressed back then...Lana Turner, Betty Grable... those babes knew how to dress. What was it they called it? 'Dressed to the nines' or something like that?"

Winnie wanted to ask her what in the hell she thought a girl living in the salt marsh would do with a fancy gown...but decided it would be futile to ask questions that would require the girl to do any sort of original thinking.

"Yes, I think that's what the rich white women used to say... I really wouldn't know. We had more...basic...needs to be met. That's why I gave all the money to the Moses Creek African Methodist Episcopal Church."

"Gave it to the church? But your career...." Rachel sounded genuinely confused as though she couldn't comprehend such a gift. She was obviously struggling to understand the reasoning behind what to her was certainly bizarre behavior. "Wait a minute!" Her face brightened as though she had solved a child's puzzle. "Of course, the Reverend Amos Fulmer... I'm guessing that little gift was all he needed to realize you were the one for him."

"OK... we're finished with the interview," Winnie said firmly and if it weren't for the pain in her hip caused by sitting so long, she would have stood to emphasize the session had reached a conclusion. "On your way out, please tell Mae I'm ready to come inside."

"But...I'm sorry...I didn't mean to offend you Miss Greer," Rachel said as she clicked off her tape recorder and gathered her note pad. "It's just that you obviously cared deeply for Reverend Fulmer...and all that money, I'm sure he would have wanted to show his appreciation for such a generous gift."

"By marrying me? Child, I truly pity you and your generation—you know no motivation but money. Not love...not family...nothing but money. And yes indeed, Reverend Fulmer was appreciative and so was everyone else in the congregation. None of the children had to go to school barefooted anymore...we got indoor plumbing in the church...we bought a bus so our choir could travel to Tampa and win the state championship... we set up a scholarship fund that to this day is helping kids from that church to get an education. We even paid for Granny Greer to have those cataracts removed so that for the last two years of her life she could see the people she loved and could watch the wood storks, and the egrets and the spoonbills feeding in the marsh. And Reverend Fulmer? He got married two months later to one of the Sunday school teachers. They had two sons—both of them preachers. One got arrested with Dr. Martin Luther King Jr. in downtown St. Augustine in '64. A deputy sheriff up in Jacksonville killed the other one because he saw him talking to a white girl one night."

Winnie was exhausted. She leaned back in her chair, closed her eyes and listened as Rachel gathered up her things. Winnie planned to just sit there breathing the warm night air until she was certain the girl was gone, then she would open her eyes and get on with her life.

"I'm sorry Miss Greer...I really am...but I just have to ask one more question. If I don't get an answer, I won't have a story...maybe I won't even have a job."

Winnie slowly opened her eyes and saw Rachel standing there clutching her tape recorder and notebook to her chest like some little schoolgirl. The flashing neon of The Strip gave her face a red glow that flared and ebbed on a four-second cycle.

"It's just that I was supposed to find out how your career began—that was the whole point of this assignment. And I'm afraid I've failed. That German spy, Mr. Miller, never got to take you to that audition and you didn't use the money you found to get started. So, please, if it's not too much trouble, could you tell me how you got started in show business? I promise that will be my last question."

Last question. Those words have a nice ring to them, Winnie thought, before summoning up the strength for the evening's last response.

"It was probably six months later, October I think, when this private train pulled into St. Augustine on a Saturday morning. Everybody in town rushed over to see who it could be and as soon as the crewman took the canvas cover off a big white Cadillac on a flatcar---they knew. Cab Calloway had come to visit. In fact, he had stopped to see me and his driver brought him out to the church and I sang for him right there. I guess he liked what he heard, because he took me on tour with him that winter. We went everywhere, and I stayed with the band all through the war. Then in 1946, I married Luther Raymond, he became my manager and...well, you know the rest of the story."

"Thank you for your time and your patience," Rachel said. "I just wanted to get that part about how you got started—I'm glad to hear that German spy wasn't responsible."

"Wait just a minute!" Winnie suddenly knew that this might very well be her last opportunity to give credit where it was due and in some small way repay an old debt. "You've got to remember there was a war on at the time and thanks to the story Michael Pomar got in the *Washington Post*, the whole country was talking about that evil Joe Miller and how he got what he deserved. If the press found out that Cab Calloway was a friend of a Nazi spy— well, his career would have been over and being a black man, the government might have lynched him. But in '45, we were in New York to play a big Victory Concert in Central Park. I got a standing ovation and backstage afterwards Cab came up to me and said:

'Winnie, that Joe Miller sure knew talent when he saw it.' Winnie laughed. "We never mentioned it again."

The glass patio door hissed open and Mae stepped out. She glared at Rachel and walked over to Winnie's side.

"It's getting late—this interview was supposed to be over thirty minutes ago," she said. "Miss Greer has to get her rest—doctor's orders."

"Yes, I know…I'm terribly sorry," Rachel said. "But she had such a wonderful life. I wanted to make sure I got the whole story."

"Had? What do you mean 'had' a wonderful life? She ain't dead—she's got a whole bunch of livin' left to do."

"I'm sure you're right," Rachel said as she backed toward the door. "She's a wonderful woman. Oh, and don't worry, I can let myself out."

Mae watched as the young reporter clumsily opened the door and then slid the glass closed behind her.

"Had a wonderful life…did you hear that Miss Greer? That girl must think you're old as Methusela."

Mae turned, placed her hands on her broad hips and shook her head slowly. Winifred Greer was sleeping soundly in her chair and each flash of neon revealed a smile of complete contentment.

Uncle Sam's

ABOUT THE AUTHOR

A graduate of West Virginia University's Perley Isaac Reed School of Journalism, Jay Humphreys has more than 25 years of writing and media relations experience. A Washington, D.C. speechwriter and briefings officer during the Carter and Reagan Years, he also worked for the Congressional Information Service and conducted media relations projects for several federal agencies. A former communications director at the University of Florida (1988-1998), he also served as the editor of FATHOM—the journal of the state university system's marine research program. His first book, "Seasons of the Sea" became a hardcover bestseller for the publisher. The parents of two sons, he and his wife enjoy exploring the beach behind their home on Anastasia Island.

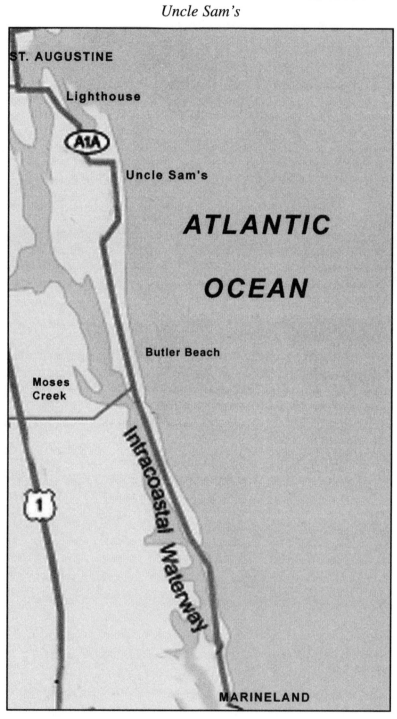

Wartime photo of U.S. Coast Guard trainees marching through
St. Augustine's City Gate.

Issued by the U.S. Office of War Information, 1942

"above and beyond the call of duty"

DORIE MILLER
*Received the Navy Cross
at Pearl Harbor, May 27, 1942*

One of America's first heroes of World War II, Doris (Dorie) Miller was serving as a mess steward aboard the battleship *USS West Virginia* at Pearl Harbor on December 7, 1941. Although the battleship was ablaze and sinking, Dorie single-handedly fired on the attacking Japanese planes with a machine gun he had not been trained to operate. He also pulled the ship's mortally wounded captain from the bridge of the sinking ship. Awarded the Navy Cross for his bravery, Dorie was killed in 1943 when his ship, the *USS Liscome Bay*, was torpedoed by a Japanese submarine. *(National Archives)*

Issued by the U.S. Adjutant General's Office, 1943